High Stakes and Bloody Business

Kailey Alessi

THE WHUMPY PRINTING PRESS

To the bats

Contents

Introduction

Welcome to WPP's fourth anthology! The people voted for vampires, and so here they are. Vampires offer the perfect fodder for whump. The blood! The fangs! The inherent emotional conflict of being forced to hurt another to survive! I am a vampire whump enthusiast, and I hope that, if you're not already, you'll be one too by the end of this anthology.

As this anthology is vampire-themed, you should expect lots of blood and biting. All stories have more specific content warnings at the beginning.

The Man in the Box

Ennis Rook Bashe

CW: Medical trauma, noncon/sexual assault, imprisonment
Whumpee: Man, Woman, Whumper: Man, Caretaker: Man, Woman

Another Monday means another batch of interview requests in my civilian email inbox. I skim the previews like a masochist. The usual patient advocacy blogs. Politicians seeking healthcare reform. Time Magazine, fucking again.

We want to know about what you've been through.

When you decide to press charges, we want to share your side of the story.

We think our readers would be fascinated by your unique story of survival and resilience...

Fuck them. If they knew a single thing about what I'd been through, they'd understand why I won't talk about it.

Why I can't go there again, even in my memories.

Although, a pesky practical thought pops up, *the money could help you make rent...*

Nope. Not going there. Sure, in terms of the apartments I've rented since getting out of the hospital, this tiny studio above an East Village K-barbecue joint is the least shitty. I've never stepped over anyone passed out on the stairs, and the water's at least lukewarm most weeks.

Still.

I'm not saying shit.

I'm staring down the dregs of my chai when my burner phone - the work one - rings. The Chumovoi Syndicate. Small-time Bratva outlet down in Coney. Last time, their guys eyed me the whole job like I was an unwrapped mini cupcake, but what choice do I have? Rent's due next week.

I pick up. "Office of Archmage Van Horn."

"Hello, little missy. Could I speak to the magician?"

A breath of power, and my voice echoes, thunder and fireworks. "I am the magician. You think to disrespect me?" Gods, I love doing that.

"Shit!" he yelps. The phone clatters from his hands.

Zino, their current leader, picks up. "Sorry about that, Miss Archmage," he says smoothly. "My employee, he's new. And he won't make that mistake again." This is Zino for "I'm going to beat the shit out of him." Overkill? Sure. But Zino's sadism is not my circus, not my monkeys.

"I assume you're not calling just to make small talk."

"I need a mage to protect a package. Boston to Brooklyn. Some of my men will be on the job, but none of them can fire lightning or call demons."

"By ground?" If it can be guarded by men without magic, why can't it go on his private jet?

"Let's just say that this is a very powerful item. A flight might be too conspicuous."

A witch bottle? A wild tome? Whatever it is, I can handle it. Even with everything that's happened to me and the tremor in my hands when I set down my mug, I'm still Valentine Van fucking Horn. "How much?"

He names a price.

A price that would cover my rent for three months.

Inside, I'm giggling and kicking my feet, but I play it cool. "Cover my transportation, and I'm in."

***

One first-class train ride later, Zino's guards pull back oaken doors as I stroll into a manor just off Harvard's campus. He and his men are waiting for me in a Colonial-style drawing room. Where I'd expect to see a coffee table, a huge steamer trunk occupies the Persian carpet. Heavy chains and locks encircle it.

"Why all the restraints? Worried whatever's inside will escape?" I joke.

Zino's cool gaze sweeps over me. "You could say that." He turns to his own mage-bodyguard. "Show Miss Valentine what she'll be guarding."

The mage kneels, feeds his power into the chains. A sense of pressure makes the room feel like it's about to implode. Finally, the spell completed, the trunk pops open.

At first I think I'm looking at a naked corpse, because no one could survive what this man suffered. His wrists have been torn open to the bone, tendons showing through shredded muscle pierced by splinters of wood. His ankles are shattered, sharp pieces of bone emerging from dark bruises, feet twisted at impossible angles. On his arms and legs, someone's flayed patches of his skin and neatly pinned it back with a staple gun. Finally, a constellation of deep stab wounds spreads over his chest, a dagger still plunged into one just above his heart.

Then – impossible, grotesque – his eyelids flutter. I've seen some pretty fucked-up shit working as a mage for hire, but my stomach still twists as I stumble back.

Not a corpse.

A vampire.

Like all vampires, he's so eerily pretty you'd marvel at him even as he drained your blood. But what draws me to him isn't his smooth, pale skin or his dark hair ruffled like feathers. It's how sad he looks. The angle of his mouth, like he's trapped in a nightmare and knows he can never wake up.

He might be conscious, aware of everything happening around him. Paralyzed and screaming silently. Struggling to accept that help still hasn't arrived.

Just like I was.

"You know who he is?" Zino demands.

Deep breath in, deep breath out. *You're not getting paid to care, Valentine.* "He's a vampire. That's all I need to know." Maybe the Court wants him for some crime? They police their own ruthlessly.

"This is Arcadian Ebenus. The missing vampire prince of New York City."

"But that's not possible." Everyone knows the vampire prince was staked by hunters during the 1920s, part of a plot to destabilize the American vampire community. His Court, his clan, have been in mourning since.

Zino smirks, putting his feet up on the table. His sneakers leave careless smudges of dirt on the priceless antique. "Don't believe everything you hear."

"If the Court finds out –"

"I know you need the money," he says softly. "How many jobs have you been offered since you staggered out of the hospital? How many repeat clients?"

None. Because no one wants to hire me with the gossip they've heard. Because, in their eyes, I'm not invincible anymore.

"If you transport the prince, I'll pay your rent for a year. Any apartment you want. And I'll tell everyone that you're just as sharp as you used to be. Wouldn't that be enough to get you back on your feet?" And, even gentler: "You need me, Valentine. Or should I tell everyone you broke down and didn't have the stomach for the job?"

Anger sparks my magic. Lightning and wind rattle the windows, the chains.

But he's right, damn him: I have no choice.

I breathe deeply, tugging my power back into my skin. "Fine. I'll help transport the vampire."

"The item," Zino corrects.

As soon as I cash his check, I'm going straight to the Court. No one deserves to be treated like this.

***

I meet Zino's convoy on the outskirts of Boston. Two hulking armored trucks look out of place on the sleepy back road where one-story suburbs fade into Massachusetts trees.

A guard lets his bulky arms dangle from the driver's seat. "Hey, pretty lady! Where you going?"

Another stubs out his cigarette. "You need a ride, little girl?"

I know I don't look like much. I'm five feet in boots, with features the supernatural society papers describe as "delicate," and I've never been able to open a jam jar without convincing a neighbor to help. But with my magic, that doesn't matter.

I'm never letting a man like them touch me again.

I breathe in the cold wind, and when I exhale, it howls around me, scattering a whirlwind of leaves. "Do you want a mage or don't you?" I snap.

The journey is remarkably calm. We take back roads, avoiding towns that might hold vampires. A noise that makes all the men jump turns out to be a passing fox. As the convoy rolls through the oak and maple forests of New England. I lean back in my seat. Maybe I'll just close my eyes for a minute. Dozing in quick snatches can help me dodge dreams.

Not this time.

I'm trapped in a tiny room, gasping for air as flames lick the walls. Outside, people pass by, unhurried, uncaring. "Help!" I scream, desperate. "Something's wrong. I'm burning up!"

"This is a delusion," a doctor explains from the doorway. "The sooner you let go of the idea that something is wrong with your body, the sooner you'll get better."

I try to run, to shove past him, but the chains attached to the walls pull taut.

I'm trapped.

Like a dog on a leash.

"You'll never leave," a nurse says placidly, robotically. "You need to stay calm and cooperate. You're not allowed to leave."

Bugs emerge from the fire. Beetles. Ants. They crawl up my baggy paper scrubs, their little spindly legs like fingernails scratching my skin-

That's when the man walks in. His suit is a slice of night, and everyone parts for him. Even the flames leave him unscathed. He kneels before me, deep blue gaze holding mine. "You're dreaming, Archmage Van Horn."

That's right.

I've been out of the hospital for almost six months now, and it humiliates me that I'm still captive in my flashbacks and dreams. I should be better than this. Stronger.

"I'm dreaming," I echo, brushing the bugs off my thighs. "I hate this."

"Would you like to leave this horrible place?"

"Anywhere but here."

***

The next thing I know, I'm outside my favorite Princeton café. It's early fall, raindrops darkening the grey stone of old buildings. A mug of chai steams on my favorite table.

No one is holding me prisoner anymore.

When my legs give out, the man catches me. He smells like sandalwood and old books. "Easy, Archmage," he murmurs, accent aristocratic and unplaceable. As I try to remember how to breathe, burying my face in the softness of his cashmere jacket, he strokes my back. "That's it. You're safe now."

He guides me into my usual chair and takes his own seat. "If it's any comfort, Archmage," he says over a mug of something dark and steaming, "you are a remarkably resilient woman."

I sip my tea. It's rich, sweet, absolutely perfect. "Mmm. Thank you, dream-guy."

He eyes me curiously, a smile playing over his lips. "You truly don't recognize me, do you?"

"Recognize –" Then it hits me. The crow-ruffled hair. His long limbs and long fingers. This is the man I saw imprisoned in a nightmare between life and death. "You're Prince Arcadian."

His smile turns into a ghost of itself. "In all these years, you're the first person I've ever been able to speak to."

I was trapped for months. He's been trapped for lifetimes. What do I even say? "I'm so sorry."

"You're also in danger, Archmage Van Horn."

That's not what I expected.

"I can overhear a little of what my captors are saying, sometimes," he says in between sipping from his mug. "There's someone who's planning to pay a great deal of money for you, preferably alive. This job is a setup. If you were to give me your blood, to allow me to free myself, we could both - "

I know how dangerous vampires are when they're awakened from torpor. There was an elder vampire in France. He'd been walled away in a tomb by an enemy. Then a group of tomb raiders stumbled upon his prison. He drained them slowly, painfully, and ripped them to shreds.

And Arcadian has been asleep for almost a century.

What lies might he tell to get free?

When I was trapped, I would have said anything to breathe fresh air again. I would have sold anyone out.

So from my own experience, I doubt his words.

"Sorry," I say, pushing my chair back, "but I'm leaving that to the experts." And, when confusion crosses his perfect face, "I will make sure you're freed. I'm going to go to the Court right after I cash my check and tell them everything so they can start looking for you. But I know enough about hungry vampires to know they can't be trusted."

I expect Arcadian to fly into a rage, fangs and fingernails sharpening. To need to wake myself up before the dream becomes a nightmare again. Instead, he just looks thoughtful. "What would I have to do to make you trust me?"

Maybe because it's a dream, because I'm half asleep, the truth falls out of my mouth. "I don't trust anyone. Not anymore."

***

The car comes to a stop, and I wake.

"Rest stop," one of the men grunts.

Another stretches his legs. "Fuck, I need a piss."

After jogging a few laps around the highway-side parking lot, I head into the rest stop and order a cup of tea. Something to cheer myself up: hibiscus, iced. My magic fills the cup, sensing and scanning it. Okay, it's not poisoned. Nothing but liquid brewed from herbs and ice made from water. They're out of straws, but a man working on his laptop hands me an unopened one he accidentally swiped.

As we take clever shortcuts through Brooklyn, the smell of the Coney Island sea in the air, I contemplate Arcadian's story. What reason would anyone have to want me taken prisoner alive? My demon enemies only want me dead, with no interest in killing me themselves. And I've never left a client unhappy.

Still. If things go bad, I have my magic. I breathe a thread of it into my hands just to soothe myself-

Pain bursts between my eyes. My head explodes. I'm leaning my forehead against the cold car window, sweaty and hyperventilating. Can't think, can't breathe. I try again, because I'm a fucking idiot, and only my seatbelt keeps me upright.

My magic.

Gone.

But how? I checked the drink for poison-

But not the paper straw, which dissolves a little even in cold liquids. The straw that a nice man so helpfully handed me when he saw me looking for one.

This is what comes of trusting anyone, even for small things.

"Hey. Can you even walk? We have a schedule to keep."

"Try to run and we'll shoot," another one of my former colleagues lets me know.

My vision greys when I stand, and I have to gasp for breath. Still, it's better than letting any of these men carry me. "I'm fine." And, when he looks skeptical, "You haven't beaten me yet."

As they carry the trunk, I follow them through the labyrinthine parking garage and into the warehouse. In the dusty semidarkness, Zino lounges on packing crates as if on a throne. "Yes, she's here. Your suggestion worked perfectly. How much is the bonus for bringing her alive again?" He covers his retro burner phone to give me a cheeky little wave, and I daydream about vaporizing his skull.

The person on the other end says something, and he looks serious. "No. You'll have nothing to worry about. Trust me, even her death will discredit her story. We'll make sure she'll never talk."

There's only one person – well, one organization – who'd be so interested in shutting me up. Why would they go to these lengths, when they know I'm too scared to press charges?

He ends the call. "That was Harker Memorial Hospital Network. They wanted to be extra sure you'll never expose their medical malpractice, that their abuse of patients misdiagnosed and shoved into their psych wards would stay just a rumor. But you wouldn't talk, would you?"

His words drag me back there. Even with my magic, I'd feel utterly defenseless right now.

"What's the plan, boss?" says one of the men now gripping my forearm to keep me from slumping to the floor.

He checks his texts on a second phone. "Put her in the storage area."

"I thought we were faking her suicide?" the guy on my other side asks. "What about the Xanax?"

From beneath the weight of how much I hate them, I try to breathe.

"Our courier got frisked going through Queens. We'll need to wait until to-morrow at least."

"People will know what you did." I find my voice, even though it shakes. "There are necromancers. I still have allies. You won't be able to get past the wards on my apartment to plant my body, and people will want to know how I died somewhere else."

He gives a sickly sweet smile. "You'll still be dead," before waving me away.

I've never given up. I'm not the sort of person who gives up. That's not how you pass the Archmage trials.

Yet I can't deny that things are looking pretty damn bleak.

"Why do you have a jail cell?" I ask as they're dragging me into one.

Zino's playing Snake on his ancient burner phone. "My old man said he bought it off a traveling circus. They used to keep lions in it. Tigers. From what I've heard, Van Horn, you're quite the wild animal yourself."

Anger makes my body tremble as I'm locked in. Normally, I'd be able to summon a towering demon to rip the building to shreds, or lightning to pierce everyone's eyes. But whatever they want to do to me, whether it's their bruising grip on my arms or the rough way they shove me to the cell's concrete floor so suddenly I can't regain my balance, all I can do is endure.

If I buy enough time, will the poison wear off? Hmm. Depends on what they used, is the problem. Odorless and tasteless narrows it down... but not by much.

What if my magic is only the first thing to turn into pain?

"Where should we put the, uh..." One of his underlings gestures to the coffin.

"It's not like it's going anywhere. Still, it should be somewhere secure, out of the way. Put it in there," Zino replies, jerking his chin at the cell next to mine.

The coffin looms silent beside me as they leave.

Maybe the rumors that dogged my life these last few months will be ignited even brighter by my death. It's a suicidal risk, but at least it's murder-suicide. And it's the only option I have.

Hands shaking, I copy the mage-signs used to unlock the trunk. Even unable to cast, I still have more magic burning in my veins than an ordinary person. The chains give way. I'm once again confronted with the man in the box.

He looks even more ghastly up close. Paper-white skin oozing around the objects shoved into him, eyes squeezed closed in agony. His lips part slightly. Last time, they were closed. Is he trying to breathe? My own chest aches in sympathy.

"Can you hear me?" I whisper. "I'm so sorry they did this to you. I wish I'd never taken this job." Not for me, but for him. His suffering was never worth my reputation. Not that there was much of it left. I'm just too fucked up to speak out and clear my name.

A grave-cold whisper of air.

Is it my imagination or the AC, or did he try breathing again in response?

As carefully as I can, I reach through the bars and ease the sharpened pieces of wood from his wrists and ankles. His tendons hang like tattered ribbons. His eyelids jolt with each shift. I know I'm hurting him. I'm no healer. Not without my magic. But if he regenerates with silver staples and rowan wood inside his body, it will only cause him more agony.

"I'm sorry," I breathe as if he can hear me, leaning to stroke his impossibly soft hair. "Just a little longer. Then you'll be free. I promise." It must feel awful not to even be able to scream.

At least I could always still scream.

"I'm almost done." Even if he can't hear me, it feels better to fill the silence, to take my mind off how his body has been ripped and shredded, torn open in a way no mortal could survive.

Finally, concentrating on the gaping wound in his bare, perfect chest, I ease the last blood-soaked piece of wood free. His whole body shudders. His chest rises and falls like he can finally breathe again before he winces and goes still.

I know what vampires are like when they emerge from torpor. He'll drain me first, driven by an unbearable thirst and hunger that feels like dying all over again. I'll feel weak, my heart racing – but I won't be able to fight off a vampire without my magic.

At least he'll use the strength my blood gives him to murder the absolute fuck out of everyone here.

I scrape my knuckles against the concrete until a drop wells up, then place it on my fingertip between his lips. Is it just my imagination, or does his tongue move against my skin?

He looks so perfect, so calm. Like he's been rescued by people who love him and his hurts are healing somewhere safe. Like any moment, he's going to open those mesmerizing navy blue eyes and murmur his gratitude.

Not like someone still in horrific agony, who's going to rip this place apart the second I awaken him as payback for his injuries.

I open my eyes on the bank of a frozen river. The cold wind whistles through lifeless trees, a snowy forest stretching as far as I can see. Not the sort of place I'd be: outside of the Five Boroughs, not a coffee shop in sight.

This isn't my dream.

And somewhere, low and hopeless, someone is crying.

People in the hospital used to cry like that, when they realized no one was coming to help.

"Archmage." A voice, barely audible, from underneath the thick ice. I follow it, and there he is.

"There you are." Relief in his voice. Like he didn't think he'd be able to find me, like he thought I'd turn and walk away. He's not the same man I saw in my last dream, looking like royalty in a perfectly tailored suit, his long hair falling in a smooth dark curtain.

This version of the Prince?

He looks like shit.

He drifts naked beneath the perfectly clear ice, loose trails of ripped bloodless skin dangling from his arms as he hugs his knees. Bruises almost as dark as his eyes paint the few places on his body still intact. The cold water moves through the hole in his chest.

I want to go to him. Break the ice and haul him to safety.

"Valentine, I'm sorry," he tells me through ruined lungs. He shifts his position slightly: blood darkens the water beneath his narrow hips. "I can't."

I kneel, touching the ice above him. "You can't wake up? Do you need more blood?" If that's what it takes to get revenge, I'll let him hurt me.

"Do you know what it's like for a vampire to emerge from torpor after so long?"

"I'm no expert on vampires." Demons, yes. The occult, sure. Vampires, well, I know the basics.

"Trying to wake up is like... barely being able to remember which way is up as the dark current rushes around you. You need to find your bearings and fight the water, and then be strong enough to punch upwards through the ice." The cold light plays over his mournful expression. "I don't know if I'm strong enough."

I can't leave him like this. Even beyond my own survival, he tried to save me. What kind of Archmage would I be if I didn't repay his kindness? "Do you need more blood? Will that make you strong enough?"

"It's not my body that's failed me. Wounds like these... I've learned to endure them. But every time I try to surface, it's like there's an anchor dragging me down."

"What do you mean?"

"I realized after a few tries there's a certain peace in total helplessness. Otherwise, I'd have to confront all of it. Everything that's happened to my body. Everything that happened while I lay here weak and helpless, everything they've done to me, everything people will say about me when they find out I've been captured by humans... There's so much to face, and no one could possibly understand. I wish I was stronger. I truly am sorry, Archmage." Arcadian's smile is the saddest thing.

No one could possibly understand.

But I do.

I tell him the story I've never told anyone. Every piece of it.

The one thing I hope might lead him out of the dark.

The night when I fumbled to dial 911 with shaking hands because I thought my head was going to explode. To my struggle to comprehend past the bright lights and spinning blurs as a doctor who didn't even examine me told me I was just crazy.

What they did to me in the psych ward when I tried to escape, and my growing comprehension and horror when the antibiotics I needed finally poured through my veins.

Then a few weeks after I was quietly released, a nurse went to the press. From there, the rumors only grew, destroying my reputation. All anyone knew was that Valentine Van Horn had gone crazy and tried to kill an innocent doctor with her bare hands. And telling the truth would mean telling them about -

About when I was raped.

I don't share any details, but he closes his eyes, and the tension leaves his shoulders. Like he's thinking "It's not just me."

"So basically, they misdiagnosed my brain infection and were content to let me rot when a few antibiotics could have saved me the whole time. How could a crazy person beg for help, right? Obviously I was just saying my head hurt for attention." Talking makes the memories rise up. But for the first time, facing them feels worthwhile. "When I finally got help, all I could think about was all that wasted time. How it wasn't fair. It felt impossible to try to make something of my life with how much I'd lost." It still feels impossible a lot of the time. "I know it feels like nothing will ever be all right again," I continue. "And that's normal. You're not alone. Whatever you're feeling, we're allies now. I'll be right here."

Those unreadable eyes search my face. Then "Move back to the bank," Arcadian says, steeling himself.

I back up.

He pounds on the ice. Once. Twice. On the third swing of his fist, it shatters into diamond shards.

Arcadian staggers from the frozen water, wraps his arms around me, and clings to me for all he's worth. I murmur soothing nothingness and stroke his raven-feather hair.

"Valentine." His voice is a whisper as he cradles me close. "You are the bravest woman I've ever met." Even though we're both shivering from the icy water, I feel warm for the first time in years, an irresistible warmth that steals up my body and seeps through my limbs. Warm and safe.

I wake to the rushing, pounding warmth of my blood being drained. His head is bent to my neck, and his vampire powers mean it doesn't hurt at all. It feels like slipping into a warm bath. Like falling asleep.

He groans, shuddering horribly and slumping against me as nerves awaken, as his ragged, dirty flesh knits itself closed. I want to offer my hand to squeeze, but when he grips the coffin's edge and it splinters, I think better of it.

At last he pulls away, panting. He looks haunted, but his posture is still that of a king. "Archmage," he murmurs, and catches me as the grey of blood loss overtakes my vision, as gravity pulls me towards the floor. "Rest now."

Now it's all up to the Prince. Dizzy and magicless, there's not a single thing I can do to help him.

But I trust him. I trust him like I've never trusted anyone else.

I wake up with my jacket under my head. The vampire leans over me, wearing blood-spattered clothes. "They're all dead. They will no longer harm you."

Oh. I'm safe, aren't I? We're both safe. "Did you have a good snack?" That's how vampires kill people, right? Draining their blood.

"I didn't want to dirty my palate with them after you."

Do I taste that good? My cheeks warm. "So... what now? I think I can make it home myself. You have enough to deal with, and I don't want to be a burden on your reputation."

He takes my hand, solemn, and helps me to my feet. "You are no burden. You are weak, you are injured, and you are the woman who saved my life. Besides, I think doors will open for the new bodyguard of the long-lost vampire prince."

I know Arcadian's road to recovery will be even harder than mine. He must feel disgusting, soaked in the grime of a hundred years, and he's still moving stiffly in a way that suggests everything aches. But we both have something we never expected: someone who understands what we've endured. Maybe even a friend.

About the Author

Ennis Rook Bashe is an Elgin and Rhysling Award finalist, TAP New York Writers' Institute Poetry Prize winner, and HWA Dark Poetry Scholarship-winning poet, novelist, game designer, and cat owner. Their chapbook *Beautiful Malady* includes work nominated for the Pushcart Prize. Find more writing and information at https://linktr.ee/ennisrooktashe.

Sister

Zi Trone

"I, Sister Therese, vow to Almighty God to live until death the counsels of chastity, poverty, obedience, and silence according to the Rule and Life of the Sisters of Our Lady of the Seven Sorrows. With our community and all the saints and angels as witnesses, I freely make my profession in your presence, Reverend Mother. Relying on His mercy, I entrust my life to the chaste, poor, and obedient Christ. I freely choose to join Our Lady at the foot of the cross, and with all my heart I give myself to this religious family, that strengthened by the grace of the Holy Spirit and the intercession of Our Lady of Sorrows and all the saints and with the support of my sisters I will fulfill my consecration and make known God's merciful love."

When I made my perpetual vows kneeling before the Reverend Mother, I felt a particular sense of peace wash over me. I felt like I was finally where I was supposed to be my entire life — in the convent, silently contemplating and praying for the world.

Of course, this was all preceded by a period of discernment and prayer. I had even felt anxious the night before, wondering whether this was truly my vocation, wondering whether I would make a good nun. I'd lived with the sisters for ten years at that point, yet Satan was still tormenting me with fears and doubts. Sometimes even through the sisters themselves; several times I received letters under my door asking me to reconsider and leave. Never maliciously, of course, more with sisterly love and a wish for me to find a life I enjoyed living.

But that day when I took the black veil, I knew I arrived home. I knew I was right where I belonged.

Giving up one's voice and social life to live in an isolated convent up north, where it was always cold and the time not spent praying was spent ploughing the snow might've seemed drastic for some. Personally, I didn't mind any of it. My voice was best used glorifying the Lord and the Blessed Virgin; if I only used it for that, that would be the most certain way to avoid falling into sins of the tongue. As for my friends and family, they might never fully understand. I must live with that. Hopefully, through my joyful letters describing my life in the convent, one day they would accept my decision.

There were many rules in the convent. A strict routine with multiple daily prayers, singing, two hours of contemplation, and mindless physical labour that allowed for even more silent prayer. The more I worked, the more I noticed it wasn't all that different from lying in my bed and contemplating the mysteries of the rosary. The saints were right in that every act performed during the day could be a hymn to God with the right intentions.

So I spent my days settling even more comfortably into my routine. The sisters and I got on well, and the well-intentioned letters trying to deter me stopped with my perpetual vows. I let the silence fill my very soul, recognising more and more that chatter only served to drown out the voice of the Spirit. I loathed the times I had to open my mouth at all outside of prayer, but of course, some talking was inevitable. Still, I tried my best to keep it to a minimum.

I was 32 when Mother Superior pulled me aside after our morning prayers, into the small room where she did administrative work for the convent. I had not a clue what she might've wanted, I only hoped she wasn't dissatisfied with the way I carried out my duties.

"It's been a year since you've taken your perpetual vows," she told me. Time flew by, I thought. It had already been a year. Eleven years in the convent. "It's time I introduce you to a new and quite special duty. It is a duty only the sisters who have taken their perpetual vows know of, and it must stay that way. Talking about it is strictly forbidden."

I must admit, I was almost giddy at the prospect. Delving even deeper into religious life and serving the convent even better sounded just perfect. "I will not talk about it to anyone," I said seriously, concealing the childlike excitement in my heart.

"Good. Please, then, follow me, Sister Therese."

Mother Superior gave me a pile of neatly folded clothes that I didn't recognise as a habit and led me out of the room and down a flight of stairs. We stopped in front of a door I'd never seen opened before and she took out a large key. I'd never asked what was behind the door; I felt like God would eventually show me if it was my place to know. And that day was the day my curiosity was finally going to be sated.

The door opened to reveal even more stairs, leading down and disappearing in the darkness. Mother Superior took a lantern from the side and lit it, — electricity was unreliable so far out and in such cold weather — leading me deeper into the heart and core of the convent.

As she asked me to close the door behind the two of us, blocking out all natural light, I attempted to stay as close to her as possible. The light of the lantern wasn't all that much, and I was quite afraid of tripping and tumbling down the seemingly infinite staircase, breaking bones and embarrassing myself in front of Mother Superior. Thankfully, that didn't happen, and we reached the bottom without issue.

"I must tell you once more," she said, coming to a stop, "whatever happens down here stays down here. If you talk about it to anyone, even to sisters who have taken their perpetual vows, you'll be breaking your vow of holy obedience. Is that perfectly clear?"

"Yes, Reverend Mother," I said, more and more eager to see what secrets lurked in the shadows.

"Good." She began walking once again and I followed close behind.

"A new one, is she?" someone said from the darkness, and my blood turned to ice in my veins.

"Is— Is there someone else here?" I asked, deciding this was an emergency worthy of talking.

Mother Superior raised her lantern, illuminating more of the room, and there I saw her for the first time. She was sitting with her knees pulled up against her chest, her long, black hair covering half her face. Her eye, the one I could see, appeared glowing red — but that must've just been an illusion of the fire. She was fitted with what looked like a dog muzzle.

"Hello, sister," she said, raising a hand to greet me. Her... chains rattled. She was chained by both wrists and ankles, and upon further inspection, I could see there was a collar around her neck as well.

"Who is this?" I asked, completely taken aback and filled with terror and pity. "Reverend Mother, we must help her! Quick, I'll—"

"There is no helping her," Mother Superior said solemnly. I begged to differ.

"We just have to find something to break the chains with!" I insisted.

"Sister Therese," she said, her eyes boring into me. "This woman is a vampire."

The world seemed to stop spinning entirely. My breath caught in my throat. "What?" I asked stupidly. Vampires didn't exist. Vampires were nothing but folklore, demons made up to scare little children into obeying and not staying out too late.

The woman burst out laughing so abruptly that I flinched. The sound was high-pitched and eerie. "This never gets old. No matter how many generations of sisters I see, that first time is always priceless." She grinned at me, baring what was undoubtedly a pair of needle-sharp fangs. I just stood there, frozen, unable to respond. "What is it, Sister Therese? Are you *scared*?"

"I— I don't understand," I stammered. "How— How long has she— How long has this been kept a secret?"

"For centuries," Mother Superior said. I couldn't tear my eyes away from the smirking woman to look at her as she talked. She didn't look a day older than maybe thirty. "The convent was founded with the express purpose of keeping her here. The Sisters of Our Lady of the Seven Sorrows have always taken care of her to the best of their abilities—"

"Hah!" She kicked her feet a little, like she was wildly amused by the explanation, then she settled into a cross-legged position. "Centuries of *taking care of me* and I still don't even get an introduction when a new sister is brought down here."

"Silence," Mother Superior boomed. "You are clothed, fed, and kept out of the sun. You are the last vampire on this earth, kept safe only by our secretive convent. If anyone knew of your whereabouts or very existence, you would be staked and burned. Show some gratitude."

The woman's grin turned into a grimace of hatred. "A stake through the heart would be more merciful than whatever your convent is doing to me," she hissed.

"What... what's her name?" I asked sheepishly.

"Victoria," the vampire cut in before Mother Superior could've answered. "My name is Victoria de Villiers." The way she said it felt defiant, like she only did so to spite the Reverend Mother. There was some pride to it, too. She must've been important at some point. Maybe even of noble descent, if there was such a thing among vampires.

"Her name matters little to us," Mother Superior said. "As I said, we clothe and feed her. That is the bulk of your duties down here in her cell, along with washing her body and hair."

"Feed... as in..."

"With blood."

I must've gone noticeably pale, because Victoria let out another shrill laugh. "She's scared, Catherine. But you have never been one for subtlety or nuance. You just rip the bandaid off, as one says."

"There's no need to coddle them. Sister Therese, hold the lantern for me. I'll show you what you must do when it's your turn down here."

I took the lantern with a shaking hand, watching wide-eyed as Mother Superior approached the chained woman. If she was as much of a monster as the folktales and those restraints suggested, she must've been one of the bravest women on the planet. And I was expected to follow in her footsteps? All the sisters who had taken their perpetual vows were?

The Reverend Mother took a blade from her pocket, raising it to the palm of her left hand. I suddenly understood why she and so many of the sisters had jagged scars across them. She slit the skin with ease, not even flinching, and I could soon see blood bubbling up to the surface. I glanced at Victoria; her eyes darkened as she followed the movement of Mother Superior, angling her head so her open mouth was right below where she squeezed the wound and let blood drip down onto her tongue.

"Your blood tastes like ash," Victoria said once she swallowed and Mother Superior stepped back. "You're getting way too old for this, Catherine."

"I don't do it much anymore, do I?" she responded gruffly. "But I must show the sister what to do, or else you'll be stuck down here without any food. You'd soon beg to be allowed a drop of my ashy blood."

Victoria's red eyes snapped to me, and I stilled entirely under her gaze. "I can't wait to taste you, sister. You look young — about the same age as I was when I was turned."

I swallowed thickly. The lump in my throat didn't budge.

Mother Superior took the lantern from my trembling hand and brought it closer to the vampire. "You can see that her clothing is held together by straps. You'll be able to remove it and give her new ones without taking off the shackles." She set the lantern on the ground and moved close to Victoria once more. "She cooperates, for the most part," she explained as she began undoing the straps. "She doesn't want to live in filth either."

"And there's no way for me to drain you dry with this muzzle on me, is there?" Victoria added.

"Besides, if anything happened to me, the next sister who came down here would likely stake her. She talks about wanting to die, but if that were the case, a sister would've already ended up with a broken neck. Those chains aren't that short."

Victoria scoffed. I watched with bated breath as Mother Superior removed all her clothing. I was so stunned I didn't even think to turn away to preserve the poor woman's dignity. I'd taken care of older sisters before, sick ones, I'd helped them change, this somehow felt no different... maybe with an air of underlying terror.

"There is a tap off to the side here," she went on, bringing the lantern over to a tap in the wall with a large bucket underneath. She turned it on and let the water fill some of it. "There is soap and a sponge. The sponge, of course, needs to be changed regularly." She threw both of those things in the bucket and turned the tap off, then brought them back to the vampire. Then she began bathing her. "I assume you don't need instructions on how to do this part."

"No, Reverend Mother," I said without thinking. It was all so surreal. Some part of my brain must've turned off, I must've only been held up by the power of the Spirit and holy obedience.

"Give me those," the Reverend Mother ordered, and I obeyed without a second thought, handing her the garments. She secured them around Victoria's body, one strap at a time. Once my head felt a little clearer, all I could think was how such clothing had to be way too breezy for the low temperature in the cell; not to mention the fact she was still wet.

"Isn't she cold?" I asked.

"She's dead," Mother Superior replied like it was obvious. And it should've been, I just couldn't think my questions through in the chaotic situation I'd found myself in. "Her body stays cold no matter what."

"And my comfort is of no priority," Victoria chimed in cheerily, but with a pointed glare towards the Reverend Mother.

"You're plenty comfortable," she said simply, then turned to me. "Is everything clear? If you have any questions, ask them now."

My mind was reeling. I had too many questions and none at the same time. The tasks were clear, I knew how to clothe and bathe people. Cutting my own palm seemed straightforward enough. I just couldn't wrap my head around the fact that I was in the same room as a vampire, a real vampire, one that had spent the last centuries down here in the dark.

"How often is she visited?" I settled on.

"Daily. But you won't have to see her more than once a week."

"Where... where can I find the... the schedule? If we're not allowed to talk about her... And if the novitiate sisters aren't ever allowed to know..."

"The schedule is on the wall with all the other duties. You will find it under 'cleaning the basement'. We had to get a little creative to keep the secret."

"Oh, I already forgot about that part," Victoria said with a chuckle. "'Cleaning the basement.' How could I forget?"

I wanted to ask more. I wanted to know the answers to questions I couldn't even formulate. "Why?" I ended up with.

Mother Superior raised an eyebrow. "Why what?"

"Why? Why is she here? Why are we doing this?"

"It is an act of mercy, Sister Therese. We're called to love all of God's creation. Even if it is beyond saving, like this one. Think of it as helping a dying sister; you've done that before, haven't you? Except she's in a perpetual limbo between life and death."

"But— But you're not merciful. This is not how we would treat a dying sister. This—"

"Perhaps I misspoke," she interrupted. "That comparison was not fair to the sisters. It wouldn't even be fair to compare the vampire to a murderer or wild beast, though she is both. She is sin incarnate. Demonic."

So why not kill her? The question died on my tongue. I couldn't say it. Even thinking it felt evil. But to spend so much time in the darkness, all alone save for about half an hour of visitation by silent sisters, for centuries... It felt cruel. It felt like torture.

But as Mother Superior had said, no matter how bad it was, Victoria seemed to want to live. So who was I to deny her that?

"I don't have any more questions," I said quietly. The Reverend Mother nodded.

"We'll go back upstairs."

"Goodbye, sister. God bless," Victoria said mockingly, and her voice sent chills down my spine. It was strange, to be so unnerved by someone while pitying her at the same time. I followed Mother Superior up the stairs and back to the main building of the convent. As agreed upon previously, I never mentioned what I saw to anyone, going back to observing the holy silence.

I couldn't see my sisters in the same light anymore. I could only categorise them one way: those who knew, and those who didn't. Not yet. And those who knew... I couldn't decide on what to think of them. To think that everyone I looked up to and loved was part of some crazy conspiracy was beyond me. Some of them gave me knowing glances once my name made it onto the basement cleaners list, but other than that, I was alone with my thoughts. Not one letter made it under my door about the situation.

What had happened in the basement truly stayed in the basement.

***

I didn't know whether to be excited or terrified the first time I was on basement cleaning duty. I grabbed the freshly washed garments and headed down to the basement door, fumbling with the key to open it. I couldn't help but wonder; were the sisters gentle with Victoria? Or were they just as scared as I was, wanting to get it over as quickly as possible? Did they see Victoria as demonic?

I lit and grabbed the lantern on my way down, holding it out like a shield. The darkness in front of me seemed to stretch on forever, and my brain wouldn't stop making up scenarios in which the vampire had escaped her chains and was only waiting for me to get to the bottom before sucking me dry, devouring me whole.

It was silly. Those restraints seemed sturdy. If she'd had a way out, she would've gotten out long ago.

"Who is it?" came the voice from the dark as I reached the bottom of the stairs. "Oh, don't answer. I know you can't."

I walked over, illuminating the woman's figure. She was leaning against the wall, half-sitting, half-lying down. Recognition sparked in her eyes as she looked at me.

"Sister Therese. The new girl. Your first time down here alone. It must be terribly scary."

For the millionth time, I was glad that my vow of silence saved me from smalltalk. I wouldn't have known what to say to a chained vampire. Instead of talking, I resorted to what I'd always resorted to — focusing on the task at hand.

I set down the lantern and took the knife from my pocket, trying to ignore the way Victoria's eyes lit up at the prospect of food. I wondered if she might need more blood than what we were giving her. Was she starving? She would've said something about it, then, wouldn't she?

I winced as I dragged the blade across my palm. I didn't cut deep enough. I gritted my teeth and did it again, deeper this time, relieved to see my blood gushing to the surface. It felt horribly rude to be standing over Victoria like that, so I crouched down, bringing my hand closer to her mouth as I let my blood drip down through the muzzle.

"Sweet as red wine," she purred once I was finished. "Sister Therese, you and I will be very good friends."

Whether to feel proud or disgusted, I didn't know. All I knew was that I had to undress her, and I didn't feel like I was up for the task. But it was my duty, and so I started as soon as my hand was bandaged.

"Do you want to know whether the sisters break their vow of silence down here with me?" she asked me as I undid the straps and pulled off her garments. "It would be the perfect crime, wouldn't it? No one would know. No one can talk about what happens down here. I can't go upstairs to rat them out."

So I wasn't safe from gossiping just because I was taking care of a vampire. But then again, what else was there in her life other than gossiping? And it must not have been too fruitful, given our vow of silence.

"Sister Lucy uses her time here as a sort of second confessional. Sister Bernadette won't stop complaining about the food and convent life in general."

My eyebrows shot up. Oh dear, was this a sin? I could feel in my heart that I was judging them. Sister Bernadette had always been particularly lax when it came to how she carried out her duties, but I never thought she resented her vocation. Maybe becoming a nun wasn't her vocation at all. Why she had decided to take her perpetual vows, then, I had no way of knowing.

No, it was silly to judge them. We were all just sinners trying our best. My face softened as I looked Victoria over. She was also just that, wasn't she? A sinner trying her best. No matter what crimes she had committed before someone chained her to that wall, no matter how heinous, she was deserving of forgiveness. Of gentle care.

No matter what my sinful nature craved — which was to turn around and run back upstairs — I decided I would care for her as though she really was a dying sister. I bathed her gently, letting her rant on and on as I worked. Sister Lucy might've treated her duty to care for Victoria as a second confessional, but she was no less chatty herself. No wonder.

"They never break the vow on the first day," she said when I was already dressing her. "I didn't expect you to, either. 'Only talk when it is necessary to carry out your duties', yada yada. And it's not necessary to talk to me. Some never break it. Some take this whole thing seriously. Being a nun and all." She suddenly grabbed my hand to stop me from working, and I could feel my heart pounding in my chest. Was this it? Was this the moment she hurt me? "You're different. You're different from the ones who resent being nuns, and you're different from the ones who take themselves too seriously."

I yanked my hand out of her hold, cradling it against my chest. Her hold would leave a bruise, no doubt. We stared at each other for a long moment, and I tried to remind myself once again that this pitiful creature was a prisoner, a dead woman in need of care. I went back to strapping the garments onto her.

"You're gentle," she said quietly. "I just have this feeling that if you were to talk... you would call me by name. You would call me Victoria."

I would, I wanted to say. *I would call you anything if it made you more comfortable. I would bring you a blanket to keep out the chill. I would like to do so much for you, no matter how afraid I am.*

Victoria sighed and leaned back against the wall once I was done dressing her. "Maybe I'm dreaming too much. I've thought that and been wrong many times before. At the end of the day, you're all the same: you're here to do your job and never talk about it again. All those sisters who have been tasked with taking care of me... Not one of them ever thought to help. Not one of them ever leaked the secret."

Before I knew it, I had reached out to place a gentle hand on her shoulder. She looked at it, then looked back at me. She seemed confused for a moment. Speechless.

I took my hand away and grabbed the dirty clothes and my lantern. I had other duties to attend to, I couldn't afford to stay and let her talk more. I just hoped that brief, comforting touch would convey how I felt about taking care of her, how I longed to make her feel more like a person instead of a monster.

"Come back soon," she called as I was leaving, "Sister Therese."

***

The second time I went downstairs, I felt a little braver. Victoria hadn't hurt me that first time, and I felt it was unlikely she would this time. Mother Superior must've been correct about her wanting to live more than she wanted to kill us all for doing this to her. Keeping her captive.

When I shone the light on her, she was curled up against the wall, visibly shivering. "Sister Therese," she said softly. "It's the dead of winter by now, isn't it? It rarely gets so unbearably cold in here. I'm usually... okay with the clothing I receive."

I nodded, pity filling my heart once more. I knelt down in front of her and grabbed my knife, slicing the flesh open to feed her. She drank hungrily.

"Some of the sisters don't feed me at all," she admitted quietly, and I could feel my heart shatter at the tone. "Can I have more? More of your blood?"

I moved my hand back above her muzzle, letting more blood drip down into her mouth. She lapped it up like a starving dog. What a miserable existence, and to think some of the sisters would make it even harder on her.

Not that I could necessarily blame them. It was painful and scary, feeding a vampire. But there were thirty of us and only one of her, surely, we could stand to spare some of our blood every week. Jesus had called us to feed the hungry. What use was our becoming nuns if we couldn't even live the Gospel?

"Thank you, sister," she said as I was bandaging my hand. She wasn't in her usual playful mood. Hunger must've made her weary. "I know it's not fair of me to ask, but I'm so cold. Is there any way you could bring a blanket with you on your next visit? Something warm. I'm so terribly cold."

The sisters would immediately know it was me who brought an extra blanket downstairs. Would Mother Superior punish me privately for it? Would I break my solemn vow of obedience by bringing the blanket? I was never instructed against it.

I decided I would try my luck the next time. Until then, there was not much I could do, except...

"What are you doing?" Victoria asked as I took her chained hands in mine, still kneeling before her. I rubbed them gently, trying to create some warmth. My hands weren't awfully warm either, but my body heat must've counted for something. "Oh," she breathed.

She let me rub her hands until I felt some sort of warmth, and then she let me place the lantern next to her, allowing her to take it and hold it up to the parts of her body that felt coldest. I watched her press her cheek against the glass and wondered just how cruel we were for not allowing her more than a few scraps of clothing.

But alas, I had to bathe her. I knew it would only serve to make her colder, but there was nothing I could do, unless I wanted to go against Mother Superior's orders.

"The water is always so cold," she commented as I scrubbed her down with the sponge. "I know hot water is hard to come by even upstairs — I've heard about it from the sisters. But still, sometimes I just wish for a bit of warmth. From anywhere. From a blanket, from the bath, from anywhere. The lantern felt very nice against my skin. Thank you, Sister Therese. Can I keep it with me a bit longer, once you're done bathing me?"

I nodded without thinking. It was just so heart-wrenching to listen to. I had other duties to attend to after basement cleaning, but I couldn't bring myself to hurry along and not let her warm her hands on the lantern's glass exterior. I sat on the ground with her, watching her desperately press her palms against the surface of it.

"Catherine doesn't even know this," she said suddenly, and I looked away from the light to look at her face. It was half-shrouded in darkness from where her fingers were blocking the flame. "But this hasn't always been my life in the convent. By the time Mother Superior of Catherine's came to show her the ropes, the tasks only included feeding, bathing, and clothing. That's what she showed you as well. That's what you'll show the new sisters, if you ever become Mother Superior. I hope, at least. But there were sisters before her, and sisters before those sisters. Different ones. Ones who thought helping me and showing me mercy included a lot more than these three tasks."

I listened intently. Maybe Victoria would answer more of my questions than Mother Superior had. Maybe she would answer the questions I knew I must've had in the back of my mind, but that I couldn't put into words. Maybe I would receive answers I didn't even want to hear.

"They performed many exorcisms on me," she said. "With priests and everything. They burned me with crosses and splashed holy water on me. They did everything to break the curse that is vampirism. I was their little experiment; if they managed to break me somehow, they could communicate it to the rest of the church and have them wage a holy war against vampires. My body... it heals. It doesn't bear the scars of those decades of constant torment. My voice is the same as it was back then, no matter how many times I'd screamed myself hoarse. Nobody knows. Nobody cares to know."

Once again, it only felt appropriate to reach out and place a hand on her shoulder. I wanted her to know I was there for her. That I was listening, and I was horrified by what I heard. That I didn't think it was right.

She huffed out a laugh. "Then the vampires slowly started disappearing. Humans stopped focusing on trying to turn us back, and they got good at killing us instead. The church decided it wouldn't waste any more energy on this little experiment that I was. When the priests stopped coming, it was the best day of my life. I thought they might even let me go. Or even stake me, hell, I wouldn't have objected. I was so broken down, I wanted nothing else but for it to end. But the sisters kept tending to me. I was still chained up. I realised there was no way out."

I scooted a little closer, despite my fears. I embraced Victoria, letting her lean her head on my chest. She let go of the lantern and curled up in my arms, and I couldn't decide whether it was the comfort or the warmth she sought from me. I hoped I could provide both.

"You're either brave or foolish," she muttered against my habit. "Or maybe I'm just not the terrifying monster I once was."

I don't see a monster anymore. I see someone tormented and broken. I see someone in need of a friend.

I held her for minutes on end. She didn't say more about her captivity, and I got lost in my silent prayers for her. I knew I needed to do everything in my power to make her stay less miserable.

When we finally parted, she handed me my lantern without another word. I knew this was likely the first hug she'd received in centuries, and I hoped it would help hold her over until I could next come visit her.

***

The third time I embarked on the journey downstairs, I had with me not only the clean garments I would dress Victoria in, but a thick blanket. My legs weren't shaking as I descended the stairs, and my lantern holding hand was steady.

"Sister Therese," she said before I even reached the bottom of the staircase. The fact that she could tell me apart now simply by my footsteps filled my heart with joy. I hoped she could sense the confidence in them. The eagerness to return.

When she saw me and saw the extra thing I was carrying, her mouth formed a little 'o'. I set the lantern down and placed the blanket on the ground to her right. She reached out to feel the material, and her lips curled into a soft smile. It was nothing like the mocking ones she gave me when I first visited her with Mother Superior; it was innocent and childlike, betraying genuine happiness.

"You might get in trouble for this," she said as she looked up at me. I shrugged, giving her a little smile in turn. She giggled. "Sister Therese, you're getting reckless. What's next? You'll break your vow of silence to talk to me?"

Her tone made it seem like it was just a cheeky little joke, but her eyes told a different story. She really wanted me to talk to her, and my mind went back to the first time I'd visited her on my own. The way she told me she thought I would call her by name.

But I could only shake my head in response. My solemn vow of silence was a vow made to God, and I felt like there was no way I could break it, even if it was to comfort Victoria. I hoped my other means of comfort would suffice.

"I can't say I'm surprised," she said with a sigh, trying to hide the disappointment in her voice. "You're a good sister. I only wish— I only wish being a good sister wasn't at odds with..." She trailed off, averting her eyes. I had a feeling I knew what she meant. I felt the same way. I wished there was a way for me to fulfil my duties that somehow included making her feel better.

I knelt down in front of her, but I didn't take out my knife this time. Instead, I reached behind her head, feeling out the mechanism holding the muzzle in place.

It was metal, which must've meant it was silver — that way, Victoria couldn't remove it herself, even if she could reach it. I, on the other hand, had no trouble getting it to open and slowly removing it.

"What are you doing?" she asked, alarmed. "What are you doing? Why did you take that off? You realise I could bite you, right?"

I nodded and put the muzzle on the ground next to me. Without it blocking half of her face, Victoria looked quite beautiful in the dancing light of the lantern. But she looked frightened.

"You'll get in so much trouble if someone finds out about this. You don't understand! What if they find out? What if they bar you from ever coming back down here? Sister Therese, I—"

I held out my arm, pulling my sleeve up and exposing my wrist. I'd thought and prayed long and hard about this, and this was the conclusion I'd come to: the only way for Victoria to properly sate her hunger and for me to know that she'd done that was to let her have control over how much she drank. And I couldn't do that through a dog muzzle.

"What are you doing?" she asked in a small voice. She certainly didn't look like a monster now. She looked lost. I didn't budge. "You can't possibly mean for me to... bite you?"

I pushed my wrist a little closer to her face. I knew what I wanted. If she really didn't want it, she could tell me, but her concern about me getting in trouble wasn't going to deter me. Some sisters were *starving* her, I needed to make sure she was well-fed.

She gingerly took my arm in her chained hands, and opened her mouth, fangs glistening in the light. She glanced at me one last time and I nodded my approval.

It hurt when her fangs sank into the delicate flesh of my wrist. I could feel her sucking on the wounds and I winced, looking away instead so I at least wouldn't pass out. Despite it having been my own offer, my heart was pounding in my chest, worst case scenarios running through my mind at a rapid speed.

But soon, she stopped. I could feel her remove her fangs and she sat back, letting go of my arm. "I can't remember the last time I fed normally," she said wistfully.

"I... I don't even know what to say. I can't believe you'd do this for me. You have a heart of gold, Sister Therese. Truly. Thank you."

I smiled at her, though my wrist still ached. It would surely bruise by the next day. I held up the muzzle and she nodded.

"Yes, put it back. Quickly."

I fastened it around her head and quickly bandaged both my wrist and my palm. It felt like lying, and I didn't particularly feel good about it, but deception was apparently running rampant in the convent, given we had a whole vampire hidden underneath it. God wouldn't look favourably on either side, I reckoned, so why not make it at least more bearable for the prisoner in our care?

Once I bathed and clothed her, I took great joy in seeing her bundle up under the thick blanket I'd brought for her. "It can't trap any heat from me," she said sadly, giving me a look I could only describe as longing. "If it's possible... Would you consider..."

I got under the blanket with her without her needing to finish the request. I could feel how cold her body was as she pressed into mine, chasing warmth that was so elusive so far up north. It was truly a shame that it was our convent that decided to keep her captive. Maybe a convent down south would've been more humane, if there was even a humane way to keep someone prisoner.

"I was religious, once," she said softly. "Back when I was human. I don't remember much — my view of it is tainted by the priests and nuns that tortured me. It was a source of comfort, I believe, at one point. A source of safety. A source of community. Is that what it's like for you? Is it safe?"

I couldn't answer right away. It used to be safe before I learned of Victoria. It used to bring me immense joy and pride to be part of a religious order. Even with all the hardships I'd faced, I was someone who could say I'd found my vocation and was happy with it.

But now? How could I be proud of being a part of this? No matter which way I looked at it, no matter the angle or lens, I just couldn't feel the same innocent joy. It wasn't safe anymore. I was caught up in a web of lies and pain. There was no way God wanted this.

"I see," she said, looking down at the lantern. "I'm sorry. I hoped it was different for you. Truly."

We stayed there, under the blanket, for the next however many minutes in silence. She didn't say anything. I couldn't say anything. There was nothing to say, really. Nothing that would've made the situation any better. Unless I could stand up and tell her 'up you go, I have the keys to your chains, you're free now,' there was nothing I could do. So we sat there, watching as the lantern burned. I tried to imagine what it would've been like for me to sit there in the darkness for days on end, weeks, months, years, decades, *centuries*. I could barely imagine a week.

"You should go," she said eventually. Of course, I knew that. My tasks weren't going to handle themselves. "Bring the blanket back up. I'm sorry I made you bring it downstairs. I don't want you to get in trouble with Catherine."

The wrath of Mother Superior was on my mind a lot, but not as much as the wrath of God if I denied a shivering prisoner her last bastion against the cold. I climbed out from under the blanket and left it with her, grabbing her dirty clothes and my lantern.

"I told you to bring it back!" she insisted, but the way she was huddled up there told me something completely different. I smiled at her and shook my head. I was ready to accept punishment if this got back to Mother Superior. "Sister Therese, this is not going to end well."

I'd known that for some time. Every visit I made down to the basement only strengthened my resolve in what I was going to do.

Before I left, I set the clothes and the lantern back down and knelt in front of Victoria, taking her hands through the blanket. I leaned my head against her pulled up knees and prayed, silently, that my plan would work out in her favour. I begged God to give us just a crumb of His infinite mercy. If Victoria was sin incarnate, a fact I believed in less and less, then I was wrong, and God would find a way to sabotage me. But until then, I had to believe she was good. Worth saving.

"Sister..." she breathed. I looked up at her, determination in my eyes. "What are you planning on doing?"

I gently patted her hands and stood back up, grabbing the clothes and lantern once more. As I made my way to the staircase, she didn't say a word. It was only when I started ascending that I heard her voice again.

"Will I see you again?"

I wished so badly that I could answer. Instead, I continued on up, ready to finish my chores for the day.

***

Mother Superior never said anything about the blanket, but I could see it was back in its place just a day after my visit to Victoria. The sister after me must've taken it away from her, a thought that made my heart break.

But I had bigger things to worry about. I looked at the schedule and planned my next moves carefully. From what Victoria had told me, the keys to her chains must've been in Mother Superior's room or office. I prayed for guidance and help in finding them, and God seemed to be on my side — when I next talked to the Reverend Mother, I spotted a special little box on her desk that I had never even considered before. Maybe it was intuition, maybe it was the Spirit, but I knew that was the box that held the keys to Victoria's freedom.

The next time I was instructed to fetch something for Mother Superior, I tried opening the box. It was locked. With a small, silent prayer for forgiveness, I grabbed the whole box and hoped Victoria would be strong enough to simply force it open.

The fourth time I went down into the basement, I was shaking in fear again. I had the box in my pocket next to the knife. I didn't hear about anyone searching for it, nor did Mother Superior summon me, but that didn't stop the anxiety from consuming me.

"Sister Therese," Victoria said softly and affectionately as I approached the bottom of the staircase. "It's you, isn't it? They took away the blanket, but I don't think that's a surprise to either of us. I hope you weren't foolish enough to bring it back."

Oh, I wasn't. I was much more foolish.

"Good," she said when I finally came into her line of sight. "Let's just do everything the normal way, shall we? Like that first time. You don't need to be my hero, Sister Therese. Nobody does. I don't wish the possible consequences on anyone kind enough to try. Besides, where would I even go? What would I do? I'm a monster. I would do nothing but go back to hurting people until someone finally staked me."

I swallowed and tried to regulate my breathing. Victoria must've seen something on my face, because her smile faltered.

"Sister? Is everything okay?"

I put down the garments and the lantern and pulled the box from my pocket. I walked over and pressed it into her shackled hands, urging her to open it. She furrowed her brows in confusion but tried regardless.

"It's locked. What's in it?"

I tapped the metal on her wrist, then gestured to the box. I gave her a look, hoping she would try again and break it open this time. She stared at me like I'd gone insane.

"It's... No. There's no way. This box— Does it really hold— But it's locked, how would you even know? If you can't even open it... But that's why you need me to, isn't it? You want me to break it open?" I nodded frantically. "I... Okay."

Victoria tried again, this time with the entirety of her vampire strength. The lid of the box popped open and a set of keys fell out, hitting the concrete floor with a jingle. I quickly snatched them up and tried them on Victoria's restraints, and they fit in the lock snugly. Soon enough, all her shackles were falling to the floor one by one. Lastly, I reached behind her head once more to undo the latch of the muzzle, freeing her from it hopefully forever.

She stared at her restraints like she couldn't fully believe they weren't attached to her anymore. After centuries of being chained up, I could only imagine the feeling. "I'm... free?"

I took a deep breath. "I will come back to open the basement door during the night," I said, uneasy that I had to break my vow. Not like it mattered more than stealing from Mother Superior.

"You spoke," she said, awe-struck. "You spoke to me for the first time in... weeks. I forgot what your voice sounded like. You'll really let me out? After I just told you I would have to go back to hurting people?"

"I'm coming with you," I said, dropping yet another bomb that seemed to shake Victoria's world in its foundations. "You'll have my blood."

"Sister Therese..."

"Let us sit. Just for a moment, before I go back up and prepare for the escape."

Victoria was all jittery from the excitement of her possible escape, but she humoured me, sitting back down on the ground next to me. "What will happen when you... I mean, you're only human. You can't... stay with me forever."

"I don't know," I admitted. "I just know that I don't think this is right. I entrusted your case to God — if He wills it, we'll make it out, and He'll make us a path."

"What if He doesn't will it?"

"Then we'll likely both die. But I'd rather die trying to save someone than live knowing I'm torturing someone innocent."

"I'm not innocent."

"You have been for the past centuries. What crimes did you commit, trapped down here?"

Victoria fell silent. "Don't get me wrong, I... I'm eager to see the moonlight again. To walk. To run. I just don't want you to regret it."

"Then don't make me," I said with a soft smile. "Victoria, I have trust in you. I'm well-aware of your nature, but many sinners have repented and changed before you. *I* have repented and changed."

"Many priests have tried to make me repent."

"They didn't love you."

Victoria stopped in her tracks, her red eyes widening. "What?"

"You cannot hate someone into repenting. You can only ever do that through love. It's the greatest commandment, to love. And I love you, with all of my heart. I believe you can change."

She looked away and squeezed her eyes shut, exhaling shakily. When she opened them again, I could see tears glistening in them. "You do have a heart of gold, don't you?"

"Any good you see in me is the work of the Holy Spirit. Without His grace, I'm nothing."

"I think I could learn to love God again," she said, voice breaking. "Through you."

"That would be the greatest gift and honour."

"Sister Therese..."

"Yes?"

"I'm so sorry."

Before I could process the words, Victoria had grabbed me by the face and slammed my head against the wall behind me. I fell to the floor in a dizzy haze, only half-comprehending that I could still see the light of the lantern and the way Victoria moved to grab it. Then she walked off with it, leaving me in the dark to pass out.

***

The next time I awoke, I found myself in a pitch black room. At first, I didn't understand where I was. The memories from before came back in bits and pieces, and soon I was in a panic, wanting to crawl my way to the stairs and up to find Victoria.

Except I'd been chained to the wall. The same restraints I had helped to get off Victoria were now binding me, by the neck and both wrists and ankles.

What had I done?

"Victoria!" I screamed into the darkness. I couldn't help but imagine the early days of her own captivity, how she must've screamed and thrashed to be let out. "Victoria!"

The door at the top of the stairs opened, and soon I heard someone descending them. I'd wanted so badly for her to come back and explain herself, but now that she was, I suddenly felt like I couldn't say a single word. I was afraid of what she would do once she reached me. I was as afraid as I'd been the first time we locked eyes.

I could see the light of the lantern as she neared the bottom of the stairs, and soon she turned the corner. She was wearing a habit instead of the clothes I helped put on her so many times. Her hair was dripping with water.

"Sister Therese," she said with a smile as she walked over. "You're awake."

"What is this?" I demanded, though my voice came out more like a plea. "Victoria, what have you done?"

"What have *I* done?" She let out a shrill laugh that made me press myself up against the wall even more. "I've done nothing but let them see divine justice while they were still here on earth. They've imprisoned me, tortured me, left me to rot—"

"What have you done to them?" I asked, increasingly anxious. "What have you done?"

She crouched down, just like I'd done many times when I visited her. She brought the lantern up to my face, drinking in whatever despair she saw on it. She looked like a different person from the one I'd admitted my foolish, naive love for. "What is it, Sister Therese? Are you *scared*?"

"Has it all been a lie? Has it all been a lie to get me to let you out?"

Her face softened and she reached out her free hand to caress my face. I didn't dare pull away. "No. No, I do think you're lovely, sister. With a heart of gold. But you must understand, I could never be truly happy until I saw those wretched women die by my hands. I painted the snow red with their blood — it's really quite pretty when the moon shines on it the right way."

"I don't know you," I said shakily, not even beginning to comprehend the fact that so many of my sisters could be lying dead upstairs; all because of me and my foolish decision not to trust Mother Superior.

She tilted her head to the side. "And I don't know you. But I do know this: I'm never letting you go, Sister Therese. And once I turn you, we'll have all the time in the world to get to know each other."

About the Author

Zi Trone is but a humble fear enthusiast with a passion for writing. An undying love for scared and crying characters has been the driving force behind hundreds of thousands of words already written, and hopefully many more to come.

Vampires Won't Hurt You

Max Browne

CW: Emotional whump

Whumpee: Woman, Whumper: N/A, Caretaker: N/A

"Mom? Dad? Can you hear me?" she whispered, her ear to the basement door.

She knew they could. She heard the light shuffle of their feet, although she couldn't see their shadows in the silvery line of light beneath the door. She pictured her mother and father exchanging glances with one another, like they did from across the dinner table: that silent, pointed communication. Worst of all, she could smell them—all that skin and meat and *blood*. It made her empty stomach twist into knots. It made her mouth water.

She didn't blame them for not answering. In fact, she knew she should stop. But she continued, "Please, I'm still here. I'm still your daughter. Nothing's—" *Nothing's changed,* she wanted to say; they all knew that wasn't true. "Please, I ... I miss you."

Her voice went small and quiet. She wasn't sure it carried through the door. She heard footsteps approaching, and it was all the more disconcerting that her heart didn't leap in surprise, instead remaining frozen behind her bloodstained blouse.

A sudden *BANG* on the door made her recoil, nearly tumbling down the stairs. "Our daughter is *dead,*" her father spat, his voice cracking. "You're going to stay down there and starve, demon." The footsteps retreated quickly. She winced as, somewhere on the second floor, a door slammed.

A sob bubbled up from within her cold chest. She covered her mouth so her parents wouldn't hear. She didn't want them to feel guilty. She understood, really. But some primal part of her—maybe the part that was fixated on the sheer amount of blood coursing through her parents' veins—wouldn't let her lie down on the concrete floor and die.

She was already dead, but still, she wanted so badly to live.

About the Author

Max Browne is a writer and editor of odd speculative fiction. When they're not writing, you can find them ... wait. Scratch that. You can't find them. They're nowhere to be found—but they did leave a nice note thanking you for reading.

Swallowed Whole

Mill Cohen

"Just do it." A chill shot down Russell's spine as he finally made the call.

He'd agonized over it for so long, *years* at this point since she'd made the offer. He just couldn't take it anymore. The sharp piercing in his neck or his chest or his wrist or his thigh, wherever she felt like sinking her teeth that night, always changing, leaving him ever-tense. Being thrown around like a helpless ragdoll, unable to offer a shred of resistance to her effortless, all-encompassing power, subject to every flick of her wrist.

It had to end. He wouldn't escape on his own, not as he was now, and at this rate, he might die before he ever got a chance to try. He needed to be stronger. He needed that same power piping through *his* veins, that same vigor in every move *he* made. And there was only one way to get that. No way around it.

What would happen when he finally returned home to his family was a problem for later.

"Oh?" Russell could *feel* the amusement radiating off her, fine-tuned to Wulfwynn's every inflection. "And I thought you'd never ask. What changed, hm?" She caressed his face as she spoke, the pointed ends of her nails trailing from behind his ear to his throat and back again, ready to carve into his skin like it was butter if she so desired.

"I just want it to stop." Russell's vision blurred with hot tears. He'd *told* himself he wouldn't cry, that he wouldn't let his last moments alive be spent crying. "That's all."

Wulfwynn's nails rested on a somewhat-fresh wound on his throat, still tender and healing. She tilted his chin up as she traced it with her finger, and he obediently looked up to the ceiling so the skin stretched taut. "Oh, Russell. You never could withstand very much, could you?" she said with faux-sympathy. "Very well. I will claim you as a vampire of my very own."

She tapped his throat. "You'll stay just like that."

Russell didn't respond, heart pounding so hard he could feel it in his temples. His last living words couldn't be an acceptance of her orders. *'That's all'* was at least better than that. Fitting, even.

Wulfwynn's fangs split his skin and buried themselves in his neck, two daggers he had to stand there and take without protest. Her head shifted, putting her teeth at an angle to widen the wounds so their edges no longer hugged the circumference of her fangs, allowing warm blood to flow freely into her mouth as she drew it out. He whimpered: it never got easier, his body screaming against the intrusion. At least this time, he knew it was the last.

It went on and on and *on,* going far beyond the usual minutes it would take. Russell found himself unable to stand, suddenly, his legs crumpling beneath him, but he didn't fall. He was caught in Wulfwynn's embrace, her arms snaking around and constricting him tight.

Just when he'd begun to drift off, the pain changed.

Bright, burning agony shot through his neck and spread like a wildfire, every beat of his heart sending it further down his limbs as the fangs retreated. Russell tried to scream, but he couldn't, Wulfwynn's hand wrapping around his throat to massage the point of the bite, the pain somehow *intensifying* under her touch.

He couldn't even try to pull away, his body sluggish and limp as the venom consumed him whole.

"You asked for this," Wulfwynn's voice sounded from what could have been miles above. "You asked to be mine."

She held him against her as he broiled from the inside out, laughing as he twitched and wept. Though it stretched on and on, mercifully, it was not as long as the bloodletting, and the fire slowly died down until only warm embers were left in his veins.

It was at that moment, when room opened up in his mind for things other than the pain, that Russell became aware his heart was no longer beating.

He staggered backward, his body finding the strength to hold him upright once more, just barely. His legs trembled like a newborn fawn's. "It's done?"

"It's done!" she agreed. "You're dead to the world."

Russell turned to bolt. He made it no more than a few steps—not even to the door—before tripping over his own feet and crashing to the floor, a dull ache radiating through him.

This wasn't right. This wasn't how being a vampire was supposed to *work.* Why did he feel weaker than he had when he was human? He was shaky and lightheaded and not even *close* to wielding the power Wulfwynn did. "I don't understand. I'm supposed to be strong!"

"Without any blood? I don't think so." Wulfwynn's footsteps got closer and closer until she gave him a nudge with her foot, turning him over onto his back.

It was foolish to ask and he knew it. He was barely thinking, his mind a jumbled haze incapable of keeping a coherent plan. His tongue flicked over the edges of his new fangs. "Can I have blood?"

The toe of her shoe tapped against the side of his head, Wulfwynn's smirk taking up his view. "Who said anything about that? A vampire doesn't require blood to *live.* No, I think I'll keep you just like this."

"What?" Russell was *cold.* The embers were all gone now and they'd taken everything with them, leaving his body entirely free of warmth. "Wait, wait, you can't—"

Wulfwynn's shoe came down hard on his chest, crushing half his ribcage and a lung in one go. The excruciating blow tore a blood-curdling scream from him, and a gasp, only one lung left to accommodate it as pain took over his whole world once more. He writhed in a feeble attempt to escape it, to give his ruined chest any relief, but she held him in place with ease.

She smiled. "You'll find that now that you're a little more durable, I can do whatever I like with you."

***

The vampire thudded to the floor the moment the stake burst through her heart, but Aspen made sure to saw her head off too, just in case. Could never be too careful about these things.

They clutched the gash in their abdomen: she hadn't gone down without a fight. They'd live, but it fucking *hurt* in the meantime. They forced deep breaths as the adrenaline wore off and the suffering truly began. At least they'd gotten the head off before then.

Aspen stood, scanning the room. Some sort of entrance hall, a few tasteful side tables hugging the walls and little bench sofas like she'd be receiving guests. Fuck, this place was *huge,* and they had to search the whole damn thing in case there were victims, which there probably were. They groaned and got to their feet.

They stumbled their way through the maze of the castle, diligently checking every room. One opened to a pile of corpses in various stages of decay, some looking and *smelling* months-old, while others had clearly been murdered just days prior. Aspen gagged and slammed the door shut, just barely managing not to vomit. They'd already lost too much water from the blood loss. They couldn't afford it.

It seemed unlikely that they'd find any living victims. But they had to be sure.

Several room-checks later, they came across the first locked door, easily broken with their hammer. When they opened it, they were sure for a second they'd found the interrupted beginnings of a second body dump, only one corpse to be found here, slumped against the wall.

Then the corpse blinked up at them.

Aspen stared. The man before them was *skeletally* thin, skin sticking to bone with nothing in between. He was covered in the scars of puncture wounds, especially concentrated around his neck, ringing his throat like a collar he couldn't take off. Fangs protruded from his slack mouth, confirmation that no, this was certainly *not* a living human.

His eyes settled on Aspen's hand, slowly reaching for the stake at their hip. "Just do it," he rasped.

"What are you?" they breathed before they could come up with something a little more sensitive.

The vampire's voice came dead and rote, his words clearly oft-repeated: "I'm a weak, pathetic toy that lives forever."

"Oh." Their hand fell from their stake. "You look... hungry."

"Never had blood. She doesn't let me," the vampire explained. He looked as though every breath was an effort, like he was forever locked in the process of dying. "Just want it to stop."

This wasn't Aspen's job. Or was it? They slayed vampires to protect people, right? From the sound of it, this one was a victim of the one they just killed. Shouldn't they be protecting him, too?

They walked closer, crouching next to the miserable vampire. "Open your mouth," they ordered as gently as they were able. "I'm gonna help you."

The vampire popped his mouth open without hesitation or even, seemingly, comprehension.

Aspen took the front of their blood-soaked shirt and raised it above his mouth, wringing its contents out like fresh-squeezed juice. The vampire's eyes went wide, and he lapped it up with fervent desperation, letting out a keening whine when the shirt ran dry.

"Please, more," he begged.

"You can have more, but not from me. There's a room where she keeps all her... deceased victims. There's some more recent ones, figure they're not using it, right? You know where that is?" Aspen took his bony hand in theirs, doing their best to heft him up.

The vampire was able to remain standing. "I do. She's... not here?"

"She's dead. I killed her." Aspen gestured to their laceration. "Parting gift."

"Dead?" His eyes were still wide as saucers.

"Yep. You go feed while I check the rest of the rooms," they instructed. "I'm getting you out of here. We'll figure it out."

The vampire gave a shaky nod. "Okay."

When Aspen finished checking the rest of the rooms–no more victims, as they'd suspected–they found the vampire at the site of their kill, staring down at his decapitated sire.

"You good?" they asked, fishing the keys from their pocket.

His voice came hollow again. "She said it would be forever. It's been... a long time. Everyone I knew is dead."

"Maybe you have grandkids?" Aspen offered.

The vampire's eyes raised from the body to meet Aspen's, the faintest hint of a smile on his lips. "...Maybe I have grandkids."

About the Author

Mill Cohen primarily writes about vampires having a bad time.

The Consequences of Walking Alone After Sunset

Max Browne

CW: Vampire feeding

Whumpee: Unspecified, Whumper: Man, Caretaker: N/A

I had thought that dying would be quicker, or would hurt less. My eyes were wide open in the dark. I counted each shadowy sidewalk crack and every tiny sprout growing between their seams. It didn't distract me as much as I'd hoped from the cold lips on my throat, the blood gushing from my carotid artery, the cadaverous fingers caressing my hair.

He was gentle, and it was agonizing. My cheeks were wet. I thought it must be blood before realizing that didn't make any sense. I tasted salt and briefly wondered what he was tasting, what I tasted like.

My lungs burned and spasmed emptily. *This is it. It's over.* The thought, accompanied by a strange mix of panic and solace, hung in my head for a few excruciating moments. Then he lowered my body to the ground.

The sidewalk was still warm from the sun, rough on my cheek. Blood trickled down my neck and soaked the collar of my shirt. His fingers skimmed lovingly through my hair. "I'll see you again soon, fledgling." My eyes slipped shut, and I waited for the relief of death.

It didn't come.

About the Author

Max Browne is a writer and editor of odd speculative fiction. When they're not writing, you can find them ... wait. Scratch that. You can't find them. They're nowhere to be found—but they did leave a nice note thanking you for reading.

The Monsters We Make

Megan Renee Doyle

CW: Character death

Whumpee: Woman, Whumper: Woman, Caretaker: N/A

The sun would rise soon, and Katarina could already feel that familiar tug against her consciousness, calling her to lose herself and let her body enter stasis until the sun set once again and she could arise as a creature of the night.

She never considered it to be real sleep—in three hundred years she'd never so much as dreamed during the day—it was like she ceased to exist for several hours until life filled the corners of her body for the velvet darkness of night. But it was a kind of rest all the same, and Katarina was tired.

To slip away easily cradled in the arms of her lover—there were worse ways to spend the day. Katarina nuzzled into Alex's soft form, feeling the gentle curve of her breast against her cheek. If only they could stay that way forever.

In a true scene of familiar domesticity, they would both retire to the caskets Katarina had made for them. The polished oak and silk-lined plush cushions had made them resemble real beds more than the final resting places they were meant to be.

Usually Katarina would insist they go to bed, resting perfectly parallel to each other, arranged for that wonderful moment in the evening when they would both wake up and see each other first thing. Even if Katarina woke first, she would lie down and enjoy the moment, counting the seconds until Alex opened her eyes.

Their bedtime rituals were wonderful, but lying together on the floor felt rather comfortable at the moment.

Besides, her own casket had been kicked over and splintered, scattering bits of shredded pink silk and loose down feathers all across the penthouse apartment.

The room was incredibly still and silent, except for the occasional wet drip hitting the hardwood floor. It could have been spilled water from the crystal vase that had crashed on its side, or it could be the blood sliding off the crimson petals of the roses inside.

Dirt and debris littered every surface. A few strands of pearls had been slashed and scattered to every corner. The velvet sofa had been slashed to ragged pieces. There were several fist-sized holes in the wall paneling, leaving deep divots in the wood. There was a torso-sized dent in the plaster by the door, probably a perfect match for Katarina's own back.

Almost nothing had escaped the destruction. Even the dining table, a giant twelve-seater made of one solid piece of wood, was leaning at a steep and precarious angle. One of its legs had been snapped completely off, leaving a lethally sharp jagged edge. Another leg was merely cracked, barely supported by its splintered pieces.

That one was especially a shame, because the table had been an antique, nearly as old as Katarina herself. She'd had it almost a hundred years, and it was not easy to move to its current location, considering she'd had to get it up five floors in the middle of the night without her neighbors noticing.

When Alex had first seen it—the first human Katarina had ever been brave enough to bring into her inner sanctum—she'd recognized its craftsmanship immediately. She ran her hand reverently across the smooth surface. Alex's hands knew exactly how much love and attention went into crafting such a stunning piece. "Is this real?" she'd asked breathlessly.

Katarina, who had been casually leaning against a doorframe and admiring the way Alex had been so impressed by her carefully curated collection of things, responded with a seemingly cavalier "Of course."

"Wow, this is all so . . ." Alex cut herself off with that adorable little blush that bloomed in her cheeks. "Sorry, I'm gushing again."

Katarina stilled her lips with a kiss and then handed her a glass—something bubbly to tickle the senses but not much alcohol to affect the blood.

Truth be told, Katarina liked it when Alex would wax poetic about what she called history. Alex, a woman who considered herself anachronistic with her era. Someone who enjoyed building furniture by hand. Studying the old masters. Always with an eye drawn curiously toward the past.

Katarina liked it when Alex asked for mundane details about her life in previous centuries. She liked it when Alex would think up some notable name and asked if Katarina had met them. She liked it when Alex got breathless at "the miracle of it all." It stroked her ego quite well.

And when Katarina had told her that all she had could be hers too, immortality and all, Alex's beautiful brown eyes had gone so wide like a sweet baby deer. Katarina wished she could replay that moment a hundred times more.

Turning Alex had been easy. Alex had enthusiastically received the bite from Katarina, knowing she was being bestowed with a rare and powerful gift. A quick bite, a little blood, a shared drink from the cup of each other's veins, and from then on the two were inextricably linked. Alex had whispered, "I love you," over and over again as the sun rose on her last night of mortality.

Katarina was able to keep her wits a little longer, and she considered herself quite happy. Alex had come into her life at the perfect time, and Alex was the perfect woman for Katarina. After all, immortality was long, and the passing time would be much sweeter when shared with another.

Alex had been initially appealing because she was fascinated with the past, but in reality she was the key to Katarina's future. A companion from this age would help her connect with the next several generations of humans. She would keep her nimble and present and grounded, which was crucial for long-term survival.

Alex would bring her enthusiasm and wonder into their life together. She would be the bridge that would help Katarina connect with the ever-evolving world. She would help her keep up while living among humans, while at the same time hanging onto Katarina for wisdom and knowledge. It was such a delicious proposition. How could Katarina let herself pass it up?

Maybe it was an ill-conceived idea to hang her emotional health and longevity on another person.

In the present moment, though, more sensations tugged at Katarina's consciousness. The blood that caked Katarina's skin was slowly transforming from slick to sticky. Whether it was her own or Alex's, she couldn't be sure. Their blood had mingled together into a syrupy wine that stained both their clothes and skin.

Katarina could feel the itch of a cut healing on her forehead. It had started as a deep gouge, nearly tearing out her eye. She'd screamed in pain but couldn't pause to assess the damage. Instead, she'd raked her own nails out like talons until she could feel flesh beneath her fingernails. Alex had to back off after that, scrabbling at the floor to get away, leaving deep scratches in the wood.

Alex opened her mouth in a feral hiss, showing her pearly white fangs still dripping with Katarina's blood.

"Oh stop that." Katarina had wiped Alex's blood dripping down her lip, though she could feel it smeared even further across her face.

Alex spat out, "Fuck you," then, like an old habit that refused to die, her lips quirked at the innuendo before her mouth twisted back into another teeth-flashing snarl.

Katarina wasn't sure exactly when they went from lovers to enemies. Like everyone else, they'd had a honeymoon period, when they couldn't stop feeling each other's bodies and sharing deep kisses and dark nights.

But Alex was always a curious creature. She valued her independence as a human, and that did not change after she became a creature of the night. She wanted to go out and hunt for blood on her own, and after Katarina taught her some of the tricks she'd picked up over the years—how to subtly separate a human from a group, how to spot a good place to feed in privacy—she let her indulge in these little urges for control. She was proud of her.

Katarina preferred to feed a little at a time; she rarely killed her victims, and she certainly never made a mess. Her habits were built from necessity—and a lot of trial and error—because she came from a time when humans still truly believed in demons and witches, and the surest way to survive was to make as few waves as possible. If she had been sloppy, sooner or later her prey would come hunting for her instead.

Alex, though, was good at hunting and taking the blood she craved. A little too good. She gorged herself on her new life. Sometimes she would decimate whole families in a single night. Sometimes she would lure pretty young things from the same club over and over again. Sometimes she fed on high-profile celebrities, just to see what their blood tasted like.

Her little bloody reign of terror kept moving in ever-tightening circles around their home. Alex laughed off Katarina's warnings. After all, what good were a few puny humans against a couple of all-powerful vampires?

Alex was better at being a monster than Katarina ever was. She wielded her beauty like a weapon. She moved much more smoothly and languidly than a human ever could—telegraphing her otherness to anyone who beheld her. She killed without discretion or guilt.

Katarina had wanted to turn Alex into a monster, so a monster Alex had become. They had fought, and it was not pretty or neat.

"You did this to me," Alex had said, spreading her arms out wide, showing Katarina the cruel destruction she'd inflicted on Alex's body, even as the flesh knitted itself back together. No matter how badly she was injured, Alex never showed whether she felt any pain. "Isn't this exactly what you wanted?"

Even covered in blood and slowly healing from gruesome injuries, Alex was a vision in white lacy lingerie. Like a bride on her wedding night. Katarina's mouth watered at the thought of her supple breasts and soft ringlets of blond hair. Of course she was everything Katarina had always dreamed of.

When did that dream become a living nightmare? Katarina had let it go on too long. Alex, who was supposed to be her tether to new generations of humans, was quickly becoming a liability who would eventually incur their wrath.

Earlier that evening, Katarina had awakened from her casket first, as she usually did. Alex drank deeply every night, and she slept just as deeply during the day.

Quietly and carefully, Katarina lifted the lid of Alex's casket. Alex lay completely still, not even breathing. If not for her full lips and rosy cheeks, she would resemble a corpse instead of looking merely asleep.

Katarina kneeled transfixed next to Alex's casket, remembering all the nights they shared. All the kisses they stole. All the times they cuddled in each other's arms. Alex was beautiful; she always had been. Lying there peacefully, she looked so soft, much like the fragile and enthusiastic woman Katarina had fallen in love with.

Caught up in the moment, Katarina hesitated.

Then, Alex's eyes flung wide open. Katarina froze, shock and dismay gluing her in place where she crouched over Alex's supine form.

Alex's gaze took her in, from the guilt-stricken look on Katarina's face to the crudely carved wooden stake in Katarina's hand, poised to plunge straight into Alex's heart.

It seemed trite to say, but all hell broke loose after that.

They fought on the floor. They fought from wall to wall. They shattered windows. They broke furniture. They pulled on each other's weaknesses with claws and words. The apartment was trashed. And any humans that were still alive after Alex's little binge last night would have long fled if they had any brains at all.

Katarina faced Alex in their little stand-off, surrounded by the crumbled mess of their lives poorly tied together. She'd tried to kill Alex, yes, and of course Alex took great exception to that. Katarina did not blame her for her anger.

Alex launched herself at Katarina; she full-body-leapt across the room. Katarina twisted, but she couldn't avoid her and was knocked down flat on her back.

Alex landed on top of her, fist plunged into the middle of her gut. Katarina screamed in pain as she felt hot liquid start to pour out of the wound.

The truth is, their relationship was probably doomed from the start.

Alex's fingers pulsed in her abdomen, causing a fresh wave of nausea-inducing agony to rip through Katarina as Alex's hand rearranged Katarina's long-neglected organs. Alex's eyes were glowing bright white with bloodlust; her lips were curled back into a rictus grin of triumph.

Katarina had found a beautiful and intelligent woman, plucked her from her youth, and in trying to mold her into something that would serve Katarina's own emotional needs—stability, safety, unending admiration—she'd twisted that perfect woman into a monster just like her. There was nothing left of the old Alex, eyes wide with wonder at the world, hands shaping beautiful wooden creations, and heart always pointing her backward toward history. She was now a creature perfect for killing, with supernatural strength and glowing beauty that would mesmerize even the most hardened heart.

And, worst of all, she completely hated Katarina, who'd made her.

Katarina reached up to claw at Alex, carving ribbons of flesh from her beautiful face. But Alex shrugged off the mutilation like she barely felt anything. Katarina could feel her strength fading. She'd lost too much blood.

Alex, still dripping from her own half-healed wounds, used her other hand to reach for Katarina's own face.

Katarina flinched, unsure what she would do, but instead Alex wiped some of the blood off Katarina's forehead.

Her touch was so gentle; Katarina wanted to cry.

Alex bent forward and planted a demure kiss on Katarina's temple. When she spoke, her breath blew hot against her face. "You gave me everything, and I will forever be thankful for that." One hand gently cupped Katarina's jaw, the barest whisper of a touch, while the other kept its iron grip on her insides. "But it's clear that we're over now."

It would be so easy to give up right then. Katarina had lived a long life, and it had been filled with moments of luxury and peace. But Katarina also had to fight for nearly every day of her life, supernaturally extended as it was. She knew deep-seated cold and hunger. She knew war and famine. She knew how to carry on when everything else had failed and sheer spite was all that drove her.

Alex had had the passion and energy of youth to lend her strength. But Katarina had lived centuries and knew unadulterated, wild, dirty, cruel *survival.*

The pain in her abdomen was blinding, but the instinct to move was still there. Katarina grabbed Alex's beautiful golden locks and pulled herself up, even as Alex's fingers dug further into her torso. She surged upward, locking their lips together in one last bloody kiss.

For a brief moment, Alex was surprised, but her body gave in to the familiar gesture, and she sank into the kiss. Her fingers inside Katarina loosened.

Katarina didn't think. She just acted. She tangled her fist in Alex's hair, her grip a tight leash keeping Alex from rearing back. Katarina's other hand shot forward, quick as lightning, punching straight through Alex's chest cavity until her fingers gripped Alex's heart from either side of her sternum. Then she yanked her whole arm back, and a split-second later she had her prize in her grasp.

Alex stared with wide eyes, even as Katarina's hold on her hair kept her pinned in place. She watched as her heart beat once—and twice—in Katarina's hand.

Then Katarina rammed it into the splintered table leg, piercing the whole thing—both Alex's heart and Katarina's palm. Katarina screamed in pain.

Alex's body collapsed lifeless to the floor.

That had been hours ago, when the moon was high and the night still young. Katarina's body had been heavily damaged, and it very slowly pulled itself back together.

Because all she could do was lie there, pressed against Alex's still corpse, she took the time to think and reflect.

Alex was dead—for real this time—Katarina had felt their connection as vampire and sire snap as surely as Alex had hit the floor.

Katarina had won, destroyed Alex before Alex could have a chance to destroy her, but the victory was hollow. Katarina knew that she'd been the cause of this whole mess.

Katarina cuddled closer to the form that used to be Alex. The shape was so familiar. The curve of Alex's hips. The softness of Alex's blond curls. The quirk of Alex's sumptuous lips. Alex was gone from this shell, even as Katarina's body naturally slotted against its form.

But the truth was, this creature hadn't been Alex in a long time. Sure, she'd been an improvement on all things Alex: hair shinier, skin smoother, smile more dazzling. But she no longer held Alex's wonder, instead carrying the confidence of one of darkness' creatures. She no longer had Alex's natural craving to experience life, knowing that she too would one day live through what future scholars would consider "history."

Alex had died when Katarina gave her her blood, and Katarina had been too eager to make it happen. Instead, Alex had come back wrong. Katarina had fallen in love with Alex as an imperfect human, and, in her haste to change her into something that would better fit her, she had killed Alex and made her hate her. And now it was too late.

The sun was rising, and the sweet oblivion of unconsciousness began to pull Katarina under. Finally, she could rest beside the familiar form of her lover. Katarina hugged Alex tightly in her arms and nuzzled her face into the crook where Alex's neck met her shoulder. She breathed in deeply, savoring her scent soured with the rusty bite of blood.

At last they could share a perfect moment together once again.

About the Author

Megan Renee Doyle (she/her) writes both long-form and short stories focused on mystery, magic, and the macabre, and she has an extra soft spot for queer ghost stories and hurt/comfort. She edits books in northern Virginia, where she lives with her blue-eyed cat surrounded by books, crafts, and stationery.

Our Light, Fading

Scarlett Skyes

CW: Character death

Whumpee: Man, Whumper: N/A, Caretaker: Woman

Every breath Lucian took was more a desperate gasp.

Cassia tried her best to sooth him, talking to him, carding fingers through his curls, but she knew that it wouldn't be much longer.

The bandage they'd hastily put on Lucian's neck had long since soaked through with blood. While the others had gone searching for a Healer, Cassia had known that it was already too late.

The damage was too great, his small body weakening quickly. The usual bright grin and brighter eyes she'd grown to love had been replaced with quiet whimpers and tears. With pain.

No. There would be no coming back from this.

So she stayed with him.

Cassia spoke softly, assuring Lucian that he wasn't alone, that everything was going to be okay. She sung him lullabies in her native tongue, hoping that even if he didn't understand them, her voice alone would bring him some semblance of comfort.

Lucian hadn't spoken, not really, any attempt to speak only making new blood drip down from his mouth.

Peta had laid Lucian on his side, and Cassia had been careful to keep him there, trying to keep him as comfortable as possible without the risk of choking on his own blood.

Lucian's breath caught, head tilting back a little.

"Shh..." Cassia said. "I've got you Little One, shh..."

Wiping away the blood from his mouth with the skirt of her dress, Cassia was a little surprised that Lucian was able to catch her gaze. His eyes were barely open, the once brilliant blue glazed with pain and exhaustion.

"Rest," Cassia said.

"Nn..."

New blood bubbled in the corner of his mouth, the bandages on his neck growing ever wetter.

Lucian tried again, his breath hitching at the effort.

"No..."

"It's okay," Cassia said. "It's okay, Little One, rest. They won't be angry. None of us will ever be angry with you."

But Lucian was already shaking his head.

He gasped sharply, no doubt having pulled at his ravaged throat. Whatever had attacked him, it was a miracle in and of itself that there had been any life left in the young teenager for them to find.

Cassia had barely seen the wound before it had been covered, but she knew full well that the two deep tears that ran down the side of his neck down to his collar bone would forever haunt her nightmares. It was a miracle that he'd even survived his neck being hurt so badly, but now he was losing strength faster than he was losing blood.

When he tried to speak once more, Cassia hushed him, soothing him through another wave of pain.

They had tried to use what few pain management concoctions that they'd had on them, but Lucian had been unable to swallow them passed the blood, and if anything the attempt to take the edge off had just made him hurt more.

Lucian shuddered strongly.

"Rest, Little One..." Cassia said.

Lucian whined, his lip trembling.

"It's okay," she mumbled. "Let go."

Just two words and it felt like Cassia was being pulled apart but he needed to hear them. He needed to know that it was okay.

"Let go, Little One."

Cassia waited for him to give into the pain, into the blood, into the nothingness. But Lucian didn't. He couldn't. While there was a part of him that seemed ready to go, ready to join the Song of the World, there was also be a part of him that was fighting hard to cling to life even though there was no way that his body could come back from this.

Even now, the ever hopeful boy was trying to hold onto that light.

Lucian's eyes flicked passed her, towards the door as if waiting for it to open. Waiting for the others, she realised.

"They won't be angry," Cassia said. "They love you. We love you. But it's okay. Everything's okay."

"Ss..." he croaked, chest hitching in a gasp. "Sca..."

"It's okay to be scared, Sweet Lucian," Cassia promised.

She loathed that she wanted him to just go already, spare the others the pain of watching him die. She loathed all of this; Lucian had only been attacked at all because he'd been so excited to explore the Night Market that he'd shot off before any of them had had a chance to catch up.

Lucian had been so happy, so bright, and now he lay in a pool of his own blood, deep tears in his neck and throat from some monster.

His breath hitched.

And again.

Cassia hummed to him, smoothed his hair away from his sweat-coated face. She saw just how pale Lucian had become, his once sun-kissed skin and adorable freckles left gaunt and sickly.

Lucian reached out his hand but it fell.

Cassia took it all the same, pressing a kiss onto it.

"We love you," she said gently. "So much. I will sing your song, Lucian, I swear it. But it's time to let go."

Lucian fought it. He fought it so hard, his hand trembling in her own. He shuddered. He wheezed. Tears slipped from his eyes, mixing with the blood.

And then he grew still.

Cassia breathed in.

Breathed out.

Then she was leaning down and kissing the boy's temple. She gently closed his empty eyes, letting her own tears fall at last.

The others would come soon, she knew.

She would let the protective spell drop from the door, the spell she'd cast to keep their companions out whether they had found a Healer or not. They would come. And they would see. See his body, see that she'd let him die.

They would be furious.

With her.

With whatever monster had done this.

With themselves.

But not with Lucian. Never with Lucian. He'd been the best of them, and while Cassia expected this to be the end of their little family, she found that she did not regret a single moment of any of it.

About the Author

Scarlett is an Australian writer who loves all things Whumpy. With a particular focus on family-based comfort, whether that be biological or found family, she loves to have a fun mix of angst and heartfelt moments where even at their lowest, a Whumpee's family is right there for them!

The Village by the Lake

Asidian Morris

CW: Imprisonment, past torture, starvation, references to death of parents and sibling

Whumpee: Man, Whumper: Man, Woman, Caretaker: Man

The moon is high and bright overhead, wide and pale as the pearl a traveling merchant brought to market once when Vale was small.

It had been the talk of Lakebury for weeks, that pearl. Anson had teased that all they'd have to do for a pretty new bauble is sell the whole village, and then they could go north, to the city, and be grand gentlemen.

They hadn't gotten it in the end, of course. No one from their village had. It was a lavish thing, that pearl — a treasure from the distant sea.

Vale hasn't thought about it in years, but the memory of that day at market settles into his thoughts like a long-lost friend coming to call. He clings to it as he runs, a welcome distraction, pulling up every scrap of detail he can remember.

If he thinks about the rich blue fabric draped over the table of the merchant's stall, he doesn't have to concentrate on the way he stumbles barefoot across the moonlit grass. If he recalls the way Anson leaned in over his shoulder to get a better look, so close that his hair brushed Vale's cheek, he doesn't have to think too deeply about the way every clumsy step tugs at the wounds along the bare skin of his back. If he remembers the other trinkets laid out on that plush velvet, pocket watches and pendants and flowers set in glass, he doesn't have to pay attention to the searing pain that shivers through him with every indrawn breath.

He doesn't have to wonder whether that breath is even needed, anymore.

The moonlit field falls away behind him, rolling waves of grass and early spring wildflowers rimed by frost.

His feet passed cold hours ago, long since creeping into numb; he's been running without pause the whole night through, what little warmth remains to him stolen by the chill in the air. Vale suspects that there's only one reason he's gotten this far, in this weather.

He doesn't think about that, either.

As long as he keeps going, it will be fine. As long as he can make it back to Lakebury, he'll have a chance to warn them, and to rest, and to explain.

He'll have to be careful, of course; he can't go to Dame Bluff or to the village blacksmith or even home, to the empty cottage his parents once owned. He knows what everyone will think. He thought it too, just a handful of months ago.

But Anson will listen. Anson will let him come inside, and sit by the fire, and drape a blanket around his shoulders.

Anson will help him hide — help him explain. Maybe even help him find a cure.

Watchful One above, *is* there a cure? Dame Bluff has been looking for decades now. Maybe there isn't one to find.

But all that's for later. For now, Vale has to get there first, and so he runs, fast as he's able, as meadows give way to forest, and forest gives way to farms, and at last the lake that lends the village its name stretches away to his left, wide and dark beneath the moon. Among the frosted grass, packed-earth roads appear, and tiny cottages stand dotted along the lakeshore.

It's one of these cottages, tucked in along the edge of the village, that Vale approaches. He creeps up carefully, picking his ginger way through the vegetable garden he helped prepare to weather the winter last year — leans up against the doorframe, trembling and exhausted, trying to force back the sting in his eyes.

The sound of his knuckles rapping at the wood is furtive and quick, pitched low enough not to carry. He waits an endless few seconds, eyes darting out toward the darkness of the village at night. Vale's just beginning to think that he hasn't been quite loud enough when the door cracks open and pulls inward.

Inside, there's a table, rustic and ungainly, made by Anson's mother. Vale's sat at that table once a week since he learned how to walk, legs swinging before he could touch the ground and then, later, feet tucked up under him in a crooked sort of perch that Anson always laughed at him for. When he was a child, Vale sat in the far chair on the left, drinking sweetened milk; then, when he was grown, it was the strong, bitter tea that Anson grows in the garden.

It's the safest place Vale knows, but it won't be safe for long. Nowhere in the village will be.

Further back in the room, the wood-burning stove has begun to gutter low, giving off the faint light of a fading fire. It casts the kitchen in shades of warm oranges and yellows, and it backlights the boy who stands in the doorway.

It's Anson, of course. His face ought to be hard to make out in the dim light, but Vale can see every detail all the same: the strong line of his jaw, and the worried crinkle of his brow, and the faint dusting of freckles across his nose.

"Vale?" he says, and his voice is a whisper, breath almost gone with disbelief.

"Surprise," says Vale, and it comes out with a tremor, a breath of air, half laugh and half something else entirely.

"We thought you were gone," says Anson. "We thought he took you."

Vale opens his mouth, a thousand thoughts on the tip of his tongue.

How to explain? How to put words to the nightmare that the last few months have been?

But before he can untangle what he means to say, before he can even begin to sort through the jumble of his own mind, Anson reaches out and takes him by the shoulders, dragging him in for a crushing hug.

It hurts. Of course it does; there isn't a single part of Vale that doesn't ache with bruises or lash marks.

But he doesn't pull away — only lifts his shaking arms and twines them around Anson's waist.

His chest hitches, slightly; he bites down on his lip. The scent is near overwhelming, rich and heady, and he's so very hungry.

"I thought you were gone," Anson is saying, and Vale can hardly hear him through the rushing in his ears. "I thought I'd never see you again."

That hitch comes again, tight and convulsive. Vale's eyes sting so badly that he has to close them, tucking his face up against Anson's chest. He's missed this, too — missed the way Anson touches him, casual and sure.

He's missed the way those calloused hands make his heart beat double-time and raise a flush of heat to burn along his cheekbones. This time, for once, that little flutter in his chest stays still and quiet.

This time, of course, his heart isn't beating at all.

"What happened?" Anson demands. "Where've you been? We sent out search parties. I looked for *months.*"

Vale takes a shaking breath in, and then another. His fingers have curled into the fabric of Anson's shirt, holding on for everything he's worth.

"You were right," he says at last, quiet.

Anson goes very still against him. "What?"

"You were right," Vale says again. "He took me."

Those gentle hands go tense; an instant later, Anson shoves him away again, holding him at arm's length. Kind, dark eyes are frantic and searching, now.

"He didn't," Anson says, strangled. "No. You're — you're the same."

"It isn't like we thought," Vale says, tripping over the words in his haste to get them out. "I *am* still the same. I'm still me." He thinks of the brighter night, of the scent of blood sharp in his nostrils, of the heart that no longer beats in his chest. "Well. Almost."

Once upon a time, Vale wouldn't have been able to make out the details in lighting this dim.

He would have missed the way Anson's eyes grow wider — the flash of betrayal — the glimmer of fear. He catches it all, volumes of explanation in fractions of a second.

"I can explain," says Vale, hushed and urgent. "But more important, there's something I have to tell you. Lord Eramastus —"

Something changes in Anson's face. Vale clocks the expression as it shifts. It's the word "lord," he thinks later. His tongue found the title by rote — by habit beaten into him by long months. When they were small, they used to poke fun of the inhabitant of the mysterious manor to the east: Eranasty, His High Creepiness, and a dozen others just as childish, a parade of nicknames with bravado to mask the fear.

They've grown, since then; things have changed. But Vale has never once used a title for the lord of the dark manor, not until the crack of the whip trained his tongue.

The betrayal in Anson's eyes washes out, replaced by resolve.

"Guards!" Anson calls, voice bellowing out across the little garden, across the cobblestone walkway, across the neighboring cottages. "Guards!"

"Wait," hisses Vale. "Don't —"

But it's too late to explain. Already lights are coming on in windows, lanterns flickering to life. Doors are cracking open, and faces appear in the gaps, frightened eyes turning their way.

Watchful One save him, but Vale knows how this is going to go.

***

Anson's stood guard in the holding pen before.

Of course he has; they've all taken turns at it, every one of them. He had his first shift when he was just a boy, barely fourteen, still not sure what to expect. He remembers the way he felt, racked by tremors that had nothing to do with the chill damp of the place, nausea growing slowly from the center of him until he'd excused himself to be sick.

He feels that same nausea now; he feels that same chill.

It's not a real holding pen, in truth. It's not the sort of place you'd keep an animal. It's too dark, too bare, too secluded.

It's not a dungeon, either, though if Lakebury had one, or even a proper guard house, those might have been a better choice.

But there's never been much by way of trouble here — aside from the ones who come back, at least. Never been much beyond childish mischief, and the occasional drunken brawl, and the ones who come at night, pale and drawn, wearing the faces of lost friends and family.

They've always been a practical people, the villagers of Lakebury.

Anson's father told him all about it: a time when the cave at the base of Livewood Hill was only a cave. When a late-night discussion had run long into the early-morning hours, and the next day the villagers had set about preparing it: a deep-carved fire pit, and anchored chains, and sturdy manacles.

It works as well as anything, truth be told. It keeps the creatures away from the villagers, and it keeps curious children from poking little noses where they don't belong — mostly, at least.

Once when Anson was very small, he asked why they didn't just put the creatures down, and Anson's father had tsked and shaken his head.

"Would you believe, old Dame Bluff still thinks she can come up with a cure? She'd have done it decades ago, if she had half a chance."

It's been ten full years since then. Dame Bluff still hasn't found a cure, but they carry on the way they always have, hauling the creatures out to the cave at the base of Livewood Hill to stay until they die in truth, putting to rest that false semblance of life.

Anson's gotten used to it. In a way, they all have.

But it's never felt so personal before.

He keeps his back to the cave's newest inhabitant, and he keeps his hand on the hilt of the hunting knife at his waist, and he tells himself he will not turn.

"Anson," says the creature, with Vale's voice. It sounds as though it's in tears, but Anson knows better. Once they've turned, the monsters can charm any human in ear range. "Anson, please."

The sobbing is a wretched sound.

It's soft and ragged and dry. It sounds exactly like Vale — exactly the way he'd sounded the night his parents came back to the village, pale shadows in the darkness, slipping out from between the trees to approach Dame Bluff's house. Vale had been all of twelve years old then, frightened and bereft.

They'd chained the both of them up together in the holding pen.

Vale had gone to see Dame Bluff every day, begging to know if she'd made any progress on the cure.

"Just look at me," Vale sobs, and the words are sloppy, near indistinguishable from the crying. "I'm still *me*. I haven't changed."

Anson wants to say something to him.

He wants to say that he knows better than to hope — that the boy who's been his best friend since they were both barely able to walk is gone, snuffed out four months ago when he was brought back to life as an abomination.

He knows better, though. He knows the rules.

You do not speak to the creatures in the holding pen. To speak to them gives them power over you.

"Anson," sobs the thing that sounds like Vale. "Anson, *please*."

Later that day, Anson will visit the guard station. For the first time since he was a lad, he will arrange for his rotation at the holding pen to be scaled back to just once a week.

When he lies down to sleep that night, the nausea and the cold close in around him like the walls of a cave.

***

A week later, the creature that looks like Vale has new bruises.

Anson isn't supposed to look, but he stands there at the cave entrance all the same, letting his eyes adjust to the gloom.

The firepit at the cave's center is still crackling merrily away from the previous shift; they've left out wooden tankards and a set of Toads and Riches dice.

And there's Vale — not Vale anymore, he corrects himself, fiercely — curled up against a wall, as far from the fire as his chain will allow him to go.

Someone's taken his shirt. The bare skin of his chest and arms is ghastly pale in the firelight, mottled by bruises that are an ugly purple-black. His chest still rises and falls with his breathing, and Anson wonders for a moment if perhaps he's made a mistake. If perhaps they've all made a mistake.

But no: there's no mistaking a lack of heartbeat, and Dame Bluff had checked the creature over well. If he still breathes — if *it* still breathes — the motion is a matter of habit only.

Anson stays frozen there for long moments, just staring.

He isn't meant to look. He isn't meant to take in the delicate curve of Vale's collar bone or the pronounced ridges of his ribs, visible now through the skin.

He shouldn't want to undo the manacles. It would be the worst kind of foolishness, to let this abomination slip out into the night.

This isn't Vale, he reminds himself harshly. Not anymore.

Perhaps Anson makes some noise, some small indrawn breath, or perhaps the scent of his blood is beacon enough. Either way, Vale's eyes flicker open and turn toward him.

All at once, the creature's expression goes earnest and pleading; all at once, its eyes fill with tears, and it scrambles gracelessly toward Anson, hands outstretched in supplication.

Watchful One above, but the things are convincing. He's almost ready to believe.

That's why they tell the stories: a sweet-tongued vampire, newly born, wearing the face of a loved one. Enchanting words, murmured reassurances, right until the fangs slip into your neck. Anson knows better. He *ought* to know better. He's heard those tales since he was old enough to walk.

He knows how vampires are.

"Anson," says the thing that looks like Vale. "I knew you'd come back. I knew you wouldn't leave —"

The creature's voice wobbles on "leave," a tiny tremor to match the subtle shift of Vale's voice when he's near tears. It's almost convincing.

Anson turns his back to the thing; he hears the clank as it comes up against the end of its chain. There's a soft scrabbling, then, as though it's trying to drag itself further.

"It's my shift," Anson says, gruffly.

He shouldn't even say that. He shouldn't give it any answer at all.

The words slip out before he can stop them, though, and then it's too late to call them back.

"Of course it is," says Vale, and his voice hitches there at the end, a shuddery indrawn breath of air, like something caught between a laugh and a sob. There's a clank of metal again and another rustle. Then Vale says, "Listen. You could let me go. I — I'd go. I wouldn't stay by the village or anything. He's coming here anyway. I don't — I don't want to be here when he gets here. No one should be here when he gets here."

Anson doesn't reply.

"I'm still *me*," says Vale, and his voice breaks on the final word. "I'm not going to — to snatch children away at night."

Anson doesn't reply.

"Or sheep," Vale hastens to add. "I wouldn't. I'd steer clear of the flocks. I'd just *go*. I'd just start walking, and I'd — I'd go, up north maybe."

Anson doesn't reply, but something in his chest clenches and turns over.

Vale's always said he wanted to see the north, in whispered confessions late at night, lying up on Anson's rooftop and staring at the stars. It's forbidden, of course; out in the heathen lands beyond the mountains, their cities are home to revels of sin, and the Watchful One is eclipsed by a veritable array of pretender gods and goddesses.

When Vale spoke of it, though, it was always with a hint of longing.

Anson's thought of it before, on idle nights: Vale in some finery, silk perhaps, or velvet. Vale in the elegant flowing sleeves so favored in the north, his sleek auburn hair pinned half up to better show the narrow line of his jaw. Vale taking hold of Anson's hand to draw him into the theatre for some grand spectacle of music and dance.

Anson presses his lips together, hard, and determinedly says nothing at all.

There's the drag of metal on stone. Then Vale says, quietly: "You could tell them I hit you with the chain. It'd be heavy, if I wrapped it around my hand. Say I knocked you sprawling, and before you knew it —"

"Stop," says Anson, and he turns around to glare at the creature that looks like Vale. "Just *stop*. I know what you're trying to do. It won't work."

The creature is on the ground, still; it hasn't risen, though it has come closer. It's on the floor at Anson's feet now, peering up at him. Perhaps it's weak from the lack of blood. Perhaps this is another act, to try and garner sympathy.

It nearly works. Vale's hair, feather-fine, doesn't frame his jaw anymore, sleek and styled; it hangs limp and matted, strands falling into his face. Vale's eyes, a peculiar shade of pale green, are wide and damp and pleading.

Every part of Anson screams for him to reach a hand out and help the creature up; every instinct in his body demands that he wipe those tears away, if they should chance to fall.

It's the hardest thing he's ever done, to curl his hand into a fist and stand there as though unaffected.

"I won't bother anyone," says the creature. "I'll just go. Please. They never have to see me again." Those wet eyes overflow, and the tears make shining tracks along the creature's cheeks. "You'll never have to see me again."

"I saw you for the last time," Anson says, stiffly, "four months ago. When you still had a heartbeat."

It takes every scrap of willpower in him, to turn away.

It takes every ounce of restraint not to do as the creature says — not to let it run free.

For half the night, the creature pleads, words soft and yearning and then wild and wavering. And then, at long last, its voice gives out, and the only sound in the cave is the crackle of the fire and the wrecked hitch of sobs.

***

Vale doesn't look up when the change of the guard arrives.

He only tucks himself further into the nook in the back wall. If he stays there, he's found, they sometimes leave him alone. If he stays there, small and quiet, he can occasionally make it through a day with no new bruises.

The bruises are nothing to the hunger, of course. That creeps in him like a live thing, like a predator in a cage, all sharp edges and endless, unceasing want.

Vale doesn't feel like a predator.

Now, a month into this captivity, he feels pathetic as a wet kitten, limbs trembling and weak, wrist bones standing out prominently at the end of too-thin arms. They haven't fed him once, and every part of him yearns for it with an intensity that cuts sharper than any blade.

He keeps thinking that it can't possibly get worse, but with each passing day, it gets worse.

Begging doesn't help, he's found. Begging gets him a boot to the ribs, or a punch to the jaw, or a belt if he's particularly unlucky and the guard is particularly dedicated.

The best he can do is ride it out — ignore the pain curled in the center of him, eating him away from the inside out, because acknowledging it, or Watchful One forbid, asking for something to quell it, is considered an affront.

And so Vale hears the footsteps, and he says nothing at all, curling himself farther into his corner.

It's quite some time before he looks up, glancing just briefly toward the flickering firelight. He's learned, this past month, which of his old friends are the most unkind to creatures like him; he can brace himself for what's to come, if nothing else.

Vale pauses, then, just staring — taking in a familiar face, lit by the flickering golden glow of the fire. Everything about Anson is as he remembers it from a better time: the strong jaw, and the straight, proud nose, and the expressive eyebrows. All of it's the same, except for perhaps those dark smudges, there beneath Anson's eyes, where there never were any before.

And yet everything is different.

Still, Anson hasn't laid a hand on him, not even once. That's more than Vale can say for any of the other guards.

"You haven't been around much," he rasps, uncurling himself from his spot by the cave wall.

Anson says nothing.

"Been a couple of —" Vale starts, and then falters to a stop. Weeks? It's weeks, he thinks — a full month, if he's counted the changing of the guard correctly — but he isn't sure. "Been a while," he settles on, eventually.

There's no reply.

After a long moment, Vale breathes out a laugh, shaky and unsure. "You know what I miss?" he says, and he doesn't wait for an answer. "It's so dumb. I miss your kitchen table. I miss staying up nights drinking tea. I don't even know if I *can* drink tea anymore."

The line of Anson's shoulders adjusts, drawing up tighter.

"Did you know, I used to hate it? I never said." With effort, Vale presses himself up to sitting — leans back against the cave wall, legs drawn up in front of him, arms hugged in around his calves. "Watchful One, but it was bitter." Vale sets his chin on his knees and smiles, crooked and a bit wistful. "But you turned eight years old and said milk was for *babies*, and I didn't want to be a baby."

Vale lets his eyes drift closed, just for a moment. "I learned to like it, though. Took me a while, but I learned. Sort of burns the tongue, you know? One of those acquired tastes." For a moment, he pauses — licks at his lips, as though he can taste the tea there. "So I miss it. Your dumb kitchen table, and your dumb garden tea, and how you used to hum when you were making it, and you'd get the notes all wrong."

When Vale opens his eyes again, he sees that Anson has turned toward him. His expression is hard to read; his face seems carved of stone, perfectly blank except for the crease between his brows.

"It figures," says Anson, finally. His voice is low and tight, the way it gets before he cries. It sounded this way the night his little sister died of pneumonia. Vale was there for that — sat with him on the back steps, leaned up against his side, as Anson spoke in halting whispers about how he'd promised her a painted top for her last birthday, and he hadn't been able to get her one, and now he'd never have the chance.

"What does?" says Vale, after a long moment of silence. He barely recognizes his own voice, nothing to it but the softest of rasps.

"Not even alive anymore, and you still never stop talking." Anson sounds tired. Exhausted, really. But there's something almost fond there underneath. "Some things never change, I guess."

"Takes more than a couple of bites to make me shut up," says Vale, wry, and Anson lifts a hand to scrub at his face.

When he lowers it again, he turns his gaze to Vale, dark eyes intent. "I didn't think you'd remember," he says. "It's not supposed to work like that."

"I know," says Vale. "But it does."

The silence stretches longer this time. There's nothing hostile in it, for once.

Vale hesitates for long moments; he doesn't have a heartbeat anymore, but he can hear Anson's, solid and steady, keeping time.

Then he says: "What if it was from the butcher," very quiet.

Anson's eyes narrow. That crease between his brows grows deeper still.

"You could take a cup before she tosses the blood next time she gets in a deer." He can hear Anson draw a sharp breath and hastens to explain. The hunger is an endless cavern inside him, bone-deep and demanding; he trips over his words in his haste. "It doesn't have to be from a *person*," says Vale. "It doesn't even have to be that much."

"Stop," says Anson, voice tight.

"I'm so hungry," says Vale, and his voice trembles, and he presses on anyway. "Just half a cup. Just a — just a sip. *Anything*, please —"

"Stop!" Anson bellows, and it echoes through the cavern like the rumble of an oncoming storm.

Vale falters to a stop, chest heaving with breaths he no longer really needs.

"I should have known better," Anson says, "than to believe your kind can think about anything but blood."

Despite Vale's best efforts, Anson won't say another word to him.

***

It's late one night, closer to dawn than sundown, when Vale feels his master approach.

The feeling scorches through him, the presence thick and choking; it presses down against his chest like a thumb digging into a bruise.

It must be close to the spring equinox; out beyond the cave, in Lakebury, there's a small choir singing the praises of the Watchful One, one of many midnight celebrations at this time of year. Vale can almost make out the lyrics, long-memorized hymns about how on this, the eve of the rebirth of the world, one must lay down their hopes for the coming year at the feet of He Who Oversees the Stars.

For the first time since Vale was a child, the words spark a sense of dread. For the first time, he *feels* watched, not by any deity, but by some roving, restless eye searching not just for him but for any who dares to live a life of their own.

The terror is so sharp, so sudden, that Vale forgets to breathe.

"He's coming," Vale whispers, the words trembling and small.

Anson turns toward him, just slightly. He hasn't spoken to Vale, not since that night when Vale made the mistake of asking for something to eat, but he *does* turn to look.

"He's coming," says Vale, and he presses himself up to sitting, trembling with the effort of it. "He's almost here."

Anson's lips firm into a thin line. "If this is some sort of trick —" he begins, but Vale is shaking his head already. Tears sting at his eyes and then spill to run down his cheeks.

"It's not," gasps Vale. "It's *not*."

He can feel it thrumming through him now, that same sick, helpless terror that roiled in him the first night he awoke without a heartbeat. His mind tries to go skittering off down dark passageways: an unlit wine cellar, and shackles on the wall, and corkscrews used for purposes they were not intended for.

However much this has destroyed him, the cave and the beatings and the slow creeping agony of hunger, it has been nothing compared to his time in Lord Eramastus's manor.

"You're not doing yourself any favors," snaps Anson. Maybe he means to say more, but before he can, there's a low rumble from the distance, like thunder, or perhaps a stampede. Vale can't begin to imagine what it might be. He doesn't want to try.

The terror inside him twists tighter, digging in like one of Lord Eramastus's corkscrews.

Anson turns toward the cave mouth, brows drawing together. He glances back at Vale. "It isn't meant to storm," he says, slowly, as though he's working through the implications of that.

For a moment, he says nothing more — only stands there, taking in the way Vale cowers against the cave wall. Then he turns back toward the entrance and rounds the corner out of sight.

He's gone for longer than Vale expects — gone for long enough to climb the hill and peer out toward the village, if he were so inclined. Vale has no sooner thought it than Anson is stumbling back inside, pale as a sheet and trembling.

"What?" says Vale. "What is it?"

Anson doesn't answer him. He paces a frantic back-and-forth beside the fire — returns to the cave entrance again. When he comes back, his face is drawn and ghastly pale. He's started to tremble.

He looks at Vale, face alight with flickering shadows from the fire pit. From outside, another of those slow rumbles fills the air.

"Promise not to bite me," says Anson, stiff.

"I can't even reach you," says Vale, and lifts his arms, the chains that shackle him to the cave floor clinking as he does.

Anson doesn't say anything at all. He approaches in two steps, three, and Vale can't quite help himself; he flinches back, eyes squeezed shut.

No blow comes. He hears the scrape of metal on metal, and when he opens his eyes again, he finds that Anson is unlocking the cuffs. One falls away, and then the next. Underneath the skin is rubbed raw and bloodless, and his arms feel oddly light without the bindings.

For a moment, Vale only stares, caught flat-footed — struck suddenly speechless.

"Let's go," says Anson.

Something twists in Vale's chest; he takes in a shaking breath. It seems impossible, that offer. Some reeling portion of his mind, caught off-kilter, wonders if this is a dream.

He makes to rise on trembling legs — gets halfway there before his knees buckle and give out beneath him.

"We don't have time for this," says Anson, voice tight and not entirely steady.

"Maybe you should have thought of that," Vale manages, "before you decided not to feed me for a month."

He braces his arm against the wall to try again, but before he has a chance, Anson scoops him up off the floor like they're ten years old again, playing at children's games: who can jump higher, and who can climb the tallest tree, and who can carry the other longer before they spill onto the forest floor, laughing.

Vale isn't laughing now. He yelps at the awkward angle, tossed upside-down over Anson's shoulder — a safety precaution, he's sure. Any other position would put him entirely too close to Anson's neck.

Even as it is, he can concentrate on little but the smell of blood as they begin to move; it burrows into him like a meat hook, sinking the sharp end through his stomach until he thinks he might black out. Dark spots dance at the corners of his vision. He blinks, and blinks again, and the ground sways beneath him with the motion of Anson's steps.

Somewhere, distantly, he's aware that people in the village are beginning to scream, a high, shrill sound carried on the spring breeze.

Not long after that, Vale smells smoke.

Then the dark spots crowd out his vision entirely, and for a long time, there is nothing at all.

***

The sound of running water wakes him, and it's Vale's first indication that he isn't where he's meant to be.

He should hear the crackling of the ever-present fire, and the low voices of the guards playing Toads and Riches, and the soft clink of metal when he moves.

Instead there's only water and somewhere, way off in the distance, the call of a whippoorwill.

When he opens his eyes, it's to daylight, the pale, buttery glow of the sky just past dawn, and for an instant, panic shoots through him.

Vale sits up with a cry, scrambling to escape the sunlight, but a moment later he realizes that he needn't have been afraid. Overhead, the thick fronds of a willow crowding the stream bank blot out all the light, swathing the grassy area in heavy shade.

For an instant, relief crowds out everything else. Vale pants, chest heaving with breaths he doesn't need, trying to come to terms with what this means.

It takes longer than it should. His thoughts feel slow and disjointed, as though they're stuck in honey that's gone crystalized with age. It's long moments before he turns from the clear waters of the stream to face the boy kneeling beside him.

Anson's brow is creased, and his head is bowed. Tears streak his cheeks, dried now; he's looking at Vale as though he's never seen him before.

"You warned me," Anson says, as though he can't seem to make the words make sense.

"Of course I warned you," snaps Vale, but his voice wavers, nearly breaking in the middle. "I've been trying to tell you. He's a *monster*!"

Anson's eyes seem to bore through him. "The whole village is gone."

"Well, it wouldn't be," says Vale. "If you'd listened to me sooner."

He feels tears sting at his eyes and he blinks them away, angry. He's not going to mourn a place that kept him chained that way. He's *not*. He rubs at his wrists, at those raw, bloodless patches where the manacles had been, as though to remind himself.

For a long moment, silence reigns. In the distance, the whippoorwill calls again.

Then Anson holds out his hand, suspended in the space between them.

Vale stares at it; his thoughts turn and tumble, honey-slow. His eyes track from the hand back up to Anson's face.

"You'll need your strength, if you're going to walk," says Anson. "You should eat something."

The words hang in the air between them like a spider web: spun silk, infinitely fragile, with all the possibility to ensnare. The hunger in Vale roars to life, a demanding thing. Need claws at his insides until they're ragged and red.

It could be a trap; it could be a test.

Vale reaches for the offered arm anyway, hands trembling — takes hold of Anson by the palm and the forearm. His eyes dart to Anson's, hardly daring to believe. He can smell the blood from here, rich and tantalizing.

If it's a test he's failed it, Vale thinks helplessly, and leans in to bite down.

The blood flows into his mouth, rich and heady, washing away all awareness but one simple fact: it's *good*. Every mouthful feels like a benediction, every swallow a blessing from the Watchful One. It's been months since Lord Eramastus first turned him, months since he's had anything at all, and every swallow quells a bit more of the aching need that's consumed him for far, far too long.

Distantly, he's aware that he's making a sound, a low keening sort of noise. He can't find it in himself in him to care.

Vale swallows, and swallows, and swallows again, the whole of him bent on this miracle of miracles: food, where for so long there's been nothing at all.

All too soon, the arm in his grasp shifts, making to pull away. Vale whines softly and only clings the tighter.

As though from a great distance, he hears Anson's voice: "We both have to be able to walk." He sounds almost apologetic.

This time, when he makes to withdraw, Vale lets him go.

For long moments, Vale can say nothing at all, lost in the sensation of having *something* to quell the endless need at long last. He licks at his lips and tastes the remnants of the flavor on them — sways, slightly, as though he's spent a night drinking something much stronger than tea.

Anson reaches out to set a hand on his shoulder, a careful touch to steady him. It takes everything in Vale not to break down weeping at how gentle it is.

Those piercing brown eyes fix him with a searching look. "Better?"

Realms better. Worlds better. Vale manages a faint nod, and tears sting at the corners of his eyes. He feels as though he's cried enough for a thousand lifetimes, these past few months.

"We should talk about what to do now," says Anson.

Vale licks at his lips again, unconsciously. "Now?"

"We can't go back to Lakebury," says Anson, and when Vale flinches, he adds: "And even if we could, I wouldn't."

For a long moment, Vale only stares at him. "What changed?" he asks, softly.

Anson looks away. There's something of shame in his face, and in the set of his shoulders. "You're still here," he says at last. "You're *you*. I always thought — I mean, they always told us —" He cuts himself off and swallows, hard. "Do you think it's always been like this?"

Vale could be cruel, if he wanted. He could drag this out — make Anson say it.

There have been dozens, over the years, confined to that cave until they starved. Some pleaded; some fought, feral and wild. All succumbed, in the end. Vale recalls his parents, pale and too-thin, not speaking a word to him that night he'd snuck out to visit them in the holding pen when he was little more than a child.

He wonders now if they'd meant it as a kindness — if they'd tried to spare him the pain that doubt might have caused.

The guards had carried him away, of course, wailing and reaching for them. Now, Vale wonders what it must have taken for them not to react. What it must have taken to pretend at indifference, so that in all the years after, Vale could think them nothing but the monsters he'd been told.

Or maybe it wasn't like that at all.

Maybe he was the exception, and it was some rare few that managed to retain a sense of self through the blood-madness. Maybe there hadn't been anything left of his parents, after all.

"I couldn't say," Vale tells him. And then, quieter: "Maybe."

A silence stretches between them. Vale fills it with images in his mind's eye: all those unfortunates, dozens of them, who ended their time shackled in that cave. Without meaning to, he shudders.

When he looks up again, he finds that Anson is watching him, expression intent and earnest. "Let's go north," he says. "To the city. We can be grand gentlemen."

Vale stares at him blankly for a moment. "You always hated that idea."

"Well." Anson huffs and rolls broad shoulders. "Things have changed."

Vale nods, slowly. Finds that he's smiling, of all things, tentative and not entirely steady. "I suppose they have."

Out beyond the sheltering branches of the willow, water glimmers in the early morning sunlight. Near to the horizon and making its slow way into the sky, the sun gleams round and bright as a pearl.

About the Author

Asidian is a writer, editor, and lover of the strange with a passion for the written word and a penchant for telling tales about humanity's ability to overcome the darkest of moments.

I Will Return To You But I May Not Be The Same

Scarlett Skyes

CW: Character death

Whumpee: Unspecified, Whumper: N/A, Caretaker: N/A

The blood felt strange as it slipped through my fingers.

It was warmer than I had expected, as if I were laying in some nice bath surrounded by candles and not just out on some street that I didn't even know the name of.

A part of me knew I should be panicking, should be fighting to stand, to run, to do anything except lay here. Some primal force was screaming at me that I was dying and yet the rest of me was strangely content.

Even as the blood pulsed with every heartbeat, with the streetlight flickering above me I could almost trick myself into thinking that maybe I was instead laying on a blanket in the countryside watching shooting stars with Jaime.

I could almost trick myself into thinking that this was okay; that if I died here on this street then at least the strange burning on my neck would ease.

The burning only grew worse as the adrenaline ebbed away, until it became outright pain.

Despite it all, I was grateful for it. It gave me something to latch onto, just like how that beast had latched onto my neck. I couldn't die here, I wouldn't. Jaime would be waiting for me, he would be waiting and I would not let him wait an eternity.

And so I stood and I took a step.

And then another.

And then I was falling, and the cooling blood was all that was left of me.

About the Author

Scarlett is an Australian writer who loves all things Whumpy. With a particular focus on family-based comfort, whether that be biological or found family, she loves to have a fun mix of angst and heartfelt moments where even at their lowest, a Whumpee's family is right there for them!

Nightfeeds

Tim Jeffreys

The baby's hungry again.

Groaning, still half asleep, I sit up in bed. One hand searches for the switch on the bedside lamp. A squeal from the Moses basket. My hand goes searching again. I find the shirt I wore the day before and toss it over the lamp. The light recedes to a soft red glow.

I turn to the sleeping form beside me. I reach out a hand and shake him. He doesn't wake. I shake him again with more force. Still nothing. I keep on until he makes a sound.

"Stefan. Stefan. It's your turn. The baby."

Stefan groans and rolls onto his side, his back to me. I shake him again.

"Stefan. It's your turn."

"Can't," he murmurs. "Tired."

"But..."

The baby starts to cry again. He's hungry, always hungry.

Throwing back the duvet, I slide my feet over the edge of the mattress. There's a chill in the room, which makes me shiver. Another cry forces me to my feet.

I notice my reflection in the mirror on the dresser top. Even in this light I look white, with shadowed eyes and wild hair strewn about my face. I feel as if I'm looking into the future, seeing myself as an old woman. That's how I feel anyway: aged, worn, tired, and horribly tired. How long will this go on? They said it would be hard but I never imagined it would be *this* hard. I don't know where I find the will at times. It must be nature, nurture, the maternal instinct, something. Before turning my eyes from my reflection, I notice that my nightgown has dark spots on it.

He's almost screaming now. He really must be hungry. I lean over, reaching into the cot, then freeze. He's fallen silent, looking up at me. I feel that chill again. I lift him out and place him on my chest.

Once the baby's fed I place him back down in the basket, and cover him with the blanket. My head feels light. I crawl back into bed and fall into unconsciousness.

It's morning when I wake again. Stefan is gone. He must have taken a turn doing a feed

in the night. He must have been careful not to wake me, knowing how tired I was, maybe feeling guilty. Leaving the bedroom in darkness, I go downstairs. Sunlight slanting in through the windows hurts my eyes. I have to draw the curtains before I make a coffee. I feel worn, tired still. As I drink my coffee, I find myself thinking that perhaps fresh air and sunlight are what I

need. I should venture out. I feel doubtful for a few moments, but then I decide yes, that's the best thing for the baby and me: we should go outside.

The baby's asleep when I put him in his buggy. He begins to stir as I draw up to the front door, so I pause, find the heaviest of his blankets and cover the buggy top completely with it. The sunlight might not be good for him, after all. I read somewhere that babies have sensitive skin, and my little one seems not to like the sun at all.

That's not true for me, of course. I love the sun. At least, I used to. Today it feels dazzling and oppressive. It blinds me and makes my skin itch. I visit a few shops along the high street, hurrying along, buying essentials. Who knows when I'll get a chance to leave the house again? Today is Tuesday and the shops are quiet. I'm thankful for this. I don't see anyone I

know until I go into the butcher shop and find Jean, one of my neighbours, there. Jean looks shocked when she sees me, but quickly tries to hide it. She has always been kind. She smiles with her mouth alone. Her eyes still look stunned. I really must look dreadful.

"Carol."

"Hello, Jean."

"How's things? How's the baby?" She glances down at the buggy, seeming surprised at the way I've covered it over.

"I was worried about the sun. I thought it might harm him."

Out of the corner of my eye, I see the butcher behind the counter, smiling as he carves up a carcass. Blood spatters the counter top. I can smell it. For some reason, it makes my stomach growl.

"Oh, a bit of sun won't harm him," Jean says. "It's not that strong today. You should take this thing off. Let us have a look at the little fella." She reaches down to lift the blanket and I surprise myself by grabbing her hand and shoving it away.

"No. Leave it."

Once again, her eyes alone betray her surprise.

She turns from me to speak to the butcher, who takes another carcass and begins lopping bits of it with his cleaver. There's more blood on the counter.

Jean turns back to me.

"Did the police ever catch the man who attacked you?"

"What? Oh that. No."

"What a terrible thing that was. It makes you scared to go to bed at night. How long ago was it now?"

"Oh, it was six or seven months ago."

"While you were pregnant as well. How awful!"

"I didn't know at the time."

Suddenly, the buggy starts shaking. And there are noises from within, little yelps and growls. Jean's eyes widen. She can't contain her shock this time. The butcher, too, has paused in his work and stares at the buggy, which shakes so much I have to grab the handles, thinking it's going to tip over on its side.

It's time to go. I say a quick goodbye, then steer the buggy out into the street, Jean and the butcher staring after me. Not until I'm almost home does the buggy stop shaking. I feel shaken myself, and tearful. Why did Jean have to bring up the attack? I've worked so hard to put it out of my mind.

When I arrive home I find Stefan there, laid out on the sofa. He's so pale I'm concerned for him. His eyes are shadowed and red rimmed.

"What're you doing here?"

"Left work early. Feeling ill."

"What's the matter?"

"Run down. Light-headed. The light hurts my eyes. Think I'm getting the flu."

"Why don't you go to bed?"

"Yes, I will. Did you go out?"

"Just for a walk. The baby got agitated."

"Why?"

"In the butchers."

"The butchers?"

"I... I think it was the smell."

Stefan sits up and looks at me soberly for a long moment. Then he stands and says:

"I'm off to bed. Wake me if you need me."

"Yes."

The clock says 3:41 when I'm woken again by the baby crying. With a sigh I turn my eyes to the cot, which I can just make out in the rooms near dark. For a moment I'm stunned by how much the cot vibrates with the kicking and flailing around inside, almost as if there's a wild animal in there.

I get up. It's automatic now: turn on light, cover lamp, legs out of bed, stand, and go to Moses basket. I don't bother trying to wake Stefan. As I'm leaning over the basket, once again

I pause, this time with a little intake of breath.

For a second the light had seemed to catch in the baby's eyes, making them glow red. Or maybe... but no, it can't be. No, it's this light. I stare at him a moment, examining his face. The child looks like my husband, though it's not his baby. Somehow, it's not. It's the child of

that thing, that man, that whatever it was that got in the house that night and attacked me.

It happened one night when Stefan was away with work. A man got into the house. At least I think it was a man. I opened my eyes in the middle of the night and saw a shape standing over me. He leaned over me and... and... and I don't want to think about that.

I felt my milk come in two days after the birth. Now my breasts feel full and heavy. But it's not my milk the little one wants. I lift him high and place him on my chest, his head against my neck. My legs feel weak. I have to sit down on the bed, leaning against the headboard. This room is cold. I feel cold. I feel the warmth draining out of me. The room is silent, but for the sound of his little slurps and swallows.

About the Author

Tim Jeffreys' short fiction has appeared in Supernatural Tales, The Alchemy Press Book of Horrors, Nightscript, Cosmic Horror Monthly, and many other places. His ghost story novella, *Holburn*, was released by Manta Press in 2022. His novel The False Ones was released by Crossroads Press in 2025.

Dear Diary

Alfie Court

CW: Character death

Whumpee: Woman, Whumper: Man, Caretaker: Man

It's strange. I never thought I was the sort of girl to write a diary. In fact, I find the concept quite insulting; why should I need reminding of my own thoughts? My better ruminations, which are at least half of them, I should think, are worthy of remembrance unaided, and the lesser ones I do not care if I forget. Certain things have transpired, however, that make it necessary to record my recollections. We cannot stop the coming of change, but I feel the need to deny it any claim over my memories. So I will preserve them, on paper if not in mind, as accurately as I can detail and as detailed as I can articulate. Thus, I see no point in recollecting my childhood musings – such as my habitual knowledge of the best spots to catch worms when I was five – most already swept away by the torrent of time. This must be a reflection of myself now, at time of writing, not a ghost of my past. So, for this first entry, I shall recount the recent events that led to this need to keep a diary.

***

I was born on April 2nd, 1678, in Darkstone, Rhode Island. There I stayed – with little to add aside from worm collecting and mud painting – until the fall of 1692, three months ago. Darkstone was even drearier than usual after a year of grim news concerning our Puritan neighbours in nearby Salem, Massachusetts: news of witchcraft and possession. Most of our Anglican community did not believe such things, but when we heard about the hangings, the more fearful folk refused to believe so many could be so misguided, that the guiltless could go to the gallows, and argued there must be some truth in the madness. That said, it had been a month since the last hanging and we all hoped it was at an end. Who could have guessed that the next ill tidings would be our own?

I still remember being stirred by the wild cries of those who woke earliest that morning, a week before All Saints' Day. Everyone gathered at the graveyard on the edge of town, which had been extended to the fringes of the woods just after the Indian War of 1675 to accommodate the fallen, our founder among them. At the spot where the miniature forest of gravestones met the far taller, ligneous trees, beneath a tombstone pertaining grandeur that looked out of place in our humble hamlet, lay Carter Darkstone himself, my grandfather.

Until that day.

We all stood staring at the unearthed grave, excavated farther than need be to reach the coffin, which had slid head-down into this deepened gulf. The casket lid was pitched a few feet away, exposing the empty interior.

Unease spread through the rest of us as most of the menfolk searched the surrounding woodlands, Father included. I asked Mother why everyone was so scared when anyone of half-able mind, with a half-adequate shovel, could steal the departed's bones without the need of witchcraft.

"No one," she snapped, "under God's eye could commit such a disdainful act. There is nothing to be gained unless devilry is involved."

I realised then how shaken she was. Of course, it was her own parent stolen away. Reminded of my relation to our defiled founder, whom I was robbed of any acquaintance with, having been born after his death, I felt more than a little afraid myself.

After Father and the others returned hours later with nothing to show for, the Minister called for a town meeting that evening, as if everyone could go about their day carefree until then. I was still too young to attend, and the subject under discussion was unlikely to permit any exception. During those long hours, I kept glancing through the dew-dripped window at the chapel, like that would somehow give me insight into what was being said within. As it happens, my curiosity did chance upon something. Sometime into the evening, who should I see meander by but Matthew, Darkstone's only Native resident, head held down in his usual manner, averting his gaze from any unfriendly observers even though there was no one about. Matthew was not his real name, of course; that he kept to himself, as was his way. Although he always seemed to contribute to the community – kept hens, attended church – he scarcely spoke with anyone. I wondered if he often excused himself from town meetings, even one called under such serious circumstances. Then I continued wondering.

***

My parents returned at nine. With all their adult minds together, all that the bickerers had agreed on was to reconvene in two days after the Minister carried out some more precise inquiries. I resolved to use that time to edge forward my suspicions about Matthew. At breakfast, I mentioned seeing him out and about during the meeting; Mother indifferently said his presence would have appended nothing; I asked if he was often absent; Father laughed, saying it would be exceptionally perceptive for anyone to notice. Some hours later, after Father had left, I asked Mother if Matthew had taken part in the search party the previous morning. I tried to sound offhanded, not just some brat spouting every half-baked theory to enter her head, but Mother saw straight through me. Seeming more upset than angry, she implored me, "Stop pointing fingers and let the grown-ups handle the situation." Looking back, I realise she only wanted to protect me, fearing I may become the focus of paranoia like the young women of Salem. At the time, however, I felt bitterly insulted.

"What grown-ups?" I replied. "Everyone is scared witless like children!"

Mother raised her voice then, responding with spite in kind: "If your elders are struggling to comprehend such plight, pray tell, what can you do, child?"

I said nothing more.

The next day, I sought out Margery, the only one in Darkstone my age. To be honest, we were not the best of friends; she did not mingle with her fellow adolescents much, meaning she tended to stay in her parents' company and confidence more than most. Through her, in exchange for a moment of rare amity with me, I learnt the sort of parental gossip that mine would never tell me; it turned out, Matthew had attended that search party. What's more, there was a reason no one suspected the outsider: he was one of the few Natives who fought on our side during the Indian War, against his own people, and had even formed a close friendship with Carter Darkstone. Satisfied that I must go unsatisfied, I was ready to abandon my suspicions until that night. Just before I was about to retire, I saw him from my window again, heading towards Darkstone's wooded fringes, carrying a heavy-looking sack of God knows what – but I dared to guess.

I planned to go directly to the Minister with my discovery, lest Mother rebuke me again. Come morning, however, she and Father told me I was to attend the meeting that evening. I nodded obediently, surprised at my luck. All became clear come dusk: every single one of Darkstone's adolescents was in attendance. I counted all my friends, fidgeting at their own parents' sides, struggling to stay still; they were all at least a year younger than me, a fact I often lorded over them. I spotted Matthew, looking less shy than usual, standing at the back. We sat towards the front – I could have made my allegations without looking at him and pretended not to know he was there, but I told myself that doing so might blemish my notion. I waited for the right moment, which could not have revealed itself any plainer; it became clear the bickerers had invited their little bickerers along because one previously discussed theory was that the desecration was some imprudent childish prank, likely as Salem's troubles hatched from the misguidings of their youth. Like a slow-burning candle, the Minister questioned us one by one, respectfully, unintentionally intimidating, the younger ones up front first. Then he came to me.

I stood up, even though those before me had not, formally declined any involvement in the desecration, then stated that I did, however, witness suspicious activity that may point to a guilty party, whom I promptly named. Mother and Father yelled my name simultaneously. I had never seen them so alarmed. It was almost satisfying. Undeterred, I laid out how I had twice seen Matthew sneaking about at a late hour, probably to avoid witnesses, glancing back at him to show I was not afraid. He could not say the same; dark features sheltered as always, but betraying unease seeping through. The crowd murmured. Mother and Father clawed at me. The Minister, less respectfully, told me to "control myself." But I had never felt so in control. I stepped into the aisle, looked Matthew in the eye and demanded he tell us what he had carried into the woods in his sack. Then came that terrible scream.

Margery fell into the aisle, directly between me and Matthew, convulsing violently. The whole town knew she was subject to fits, but never as bad as this. There were more screams as most of the congregation fled the hall like the Devil was on their tails. Thank God it was Margery they were eschewing, else she would have been trampled. Dropping all formality, the Minister bid those who stayed and gawked to leave, except for some village officials, Margery's parents, Matthew, who had barely moved, and Father, who told Mother to take me home. Simply stunned, I let her lead me away.

I wish not to detail my bitter argument with Mother as soon as we got home – I cannot, for that dreadful memory would leave this first entry sodden – even if that means I forget it forever. I hope I do. That said, greater was the hurt when Father returned, coldly told me I was not to say another word against Matthew and sent me to bed. I would never hear a warm word from him again.

***

The following morning, Margery and her family had left Darkstone. No doubt, in light of recent events, they dreaded the magnified return of the paranoiac speculation that had surrounded her condition in the past, subsided to tattle until now. I confess, her convulsions were what prevented me from offering her genuine friendship. Not out of prejudice – I just feared being nearby whenever it happened – honestly, I felt for her. And then she was gone.

Her departure was hardly Darkstone's greatest concern that morning. We awoke to the news that a number of livestock had disappeared – eight hens and one piglet – a few replaced by a smear of blood, substantial for a small animal, otherwise without a trace. Several farmers had noticed their livestock was unusually quiet before bed; others said they slept too near their pens to slumber through any ransack; and not a single egg was left for us overnight. Therefore, the smarter bickerers concluded this mass theft must have occurred, miraculously, whilst everyone had been attending the evening's cut-short meeting. That cleared Matthew of any suspicion, lest I hope Margery's absence draw attention back to him. Most believed the thieves, for there must have been more than one to steal away nine animals so quickly, simply must have been outsiders. Of course, some thought there was "other work" at play, noting the adjacent occurrence of Margery's head-turning fit, failing to note that by sending everyone fleeing from the chapel, she may have nearly had the thieves caught in the act.

More aimless debates and vain searches proceeded over the next couple of days. Left shamefaced by my performance in the chapel, I adopted Matthew's head-down demeanour and avoided him as instructed. I began to feel sorry for him, thinking my accusation must have indeed been unfounded. Then, on All Hallows Eve, I saw him.

Three hours before midnight marked All Saints' Day, Mother, capable of a kind word by then, unlike Father, sent me to fetch some water from the well. I was returning when I spotted Matthew heading for the woods, hauling a large sack again. He had not seen me. No one else was about. My mind spun a cyclone of zeal and doubt. I was a few feet from home. Mother and Father were in their room. Wavering vanquished, I opened the door, placed the brimming bucket inside and closed the door from the outside. They would think they had heard me coming in. Any longer and I would have lost sight of him. That fear of losing my chance to act was all it took for me to make the choice that changed my life forever.

***

Making no sound, I rushed to the spot where I saw Matthew disappear into the trees. The woods stood tall – a wall of shadows, so much more uninviting lacking daylight. I saw movement up ahead and followed through the undergrowth, where it was formidable to tread lightly. I could not get any closer lest he hear my twig-snapping footsteps, nor stray too far behind without losing him. This tailing persisted a painful hour or so, keeping Matthew just beyond the borders of my sight, a shimmer in the black curtains ahead. My heart lifted as the dark mass of trees spaced out and the moon graced us with some luminescence. I was losing my cover, but with a better view across the open space, I could stalk Matthew at a greater distance. That was until we came to an area of rocky terrain about the wide peak of the hill where the trees stopped altogether. Thankfully, this was the end of Matthew's trek.

From the tree line, I watched him ascend a large boulder in a few strides – most would have needed to use their hands to climb its steep sides. His form stood against the charcoal sky, nothing above but the fullest of moons. All was below him, and with a slow leer, he took it all in. Even at night, his view over hill and dale must have been stupendous.

Suddenly, he spoke. "I'm here. I've come." His deep voice erupted forth and flooded into the trees. I feared he must have been talking to me, the only other soul for miles, crouching in some bushes a hundred feet away. Then he withdrew from his sack and held up in one hand, by their broken necks, two unplucked hens. "I've brought more. All I have left. This can't go on!"

I turned with a start. There was nothing there. Still, I heard a distinct rustling, spread out amongst the trees, like lots of little things getting closer. They sprang from the branches above, flying in sync like swallows: at least three dozen bats.

They conversed above Matthew's head in a moonlit dance. Most strange, yet most majestic.

"Well?" Matthew appeared to be calling up to them. "Won't you come down? Talk?"

"Wait!"

That word was like a whisper howled by the wind on that still, breathless night.

The bats darted to the side, converging even closer together, then circled round to the trees – no, to me! They swarmed me, skimming against my head and arms and legs, the gust from their wings watering my eyes. I was forced, screaming, out into the open, and the swarm came with me, like they knew my movements before I did. The entangling tempest impelled me forward until I was before the boulder, then flew upward, leaving me to fall to my knees, blood oozing from several cuts on my cheeks. I looked up to see my awe reflected in Matthew's face, more expressive than I had ever seen him. The bats dived between us. At first, I thought the deranged creatures were plummeting into the ground, but then I saw they stopped just above, hovering. They converged ever closer, more than a flurry of flying animals should be able, their surge fashioning the shape of a man. The mass of black blurs merged to become one, which distilled into the form of a dark figure, with dark clothes, dark hair and a pale set face.

He might have been handsome had he not looked half dead; ashen skin flaking like a rash, spindly hair greying and sparse, yellow nails long and curled at the ends. His eyes were old, owlish, all-knowing. He stood at least six feet with broad shoulders, imposing as he looked down on me with a malicious smile, as if I were a warm roast and he was famished.

"So, who is this unfortunate one? Getting herself lost in the woods – now found." The voice on the wind was now coming from his mouth, deep, composed and unsettlingly soft.

"That's her, Abigail's child," Matthew said, with meaning. The man turned his head with sudden urgency. "She's your granddaughter."

He turned back to me, his expression completely changed, stunned. I must have looked a terrified little thing, staring up at him, unbelieving, as we both struggled to perceive one another in light of Matthew's impossible words. I had two grandfathers buried in that cemetery; only one grave was now empty. But I had thought Carter Darkstone was – at least partly – in Matthew's sack, moreover entirely deceased, unlike the thing towering above me.

"Why are you here? Why *you?*"

I had turned into a quivering creature, incapable of speech. Matthew answered for me. "She must have followed me. I told you she suspected me."

The spectral face took on a look of weary contemplation. "For twenty years you have served me well, only to fail me now, here, like this."

He was addressing Matthew without looking at him. Still, his words struck.

"I'm sorry," was all Matthew could muster.

"As am I, dear Matthew. But we both know those poultry won't sustain me." He smiled at me with a sadness corresponding to his black attire. "And yet, I will not sacrifice my kin. You have been a loyal friend, Matthew, and this grieves me to say, but your first blunder will be your last."

In his last moments, Matthew's fear turned to hurt. "Carter, I—"

It happened in an instant. One moment, Carter was in front of me, mourning eyes still locked with mine; the next, quicker than anything my eyes could track, he was atop the boulder, burying his head into Matthew's neck. A crimson tide leapt into the air in a display vile enough to shock me back to myself.

I still remember the awful gargling sound behind me as I ran – Matthew suppressing his dying scream, maybe, through pain and bile, as not to risk waking those sleeping soundly miles below out of some undying loyalty. The noise stopped as I breached the treeline. Glancing over my shoulder, I saw no one atop the boulder. Matthew may have fallen, but where was his killer? I looked forward again just as something fell from the heavens, blocking my flight. Carter Darkstone loomed before me.

He was changed: His skin was no longer mottled. Colour had returned to his ivory face and umber hair. His nails were white, straight to a sharp point, as were his canines, I noticed. The moonlight peaking through the trees glistened off the thick, red droplets dangling from his teeth. He was alive, fully, and young – no older than my father. And by his crescent grin, he felt it.

"Will you kill me too?"

At those few words I could string together, he laughed – raucous, maniacal, genuinely amused. "If I were, there would have been no need to kill poor Matthew. Rest assured, one of you had to die. In a way, I just saved your life." I thought he was exchanging some jest I was too young to understand. "You need not fear me, little one. As you can see, I am full – whole again. Half your town's livestock barely lasted me a few days; feast on human blood, and we need not feed again until three full moons pass."

"We?"

"Ah, I'm getting ahead of myself. I won't lie to you, it will be a cruel life, but I cannot have you running back to Darkstone and announcing my existence to all."

Suddenly, and seemingly without taking a step, he was a foot closer, standing toe-to-toe with me.

"I wish there was another way. I'm sorry."

And he was. I could see it in his eyes, drained of any pretence of pleasure. He took my arm in one hand and, with the other, tilted my head to the opposing shoulder, making way for his teeth to sink into my neck. I thought that was it. Then I knew – I felt it somehow – this was not the same fate Matthew suffered. No blood left my body; something was coming in. A darkness. I looked up at the treetops meeting the night sky. All smeared into a single shadow.

***

When I woke, I instantly felt changed. Like I had slept through a restless voyage, pressing all manner of seasickness upon my landlubber body and soul, and had come out the other side dissimilar to whatever I was before. But it was still dark, over the same sleeping forest that had surrounded me my whole life, or so it appeared. Carter was sitting next to me in the high crevice in which I awoke.

I should not have been surprised when he revealed it was the following night and that although I had never been sea-bound, we were already many miles from Darkstone.

Carter told me everything then. He was born during the third century. Things were different back then, he said, more wondrous, daring and free – order and idols less revered. He had risen against the ruthless chieftain of his tribe, who by some malign had gained the secret of immortality at the cost of living off the blood of his fellow man. As punishment for his defiance, the tyrant inflicted Carter with this deathlessness the same way he had just passed it onto me. Only then, to my horror, did I realise what he had done to me.

"You mean, I am now cursed with this devilry?"

"Devilry?" Carter laughed. "If that's what it is … If ever I die, if that day ever comes, the Devil might have the grace to let me know. Until then, I'm afraid its origin must remain a mystery."

He went on telling his tale, of how he went on living, years into decades, century after century, fleeing from one land to the next whenever his ravenous nature was exposed. He had hoped things would be different in the New World, where others fled to escape persecution. Alas, the lack of populace proved too laborious; to sustain ourselves, we must sacrifice someone every three months, forevermore.

"But how can you live with yourself?" I asked, aggrieved. "Relishing the lifetimes you've robbed from others!"

With a heavy heart, Carter told me there is no alternative; death is not the consequence of our starvation – not our death. If we allow ourselves to waste away, eventually we lose our minds and go into a feral state, gluttonously and mercilessly overcompensating on human blood. Carter avoided this the same way he ultimately defeated his predecessor: by having the unlikely confidant he found in Matthew bury him upside down, putting him into an endless sleep, then dig him up two decades hence so he could sneak away, had famishment not caught up with him. In the end, Matthew was the solution to that problem, too. Rather than feed on the colony he had founded and come to cherish, aside that regrettable exception, Carter chose to fake his death and disappear.

Faced with the same choice, how could I not follow his lead?

Since that dusk when I awoke to a life with no dawn, he has become something of a paternal figure. I think he has been waiting for such a companion for a long while – a child he won't outlive. We journey only at night for sunlight burns our skin, suppressing our unnatural abilities, like those Carter demonstrated that night. I soon discovered the food and drink that once fulfilled me now tastes rancid and seems to turn to ash as it goes down, until it comes back up. Yet for a while, I felt no hunger or thirst. I asked Carter how that was possible, to learn that he had forced what was left of Matthew's blood down my throat as I slept. I was appalled at first, but have come to understand what must be done. Craving rises within me. After travelling all winter, we are nearing the West Indies, chasing rumours of distant colonies. Very soon, I shall see the sea, and just in time for my first feast.

***

I can never go back. Better Mother and Father think me dead and remember me as I was rather than the monster I will become. Oh, but how I miss them! It is almost a comfort knowing I need not suffer such griefs in time; our lives are indefinite, but our minds can still only retain as much as mortals'. Carter says that if one lives long enough, slowly but surely, the details of the past are obscured beyond recollection, previous kindred feelings become unfamiliar, until one's former self is no more than a stranger. An echo of a dream.

And that, dear diary, is the purpose of your existence. In a blink, what would have been my whole life will be in the past, memories lost to the void like shadows in the dark. I vow to document it all, so that I may rediscover the life I had, and all subsequent lifetimes. This is to be the first of many entries in the first of many diaries. So many that eventually I may need an entire library of my own. I'm going to be around for quite some time.

About the Author

Alfie is a London-born, -bred and -based writer and filmmaker. His short film "Boys Don't Cry" received several awards. His short stories include "The Beasts of Bethnal Green" – published in the 35th issue of Tigershark Publishing, and "She Hears Voices" – published in the most recent issue of Eternal Haunted Summer.

Into the Sun

Aiden E. Messer

CW: Suicidal ideation, hand whump, graphic torture
Whumpee: Man, Whumper: Man, Caretaker: Man

Nicolai watched as his family walked away into the sun, a single tear running down his pale cheek.

His family.

That was how he used to think of them, but obviously, he'd been mistaken, and now he was alone again. He didn't understand what was wrong with him, because there had to be something wrong, right? Why would everyone keep abandoning him otherwise? An orphaned kid left to fend for himself on the streets. A young man with no friends and no future.

For a blessed couple of hours, when he met the vampire who sired him, he thought that everything would change. That someone was finally going to take care of him. Once the first shock had passed, he'd offered his neck willingly, clenching his teeth as fangs sank into his flesh. The pain was severe, but he forced himself to stay still, telling himself again and again that it was worth it. That he wouldn't be alone anymore.

When he was done drinking, his sire left without another word, leaving him to crumble on the cold hard floor, trembling and crying in incomprehension. The vampire had had no intention of taking him in, he just wanted to feed and Nicolai had been desperate enough to become an easy prey.

His transformation into a vampire had changed him, giving him an aura that made him incredibly attractive to humans. It made things easier for him, but he promised himself he wouldn't abuse it. Since then, he had sired three vampires : Lucia, Soran, and Tessa.

His lovers.

His family.

He had chosen them carefully, studying them for months to make sure he wouldn't regret his choice. After all, once he'd turned them, he wouldn't leave them, so they'd be together for eternity. Once certain of his choice, he approached them and offered them his love. He sincerely believed they loved him back, but it wasn't true. He thought back to the last few hours.

Tessa's ex-girlfriend had found them. He hadn't paid her any mind when he'd seduced Tessa. After all, she was so insignificant, she couldn't compare to the eternal love he was offering. He knew Tessa would soon forget her, forget her human life. It meant nothing. She'd be so much happier with him anyway. At least, that was what he had thought.

There was only one cure for vampirism: a true love kiss under the sun. Tessa's girlfriend had convinced her to give it a try. Nicolai had tried to stop them, convinced that she would be destroyed, but they had been quicker. Against all odds, it worked. Nicolai couldn't understand how this girl could be Tessa's true love instead of him, but before he had time to process the information, Lucia had grabbed Soran's hand and pulled him into the sun. She'd kissed him, and both of them had turned back into humans. None of it made sense. It was him they were supposed to love. Why would they want to leave him?

"Why?" he asked. "You love me... I thought..."

Lucia turned to him.

"We never loved you, Nicolai. We were trapped by you."

"Who could love a monster like you?" Soran added. "You tricked us. Bewitched us with your charm and kept us prisoners here. And you dare call it love? You stole our lives from us."

They left without another word, leaving him in the shadows.

Alone.

Nicolai didn't have the strength to keep going. He curled up deep in the shadows of his lair and closed his eyes. Time passed in a blur. Dust covered his motionless body. Insects crawled over him. He felt a spider spinning a web between his elbow and knee, but he didn't chase it away. It was company, and he didn't have the strength to move anyway. Not consuming blood for so long had weakened him, and his desperation had drained what little energy he had left.

When footsteps echoed through the halls, he didn't raise his head, thinking it must be another hallucination.

"Well well well, what do we have here?" an amused voice sounded above him.

Maybe it wasn't a hallucination after all, but still, Nicolai felt no desire to move. Getting killed by a hunter wouldn't be so bad, after all. What else could he hope for now, if not for the cold, peaceful embrace of Death?

He felt a strong hand grab his hair, forcefully lifting his head. Nicolai blinked until his eyes were able to focus enough to make out the face in front of him. It was a hunter indeed, and a cruel looking one at that. Long messy hair, piercing brown eyes filled with contempt, strong jawline, mouth twisted in a sadistic sneer. Nicolai could tell just by looking at him that he wouldn't get a quick death, but maybe that was what a wretched creature like him deserved. As long as he died in the end, he didn't mind.

"Look at you," the hunter sneered. "Too weak to even resist. That's too bad, a kill without the thrill of the hunt loses much of its interest. Oh well, there are other ways to have fun."

The hunter grabbed a flask of holy water from his belt and tilted it over the vampire's right wrist. A pained groan escaped Nicolai's lips as the first drop made contact with his skin, causing it to sizzle and sear. The first sound he'd produced in decades.

More drops followed. A guttural scream tore from Nicolai's throat as his skin bubbled and melted. Screaming after such a long time spent in silence felt like his vocal chords were on fire. Soon, he could see his bones peering under layers of ruined flesh and tendons. The grotesque view made him retch, but nothing came out of his empty stomach. He didn't want to die anymore. Or maybe he did, but the pain was too much. He couldn't take it. He just couldn't.

The hunter finished emptying the flask on his hand, laughing as Nicolai's fingernails fell from their liquefied beds, leaving his hand a bloody, useless mess.

"Please..." Nicolai uttered, his voice feeble and scared.

"Please what, Dracula?" the hunter mocked. "Please melt more of my disgusting, impure body? Please make me scream some more? With great pleasure."

Nicolai whimpered. If his tear ducts hadn't dried up long ago, he knew he would be crying right now.

The hunter grabbed a vial filled with a thin white powder. As soon as he opened it, the foul stench of garlic invaded the room. Nicolai's nose and lungs itched as he inhaled some particles. The hunter sprinkled the powder over his already mangled arm and hand. The pain was so intense Nicolai's vision went white for a few seconds. He was shaking violently, his pale flesh taking on a greenish hue. When his vision came back, the hunter was tilting Nicolai's head back and pushed the powder down his nasal canal.

It burned.

His whole chest was on fire, and the worst part was that he knew it wasn't enough to kill him, and he could see that the hunter knew that too.

He coughed violently, blood dripping from his lips, mixing with the hateful powder.

A second hunter entered the room. Nicolai huddled in on himself. He couldn't take any more. It was too painful.

"What the fuck are you doing, Jeff?" the second hunter asked the first one.

"What does it look like, Greg?" Jeff replied. "I'm giving the monster what it deserves."

"I'm done. I'm fucking done," Greg spat. "I enrolled to keep the streets safe, not to fucking torture people! Look at him! He's harmless!"

"He's a vampire, Greg. A fucking bloodthirsty monster! I knew you were too soft for this job."

"I killed my fair share of vampires, you know that. Doesn't mean I have to condone torturing one that's already on the ground. He was human before, for fuck's sake!"

Jeff shook his head and reached for a new torture instrument, but to Nicolai's surprise, Greg didn't let him. He lunged at his companion, grabbing him by the wrist. Jeff shook his wrist free and went to punch Greg in the face. Greg swiftly avoided the blow before delivering one of his own. This one hit Jeff squarely in the jaw, knocking him unconscious. Greg then kneeled down in front of a shivering, cowering Nicolai.

"It's okay, I won't hurt you," Greg said softly. "I'll take you to my place where you can heal. If you try to hurt me, or anyone else, I won't hesitate to kill you. But I don't think you will. You just need someone to take care of you, don't you?"

Nicolai was too overwhelmed by the hunter's words to answer. He just nodded, and let the hunter wrap him protectively in his long coat to shield him from the light as he carried him outside, walking away into the sun.

About the Author

According to one of the children Aiden works with, if they were a teacher, they would be as tall as a human. They are not a teacher. Aiden studied psychology and always had a penchant for horror and the macabre. They like to combine these subjects in their books.

A Boy and His Wolf

Scarlett Skyes

CW: Violence, child death, past child abandonment, character death
Whumpee: Man, Whumper: Unspecified, Caretaker: Man

The scream had been little more than a choked sob and yet before Fenn had really even registered it, he was already launching himself towards the horrid sound.

New sounds echoed instead, his bones cracking and popping, skin stretching and morphing as he ran, but he shoved aside the hellish pain that tore through him as he shifted into his wolf form too quickly because he knew that voice. The fire lacing his veins, his soul, did not matter, not when Channon, his little Channon, had been forced to make that sound.

Faster, he needed to be faster.

Channon was in danger, Channon was hurt and Fenn needed to be there, he needed to get to his boy, he needed to keep his Little Wolf safe.

Fenn's legs screamed, not yet ready to accept his full weight let alone run, yet the pain only spurred him onwards. This hurt was nothing compared what he was going to bring to whatever had brought that sound out of his little Channon.

The trees around him blurred but all at once he saw the shadowy figure hovering over a prone form and Fenn was launching himself towards it.

Teeth tore into flesh but the scream that erupted wasn't from the foul beast, but from the boy beneath it and Channon only screamed again as Fenn was thrown away, flying through the air and colliding with something hard before he could catch himself on anything.

Fenn shot back into action but this time he didn't even reach the monster before the beast was darting towards him faster than anything should be capable of, its entire weight slamming into him and sending him flying once more.

Another scream, this one more of a howl, and Fenn only distantly knew that it had come from himself, the need to protect his little Channon cancelling out all else, even the pain.

Fenn threw himself towards the beast once more except he hadn't made it a single step before he was collapsing back down onto the ground, his legs having buckled beneath his weight.

He tried to rise only to fail again, his whole body protesting as pain slammed through him after all. Fenn shuddered, his ribs shattered, but still he tried to stand because Channon was right there, he was right there and he was in pain and- and there was blood.

There was so much blood.

Fenn didn't know how he hadn't even smelled it but now the stench hit him all at once, his focus locking not only on the red that surrounded his little Channon but the iron that hung heavy in the air.

Blood.

Channon was covered in blood.

New red filled Fenn's vision and he was all at once latched onto flesh once more, the beast finally giving its own roar of pain as Fenn bit deep into its shoulder. The beast tried to throw Fenn but Fenn just shut his jaw tighter, sinking in until it met bone.

The moment the monster was even somewhat subdued Fenn's claws were ripping through its back, but the small victory did not matter because it let the beast impossibly slip away from Fenn's grasp.

Instead of going towards Channon, the shadow was flying towards Fenn but Fenn was ready for it, diving to the left just as the beast's own claw-like nails swiped right. Fenn was able to pivot faster, throwing his entire body towards the beast and pinning it to the ground, his teeth already sinking into what on a human would have been the jugular.

It wasn't the familiar taste of blood that erupted into Fenn's mouth, but something almost like an acid, but Fenn did not let go, if anything biting down harder onto it.

The beast really did scream then, the sound echoing in Fenn's ear as he tightened his hold even more.

A fist slammed into Fenn's side and his entire world pulsed white but still Fenn refused to let up because he needed to protect, all the pain in the world would not matter, Fenn would take it all on if it meant protecting his own.

Claws, no, nails, dug into Fenn's side but Fenn just bit down even harder.

The beast thrashed, screeched, thrashed again, went still.

Fenn did not let up, he knew better than to expect a monster to go down so easily, but only swiped a claw down the beast's arm, tearing through what didn't really look like shadows now so much as fabric.

A new sound, a pained rasp, and Fenn was letting go.

The beast remained frozen where it lay as Fenn surged towards the boy on the ground, the scent of fresh blood ever thicker.

Channon was still curled up, a hand clutching onto his neck but even that wasn't enough to hide the two deep gashes that ran down from his neck to his shoulder. His eyes were screwed shut, his breathing ragged, and all at once Fenn was shifting back into human form and pulling Channon up into his arms.

The boy jolted hard, trying to pull away but Fenn didn't let him, cupping his cheek instead.

"Chann, Chann look at me, look at me, you're okay, it's okay,"

Channon stiffened, his trembling stopping if only for a moment before it was back again. His eyes cracked open, only a little, before all at once they were wide and staring straight at Fenn.

"You're hurt!" Channon cried.

Even in Channon's misplaced worry, his voice sounded wrong. His breath hitched, and then again, pain overtaking all else. A hand curled into Fenn's but instead of forcing it away from Channon's face, Channon kept it there as if terrified of Fenn letting go of him.

"Fenn," Channon tried again but it was wrong, all of it was wrong.

"Easy, easy, Little Wolf," Fenn said. "Shh, I've got you."

But Channon was already shaking his head, still not letting Fenn let go of his face.

"You're hurt," the boy croaked.

Fenn didn't mention, he could not mention, that the two of them sat in a pool of Channon's own blood.

Even Channon's blinks were wrong, each one seemingly harder to come back from than the last.

Fenn tugged him closer, readjusting so that his little Channon could be more comfortable, but the movement only made Channon hiss, his entire body coiling. Fenn hushed him, hating that Channon had finally let go of Fenn's hand even though it meant he could now run fingers through Channon's hair.

Even Channon's hair was not free from the blood. They would need to wash it, Fenn realised distantly, and if it was anything like the last time he had tried to get the boy to bathe in the river it was going to be a fucking nightmare.

"Hey, hey," Fenn snapped. "Eyes open."

Channon's eyes opened again but just as quickly his blinks were slowing once more, his head dipping against the crook of Fenn's shoulder. The hand that had been pressed against Channon's wound had loosened to the point of uselessness and before it could fully slip down Fenn readjusted his hold again. It was awkward trying to brace Channon with one arm while also trying to card fingers through his hair, using his other hand to put pressure onto the boy's neck, but Fenn had no other choice.

Of course, Channon had made another godawful sound as Fenn so much as grazed against his neck but he did not let that keep him from pressing down hard onto it. Even when Channon thrashed, trying to get away from the pain, Fenn did not let him.

"Easy, easy Little Wolf," he murmured, "I've got you. Just breathe, I've got you."

If Channon had indeed been a little wolf, the tears in his flesh might have mended just as Fenn's own body slowly stitched itself together, but Channon wasn't a shifter, he was just a human boy and humans don't heal, not like that.

Not without help.

The mere thought of taking Channon anywhere utterly terrified Fenn, they'd managed the last several years in this forest just fine by themselves, but he knew that even makeshift bandages were not going to be enough to stem the bleeding this time. They would need to go to a human settlement, definitely not the one that had cast Channon out so long ago, but somewhere safe away from all the blood.

Blood.

There was so much blood.

Fenn almost felt sick from the stench because this wasn't like the blood he smelled when he went hunting. There was something wrong with it, not just the fact that it was Channon's own.

"You're hurt," Channon said again.

"Shut up."

"But you're hurt," Channon said. "I can... I can help, promise."

"All you need to do is stay with me," Fenn said. "It's going to hurt, but you need to stay with me."

"I'm okay," Channon said. "I... I'm okay."

But even with the reassurance, Fenn could not be convinced, not when Channon's eyes were glazing over, his weight slowly shifting until he grew heavier in Fenn's arms.

"I can walk," Channon said.

Fenn snorted.

"Damn Kid," he said fondly.

As Fenn stood, Channon's energy was all at once back if only for his hands to latch onto Fenn's neck, his nails digging in. Fenn brushed aside the pain, even the pain of his slowly reforming ribs grinding against one another, focusing instead on taking a step forward and then another.

Just as quickly as Channon's strength had returned, it had waned once more. "Fenn..."

"I've got you," Fenn said. "Rest, but don't sleep."

Channon opened his mouth to argue, no doubt wanting to ask how you could rest without fully sleeping, but he only blinked slowly again, his grip on Fenn's neck loosening.

Every step was agony, less so because of Fenn's body trying to repair itself and more because with every step Channon only grew weaker.

There was still blood coming from the deep gashes but it was not pouring out so much as seeping. Channon had already lost so much, and with how small he was he couldn't possibly have much more to lose.

He was still blinking but even that grew sluggish and when Channon mumbled something, even Fenn's sharpened hearing was incapable of understanding what he had said.

Channon was barely looking around at all by the time they reached and crossed the river and as Fenn readjusted his hold once more in the hopes of making him more comfortable, Channon had barely so much as breathed let alone whimpered.

They were still hours away from the closest town when Channon shifted a little, his head barely able to rise up from Fenn's shoulder.

"Fenn?"

"Rest, Little Wolf."

"Fenn... I... I'm really tired. Can I sleep?"

"Not yet."

Channon hummed. He didn't really set his head back down, it had instead fallen against Fenn's shoulder once more but his whole body had jolted as pain apparently lanced through him, no doubt from the movement of his injured neck.

"Easy," Fenn rumbled.

"Sorry," Channon said.

Fenn held him a little tighter, barely pressing his lips against Channon's forehead before he was looking out around them again to make sure that there were no more beasts coming to hurt his Little Wolf.

It was both an eternity and barely a moment before Channon was speaking again, but this time it was little more than a whisper.

"Fenn?"

"Yes, Channon?"

"Your arms are nice and warm."

Not really knowing how the damn kid expected Fenn to respond to that, Fenn just climbed up and over a fallen tree. This time Channon didn't even flinch from the strange movement, the only sign that he registered it at all the smallest of breaths passing through him.

Each time Fenn reminded Channon that he was only to rest, and not sleep, Channon had only grown weaker. What had once been clear acknowledgements of the command had become simple small nods until at some point even that had seemed too much for him.

Fenn still said it occasionally, he still roused Channon every time his eyes were closed for too long, but mostly Fenn just focused on walking.

Just as Channon's moments of awareness had become few and far between, so too was Fenn's dwindling hope.

He needed to get Channon to a healer, he needed to make sure that his Little Wolf was okay, he needed to do a thousand things to make it up to the boy and yet it was almost as if Fenn's body was starting to fight against him.

His steps had become slower, no matter how many times he forced himself to speed up again. The town was still hours away, the sun would set soon and it would only make the journey all the harder on Channon.

Fenn needed to keep walking, he needed to keep going and get his boy to safety, he needed to make this right.

"Fenn?"

The sound had barely been more than an exhale, this time, almost like Fenn had imagined it.

Fenn took another step forward.

And another.

Onwards, he needed to go onwards. He could not stop, not even for a moment, not when Channon was depending on his strength now more than ever.

"Fenn..."

"I'm here, Little Wolf."

"Cold."

"I'll make a fire soon as we get to the town," Fenn said.

Channon's lip wobbled but Fenn looked away and took another step.

And another.

A third step and he was stopping but he couldn't stop, he couldn't, not now and not ever.

"Fenn."

Fenn held him tighter.

"It's going to be okay," Fenn said. "Everything... Everything's going to be okay, Chann, just hold on a little longer."

"Fenn."

"Save your strength, the humans are still a few hours away."

"I know," Channon mumbled.

Channon did not speak again, not even when Fenn continued onwards.

Fenn did not know when Channon had stopped trembling, the realisation only dawning on him gods know how much later after he'd lost the ability to do even that. He was still breathing, how he was still breathing, still alive, even after hours suffering from such significant blood loss Fenn did not know but Fenn clung onto the knowledge that his Little Wolf had not yet abandoned him all the same.

Cradling Channon close, counting his every slow breath, Fenn felt something hot roll down the side of his own face.

Tired eyes flicked up to Fenn. Channon's body tensed then, as if he had tried to raise a hand to wipe the tear away but then it was relaxing once more, simply unable to summon the strength.

Fenn did not take another step towards the town. He took Channon to the biggest tree that he could find instead, careful as he set the boy down. Channon really did reach for Fenn then, but his meagre strength failed him. Before his hand could fall, Fenn clasped it, bringing it up to his lips and pressing a kiss against it.

It had been a tree like this that Fenn had found Channon by. That had been an eternity ago and yet also mere moments. An eternity full of annoyances, full of confusing arguments that could only come from a Pack comprising of nothing more than a wolf and a boy. An eternity full of laughter, full of life. An eternity that was bleeding out right before Fenn's very eyes.

Channon's chest was barely moving at all anymore, each breath shallower than the last.

Fenn let the shift come onto him slowly this time, feeling his bones readjust and settle into a new form, human-like skin changing into that of a wolf. Channon tried to curl towards him but he seemed unable so Fenn was careful in laying himself down around the boy, gently nudging Channon's smaller body into what Fenn could only hope was a more comfortable position.

A hand curled into Fenn's fur, Channon's head cushioned against Fenn.

"Fenn."

It was even less than a whisper this time but Channon did not need to speak for Fenn to know that the boy loved him, just like how he hoped that Channon too understood just how much he had come to mean to Fenn.

His little Channon, his Little Wolf, slept, and Fenn could do nothing except keep him warm.

***

Fenn woke slowly.

He kept his eyes closed a moment longer, then another, and another, not wanting to wake to a world without his Little Channon in it.

Eventually of course he would need to get up.

He would get up and he would see for certain that his Little Wolf was gone and a part of Fenn would be gone alongside him. There would be no more curling close to campfires together, Channon leaned up against Fenn's much larger form, wolf or otherwise. There would be no more days spent trying to harass Channon into washing up in the river, days where Fenn wouldn't even mind getting absolutely soaked because it always made Channon laugh and gods did Fenn want to hear that sound again just one more time.

Fenn woke not with his boy but with a rage deep in his heart, one that would not abate until every single monster like the one who had taken his Little Wolf was vanquished.

He shifted into his human form, knowing that he would need the dexterity to take Channon's body and-

Fenn scrambled up, his heart rabbiting right out of his chest because Channon wasn't there. His boy, his sweet boy, his Little Wolf, was gone. It wasn't only rage that swelled then, but abject fury, because another monster must have come in the night to take what remained of his boy away from him.

A roar ripped through him, low and primal, his nails sharpening into claws as he readied to shift fully back into a wolf once more so he could rip the throat of whatever the fuck had dared touch his little Channon except Channon wasn't gone, he was sitting cross legged in front of him, using a stick to draw into the dirt.

The false memory of Channon glanced up, because it must be a memory, gave that wide toothed smile of his and Fenn's every instinct screamed at him that something was wrong.

"You're finally up!" Channon said. "It's about time!"

It is a Changeling, it must be, a Changeling that had stolen Channon's form as their own and was going to pay the price for dishonouring the dead boy like that.

Fenn stalked towards the monster but then Channon cocked his head like he always did whenever he was amused except now instead of focusing on Channon's smile, Fenn's gaze locked onto the two large gashes that ran down Channon's neck.

A dream of Channon would not have those gashes, Fenn would not let himself tolerate otherwise. If Fenn was to dream of his boy, it would be as he had been, not as he had become.

How he had succumbed.

"Can we go hunting?" Channon said. "I'm hungry."

Channon didn't hunt, not really, though he always insisted on being involved whenever Fenn went off to get them food. Channon always insisted that he be involved, period. Needy little shit the brat had been, one that Fenn had let die but Channon wasn't dead, he was setting down the stick and drumming fingers onto his knees the way he always had when he was looking forward to a meal.

It was a Changeling, or some other monster, it had to be.

Channon was dead.

He had grown cold, he had stopped breathing, he had died, this... this wasn't Channon. Channon was just a boy, a human mortal boy, and he had died because Fenn hadn't been strong enough to save him.

"Fenn?"

"You... You're not real."

Channon blinked. He tilted his head to the other side now, though it wasn't quite enough to fully hide the two deep gashes. The wound had closed over, more than it ever could have in a single night even if Channon had survived the injury. It had scarred, not disappeared entirely, but even so it should have never looked like the marred discoloured but still clearly healed flesh it had become.

"You're not real," Fenn said again, even more firmly.

The grin dropped then, Channon's head dropping fully also.

"I..." Channon swallowed roughly. "Did I do something wrong?"

"Of course not," Fenn snapped, before he realised he was saying it.

The grin was back in an instant and Channon was not only all at once on his feet but he was holding Fenn's hand before Fenn even saw him move. Fenn scrambled back, his claws once again descending alongside his teeth, ready to tear the threat apart piece by piece except it wasn't a threat, it... it was Channon.

Channon wasn't dead, he...

"No," Fenn breathed.

"Fenn?"

"No, that... That can't be, you can't..."

"So, are we going hunting?" Channon asked. "Or can we go exploring? You know you promised me that we can see the cave when I was fast enough to get away from the cave-dwellers. And look! I'm fast enough now!"

Channon shot off to the left, scaling a tree before all at once sitting perched on a fallen one to Fenn's right.

Monster.

This was a monster.

No. No, it was Channon.

Channon had become a monster.

Fuck no, Channon was Channon. He was simply... faster... now?

"Little Wolf..."

Channon was all at once right in front of Fenn, far too close in his space for comfort. Fenn knelt down, setting a hand on Channon's shoulder. Channon rocked on his heels, glancing around before finally meeting Fenn's gaze. Channon only could hold it for a moment, but that was all that Fenn had needed anyway.

Channon's eyes were wrong. They were sharper, somehow, more focused even if the boy himself was still looking around them in wonder.

"Channon," Fenn said. "Do you remember what happened yesterday?"

Channon opened his mouth to reply instantly but he hesitated instead. When Channon's gaze dropped this time, his head did not rise again.

"I'm like you now," Channon mumbled. "I thought you would be happy with that. I won't slow you down anymore."

Except Channon wasn't like Fenn, not really.

One hand still on Channon's shoulder, his other raised up to Channon's chest. Channon was breathing, he was, but... but Fenn could not feel the familiar thumping in Channon's chest. The breathing was instinctual, Fenn realised distantly, Channon hadn't yet realised he didn't need to do it anymore.

A monster.

His boy had been taken from him and had been replaced with a monster without a beating heart.

Channon's skin was cold when Fenn cupped his cheek but that didn't matter because Channon leant into the touch and it was *everything*. This wasn't a monster. It was Channon. Channon was alive, at least, alive in the only sense that mattered; he was *here*.

There was still blood on Channon's neck and clothes, so much blood, more blood than any human could survive without.

"Channon," Fenn said.

"You're upset," Channon said. "I... I messed up, didn't I?"

"No," Fen said. "No, Kid, no, you just. . Got hurt. Really badly. But everything's okay now."

"So we can go hunting then?"

"We need to get you cleaned up first," Fenn said.

Channon scowled but the expression only lasted a moment before he was rocking on his heels again, a too-wide smile showing off teeth that were far sharper than they had been yesterday.

"Then we can hunt? I'm hungry, like, really really hungry."

Even now, Channon was weak, Fenn realised distantly. His gaze wasn't latching onto every single moving thing around them simply because Channon was always enraptured by the world around them; he was looking for prey.

Now that Channon was... different, his body needed to make up the energy it had lost in making the changes necessary to bring Channon back to him. Channon needed to eat. No, not eat. Feed. Revulsion curled within Fenn but Fenn shoved it all aside because this was Channon dammit, old tales of monstrous vampires meant nothing compared to what he felt for this boy.

The scent of blood was still thick on the air, even though most of it had dried in the hours that they had slept for, but even that felt distinctly different now, almost like the acid that had poured into his mouth when he had torn into the beast that had attacked his Little Wolf.

"We will hunt," Fenn said. "But this time, we hunt together."

"We always hunt together," Channon said. "Because you're my Fenn."

There might come a time when Channon will realise just how much things have changed. Fenn will grow old, slower than a human certainly, but he will grow old and weak and weary and his Little Wolf will remain in this form.

There might even come a time when Channon resents Fenn for not putting him out of his misery sooner, but for now none of that mattered because by some mercy his boy, his Little Wolf, his little Channon, had come back to him.

Fenn stood fully, leaning down just enough to peck Channon on the top of his head.

Channon made a show of being annoyed by the show of affection but he was unable to hide his bright grin, growing ever brighter when Fenn ruffled his hair.

It wasn't a scream that echoed across their forest then, but a chorus of laughter, not only from the boy turned something more but the man turned wolf too.

About the Author

Scarlett is an Australian writer who loves all things Whumpy. With a particular focus on family-based comfort, whether that be biological or found family, she loves to have a fun mix of angst and heartfelt moments where even at their lowest, a Whumpee's family is right there for them!

Orchid

P.C.M. Vandermeer

CW: Character death, religion

Whumpee: Woman, Whumper: Woman, Caretaker: Woman

Finally, no bloodlust tonight – oh, to be free from it! The raindrops drum against the stained-glass windows, but even their constant flood won't drown out Aveline's beautiful song. Her hums fill the library hall just as daylight will in a few hours. But at this hour, way past midnight, it is only the two of them in this part of the college. Their time is always short and sweet.

When lightning strikes right outside the castle, Aveline's voice shakes with a chuckle. "Heavens, what a night!"

"Not a night to meet outside," Orchid concurs. She can hear Aveline's chuckle deep in her chest, where she rests her heavy head.

They both shift where they're sitting on the oak wood floor. "Too bad we cannot roam your beloved graveyard," says Aveline, who thinks that Orchid's name is Olivia.

"But this way I got you to do my portrait again."

"Which you could hardly wait for, I reckon!"

Orchid smiles. "That is true. Oh" – she freezes – "hush!"

"What is it?"

Yes, good question. Orchid's senses bounce back from the cold stone walls, the rain now duller behind the heavy velvet drapes. In her miserable state, hearing is more difficult than usual. "Nothing," she says, barely back in the present. "I thought I heard something."

"The rain?"

"No, the mouse you keep hidden in your room!" Their giggles mingle with the raindrops.

Despite the pain, Orchid is in a cheerful mood. She rejoices in experiencing Aveline's classically trained artistry. The thick drawing papers lie on the floor beside the suitcase Aveline used to bring her utensils into the library. Additionally, kindly, her sketches show Orchid that she still looks the same: short black hair, high cheekbones, and a nose that's a little too sharp. The last time she has seen herself was in a portrait done by Aveline, too, an oil painting for her art classes.

These here pencil drawings are less elegant, rougher, and more intimate.

Orchid aches against Aveline's chest. Despite the crucifix necklace pulsating above her with power and doom, this place is the most beautiful on Earth. With its warmth above a beating heart, it has become paradise and purgatory alike.

Tonight, curiously, Aveline's heart beats quicker than usual.

Orchid dreads the question: For how much longer can they keep this up?

"Can you kiss me?"

Aveline leans down and does as Orchid asks. She never interrogates her, or at least only in the most trivial ways. 'What do you mean?' she would often ask, just to make Orchid blush after a compliment, metaphorically. Blood has left her cold cheeks long ago after all. But Aveline doesn't know that.

She does not know that every visit with her means both torture and relief but never something normal.

Her faith had been nurtured from an early age in her family, then school, and now college. It fumes around her like poison. Around Aveline, Orchid finds her breath growing shallow. Her chest tightens whenever she steals a glance at Aveline's forbiddingly curved neck and – worse – further down, where the small crucifix rests between her collarbones like a guard dog.

Her environment, too, is needles in Orchid's body. From the sacred ground of the college's chapel to the dark Gothic corridors with even more crucifixes, the stench won't leave her. Every blessing said by her with only the best intentions is another stone driven between Orchid's shoulder blades. Some nights, the pain grows so grand that she debates not coming to the college at all. But that would mean leaving Aveline alone, not seeing her, and to instead have this dead heart torn with yearning for her. The on-site pain is worth it.

It is so bad that it drowns out the bloodlust.

An unexpected side effect, at first. Now, Orchid would never want to go back.

More and more, she finds herself resting beneath that weight, not wanting to fight it. She never really has, but tonight it seems truer than ever. Fighting it means not letting herself get lost in Aveline's love.

And having to feed. Drinking that dreaded liquid copper. Having to kill for it.

With Aveline above her, the entire sun could crush Orchid, and she would still sigh and sing of its warmth. It is paradoxical. And scary. Orchid fears not knowing her limits.

The others have warned her, as soon as they found out for just how long she goes without drinking by now. Nightshade's words echo in her mind: 'If you do not leave the mortal, she will eat you alive. You need to feed.'

You could count the times Nightshade has ever been wrong on one hand. Her perception and empathy are too sharp to be dulled by excuses or hope. Orchid loves her for these characteristics, but Nightshade would never be able to understand her love for Aveline, or the all-encompassing satisfaction she instils in her. This distance has made it easier for Orchid to apologise for her 'overbearing family' – that's the way she describes the flock – whenever Aveline complained about only ever being able to meet after sunset. But in turn, Aveline talks ill of her college and its strict rules, too. Orchid does not know the rules in particular, but she is quick-witted enough to understand that romancing a fellow woman would get Aveline into serious trouble if they were ever found out.

"Your lips are cold."

Orchid blinks and meets Aveline's eyes. "They always are, aren't they?" she smiles.

Aveline mirrors the sentiment. She looks like a fairy, golden and mysterious. Orchid melts a little closer into her deathly embrace.

More weight – more warmth.

Just when Orchid decides, 'I shall stay like this forever,' Aveline inhales deeply above her. "Alright. I will speak up now."

Orchid shifts. "About what?" she asks, courting nonchalance to will away Aveline's sudden determination, despite knowing it'd be fruitless. Once this woman has made up her mind about something, it sticks. Such is the case now, it seems.

Aveline makes Orchid sit up straight and takes her hands. "I've lied to you about the suitcase, my dearest."

"Ah?"

"I've prepared everything. I wanted to wait for the rain to stop until we could go but – so be it!"

Orchid searches her grey eyes for clues, but Aveline's mouth is quicker: "Let us leave now."

"Leave? Whereto?"

"I don't know!" Aveline sighs, as though not knowing was the greatest bliss. "Let us just leave this cursed place and go wherever we please."

"You cannot run away," Orchid begins, but Aveline's warm hand is on her cheek in no time, as are her lips.

"My dearest Olivia, what do we have to lose? I realise how this sounds, but I see no other way to go on living." Her round face breaks into a helplessly joyous smile. "I was so excited to tell you! I am ready to leave this cursed place behind and be with you all the time. I have enough money from my family to take us to the coast and even pay a ship. Should worst come to worst, I shall sell my red gown, even though it is my favourite and matches your cravat so well." She slows herself. "The point is, I don't know what will come after, but together, we will see. Together. I have faith in us."

Orchid wants to cry. She should have known it would have come to this one day. She herself would've pulled out her fangs with pliers if it meant being with Aveline forever, only to find that this golden sunray of a human did not mind their sharpness.

Of course *this human* would want to run away with her, because she does not know that her eternity is not the same as Orchid's.

'You cannot have faith in us. You mustn't throw your precious life away like that – you only have this one – how foolish! And yet you are the last one to blame,' Orchid wants to sigh, and break down in Aveline's arms as she does.

It doesn't come to that.

Instead of raindrops, or Aveline's beautiful song, a grindstone voice now fills the library, so loud that Aveline ducks her head.

"Who do you think you are? Repent now, child, and your father won't have to know!"

"Quick," Aveline breathes, Orchid's hand still in hers. Together, they crawl away from the suitcase. "I hoped it wouldn't come to this," Aveline cries along the bookshelves. "Oh, we should have left right away!"

"It's not your fault," Orchid says. Trying to plan their escape route is discouraging: There is only one door in or out of the library. No secret escapes either. The college had blocked the last secret pathway over a century ago.

Blasted modernity.

"Miss Allistor! Come forth now and punishment will be minimal," now says a female voice, just as strict as the male one from before.

'The windows,' Orchid thinks as lightning strikes outside. Neither glass nor heights have ever held her back. Still, her eyes flutter back to Aveline. Would it be wise to reveal herself in front of her like that?

Yes, it would, wouldn't it? Because if Aveline won't understand, then who, in this entire wide world, would?

"Got you!"

Aveline lets out a scream. A human has grabbed her by the wrist, holding it up high.

"Let go of her!" Orchid hisses – but her voice burns in her throat. She reaches out to wrestle the man from where she's crawling, but his foot pushes her further down, deeper than any stones on her back could've managed to do.

She is too weak.

The man forces Aveline back to the corridor, to the door, where people with lamps and frowns are waiting to receive her. He marches right over the papers on the floor.

"The council might want those as evidence," the elderly woman says.

"Against what crime?" Aveline cries.

"Silence! You know very well of what we speak! It does not need repeating."

"Oh, do explain it to me, you witch!" Aveline all but spits. She's writhing and screaming against her captor – Orchid has never experienced her like this. As though the sun had turned into a solar eclipse. Gone is the poise, the grace. Right now, Aveline is fury.

What have they turned her into? Has she always been like this deep down? Or has this been Orchid's dark influence?

"Stop it," she creaks.

"Silence! Take her away."

Orchid scrambles to follow them, but she can only drag her legs as though they were but broken bones. "Don't let them take you – Aveline!"

"Olivia!"

It is then when the fury's song dies. The man hits Aveline on her head and her body collapses. Orchid watches. For what feels like eternity, her dead eyes are still on Aveline's limp back.

She leaps. The old woman is closest. She flashes the lamp in front of Orchid, but the winds of darkness douse it immediately.

Orchid clasps her grey head. She embraces it tight to sink her claws into the wrinkled skin. The old body sinks quickly. Next is the old man, as well as a younger student who is entering the library door behind him. Orchid scratches their eyes, not so badly that they'd fall from their skulls, but thoroughly enough to drown them in blood. It splashes onto the candles, clearing the way for darkness and screams to take over entirely.

Her fangs ache.

In her rage, she flies, bends down, bites, and sucks. She spits out the eyeball. She leaps through the prayers the last human is speaking in the face of evil. They slow her down. Immobilise her legs. She cannot get a hold of his neck. She forces him against the archivolt of the library doors where his head won't move.

Now she rips out his throat, life spilling out of him. She spits out the cartilage of his Adam's apple and stares at the red fountain she has created by her feet.

Her teeth, still aching. The stench of copper is unbearable.

The night has become silent. This affair could not have taken long, and yet the storm is over. Orchid's eyes flutter.

She had not heard the intruders coming. This is her fault.

She turns around. "Aveline?"

A new sound: a stifled sob.

"Aveline? Where are you? Are you hurt?"

Orchid sees her gown from behind a bookshelf. Clever of Aveline to get herself to safety as soon as she has regained consciousness. Good. "We can leave now," Orchid tells her. All tension has left her shoulders. The night is bright and clear once more. Finally, they are alone and free to leave.

Leaving would be good.

"Aveline?"

"Don't touch me!"

A deafening force punches Orchid to her knees. Lightning strikes in the storm-less air. Her head as heavy as stone, she glimpses upwards. Aveline is holding forward a crucifix, like a sword. To keep her at a distance. Behind it, her face is a grimace of fear.

What?

Oh.

So, this is how it happens. So soon?

Against all instincts, against better judgement, Orchid begs: "No, please..."

"Don't! Holy Father, don't let it come close to me! Protect me, Holy Father, cast away the spawn of hell! Forgive me – *forgive me, Father* – spare me and destroy it!"

Tears of blood blind Orchid's eyes. She's too weak. "Aveline... It's me..."

"*Begone!* Lord, I give myself over to you – our Father, who art in heaven, hallowed be thy name – thy kingdom come, thy will be done, on earth as it is in heaven...!"

And so, for a last time Aveline's song fades. No sweet melody, no furious symphony – just fear.

Perhaps the sound disappears so gradually because she inched away, without taking her eyes off the devil she has discovered.

Perhaps it is just because Orchid herself is fading away. Her body may have been weighed down by stones before, but now it turns into stone itself. Bloodless.

How miserable, to end beneath a shrieking sun.

Before daybreak, Nightshade and Violet come through the stained-glass windows and pick her up. They take her back to the flock. No one shames her, not the Count, not even Nightshade.

In fact, she offers to help Orchid recover. Her hands are cold but gentle. Orchid wonders if her own hands have felt like that, as she has a lot of time to think these days.

She helps her feed, though the taste is foul inside Orchid's mouth, worse than ever before.

Nightshade lowers the raven's corpse. "You'll have to relearn to consume regularly now."

"I see."

"I'm sorry."

Orchid gives her a smile. "Please don't be."

Any movement is cruel and would stay this way for a long time, even drinking hurts her. Flying is impossible. But she has no need to do that anymore anyway. Where would she go?

Briefly, she regrets how quick she has been to leave the flock. Nightshade points out to her that Aveline herself has not wasted a single thought on how Orchid would feel leaving her entire family behind.

Orchid cannot argue with that assessment. But she does not want to continue that line of thinking. She wishes her head had turned to stone after all.

"You need to come inside." Nightshade reminds her every morning – not as a warning but as counsel.

Not only that, but feeding is due, too. Orchid hears her but keeps watching the sun rise behind the trees. They're forked like veins. "I know. Just... a little longer."

About the Author

Being queer in a heteronormative world, P.C.M. Vandermeer finds comfort and joy in writing queer stories. She is a rescue dog mum and enjoyer of speculative fiction – especially when it includes monsters and body horror.

Starving for Salvation

E.J. LeRoy

CW: Starvation, disordered eating, hospice setting

Whumpee: Man, Whumper: N/A, Caretaker: Woman

"Are you a real vampire?"

Matty's temples pounded along with every other part of him where blood should have flowed but no longer did. He grasped his bedsheet with both hands in the futile hope that the texture of the fabric would somehow lessen the relentless gnawing under every inch of his anorexic flesh. It was one thing to be undead but another to be on his 103rd day of repentant starvation at St. Camillus de Lellis Hospice Center. He pressed his dry lips together and closed his eyes tighter. His throat burned, having received no liquid since Eucharist the night before. Constant hunger made his fangs scream for relief that would never come again. To be awakened by a voice clearly belonging to a child meant this had to be the middle of the day, a dreadful time for an already suffering vampire to be conscious.

"I said, 'Are you a real vampire?'"

Holding back a groan, Matty struggled to open one eye. A little girl with a comically large side ponytail stood at the foot of his bed. Opening his other eye, he noted that the girl wore an oversized T-shirt with the starfish logo of an aquarium and a shark tooth necklace. In one hand, she clutched the gooey stick of a dripping orange cream bar. Her eyes remained focused on Matty as she licked her frozen treat. She was clearly one of those children who licked rather than bit into desserts to make them last longer, only to lose a great deal of the juice as it melted.

Matty swallowed, wishing that the droplets of juice from the girl's melting cream bar would miraculously fly into his throat. That was a stupid pseudo-prayer. Only human blood could quench his thirst, and even before his act of perfect contrition, he never fed on children. Nothing would pass through his parched lips until he received Eucharist again tonight. He closed his eyes, silently praying a Hail Mary that he would not seek the Blood of Christ to merely satisfy his appetite.

"I said-"

"Yes, child," Matty said, forcing himself to open his eyes again, "I am a vampire."

The girl nibbled on the edge of her cream bar, probably realizing she would lose it to melting otherwise. "My name isn't 'child.'" She took a bigger bite and spoke with her mouth full. "My name is Nevaeh. That's Heaven spelled backwards. I'm six, and I'm on summer vacation."

Maybe if he ignored her, she would become bored and go away. Matty turned his head toward the curtained window, nearly igniting a migraine. A lightning bolt of pain shot down the side of his neck into his shoulder. He inhaled sharply, not wanting to display his newest form of agony with theatrical groans. Every day since he checked himself into hospice by order of the parish priest, Fr. Tomás, his pain increased. He wasn't like human hospice residents whose pain often faded as death neared, even in the midst of starvation. Matty's vampiric body would torture him worse and worse until he succumbed to the temptation to feed or the Lord saw fit to take him home. Already, he had miraculously survived more than one hundred days by daily consumption of His Blood. He received His Body too, another miracle considering he hadn't been able to consume solid food in over four hundred years. Other than that, he ate and drank nothing.

"What's your name?"

It had been foolish to think that the inquisitive little chit would leave him in relative peace. Warily, Matty glanced at the stream of light illuminating part of the floor. As he suspected, it was the middle of the day. At least the sun wouldn't hurt him as he lay in bed. The staff had made sure of that by installing thick curtains. Still, the time of day instinctively made him shudder. With effort, he turned his head again to regard the girl, if only to distract himself from his unease about the sun.

"My name is Matty."

Nevaeh wrinkled her nose. "Maddy? That's a girl's name."

Matty wondered if God sent this annoying child to his room during the most brutal time of day for a reason. Was she some kind of test to help him exercise the Christian virtue of forbearance? If she was, Matty supposed he would have to be good natured about her presence. But the cramps in his legs didn't make kindness easy.

"My name is *Matty*, spelled with two t's. That's a boy's name."

Nevaeh pursed her lips and then licked her orange cream bar a couple of times. "How old are you?"

Despite his ever-increasing hunger resembling an internal implosion, Matty couldn't help being amused by Nevaeh's impertinent question. She was either too young to know not to ask adults their ages or too old to care about social conventions.

"I'm four hundred fifty years old."

Nevaeh stopped licking her treat and stared at him wide-eyed. "Wow, that's pretty old. Older than my grandma, even." She took a bite of her orange cream bar. A small sticky puddle of it had formed on the floor some time ago.

With supreme effort, Matty tucked the bedsheet around himself. He heard the air conditioner turn on and knew his room would become agonizingly cold within minutes. Unfortunately, his quilt lay at his feet, and sitting up to reach for it required more strength than he currently possessed. Still, he would try, no matter how much it hurt. Panting, he hoisted himself onto his elbows. His whole body protested the effort, punishing him with throbbing shockwaves in all four limbs and sharp aches everywhere else. He barely resisted the temptation to curse himself and the heavens for his excruciating feebleness.

"Here," Nevaeh said, giving him the quilt with her free hand. She managed to let her cream bar drip on it, but Matty didn't care. Surprised by her charitable gesture, he forgot his agony for the briefest moment.

"Thank you," he said, lying back down. The soft thud of his head against the pillow rattled his brain. His shoulder blades and back warred with the mattress springs beneath them. Matty ran his fingertips over the patchwork, letting the texture of the quilt's stitches distract him from the various pangs inhabiting him.

"So, how old were you when you got turned?" Nevaeh said after a long silence, startling him. Anyone young enough to wear a side ponytail shouldn't have had an inkling of such things.

"Child, what do you know about getting turned?"

"My name is *Nevaeh*," she said, obviously irritated with being called "child."

"Forgive me, Nevaeh." Offering an apology while slowly dying had to be among the worst Christian trials. Matty often wondered how the martyred saints not only asked for forgiveness in the midst of torture but extended it to their assailants. He would meditate upon this during his next Rosary.

"So, how old were you?"

Matty wondered if he should entertain this line of conversation with a six-year-old. Frankly, he didn't want to discuss *anything* with the air conditioner running. Unable to generate much heat from a prolonged lack of nourishment, Matty shivered violently, despite the bedsheet and quilt covering what remained of his frail form.

"I was twenty-one," Matty said, trying to distract himself from the polar chill permeating his bed coverings. "But how do you know about turning?"

"My brother, Raphael, knows everything about vampires. He's eight-and-a-half. Actually, he's eight-and-three-quarters, but I forget sometimes." Nevaeh chomped on her orange cream bar, likely aware that she better hurry up and finish before the rest of it became a sticky puddle.

"He wanted to be a vampire for Halloween, but Mom wouldn't let him. She said that it was bad to want to be a vampire, even in pretend. So, Raphael decided to be a fruit bat instead. That way, he still got to wear the fangs that George gave him at school, because fruit bats have fangs too. And Mom couldn't really argue with that."

Nevaeh's talk of fangs brought attention to the white-hot torment in Matty's own fangs that hadn't pierced flesh in 104 days. "Your mother's right." Matty closed his eyes for a moment, bracing himself against an incoming wave of abdominal pain. "It's bad to be a vampire, even in play."

"So, how come you're a vampire then?"

Matty clutched his quilt, as though doing so could ease his myriad of afflictions. His belly acted like it was trying to suck itself into oblivion, and his spine felt like it was being ground into fine powder. He swallowed, his throat scratching and burning like it was full of sawdust. Tears threatened to form. Matty often cried from all the merciless physical and emotional hurt that increased each day, but he did his best not to show the extent of his suffering to visitors and staff. Even before he repented, he never liked to upset anyone. Besides, he wanted to offer his hidden grief for the Holy Souls in Purgatory. After all, he must have put so many people into that horrid place when he fed upon them.

"Did you get bitten by a cursed vampire bat, like in the movie *Curse of the Night Bat*?"

Matty hadn't seen *Curse of the Night Bat*, but he had certainly heard of it. He also knew that its content was questionable for a six-year-old at best. Moreover, it was just a fantasy.

"No, I wasn't bitten by a bat. I was bitten by a vampire." Matty sighed, remembering how Helewis deceived him. He used to lament how if he hadn't sinned in the first place, she never would have had a chance to turn him. But that was unproductive, so he prayed for her soul instead.

Nevaeh wiped her mouth on her sleeve and then resumed munching on her half-eaten-half-melted orange cream bar. "Did you want to be a vampire?"

"No, never. But I..." Matty stopped himself from saying he didn't have a choice. While he certainly didn't choose to be turned, he did choose to partake in sins of the flesh that left him vulnerable to Helewis's attack in the barn. Of course, he wasn't going to tell a six-year-old *that*. Still, he figured he better offer some age-appropriate explanation for his turning because Nevaeh was sure to ask. And as long as Matty kept talking, maybe he wouldn't notice the frigid temperature of the room, or that it was the middle of the day, leaving him extra fatigued and anxious.

"You see, the vampire who turned me wanted to keep me forever as her... Well, I guess you could say she wanted me to be like a fairy tale prince who never got old." Worried he might have made his unexpected transformation sound too glamorous, he added, "But that was a very bad thing because vampires... Well, I guess you know how vampires eat."

"Yeah, they drink people's blood."

Hearing the truth from one so young unleashed vile memories of his 450 years of terror. Convincing himself he wasn't truly evil, he fed from condemned criminals, mortally wounded soldiers on battlefields, rogues, and random persons of seemingly little importance. He never attacked children, people he befriended, or anyone he bedded. But every one of his victims had an immortal soul and a gift of life that wasn't his to take, even when those lives were near their natural end anyhow. Sobs of profound regret threatened to wrack Matty's body and soul, but he held back. Once his little visitor left, he would funnel that overflowing river of sorrow into prayer.

"Mom said you don't feed off of people anymore." Nevaeh finished her cream bar but held on to the stick, even though there was a garbage can in the room. "So, you're pretty much dying."

Somehow, Nevaeh's lack of tact made him smile. The corners of his lips cracked, one more little source of penitential pain. "Yes, Nevaeh. I'm dying from starvation because it's wrong to feed from people. Only God sustains me now."

Nevaeh opened her mouth like yet another question wanted to pop out of it, but Paula, one of the nurses, entered the room.

"Nevaeh," Paula said, taking her hand, "I've been looking all over for you. You know you're not supposed to go into residents' rooms. Matty, I'm so sorry if my daughter disturbed you. I thought she was downstairs in the kitchen. It's summer break, and I wasn't able to get a babysitter today. Plus, we don't have air conditioning at home, and with this record heat, I-"

"It's all right, Paula. We had a nice visit."

"Yeah," Nevaeh said, nodding. "Matty's really nice for a vampire." She smiled at Matty, who returned her joyful expression despite undergoing his own private purgatory.

"That's fine, dear, but we need to go downstairs to let Matty rest now. Vampires need to sleep during the day."

"Okay." Nevaeh stretched out the word in resignation, her smile suddenly replaced with a pout. "But can we at least bring Matty an extra blanket? He's been shivering."

Paula's mouth flapped like a fish out of water. "Oh, yes. Of course. Sorry, Matty, I should have realized that the air conditioning would be hard on you. I'll come back in just a minute with another blanket."

"Take your time," Matty said, strangely warmed by Nevaeh's attentiveness to his needs. "I planned on saying a Rosary before going back to sleep."

Breaking away from her mother's grasp, Nevaeh skipped over to Matty's nightstand.

"I know it's not like in the movies," Nevaeh said, handing him his Rosary. "Touching a Rosary isn't going to make you burst into flames. And the sun just really, really hurts instead of turning you into a pile of ash."

Matty held back an amused laugh, not wanting to hurt Nevaeh's feelings. No matter what the time period, children disliked when adults laughed at their sincerity.

"All right, that's enough," Paula said, taking Nevaeh's hand again. "Say goodbye to Matty now."

"Okay," Nevaeh said in that childish drawl again. "Goodbye, Matty. I'll pray for you so you can go to Heaven soon. Don't worry. I don't think it'll be much longer now."

Paula tugged Nevaeh toward the door, probably embarrassed that her daughter had no filters. At this point in his torturous transition from undead existence to totally dead, Matty found the six-year-old's candor oddly refreshing.

"Goodbye, Nevaeh," he said. "And thank you for your prayers."

When Paula and Nevaeh left the room, Matty made himself as comfortable as possible. Everything still hurt, the air conditioning practically blew right through him, and the light peeking through the thick curtains continued to induce anxiety, but he had gained enough strength to muddle through another day. Although Nevaeh seemed convinced that he didn't have long to live, Matty honestly had no idea how much longer he would survive. In the meantime, he thanked God for sending him a little slice of backwards Heaven to make the journey easier.

About the Author

E.J. LeRoy is a freelance writer, poet, and aspiring novelist whose work has appeared in *Androids and Dragons*, *Fiction on the Web*, *Horrific Scribes*, *Neon Dystopia*, *NonBinary Review*, and several speculative fiction anthologies. LeRoy also published the novelette *Fusion*. Visit the author's website at https://ejleroy. weebly.com/

What Fuels Those Bodies

P.C.M. Vandermeer

CW: Character death

Whumpee: Man, Whumper: Man, Caretaker: N/A

Automated Workshop Log for 20 October 2464

» Dr. Tallasios returned to the workshop with a new idea to combat the missing research funds. He said, "You've heard of that billionaire O'Sullivan guy, haven't you?"

Mr. Nakano said, "I have. Unfortunately. Hasn't he always been against electronic fuels, and regenerative technologies in general?"

"Correct, dear Nakano. Unless he can make it funny!" Dr. Tallasios barked in amusement before continuing to say, "And he would find it funny to use blood as fuel."

Mr. Nakano had not answered right away, arms crossed. "That *is* regenerative, I guess."

"Correct again, dear Nakano."

"And he is thinking of this now because Halloween is coming up?"

"Third time lucky! A vampiric android! What do you make of that?"

"A whole lot of work," Nakano sighed. He smiled when Dr. Tallasios grabbed him by the shoulders and convinced him to start workshopping [violence detected – note deleted]. «

***

Automated Workshop Log for 24 October 2464

» "What in God's name is that?"

"Right? Isn't she a beauty?"

"'She'? Those cables and... Wait, did you steal an android?"

"What? Oh, dear Nakano, no. I would never waste my precious criminal energy on something as trivial as that. No, she was shorted out – but nothing we can't fix, while we make her ready and scary," grinned Dr. Tallasios, then paused. "Don't give me that look. I promise faithfully that I did not steal her."

"All right, all right." Mr. Nakano stepped closer to inspect the android model. "I suppose we could carve something out of this mess."

"That's the spirit!" «

***

Automated Workshop Log for 31 December 2464

» "This is Hijiri Nakano, recording the progress on the android Carmilla. The teeth pumps aren't quite working the way we want them to. I've cut myself again today. Fuel distribution is giving me a headache, too. Tallasios has asked me to join his New Year's Eve party instead of working, so I will go now. He has been in high spirits lately, and I would like to keep him that way." «

***

Automated Workshop Log for 3 May 2465

» "I wouldn't worry about all that now. By next week, it's over for us."

"What? Nakano, why would you say that?"

Mr. Nakano held up an empty blood bag.

"Ahh, I understand. Don't worry about it! Lucky for us, I've already ordered a new conveyance."

"What? How?"

"Leave all of that to me, dear Nakano. Work will continue as usual." Dr. Tallasios leaned in. He patted Mr. Nakano's cheek. «

***

Automated Workshop Log for 26 July 2465

» "The distribution doesn't work like that. I told you, remember?"

"You should've refined the filter pumps to 0.05!"

"We can't go smaller. It won't work."

Dr. Tallasios let out a scream and hit Mr. Nakano's face [violence detected]. "You small-minded fucking imbecile! Can you not see we're working on something bigger here? Try harder!"

On the ground, Mr. Nakano waited for a few moments before he spoke again: "Maybe some things aren't meant to be. You should know that. I'm out of here."

To inform authorities, please enter security code Beta. «

***

Automated Workshop Log for 18 September 2465

» "Tallasios here, recording. Carmilla is as dead as a stone. Nakano is speaking to the committee and trying to keep them from asking too many questions. But I don't know what he's telling them this time. I don't know anything anymore about what's going on inside his stupid little head. Despite what he's saying, he isn't in this, mentally. His heart isn't either. Part of me wants to stop. But I can't be away from him. And he not from me, obviously. And if this truly works, Carmilla could be a breakthrough for regenerative technology all over the world. She might have started as a wacky idea, but by now she belongs to us, not that clown O'Sullivan. Our work is so much bigger than him. Even if we won't make it in time for October, this'll be huge! And with such a patent, we would never have a single worry again in our lives. We'll finally make it. Just the two of us. So, I'm marching on. We cannot be wrong with this." «

***

Automated Workshop Log for 24 October 2465

» Dr. Tallasios stepped back. "Hello, Carmilla?"

"Hello, Doctor. How are you?"

"Ha!"

"What a fine evening this is."

"*Ha!* Nakano, did you hear? Nakano–" Dr. Tallasios kissed Mr. Nakano. "We did it!"

Mr. Nakano laughed. "Yes. Incredible!"

"She's perfect! Oh, you're perfect, my dear! Look at you! Smile, Carmilla! God, Nakano, those fangs will be the showstopper! You've truly outdone yourself."

Mr. Nakano said, "I couldn't have done it without you, you know."

"I do! Now, let's celebrate! Champagne for the two of us, and a fresh blood bag for dear Carmilla!" Dr. Tallasios let out a scream of joy. «

***

Automated Workshop Log for 31 October 2465

» The android attacked Mr. O'Sullivan first [violence detected]. The entire first row had their throats slashed, three had their necks broken. Dr. Tallasios left for the corridor. The android refueled by drinking from Mrs. Sutrack's neck. It continued its attack in rows two and three. Its speed surpassed everyone else's. Finally, Mr. Nakano held it in place and yelled, "Carmilla, no! Stop!"

The android broke Mr. Nakano's legs before refueling. It bit through his stomach, his chest, his neck. Approximated blood loss: unclear. "Please, help!" Mr. Nakano cried.

By midnight, there were twenty-one dead bodies. Dr. Tallasios returned to Room 3b and cradled a corpse. "No! Dear Nakano," he cried. "Dear Nakano. Hijiri."

Mr. Nakano's life signs ceased at 2207 hours.

Dr. Tallasios' life signs are active within a 100-kilometer radius.

The android's non-existent life signs make detection impossible. To inform authorities, please enter security code Beta.

To inform authorities, please enter security code Beta.

To inform *authorit–*

About the Author

Being queer in a heteronormative world, P.C.M. Vandermeer finds comfort and joy in writing queer stories. She is a rescue dog mum and enjoyer of speculative fiction – especially when it includes monsters and body horror.

The Lady of the Lake

Randall Madden

CW: Character death

Whumpee: Man, Whumper: Woman. Caretaker: Woman

"She's been down there for centuries."

The sky still fell toward the absolute dark of a cloudy night, and the air was blisteringly cold. Every time the wind gusted across the surface of the frozen lake, my eyelashes tried to freeze together, and I gasped for air inside my scarf. I fought the overwhelming urge to turn my back on the whole endeavor, to go back to the Jeep and hide in its warmth until the rest of the group came to their senses.

Our tiny circle of five huddled on the face of the dead lake. Ice and snow crunched under boots as we shuffled back and forth in a vain attempt to generate some heat, breath clouding around our faces only to be snatched away in the vicious wind. I pulled my toboggan down over my eyebrows and risked a glance down at the frozen lake.

A flashlight beam danced in the frozen fractals of ice that we surrounded like sojourners at a campfire, just barely revealing the shadow of a person underneath. My breath caught in my throat once more, but this time it had nothing to do with the cold.

Bobby dropped onto his knees and wiped some of the loose debris and snow away from the lake's surface. As more flashlight beams trained on the ice, the face of an impossibly beautiful woman became visible. She was pale—and obviously dead—but somehow her face seemed ready to explode with an unquenchable vitality. We all held our breath as we took in her raven hair and violet lips, her shadowed eyes mercifully closed from view. She seemed ready to move at any moment, and none of the panic of what must have been a drowning death showed in her dainty cheekbones.

More than any corpse I had seen in a dozen funeral homes, she seemed to be merely sleeping. The gentle curve of her lip reminded me of mother, and the deathly pallor that their skin shared only amplified the image. It had been so many years since I tiptoed to see my mother in the casket, but the image still lingered. The figure locked away in ice brought it back full force.

"The Lady of the Lake," Terrance said, but no one laughed. Though her aching beauty made her alluring in a way that I could not describe, somehow, she seemed inhuman. Almost monstrous. Even the ancient black dress that clung tightly to her curves did nothing to disguise the animalistic aura that seemed to pulse through the ice.

"We're really gonna do this?" Jake looked around the circle. "I really thought this hunt was a waste of time, but...we're really gonna try the ritual?"

"Grow a pair," Sam said, opening the tattered leather book he had produced from his jacket pocket. "Shine your light over here."

They started the ritual, but I couldn't look away from her face. Even when the words started to hiss from their mouths, unnatural and painful to hear, I was enraptured by the unholy splendor dwelling less than a foot away. Tears froze to my cheek at the idea that this creature once walked the earth, that I might have known her then. Maybe even *had* her.

"The blood, Terrance. You agreed."

"Yeah, yeah."

Terrance cursed, and I blinked as droplets of darkness scattered on the ice above her face. Was it my imagination, or did her cheek twitch?

More. I need more.

Bobby removed his glove to spread the bloody pattern into shapes, impossible shapes that broke something loose in the back of my mind. I tried to stare past them at her face, even though my vision grew blurry. A sudden, raging headache worked to erode my thoughts.

This won't work. I. Need. More.

"Garret, what the fuck are you doing, man?"

I started and looked away, blinking against the bite of the wind. Immediately, I saw the glint of a knife in Terrance's hand.

"What?"

"You zoned out, dude. Are you okay?"

"Yeah, yeah. I'm fine."

It had been so long since I saw her face. My eyes tracked back across the smeared blood droplets, over Bobby's hunched shoulder where he continued to scribble. Along the flowing curves of her dress, her body...

I want you, Garret.

Her eyes were open.

"Shit!" I gasped in the cold air and slipped on the ice. As I fell my heart raced at the momentary link with those impossibly black eyes.

They were the most beautiful thing I'd ever seen.

Free me. I need more. I will comfort you...

"Dude, are you okay?"

Terrance offered his free hand to help me up. I took it, shaking, and smiled.

"Thanks, man."

"No prob –"

I grabbed the knife from his grasp, cutting my hand in the process. Terrance opened his mouth to protest, but it was too late. I turned back to my lady in the ice, her black eyes meeting mine once more, her lip twisting in a faint smile.

Kill him. He's going to take me from you.

I grabbed Bobby's forehead and wrenched his head back, then plunged the knife into the side of his throat. Crazed shouts of confusion echoed across the ice.

"Oh my god!"

"What the fuck!"

Bobby gargled as a hot spray of crimson gushed from his throat, steaming violently into the frigid air. The blood turned black and hissed as it dissolved the ice, flowing down through cracks that looked like bulging veins, feeding the black heart beneath the lake.

Thank you, my love. **More.** *More, and I can be with you, soon...*

Terrance's eyes were terrified and confused as I turned and plunged his knife at his throat. My aim wasn't as good this time, hand slippery with Bobby's life, and he howled as I stuck the blade into his shoulder instead. I grunted with the effort of wrestling him to the ground. Jake and Sam pulled at my arms, but we were lost in a shadowy scuffle, and they couldn't stop me as I plunged the knife into Terrance's thigh. I yanked it free, and his blood spurted out in a fountain to join Bobby's. He cried into the night as I stabbed him again and again. The bludgeoning from the other two couldn't stop me.

"Oh, shit..."

The pressure on me slackened; Terrance was dead, and the other two had become little more than footsteps racing away into the darkness. As I looked up, I saw why they had run.

The dark lady was floating above the lake, her prison a thawed crater filled with meltwater and congealing gore. Her unblemished skin beckoned to me, and I stood to move into her embrace.

Come to me, my love.

I smiled. There was time now. It was just the two of us. I wrapped my arms around her waist, sighing as her hand pushed my face gently into her breasts.

I didn't even mind when her distended jaw tore out the side of my neck. She fed deeply of me, satiated her hunger, and we became one.

About the Author

Randall Madden was born and raised in rural Tennessee. From an early age, his writing interests have included fantasy, science fiction, and horror, with an occasional twist of humor. He received his MFA in Creative Writing at Southern New Hampshire University.

Lover's Collar

Kras Nebula

CW: nonconsensual touching, mind control, abusive relationships, self-harm

Whumpee: Man, Whumper: Man, Caretaker: N/A

Sajjad surfaced from the depths of death, certain he was dying all over again. Fire spread out from his chest and down through his limbs, and set them writhing in a desperate attempt to escape the pain. He took a breath as though he had just breached the surface after drowning— a huge, deep gulp of air in a desperate attempt to ease the clawing agony in his chest. His eyes were stretched wide, staring sightlessly up at a ceiling he might have recognized— dark paint chipping away with age, chandelier unlit, unmoving, and crusted with grime— were it not for the corrosive pain melting him from the inside out. One hand twisted in his shirt, his mind unable to comprehend the undone buttons or loose fabric, instead convinced that it was too tightly wrapped around him. His other hand clawed at the sweat-soaked sheets of the bed beneath him, scrabbling for purchase against the pounding desperation taking hold in his chest. He was suffocating, he was certain of it— he took in another gulp of air— somehow he wasn't getting enough oxygen, even though he was equally certain he was hyperventilating— another gasping breath— and everything was so loud and there was a scent filling his nose— *breathe*— like smoke and ash but no, no, no, this was different this was—

Blood.

With recognition came clarity, and with clarity the unnamed agony announced itself: Hunger.

Sajjad's senses narrowed to a point in the room; there was blood, not far; he could almost *feel* it; it was what he needed to end the pain. He let go of his shirt, planted his hands on either side of him against the mattress, and surged forward with singular animal intent—

"Stop."

Only for a command to tighten like a rope around his neck, freezing him perfectly in place. His muscles locked, his desperate breaths caught in his chest, the promised cure for his pain perfectly out of reach.

"Calm down. Lie still."

Sajjad *bucked* against the control, but was forced back down like a disobedient dog. His thrashes were muted as his body turned against him, coercing him to stillness despite the desperate hunger still clawing in his chest. There was no relief, only wave after wave of an endless ocean of agony until, slowly, the ringing in his ears began to fade and his gasps turned back into breaths. His eyesight began to clear, the fog began to pull back from his mind, and he began to shudder in exhaustion instead of desire.

"Are you back with me?"

Sajjad froze, struck with two thoughts at once. The first was that, though he had expected his heart to *thud* in response to the voice, he could no longer feel any sort of heartbeat at all. The second was that he knew that voice, and he knew it intimately. His gut twisted in revulsion as he realized just whose bed he was lying in, and just whose mouth had been on his neck, as memories of the previous night began surfacing from the dark sea of his mind. Flashes of meeting with the vampire, flashes of making deals to secure his revenge and promises of freedom, flashes of blood soaking the furniture and tender, pristine touches trailing down his jaw—

"What—" His voice broke into a cough; his throat ached as though he had been screaming for hours, but still he attempted to speak. "What have you done to me?"

"There we go." The voice came from somewhere at the foot of the bed, right where Sajjad had pinpointed the scent of blood. "The change can be quite disorienting at first, I know, but you're doing *so good*. Now. **You may get up, but do not leave the bed.**"

The collar around his neck loosened, and the grip it had held on his muscles relaxed all at once. For a moment he simply lay there, shuddering and staring up at the ceiling, taking stock of himself. His thick black hair was sweat-soaked, and plastered against his forehead and the back of his neck; his clothes were rumpled, the first several buttons of his shirt undone, and the collar felt crusty in a way he did not have it in him to investigate; he *ached,* as though he'd run for miles without rest; his heart did not beat in his chest, and he was laid in the bed of the monster responsible.

With weak, shaking arms, Sajjad carefully levered himself into a seated position. Carmine Riviera sat in an ornate chair a few feet from the foot of his bed, his clothes pressed and perfect, his white hair freshly combed, his luminous red eyes burning into Sajjad's own. They outshone the dim light emanating from the candles carelessly placed around the room; it was difficult to say what time it was, as heavy curtains covered the singular large window, keeping the room safely dark. Sajjad had no idea how old Carmine truly was, he'd never asked, but the furniture and rugs had begun to show the wear of ages past, to say nothing of the dust gathering in the corners and elaborate detailing. As it was, Carmine in all his pale perfectness sat in stark contrast to the dreary disarray of his room, leaning forward on his crossed legs with a pleased smirk on his lips.

"You didn't answer my question," Sajjad rasped, finally finding his voice once more.

Carmine's smile grew. "I gave you a gift," he purred. "Consider it a bonus for what I did to the Maranzanos for you. I know you want me to say it out loud, but you can feel the proof for yourself..." He raised two delicate fingers and tapped the side of his neck. Jad mindlessly moved his own hand to the two perfect scars along his own neck, but all he could see was the yellow scarf wrapped loosely around Carmine's pale throat.

"...That's my scarf." That had been his *mother's* scarf. The only thing he'd had left of her.

"Is it?" Carmine twirled the ends lazily about, pleasantly disinterested in anything Jad could say. "I hadn't noticed."

Red colored Sajjad's vision, but when he tried to fling himself from the bed to throttle the monster before him his muscles locked tight, the mental collar around his throat tethering him to the bed. "*You used me,*" Sajjad spat, hands shaking with rage.

"And you knew that going in," Carmine said, examining his nails. "You knew what I was when you came to me for help, you knew exactly what you were doing when you asked me to kill all those people. I could have simply spirited you away from that house and all its horrors— but, no, you wanted *revenge*. And I delivered! The Maranzanos are no more, and now your dear old mother can rest in peace. But..." Carmine stood in one fluid motion and strode easily to the bed, playfully flicking Sajjad's nose. "Sometimes you have to pay the piper." Sajjad had a sudden, violent fantasy of tearing Carmine's arm off with his teeth.

The worst part was, Carmine wasn't wrong. Sajjad had known what Carmine was when they'd met, he wasn't stupid. He had been desperate, though, and Carmine had been so gentle and understanding that Sajjad had ignored the vampire's teeth in favor of getting what they both wanted. Except, it seemed, Sajjad had misunderstood just what exactly it was that Carmine had wanted.

"I'm going to kill you." Carmine was unsurprised by his growl. If anything, his eyebrows quirked up as though he'd seen a particularly cute puppy. "I will find a way," Sajjad promised, "*and I will kill you—*"

"**Stand up.** Come on, off the bed." Sajjad's rage died in his throat as the collar tightened to a strangle, and his body was no longer his own. He was moved off the bed, placing his bare feet on the cold stone floor. "You see those curtains over there?" Carmine gestured to the large window, and dread began to slowly but surely pool in Sajjad's stomach. "**I want you to open them.**"

Sajjad stumbled forward as the collar tightened, but whatever resistance he could muster wasn't enough. His breathing picked up as he dropped against the wall next to the window, and it was with trembling hands that he pulled the heavy curtains aside. He flinched back at the sudden stream of light into the dark room; golden hour. He'd been dead for almost a full day, then. The last rays of sunlight cut a sharp line across Carmine's room, catching on the dust particles hanging in the air.

Carmine strode over and leaned casually against the wall on the opposite side of the window. "**Now**..." He rolled the word in his mouth. "**Stick your arm into the light.**"

Sajjad *thrashed*, but the collar snapped tight. He dug his feet in, grabbed his arm so hard he dug bloody rivulets into it, but there was nothing he could do. Sajjad choked back a scream as his fingers entered the sunbeam, flesh sizzling upon contact, smoke beginning to rise from his skin. The longer it lingered, the more the sunlight seared and charred.

"*Alright*," he choked out, still desperately fighting the command, "alright *you made your point.*"

Carmine said nothing, simply watched, his pleasant smile never leaving his lips.

"*Stop*-!" It had been mere seconds, and already the blinding pain had reduced Sajjad to begging. It was as though his arm was being held to flames, and no matter what he did he couldn't pull it away. "*Stop!*" His knees buckled and he collapsed to the floor, but the power of the bond that had been forced on him continued to hold his arm aloft, continued to let his flesh sizzle and melt and *burn*. He clawed at his own flesh, buried his face in the crook of his elbow and *sobbed*.

"**Alright, that's enough.**" Sajjad dropped to the floor as though his strings had been cut, and immediately curled around his burnt arm. In his periphery Carmine closed the curtains, returning them both to blessed darkness. "Come on now, that wasn't that bad."

Sajjad flinched violently as a hand carded gently through his sweaty hair. "F... Fuck—"

"Shhhhh."

The words crumbled to ash in his throat, and Sajjad thumped his forehead against the floor in defeat.

"That's better." Carmine was gentle as he wiped the tears from Sajjad's face, was almost caring as he cradled Sajjad in his arms, and Sajjad was sick to his stomach even as he leaned into the touch.

Part of him wanted to ask why Carmine had done any of this, but there would be no answer that would satisfy him. It had been a power move, plain and simple. Sajjad knew power moves, he'd dealt with them for the past eight years with the Maranzanos. He could deal with them a little longer, though how long 'longer' was, now that he was immortal, was a question he didn't have the answer to.

"I'm sure you must be hungry," Carmine said into his hair, and Sajjad couldn't stop how he tensed. He *was* hungry. Starving. In light of everything else, he had forgotten the scent that had claimed his entire being when he'd woken up, but now— Carmine had reached into his shirt pocket and pulled out a bag—

Blood.

The agonizing hunger from before twisted Sajjad's stomach, but already the fear of retaliation should he lunge for it had sunk in. He was sick of his body moving beyond his control, but the hunger was so, *so* loud. He fisted his uninjured hand in Carmine's shirt, eyes locked on the bag.

"Here, it's for you." Carmine plucked the hand from his shirt and placed the revolting bag into it, as though it were a gift, as though he hadn't placed the desperation in Sajjad in the first place, and Sajjad couldn't find it in himself to care, he was so, so, *so* hungry, and with an eagerness that disgusted him he brought the bag up to his lips—

"Before you drink, however," Carmine's voice cut through him like a knife, the collar tightening to a strangle. **"I think we need to lay down some ground rules."** Sajjad's hands shook, his jaw ached, his stomach was a mass of writhing agony, and though he held the blood bag in his hands, he could not force it to his mouth. "**First: you may not drink without my permission. Second: you may only drink blood I give you.**" With every new order, Sajjad could feel the collar tighten further like a noose. "**Third: you may not try to kill me, or yourself.** I doubt you'd be able to do the former, but I'd rather not deal with it all together. Besides, if you somehow managed to succeed, you'd kill yourself alongside me." Carmine continued to idly comb through Sajjad's hair like a favorite pet, even while he trembled in his lap. "Alright, **you may drink now.**"

Sajjad slumped as the collar loosened, but hesitated with the bag at his mouth, shaking. "Whose... whose blood is this?" He didn't want to know, but he couldn't help but ask.

Carmine smiled pleasantly, brushing Sajjad's hair behind his ear. "Does it matter? **Drink.**"

Sajjad placed the bag in his mouth, and drank.

About the Author

Kras Nebula is a little guy who's been writing things since they were even littler. They are a lover of everything sci-fi and fantasy. When not writing, they're probably playing with fiber like a horrid gremlin, or camping, also like a horrid gremlin.

The Footman

Lady Wallace

CW: Slavery, bigotry, fantasy racism, mentions of past child abuse (physical beatings/dehumanization)

Whumpee: Man, Whumper: Man, Woman, Caretaker: Woman

Helena stepped out of the carriage with the aid of the driver's offered hand, releasing her skirts as she smoothed them down from the ride.

Her aunt huffed as she exited behind her in a slightly less graceful swoosh of skirts.

"I don't see why you decided coming *here* was the best place to find a new footman," the older woman muttered as she adjusted her large, feathered hat. "You really want to bring one of those beasts into your house?"

"Dhampirs make good serving staff—Rose is testament to that," Helena replied with quiet determination.

Her aunt let out another obvious huff. "And I have my opinions on that one as well."

Helena ignored her pointed disapproval. "Well, Auntie, as a woman running my own estate, I would feel more secure with a footman who could also act as a bodyguard as part of his household duties should need arise."

Her aunt still had a disapproving look on her face. "It's precisely because you're a young woman living alone that I worry about you bringing one of those creatures into your house. You think your maids or the kitchen boy will protect you if he decides to go wild in a fit of bloodlust one day?"

Helena kept her silence, well used to her aunt's opinions. While she knew that it was possible for dhampirs to go into fits of bloodlust just like vampires, that was only generally in cases where they were abused and starved. And Helena had no intent to treat her new footman any differently than her other staff members.

"Come along, Auntie, it will only grow later if we wait."

Her aunt huffed again but followed Helena into the large building.

The opulent establishment was usually used as an auction house, but that evening, a different kind of sale was open.

As Helena stepped inside, she could see the mingling crowds, the air heavy with the press of bodies, the rustle of women's dresses and the scent of men's cologne. Human and vampire nobility both lingered in the large ballroom where refreshments were being served.

Helena declined champagne as her aunt took a glass. She wasn't interested in mingling, glancing instead toward the door that led to the buyers' hall on the other side of the room. She began to head in that direction and the footman opened it for her as she stepped inside.

The sounds of the conversation out in the ballroom dimmed and were soon replaced by the sounds of chains dragging, locks being removed from cages, and the voice of a salesman.

"She's a good fit for the kitchens—had her fangs filed down as well so she won't attract attention."

Helena soon found herself surrounded by multiple large cages, and other interested shoppers. She pressed her gloved hands together in front of her, schooling her expression.

It never ceased to disgust her that, while slavery had been as good as abolished in this country decades ago, it was still common custom to treat dhampirs little better than animals.

They were stuck in an unfortunate space between humans and vampires. Too beastly to be considered human, and without the pure blood to be considered vampires, they were outcasts from both corners, treated and sold as slaves with little to no rights if they were unlucky enough to be masterless.

The vampires considered all of them bastards since marrying or, God forbid, siring a child with, a human was highly frowned upon in their society, and though vampires were well integrated and established into the society as a whole, humans would never fully trust them, even with the Hunters who worked tirelessly to keep the status quo between the two worlds.

Dhampirs, caught in the middle, half human, and half vampire, were in a purgatory of their own; the lucky ones hiding what they were for the majority of their lives, and the unlucky ones being taken off the streets and sold in auction houses like this.

Helena looked around, hiding her distaste with well-practiced ease despite how much the sight of them in cages turned her stomach, as she perused the potential dhampirs.

A lot of them were painfully young, some of them struggled in the cages, most of them already feral, or at least driven that way by their captors through poor treatment and lack of proper feeding. These would likely be sold to those looking for hard labor in factories and though Helena hated to think of them meeting that fate, they would admittedly not be a good fit for a footman.

The dhampir in the last cage was different though. He sat silently, watching the proceedings with wary eyes. He was a young man with dark hair, perhaps in his late twenties, handsome features from what Helena could see past the muzzle, overall, rather unassuming.

His eyes turned up to meet hers as she approached the cage before looking down quickly. Not before she had caught the light hazel tint in them instead of the garnet eyes that the dhampirs who had been worked into a blood frenzy showed. So, he wasn't feral, then—why the muzzle? Helena wondered as she stopped by the cage.

Her aunt let out a distressed sound, jumping as one of the dhampirs down the row slammed a hand against his cage as the salesman tried to show him off.

"I will wait outside," the older woman said. "I don't wish to be around these beasts anymore."

Helena nodded, letting her go as she glanced at the dhampir again before turning toward one of the attendants. "Excuse me, is there any information about this dhampir?"

The attendant nodded and plucked a book from his pocket. "Yes, Number 23, let's see...he was put up for auction by his former employer after only three weeks of service. He worked as a footman. Tried to hide his nature, but when his employer found out he was not interested in having a dhampir in the house around his small children."

"I see. And before that employment?"

"Unknown, my lady. But he does have scars on his back so it is to be assumed he is a runaway," the attendant said.

Helena furrowed her brow, noticing the dhampir's shoulders stiffen slightly. "Did he tell you that himself?" she asked.

"We haven't been able to get anything out of him, my lady."

"And the muzzle?"

"A precaution because of the scars."

"But he has not bitten anyone or shown violent tendencies?"

"Not that we have seen, my lady."

Helena nodded, considering briefly, before she made up her mind. "I will take him then."

The attendant looked slightly surprised. "This one, my lady? Are you sure you don't want one of the maids? Or, this young boy would be perfect for a runner or for your scullery..."

"I already have a perfectly good maid and scullery boy, I am in need of a footman," Helena cut in pointedly as she turned to the dhampir. "You have proper training?"

The dhampir looked up in surprise at being addressed directly and nodded before respectfully lowering his eyes again.

Helena turned back to the attendant. "Then it is settled. How much are you asking for him?"

After settling the purchase, Helena returned to the ballroom to find her aunt. The older woman was talking to a friend of hers about the latest gossip as Helena approached.

"I'm ready to leave if you are, Auntie. They're bringing the dhampir out to the carriage."

Her aunt gave her a slightly disapproving sigh as she bid goodnight to her friend. "So, you really bought one of those creatures?"

"Yes, Aunt."

The older woman side-eyed her pointedly. "This isn't another one of your little hobbies, is it, my dear?"

"I have no idea what you mean, Auntie."

Her aunt huffed, pulling out her fan and fluttering it in front of her face. "You're just like your father."

Helena hid a small smile as she turned toward the front of the building.

The carriage was waiting as she stepped out into the night and she saw the attendants unloading the dhampir's cage next to it.

The driver turned to her as he saw her appear. "My lady, I don't think we have room for the cage..."

"That cage won't be necessary," Helena said instantly, turning toward the attendants.

"Helena," her aunt hissed, eyeing the dhampir distrustfully.

"Dhampirs can be troublesome, my lady," one of the attendants protested. "If he—"

"I'm aware. The keys to his muzzle and manacles, please," Helena said, holding out a hand so the attendant could brook no argument.

The attendant handed it to her silently before his companion opened the cage.

The dhampir crawled out with some difficulty due to his bound hands, straightening stiffly. Helena looked up at him. He was a lot taller than she had originally thought. She barely came up to his shoulder.

She beckoned to him. "Come."

He dutifully stepped closer and Helena reached out to unlock his hands before motioning for him to bend so she could unlock the muzzle as well.

"Helena!" her aunt protested again but Helena had already unlocked the muzzle from his face, revealing a sharp jaw and bruised lips that parted in a relieved sigh as the muzzle was removed.

"Thank you, my lady," he said hoarsely.

Helena nodded. "You can sit with the coachman."

He dipped his head in a small bow and climbed up onto the driver's bench as Helena climbed into the carriage next to her aunt, tossing the muzzle onto the seat beside her with disgust. It was the kind that had a silver bit in it, purposefully made to cause constant pain to dhampirs when they were forced to wear them.

"I can't help but fear for you, my dear, taking that beast into your house," her aunt said.

"I assure you I will be quite fine, Auntie," Helena replied. "The attendant said there was no record of violent tendencies. Need I remind you that father employed many dhampirs? I grew up with one as a nurse."

"Yes, yes, I'm well aware. I worried so much over you for that," her aunt shook her head, pressing her hand dramatically to her bosom. "Just...make sure to keep precautionary measures in place. You never know when they can snap."

Helena politely ignored her aunt as they drove through the lamplit streets.

The driver stopped at her aunt's townhouse and the older woman exited.

"Good luck with your new footman, dear. Please call round soon to let me know you're well."

Helena promised to visit soon before signaling the driver to continue.

It was late by the time they got back to the manor house and Helena stepped out of the carriage.

"Thank you, Cartwright, that's all for tonight," she told the coachman.

"My lady," the man said, tugging on his cap before he drove the carriage around to the carriage house.

The dhampir stood by silently, awaiting Helena's orders.

She motioned to him. "Come along." She hesitated slightly, and met his eyes. "I never asked your name."

He dipped his head a bit. "Victor, my lady."

Helena nodded. "Victor. Good. Come along then, Victor."

He followed her inside, looking around respectfully.

Rose trotted downstairs as she heard the door open. "My lady, I have your nightclothes set out for you. Would you like some tea before bed?"

"Thank you, Rose. My tea can wait for now. If you would please get Victor something to eat."

"Yes, of course," Rose said and nodded to the tall man. "You'll be the new footman, correct?"

"Yes, miss," Victor replied quietly.

Helena turned to the dhampir. "Rose is my head maid. She'll be the one you'll be working with the most."

Victor nodded politely to Rose. "It's nice to meet you, Miss Rose."

Helena left Rose to handle her new hire and headed toward the linen closet, pulling out a basket of medical supplies she kept for emergencies.

She took it toward the kitchen where Rose had sat Victor down, making him tea and a sandwich.

"There's blood if you need it. We have an order sent every Tuesday," Rose told him. "I'll have the butcher send extra from now on, of course."

Victor looked at her with slight surprise before he seemed to realize something and nodded gratefully.

"Will that suffice?" Helena asked as she came into the kitchen.

Victor started to stand but Helena waved her hand at him, setting the basket on the table.

"Your duties do not start until tomorrow. For now, allow me to tend your injuries."

"My lady, that's unnecessary…"

"I insist," Helena said firmly, leaving no room for argument.

Victor obediently sat still as she tended to the abrasions around his wrists, spreading ointment on them before wrapping them in gauze. He seemed to have relaxed some, though he stayed silent as Helena finished.

"Tomorrow I will have you fitted for uniforms. Please make a list of all the essentials you will need and I'll have the boy pick them up first thing," she told Victor as she put away the medical supplies.

"Yes, my lady."

Helena turned back to Rose. "Show him around and take him to his room when you're done. That one in the back should be good."

"Yes, my lady, I will go and get it ready now."

She hurried out of the kitchen and Helena was about to leave when Victor spoke up.

"Since I am not officially on duty yet, my lady, may I ask a question?"

Helena cocked her head. "You never need to hesitate to ask me anything, Victor."

He pressed his lips together softly before saying, "May I ask why you chose me? Instead of a more…reputable footman?"

"Are you un-reputable then, Victor?"

He looked slightly uncomfortable. "I would not say so, my lady, however, some find my very existence to be undeserving of reputation."

"I assure you that is not how I see it," Helena told him firmly. "My father made his home a refuge for dhampirs to work for a wage as any other person has the right to, and I intend to do the same. As long as you are under my employ, you need not worry about such things."

He glanced down at his bandaged wrists. "Your stance is rare, yet greatly appreciated, my lady."

Helena reached into her pocket and pulled out the certificate of purchase the auction house had given her. She handed it to Victor. "I want you to keep this on you at all times, especially when you leave the house."

He looked genuinely shocked, making no move to take the paper. "Why are you giving this to me?"

"I would rather give you full autonomy, but society refuses to allow that." She placed it by his empty plate. "So instead, keep this paper to prove that you were purchased by me and are now in my employ. By law, no one will be able to touch you then."

She could not read the look on his face as he finally accepted the paper, slipping it into the pocket of his waistcoat. "I will make sure not to lose it, my lady."

Helena smiled. "I hope that you will be happy here, Victor. Now, I'll bid you goodnight. Rose will give you your instructions in the morning and show you what your duties will be."

She started to make her way out of the kitchen before turning back. "By the way, my apologies for not introducing myself earlier. My name is Helena Harrington."

***

Once Victor was shown to his room by Rose, he took in the space. It was larger than the room he had been allotted at his previous employment, comfortable, if a bit bare, as would obviously be the case since he had no worldly possessions to bring. He saw that nightclothes had been set out for him as well as a fresh outfit for the next day. The sheets of the bed were clean and smelled of soap and there was hot water in the basin on the vanity, steaming pleasantly.

Victor walked over to it and washed his face, embarrassed by the slight stubble that had grown on his chin. A razor would have to be added to his list of needs. He would need to finish that tonight as well...

He sat down at the small writing desk in the corner of the room but before he began, he took the certificate of purchase out of his pocket, unfolding it and reading over it.

He didn't truly know how to feel about it. While his previous employer hadn't been cruel, he had cast Victor aside as soon as he found out about his true nature.

Victor was well aware of how much worse it could have been for him after having omitted the fact he was a dhampir on his application. Ending up in the auction house hadn't been the worst outcome—he knew all too well how much worse it could get.

But fortune truly seemed to be shining down on him considering the fact that he had ended up in the employ of someone like Lady Helena.

He thought of the sharp-featured young woman, elegant, shrewd, and seemingly kind. He vowed to do his best serving her and to not somehow mess this employment up like the last one.

***

The first week, Victor learned his duties, Lady Helena's schedule, and what would be expected of him as footman. He was fitted for uniforms and was soon looking the part in his perfectly tailored tailed coat, shined shoes, and clean gloves.

He easily befriended Rose as well as the other servants. They seemed to be a little family of their own here, working for the lone Lady of the house.

He fell in easily with Lady Helena as well. He appreciated her straightforwardness, not afraid to tell him if he needed to change something or if he had done something incorrectly, but she was always patient and he never felt like he would be needlessly punished for a minor issue. He learned to make her tea and her favorite snacks. He prepared her schedule every day, managed her appointments, accompanied her into town, and performed whatever other tasks she asked of him.

He was...comfortable for the first time that he could remember aside from the brief stint of first working for his former employer. Even knowing his true nature, Helena looked at him the way the former family had before they knew what he was. He would always remember how the heavily pregnant wife had looked at him after he'd been discovered drinking blood as opposed to how she had trusted him to help her with all her needs before that. The look of fear and betrayal. It was nice not to have those looks thrown at him all the time and when he was running errands in town, everyone assumed he was human.

Perhaps he grew too comfortable as the months stretched on. One day, Lady Helena's Aunt Constance came to visit. He could tell she distrusted him, especially when she asked Helena right in front of him as he served tea if he had been acting tame.

"Auntie, he's not a dog," Helena said firmly. "Victor is my footman and as far as his service I have no complaints."

She cast him a smile and he cast his eyes down as he handed her a cup of tea.

"He still has a wild look about him," her aunt muttered as she sipped her tea. "Perhaps you should at least have him cut his hair so that it looks a little less rakish."

Helena seemed amused. "Victor, would you prefer a haircut?"

"Whatever pleases my lady," he replied simply, feeling a little self-conscious. Perhaps his hair was a little long for the current style, but he always combed it back as was appropriate of his station.

"Well then, I don't have any issue with it as is, I think it suits you," Helena said simply.

Victor paused briefly as he returned the tea pot back to the tray, then retreated to the kitchens, feeling just a bit in an odd way.

"Don't mind Lady Constance, she is simply worried about Lady Helena's well-being," Rose said the instant he entered the room as if she had been listening in.

"I don't mind her," Victor replied sincerely. "I would rather cautionary distrust than open hostility."

Rose smiled at him in a way that showed her dainty fangs. "Very few are like Lady Helena and her father."

Victor inclined his head with interest at the mention of Lady Helena's father. He had seen the man's portrait where it hung over the fireplace in the parlor and thought he bore a striking resemblance to his daughter. But other than that, he didn't know much about the man.

"Did you work for the previous lord?" he asked.

Rose nodded. "Briefly, yes. He took me in when I was just a girl in need of steady employment after my grandmother died. Lord Harrington did the same thing that Lady Helena does. He was very active in the rights of dhampirs. It is truly a shame that the fever took him before his time, but Lady Helena is happy to follow in his footsteps."

Victor digested this information with interest as he accepted the plate of biscuits that Rose handed him to bring to the parlor.

"All you really need to know is that here, we are safe," Rose told him. "And that is truly a comfort."

"Indeed," he replied and made his way back to the parlor with the baked goods and a fresh pot of tea.

As he was refreshing the ladies' cups, the bell on the door rang.

"Allow me, my lady," he said and headed to the foyer, opening the door to find a messenger boy waiting.

He handed over a blank envelope. "For Miss Helena's eyes only," the boy said firmly.

Victor took the letter and passed the boy some coins. "Be on your way."

He scampered off, and Victor returned to the parlor, schooling his curiosity as he handed over the letter.

"A boy brought this, my lady."

"Thank you, Victor," Helena said, barely glancing at the letter before she tucked it into the day planner that was sitting on the small table by her chair. "You're dismissed to work on any other duties that need seen to."

He nodded, bowing slightly, before he made his retreat.

***

The rest of the afternoon proceeded normally, dinner happened as it usually did in the Harrington manor. Rose would cook with the aid of the scullery boy

Daniel, Victor would serve it, and then all of the servants would sit down with Lady Helena to eat.

It had shocked him at first, but she insisted that she hated eating alone so as long as she had no company, she preferred that the serving staff would eat with her. They often used it as time to discuss the daily duties or any concerns that needed to be seen to.

Victor still recalled his first night eating with the lady of the house, so nervous that he had dropped his knife on the table cloth. The sight of the stain on the linen had brought back memories of previous employments—accidents followed by loud berating and pain.

He had apologized profusely, offering to clean the mess while everyone ate, but Lady Helena had insisted he finish eating first.

"It's not the first time someone has dropped silverware on the tablecloth," she assured him. "No harm has been done."

It still baffled him when he thought of how different his new employer was to some of those he served in the past.

That night, nothing unusual was said at dinner. Victor finished the rest of his duties that evening before retiring to his room, dressing for the night and reaching for his glasses so he could read before bed.

However, as he began to fall asleep with the book on his chest just past midnight, a soft, yet insistent knock came on his door.

At first, he assumed it would be Rose needing help with some household emergency, so he got up quickly, just barely grabbing his robe as he opened the door.

To his shock, it was Lady Helena, dressed in a plain grey dress and dark cloak.

"My lady." He snatched his glasses off to see better, taken aback. "Is something wrong?"

"I need your assistance," Lady Helena said simply. "You must not ask questions at this time, do you understand?"

Victor nodded.

"Get dressed—not in your uniform. Meet me out front."

She left almost instantly and Victor stood there for a brief moment, gathering himself before he swiftly dressed, pulling his normal off-duty clothes from his wardrobe.

He hurried out front where Lady Helena stood alone under the moonlight. She turned to him as he arrived and handed him another cloak.

"Put this on."

He swung it around his shoulders and pulled his hood up as she had. She nodded in approval.

"Follow me and stay quiet, I will explain on the way."

"My lady," he nodded.

"You should refer to me as Helena only for the time being," she said then.

He frowned, and though he was currently bursting with questions, it wasn't his place to ask. He trusted that she would explain in time, and if not, well, it wasn't really his business to do more than obey.

The coach was already waiting and to his surprise, Helena picked up her skirts and climbed up onto the driver's seat, motioning for him to follow.

"Do you know how to drive, Victor?"

"Yes, my lady—ah—Helena."

The name felt strange on his tongue, but the darkness hid his discomfort. He climbed into the seat and took up the reins.

Helena guided him through the streets until he realized they were making their way toward the Thames. The strong scent of the river was rank in his nostrils as he pulled the coach to a halt where Helena bid him near one of the docks.

"Now we wait," she said.

The place was deserted, and he had to refrain from asking questions. The entire set-up was rather nefarious. Was his lady in some sort of trouble? Or did she engage in illegal dealings? The thoughts raced in his head, admittingly none of them adding up.

Then he heard the soft swish of oars in the river and glanced over to see a small boat approaching the dock.

Helena dismounted from the carriage before he could hand her down and he followed quickly as she stood on the dock, catching the rope one of the figures threw to her.

Three cloaked figures bobbed in the small boat; two adults and one a lot smaller. A man jumped to the dock and reached for the other two. Victor could see the shine of red in the man's eyes and instantly went on the alert. He could sense the bloodlust in him, and though it was not as strong in the others, they were obviously also dhampirs.

Understanding began to dawn in Victor.

"Thank you, miss, thank you," the dhampir woman said, holding the small figure close, reaching for Helena's hand. "My husband, daughter, and I are in your debt—"

The man pushed forward then, holding his wife back as his nostrils flared. "She's not one of us, Grace, we can't trust her!"

Victor didn't interfere, but stood, poised to intervene, as he watched Helena raise a hand.

"I assure you that I am on your side," she said simply. "But you need to come with me now so that you can make your train."

He gritted his teeth, fangs bared. "How do we know you're not just going to turn us in?"

"Jeremy, we were told she could help," the woman said, reaching out for her husband, but he stepped further in front of her.

"No, we were expecting one of *us*," he snarled, eyes glinting again. "I don't trust humans. All of you are full of lies." He reached into his coat and pulled out a knife.

Victor moved instantly with the flash of steel. His arm shot out across Helena's chest, catching the blade before it could hit her. He felt the hot burn of steel, but ignored it, reaching with his other hand to grab the dhampir's wrist and wrenching hard.

The dhampir cried out and the knife hit the dock with a dull clatter. Victor twisted his arm around to pin at his back and wrapped his other hand around the dhampir's throat.

"You are starving, I understand, but if you cannot refrain from harming the one who is trying to help you, then I will be forced to leave you in the river. You do not want to make your wife a widow and leave your child fatherless, I imagine?"

The dhampir woman was sobbing quietly as she held their daughter. "Jeremy, please. They're here to help."

Helena moved to wrap an arm around her.

"Release him, Victor," she said simply.

Victor eyed the dhampir for a long second before he finally released him. The man staggered, but went to his wife, holding her close.

Helena stepped away, motioning toward the coach. "There is blood under the seats for you in the carriage. I suggest you drink it."

The dhampir let out a shaky sigh. "Thank you... I—"

"Apologize by living a fulfilling life far from here," Helena cut in quickly. "We are not all against you."

He bowed his head, obviously humbled as he helped his wife into the coach with their daughter and their luggage.

Victor could not help but watch his lady in great respect. She had barely even flinched when Jeremy had come at her.

"Are you alright, Victor?"

He came back to himself as he realized she was looking up at him. It was only then that he felt the trickle of blood running down his arm, soaking into his glove.

Helena was already retrieving a handkerchief from her pocket and tying it around his arm.

"Are you always so cavalier with your wellbeing, my lady?" he asked before he could stop himself, realizing he was speaking out of turn.

She paused, seeming herself to be surprised at his words. "In my experience it does little good to show fear to anyone. Besides," she tied the handkerchief in a neat knot before looking up at him, her grey-blue eyes catching the starlight perfectly. "I trusted my reliable footman to protect me if needed."

Victor pressed his lips together into a thin line.

"You were, however a little rough with Mr. Jeremy in front of his wife and child. His concern was valid after all."

"My apologies," Victor replied, lowering his head. "Without knowing the situation—"

"We will talk later."

Helena passed him and Victor just barely managed to offer her a hand up onto the bench this time. He climbed up beside her and took the reins.

"The train station?" he asked.

She nodded.

He drove there and by the time they dropped the dhampir family off, they looked more refreshed, the bloodlust no longer apparent.

Victor didn't say anything on the ride back to the manor, and the groom, Cartwright, took the horse and carriage as soon as they returned so all he could do was follow Lady Helena back inside.

"Meet me in the kitchen," she said simply.

He went to the kitchen dutifully. It was dark, Rose having gone to bed hours ago, so he turned the gas lamps on and was about to start the kettle boiling for tea when he remembered his bloody gloves. He sighed and removed them, tucking them into the pocket of his overcoat. He tsked as he glanced at the new slice in his sleeve too. He would have to mend that as well.

Helena returned with the medical basket and set it on the table.

"Please sit down and allow me to look at your wound," she said, already reaching for the makeshift bandage.

Victor sat on the bench, taking his overcoat off and rolling up his sleeve. He winced as blood trickled down his forearm.

"My lady, perhaps I should—"

"Don't argue," she said simply, taking her own cloak off finally and going to wash her hands in a businesslike manner.

Victor closed his mouth and allowed her to sit next to him, holding his arm out for her to tend.

"It wasn't silver so it will heal quickly," he said quietly.

"Regardless, you should have an extra serving of blood to bring your strength back and stave off potential fever."

He pursed his lips, then broached, "My lady, may I ask a question now?"

She paused in her cleaning of the wound. "You may."

He took a deep breath. "How often do you do this?"

She exhaled slowly, but didn't reprimand him. She turned back to the basket and rummaged around until she found what she was looking for. "I am merely carrying on where my father left off," she said. "He set up several safe routes for dhampirs and became a...ferrier of souls, I suppose you could say."

"And that family, where do they go now?"

"There is a halfway house out in the country," Helena said as she painted his wound with a stinging tincture. "An old lady there takes them in and gives them a place to stay until they can establish themselves."

Victor was silent for a long moment before he said, "I think you're very brave, my lady."

She laughed lightly. "You think I'm foolish."

He was shocked at her words. "Not at all," he insisted sincerely. "I...think that what you do is admirable. Many would not, especially those in your position."

"Well, it is precisely because of my position that I take the opportunity to help those I can," she said simply.

"I ask only one thing, my lady," he pressed on.

She raised an eyebrow, reaching for a roll of bandages. "Oh? And what might that be, Victor?"

He watched as she slowly wrapped the bandage around his forearm. "That you do not go on these missions unaccompanied."

She seemed to relax a little as if having expected him to say something else. "I have no need to go alone. After all, I have my trusted footman, don't I?"

"Always, my lady," he said quietly with all sincerity as he watched her tie a neat little bow on his bandage.

They both sat there in silence for a brief moment before Helena stood, gathering the unused supplies back into her basket. "Make sure you drink some blood before retiring, Victor," she reminded. "Good night."

"Good night, my lady," he replied, watching her shadow disappear down the hall.

Something had changed between them that night, some kind of understanding. But he did not quite know what it was, nor did he think it was a good idea to probe further. It wasn't his place to question his lady's intentions. It was his place to do as she said, so he drank some blood and went to bed as prescribed.

***

The midnight missions were rare, but several more occurred in the months that followed. It became second nature for Victor to accompany Helena out on her ferrying missions and he understood now Rose's attentiveness in always keeping extra blood and other supplies around. Sometimes they even sheltered some of the runaways if they could not get out of the city right away, in which case discretion was key when it came to the household.

It was in his sixth month serving Lady Helena that she finally asked him to do a mission alone.

"There is a girl who is in desperate need of assistance," she told him. "But I must attend a dinner party tonight that would be quite inappropriate of me to miss so I cannot go. Please see that she gets to the two o'clock train safely without anyone following her."

"Where am I meeting her?" Victor asked.

Helena handed him a card with the address. "She currently has a room at this hotel, but there are people actively looking for her—potentially hired thugs. You must be careful to go as undetected as possible, Victor."

"Understood."

When the time came, he dressed in plain but respectable clothes with a cap to hide his features. It was a Friday night and parties were prevalent in the town-houses. Perhaps it was better this way though—a couple would not elicit much notice walking about after midnight. Victor took off on the horse alone, planning on stabling it at the hotel and walking his charge to the train station.

The hotel was mostly deserted this time of night, but there was one rather rough-looking man sitting in the lobby. Victor eyed him warily. On his belt, he could see the brief flash of a silver stake under his coat and a crucifix dangling next to it. A freelance hunter, he would guess, from the lack of badges.

He didn't let his eyes linger, but passed toward the stairs. It was doubtful that the man staying there was a coincidence. Helena had been right in that there were people hunting this girl.

He climbed to the right floor and found the room on the card. He knocked three times then spoke quietly through the door.

"Miss, I was sent by Lady Helena."

It was a brief moment before he heard the latch open to reveal a trembling girl. "You're Victor?" she asked.

He nodded, taking off his cap. He allowed his eyes to shine red and showed his fangs. She seemed to relax a little and she stepped aside to let him in.

"Do you have all your things?" he asked, glancing toward the pile of clothes and belongings that sat on the bed.

"I'm so sorry, I'm just such a mess; my maid wasn't able to come with me and…" She started crying, and Victor stepped forward to hand her a handkerchief.

"I know this is difficult," he said gently. "But you'll be safe soon enough. What is your name?"

She sniffed. "Lillian Chambers—well, perhaps just Lillian now."

"Allow me to help you, Miss Lillian," Victor said as he began to neatly fold away her clothes into her carpet bags. "Do you have your ticket?"

She nodded. "Miss Helena gave it to me."

"Good. Now, I do not want you to be alarmed, Miss Lillian, but we might have to escape a little carefully. There are hired hunters sitting in the lobby."

She gasped, but the fury suddenly outweighed the fear. "I knew she would send those men after me!" She looked up at Victor. "My stepmother... ever since my father died, she has been trying her best to be rid of me. I've been trying to get away to meet my fiancé—he went ahead to secure a place for us but...I can't seem to escape her."

"You will tonight," Victor said firmly. "Your fiancé is a good man?"

"Yes," she said with a small smile. "He is human and he will provide a safety net for me."

"I am glad to hear it." Victor closed her carpetbag and Lillian grabbed her reticule.

"Is it nice working for Miss Helena? I would imagine that brings a feeling of security in itself."

He couldn't help the small smile. "Indeed. I have never been more content. It is important for us to find people who see us for who we really are, isn't it?"

Lillian blinked a little. "Oh—are you Miss Helena's intended?"

Victor's lips parted in shock. "No, no, I am simply her footman. I simply meant, that it was fortunate for her to take me on as an employee."

"Ah, I apologize for the misunderstanding," Lillian said, flushing a little.

Victor cleared his throat and pulled her carpetbag off the bed. "We need to leave or you'll miss your train."

Lillian nodded and Victor went to the door, cracking it to check outside before opening it fully and beckoning her forward.

"Come, we will head out the back."

She slipped out beside him and Victor led her to the staff's stairwell heading down into the laundry before coming out behind the hotel in the mews.

Victor offered her his arm. "Put your arm through mine. We will look like just another couple leaving a party."

She tucked her hand through his elbow and he could feel the small tremors that still ran through her.

He caught movement out of the corner of his eye for a brief moment. Noting it, he continued without saying anything. Then another figure appeared on the other side of the street. He quickened his pace just slightly.

"Do not fret, miss, but we have picked up some shadows," he murmured.

He felt Lillian tense instantly. "Hunters?"

He nodded once, catching the sound of a third pair of footsteps joining the others.

Victor looked around. The station was at least another ten minutes by foot and he wasn't so sure that they didn't have men hiding there either. But perhaps if he could keep these hunters distracted...

There was a cab parked up ahead, the driver looking like he was dozing off.

Victor suddenly urged Lillian on into a trot. "Come, hurry."

She ran beside him, and Victor slapped the side of the cab to startle the driver awake.

"Wot do ya want, gov?" the man grumbled.

Victor was already helping Lillian into the cab with her bag. "The lady needs to get to the station or she'll miss her train," he said, handing over a handful of coin that far exceeded the cost of the trip as the pounding footsteps of the hunters behind him drew closer. "Quickly."

"Victor, those hunters—"

"Be careful and watch your surroundings," Victor cut Lillian off before closing the door.

The cab driver cracked his whip and the horse trotted off at a good clip.

Victor turned, seeing the hunters come to a halt, annoyance on their faces, as they watched the cab drive off.

Victor stood his ground.

One of the hunters was already pulling a stake. "Another 'alfblood, huh? You another one of 'er lovers then?"

Victor narrowed his eyes but didn't reply.

The hunter spat on the ground. "Well, the little lady won't get far. We'll deal with you and then go pick 'er up from the train station."

Victor gave them a dark look, shifting his feet to brace himself. "I'm afraid that I cannot allow you gentlemen to do that."

"Well, don't you speak pretty," another hunter, with a large scar across his face, snorted, casually swinging his crucifix in one hand. "I bet you would fetch a pretty penny for a dham—if there's anything left of you by the time we're done."

Victor wasn't fazed. It was fifteen minutes until 2, and as long as he could keep them distracted until then, they wouldn't get to Lillian in time to stop her.

"I am rightfully employed," he said calmly, reaching into his coat pocket. "It would be illegal to injure me—you would have to pay my mistress for property damage."

His hand slid into his pocket where his billfold resided, but then he thought of something. If they saw Lady Helena's name on the papers, then she could be implicated in Miss Lillian's escape. It would destroy her whole operation and he couldn't allow that.

He drew his hand away, faking panic as if the proclaimed papers were missing.

The hunters watched with cruel glee and began to circle him, closing in.

Victor felt the sudden sense of fight or flight kick in, but he forced himself to stay calm. He could not fight them if he didn't want to be instantly put to death. He could only prove his innocence if he didn't attack.

The hunters knew this, and he hoped that he might be alive to have the chance to defend himself.

"Looks like the 'alfblood is a liar as well as a blood sucker," one of the hunters jeered and grabbed Victor by the back of the collar, tugging him down. "Let's go somewhere more quiet to continue this discussion."

They dragged him down an alley and threw him into a pile of empty crates. Victor barely caught himself before they started kicking him with heavy blows that left behind dark bruises.

One wrenched him up by his hair, a silver stake pressed to the underside of his chin, burning against his flesh. He gritted his teeth.

"Where's the girl going?"

"I don't know," Victor replied honestly.

He cried out as one of the other hunters threw holy water at him. He raised his arm but some still hit his face and neck, the rest soaked into his clothes to start slowly burning his flesh beneath. A heavy boot to his stomach left him doubled over and gasping.

"Speak, you bastard halfblood or we'll burn your eyes out!" snarled the hunter who still held a fistful of his hair. "We don't get paid the full amount for our services unless we bring the girl back."

Victor glowered upward. "Then I supposed you'll have to settle for half."

Fury flashed in the hunter's eyes. He grabbed Victor's wrist and slammed it against the crates, driving the silver stake through his arm and pinning him to the wood below.

Victor gave a breathless scream at the agony, instinctively reaching for the stake with his other hand before the hunter with the scar grabbed his arm and slammed him back against the crate.

"It can get worse, you bloody dham," the man said darkly. "If you 'aven't experienced pain before, I promise you will now."

"What's going on down here?"

Victor looked up to see a policeman standing at the head of the alley as all the hunters turned to look at him.

"Just business, officer," one said, tipping his cap, and subtly pulling his coat aside to show his hunting paraphernalia.

The policeman didn't look convinced. "I need to see your credentials..."

Victor took the opportunity of their distraction, and ripped the stake from his arm with a bitten back cry, the silver burning his palm. He rolled over and scrambled to his feet.

"Oi!"

The hunters lunged, and one fired a gun as Victor sprinted away. He grunted as the bullet sliced across his side, hot blood dripping down his hip as he ran but he kept going, disregarding the pain.

He didn't stop until he got several streets away, collapsing against a stone wall concealed by some neatly trimmed bushes. He was likely next to a residence, but he didn't care at the moment. He tugged his overcoat off, so the holy water would stop burning him, gasping as every movement sent agony through his wrist and side—breathing felt like a dagger piercing him. He pressed his arm to his chest, yanking a handkerchief out of his pocket and clumsily wrapping it around the wound in a poor attempt to stop the bleeding.

But he still felt a bit of triumph surge through him as he heard the sound of distant church bells strike two. Miss Lillian had gotten away and that was all that mattered.

Victor pushed himself back upright and staggered to a safer location. He could feel his energy draining with his blood. The manor was too far for him to get to in his current condition. He would have to find a cab or...

The thought of Lady Helena's expression when she saw the state of him put his stomach in knots. He was not supposed to worry her, but she needed to know that he had fulfilled his mission, that Lillian was safely on her way to her fiancé.

A wave of dizziness struck him and he just barely staggered to a concealed space that seemed to be the backside of a stable.

Perhaps he would just rest here for a few moments before heading back.

***

Helena returned very late—or rather, very early in the morning—after the party at her aunt's. It had been just as tedious as she had expected, more of her aunt introducing her to eligible bachelors which resulted in copious dances and interminable small talk.

She was admittedly anxious to find out how Victor's mission had gone. Lillian was such a sweet girl and when her maid had approached Helena about her stepmother's plans for her, she knew she couldn't leave the girl without aid.

It was long past 2 in the morning by the time she got home so if all had gone well, Lillian should already be well on her way to the north to meet up with her fiancé.

Cartwright saw to the horse and carriage as Helena made her way inside, greeted almost instantly by Rose.

"Rose, I told you not to wait up for me," she said as the maid took her cloak.

"I was up finishing some mending, my lady," she said nonchalantly. "How was the party?"

"Tedious," Helena said, instantly looking around. "Where is Victor? I wish to speak to him."

Rose's lips pressed into a thin line. "He has not yet returned, my lady."

Helena frowned and again checked the time. "But it is nearly four in the morning! He should have been done with the mission by now…"

"I've had no word," Rose said grimly. "Don't fret though, Lady Helena, you know Mr. Victor is a very capable soul."

"Yes, he is," Helena replied. "But capability does not guarantee safety."

She reached for her cloak again, but Rose stopped her. "Please, my lady, Mr. Victor would not want you out there looking for him. Besides, if he was forced to go into hiding with the girl, you might cause a disruption."

Helena pursed her lips, but saw the logic in the maid's words. "You're right. We will wait, and pray that all is well and that he returns safely."

Rose nodded. "You should get out of that gown at least, my lady. I'll put the kettle on for tea as well—I'll be up in a moment to fix your hair."

Rose bustled off to the kitchen as Helena stood in the foyer, a bit at a loss. The rational part of her brain was telling her that Victor had likely been delayed and would be home before dawn. Her heart, on the other hand, was telling her that something was gravely wrong and that her footman was in trouble.

But Rose was right either way, she could do little until the morning, so it was best to get a couple hours of sleep at least—it was likely she would need it by the time the sun rose.

***

Victor had still not returned by the time Helena woke from her restless sleep. Cartwright informed her that the horse the footman had taken was also still missing. She wasted little time in taking the driver into town to search for her wayward footman, starting at the hotel Lillian had been staying at.

Sure enough, Cartwright found the horse lodged in the stables with a very disgruntled groom. Helena left Cartwright to speak with the man and found out that the horse had been left overnight and the stable boy had been asleep and hadn't accepted any pay for it.

Helena offered the money, but the man wasn't able to give any further information as he had been home the night before.

Helena brooded over her next move. She very much needed to find Victor, especially if he was in some trouble, but any line of questioning might put him and possibly Lillian in even more trouble. If she asked at the train station whether anyone remembered Lillian getting on the train then she risked someone with ill intentions remembering the girl and if Lillian and Victor were still in hiding somewhere then Helena would want to avoid that at all costs.

There was one option open to her, however.

"Cartwright, let's go to see the Hunters," she said decisively.

The city office was tucked about a street over from the Central London police station. It was recognizable only by its crest in bronze above the door: a cross with a blade and a stake in an X behind it.

Helena made her way inside and found only a young man with dark hair and striking blue eyes sitting at the front desk. He had been writing something, but he looked up as she came in.

"How can I help you, miss?" he asked.

"My footman has gone missing, I need him found."

The young man pursed his lips. "I believe that is a job for the police—"

"He's a dhampir."

The young Hunter cocked his head to the side. "Understood. Do you have reason to believe he has run away?"

"I sent him on an errand he never returned from. He should have his papers of employment on him."

"Where was he last seen?" the Hunter asked, writing notes as he spoke.

"At the Central Hotel, his horse was left there at least."

"Do you have reason to believe he is in any trouble with the law?"

"No, I have had no complaints about Victor in the six months he's been in my employ."

"Has he experienced bloodlust in that time?"

Helena shook her head. "I make sure my employees are always well provided for." She paused then, with some decision, she added. "I heard there were free-lance hunters in the city. I worry that he might have run afoul of them."

The young man's brow knitted. "We are already aware of the issue and are working to neutralize it. It is illegal to work as an unlicensed hunter in London so rest assured that if they had anything to do with your footman's disappearance, they will receive the proper punishments."

He wrote some more notes before glancing back up at her. "May I have your name, miss?"

She handed him her calling card and he looked at it in surprise. "Ah, Lady Harrington? Are you related to Sir George Harrington?"

"My father," Helena said with a small smile.

"I see." He seemed intrigued. "We will do all we can to find your footman, my lady. In the meantime, if you have any questions or discover anything, please call the office. You can ask for Aubrey—I'm usually here."

"Thank you for your assistance, Aubrey," Helena replied gratefully.

She returned to the carriage and Cartwright drove them back to the manor. There was nothing more they could do. She was at least consoled by the fact that with the Hunters looking for Victor they would be an impartial party. They couldn't kill or harm him unless he attacked them directly and even if he'd been forced to hurt someone in self-defense they would make sure he stood trial.

Now without an occupation, Helena felt even more exhausted by the time she returned home. Rose came to greet her as always, already bundling her off into the parlor.

"Still didn't find him, my lady?"

Helena shook her head. "No. But I opened a case with the Hunters. There's nothing more that I can do."

Rose nodded. "Please sit and have some lunch, Lady Helena. It will do you good."

Helena wasn't very hungry, but she knew Rose would insist so she took her seat in the parlor and tried to eat sandwiches and tea.

She had barely gotten halfway through with her meal before Daniel ran in, panic on his face.

"Mr. Victor is lying out in the back garden!" he shouted, skidding to a halt.

Helena was on her feet instantly, nearly tipping over the teacup in her haste. She and Rose both ran after the boy, flinging open the door to the garden.

Helena looked around frantically before Daniel pointed. "There!"

A still figure lay in the shadows of a large topiary. Rose gasped and clapped a hand over her mouth.

Helena simply felt her insides freeze as she cautiously made her way over to the footman.

"My lady, wait," Rose tried to warn her but Helena crouched and took hold of Victor's shoulder, turning him onto his back.

To her relief, he groaned and his eyes fluttered open, red. Rose reached out to pull her away, but Victor made no threatening move, simply letting out a sigh of relief.

"My lady," he murmured. "Miss Lillian is safe."

He then seemed to pass out again, breath whistling slightly in his chest.

"Get Cartwright," Helena snapped at Daniel. "Rose, gather medical supplies and bring them to Victor's room."

She crouched again, as she was left alone with the footman. His clothing was covered in blood and she couldn't yet tell if it was his or someone else's. However, if the bruises on his face were any indication...

Cartwright came swiftly with Daniel on his heels. The groom uttered an oath before apologizing to Helena.

"Can you carry him to his room?" Helena asked.

"I can try," the groom said.

He reached down and got his arms under Victor's, lifting him up with Daniel's help. The footman was a head taller than him, but Cartwright was stout and managed to mostly support Victor's weight.

Helena hurried ahead to the footman's quarters where Rose was already setting out the medical supplies, laying old sheets across Victor's bed.

"I have water heating, my lady," she said.

Helena nodded gratefully and held the door open for Cartwright to get through with Victor.

The groom motioned to Daniel. "Help me get his coat off."

The boy did as he asked and Helena felt ill as she was finally able to see the injuries Victor had sustained through his torn shirt and waistcoat. The skin on his neck and one side of his face looked raw and red as well, a bit blistered in places—likely holy water burns.

"It was definitely those thugs who attacked him," she said darkly and reached for Victor's coat, checking the pockets. Her finger found his folded papers and she pulled them out with pursed lips, setting them on the desk.

"Rose, call for the doctor."

"Yes, my lady."

Rose hurried out of the room and Helena turned back to see the groom and the boy leaning over Victor, trying to get him to wake. He seemed to have no energy, however, laying comatose as his wounds bled sluggishly.

Helena made her way to the kitchen to fetch the hot water, carrying the kettle back to the room and pouring it into the waiting basin.

Rose returned. "The doctor is on his way, my lady."

Helena nodded. "Cartwright, is he actively bleeding?"

"I don't think so, my lady, it seems he was able to stem the blood for the most part."

Helena refused to let her growing fury show. The fact that the only thing Victor had done since getting back was to assure her that he had not failed his mission...

She clenched her hands, schooling her expression. "Cartwright, stay on hand in case the doctor needs assistance with him."

They waited for the doctor to arrive, all of them feeling helpless, and as Rose showed the man into the footman's room the doctor did a double take.

"My, your man seems to have gotten into quite a spot of trouble," he said warily, setting his bag down as he started to pull several items from it. "What exactly happened to him?" He reached down to start unbuttoning Victor's shirt, inspecting the wounds.

"He was attacked by thugs," Helena said simply.

"Quite a brutal beating," the doctor murmured before he reached out to peel open one of Victor's eyelids.

The doctor almost instantly staggered back in horror as he saw the crimson pupil. "A-a dhampir? My lady, I do not work on dhampirs or vampires."

Helena's jaw clenched, feeling the fury rise further. "I will pay you extra for the trouble."

But the doctor was already packing his bag again. "I'm sorry, Lady Harrington, I have a family and do not care to risk my life while saving others."

Victor let out a soft moan, head lolling on the pillows, still appearing to be in quite a bit of pain.

"Very well then," Helena said firmly, tucking up her sleeves. "I will tend him myself."

"My lady..." Rose began, then stopped, knowing how determined her mistress was. "I will help."

The doctor shook his head. "I would not advise it, my lady. He could snap at any moment in his condition."

"Frankly, doctor, I'm not interested in your opinion—you already said your piece," Helena spoke sharply. "You may see yourself out."

With Cartwright and Daniel helping to remove Victor's clothes as modestly as possible, Helena and Rose brought the basin over and began to clean the blood from the injured footman's body. The fury only mounted as Helena saw the amount of injuries he'd sustained. He had been beaten bloody, the crimson and violet bruises across his chest and stomach were horrible. Cartwright confirmed cracked ribs, and the graze on his hip and the garish puncture wound in his wrist showed signs of singed flesh confirming that silver weapons had been used.

His clothes seemed to have protected him from the holy water for the most part but Helena applied cream to his face and neck where the burns were the worst.

She also finally saw the scars on his back. They were old and stretched as if he had gotten them when his body was a lot smaller. The sight made her heart clench, wetness pricking at her eyes.

Victor mercifully stayed unconscious through the tending, but he did let out small sounds of discomfort and pain and seemed to be getting more restless.

"He'll need blood, my lady," Rose said. "It will aid in his recovery."

"Yes, of course. Please go fetch him some."

As Rose left, Cartwright and Daniel got Victor into a clean shirt while Helena cleaned up the dirty rags and other supplies for them to remove.

Rose returned with a mug and spoon. "I got him the blood, my lady. I warmed it for him."

"Thank you, I think we'll need to feed him," Helena said, taking a seat on the edge of the bed. "Rose, could you prop him up?"

The maid nodded and sat on the other side of the bed, shifting Victor up against her shoulder. He stirred a little, his eyes fluttering.

"Victor?" Helena tried, holding the blood a little closer so he could smell it.

He blinked his eyes open, the red very apparent. He let out a shuddering breath. "My lady?"

"I need you to drink this, Victor," Helena said firmly, holding the spoon to his lips.

He didn't seem to have the energy to protest and simply sipped the blood dutifully. Helena fed it to him spoonful by spoonful until it was gone and Victor seemed unable to stay conscious another second. She and Rose lay him back down and tucked him under the covers.

"Do you think that will help him?"

Rose watched the footman, plumping his pillows in a businesslike manner. "We shall see, my lady. He may need fresh blood for injuries like this, but Mr. Victor is strong, it might be enough."

Helena pressed her lips together then forced herself to stop staring at Victor's face. She and Rose left the room and Helena found Daniel hovering in the hallway, forcing a kind smile onto her face for the boy.

"Daniel, if you could please sit by Victor and keep an eye on him?"

The boy looked grateful for the occupation and slipped back into the footman's room.

Helena went into her office and called the Hunter's station. The voice that answered the other line sounded familiar.

"This is Lady Helena, is this Aubrey?"

"It is, my lady, but you're calling so soon, we haven't yet been able to start the investigation—"

"I called to inform you that my footman has returned. He was here when I got back," she said. "However, he is in very poor condition after a run-in with those freelance hunters and I will be pressing charges should you catch them."

A sharp breath came from the other end of the line. "My sincere apologies, my lady. Our team is currently trying to find them, but I will warn you that it looks like they might have left town already."

"Then it seems that this city needs to be more firm in their rules about unlicensed hunting," Helena snapped. "My footman had his papers of employment on him. Attacking him is against the law and I assure you he would not have provoked them."

"I share your sentiment, my lady, I assure you," the young man said sympathetically. "However, it is not up to me how things are run in this city. I will do all I can to persuade my colleagues to look into this as far as they can."

Helena schooled her anger and took a deep breath. "I appreciate your attentiveness, Aubrey. Please let me know if there are any developments."

She ended the call, then sat down, brooding, her stomach roiling as the fresh images of Victor's wounds continuously flashed through her head. It wasn't just the fury of what had happened; seeing him like that, injured so badly...it had scared her. Scared her in ways she hadn't felt since she had seen her father dying in his own bed.

She realized her hands were shaking a bit and she clasped them in her lap.

Rose brought her a cup of tea and she gratefully sipped it.

"I'm sure Mr. Victor will be all right," the maid said after a long moment.

Helena simply nodded. The only thing she could control at the moment were her own emotions and she was determined to do so.

***

By that night, however, Victor only seemed to take a turn for the worse, a fever stubbornly setting in. Rose dutifully took a turn beside him, bathing his brow in an attempt to cool him down.

"He's quite warm," she said worriedly when Helena went to check on her later in the night.

Helena frowned. "Do you think it is an infection or simply exhaustion?"

"It's hard to tell, my lady," the maid replied, pursing her lips as Victor moaned softly in his sleep, shifting as his face pinched with pain.

Helena sighed and took the pitcher of water from the vanity and refilled the bowl by Victor's bedside. "You should get some rest, Rose, I'll take over for now."

"But my lady—"

"Please. I won't be sleeping anyway so you should get some rest if you can."

Rose knew it would be pointless to argue with her, so she stood up, stretching out her back.

"Please let me know if you need anything, my lady," she said. "And do wake Daniel if you need to get some rest."

Helena took up the seat Rose had left by the side of the bed and began to bathe Victor's brow again. He looked so pale, his dark hair lank over his forehead. Helena reached out to swipe it away before she realized what she was doing. She paused but didn't remove her hand, feeling how hot he was. Victor shifted, leaning into her touch just slightly, before she finally pulled her hand away and replaced it once again with the cloth.

She spent the night reading at his bedside, watching the footman grow more and more restless as the night went on. She seemed unable to bring his fever down at all, and the longer the night stretched on, he seemed to be trapped in some nightmare he was unable to escape.

Helena reached out to adjust his blankets, pulling his collar open to cool him off.

She gasped as a hand suddenly wrapped around her wrist and she found herself looking down into Victor's crimson eyes, bright with the fever and...terror?

Helena froze and he blinked a couple times before his grip loosened. "My...lady?"

"Victor, you're safe, you're back home," she said quietly, pulling her hand free.

He still seemed slightly confused, looking around. "But, my lady, why... are you here?"

"Hush," she said quietly. "I'm simply looking after you. How are you feeling?"

Victor swallowed hard, his eyes shifting away in discomfort. "I am...very weak at the moment. You...should not be here." He seemed restless, swallowing thickly, holding his breath slightly as if to cut off his senses.

She knew he needed blood. His eyes were still fully red. She remembered what Rose had said earlier about him possibly needing fresh blood. Her heart beat a little faster on instinct and she saw him let out a small, shuddering breath.

"Victor, would fresh blood help?" she asked him finally.

His eyes fluttered open again. "It would be...the best, but I can survive on the butcher's blood—"

"No," Helena cut in firmly and got up to retrieve a penknife from Victor's desk before returning to sit by the bed. "You need fresh blood for your wounds. Please, allow me."

"My lady, no." He tried to reach out and push the knife away from her arm as she tugged her sleeve up. "That...would hardly be appropriate."

"It's not the first time I have given blood to a dhampir in need, Victor," she assured him, sinking the tip of the blade into her forearm and letting blood bead on her skin. "It's all right. Please. You need it."

He tried to turn away. "I can't...please...my lady I am so close to losing myself, I might hurt you."

"Victor, I insist."

She slid her hand behind his head to lift him up and brought her arm to his lips.

Victor exhaled shakily, nostrils flaring at the scent and was unable to resist leaning forward as the drop of blood began to drip down his arm.

Instinct seemed to take over. He caught the drop on his tongue and settled his mouth against the cut. A shudder ran through Helena's body as he started drinking. He was careful not to allow his fangs to touch her skin but his hunger was apparent. His hand instinctively came up to cup the back of her arm to steady himself, his touch delicate, almost ghosting over her skin.

By the time he finished drinking, he had gained some of the color back on his face and she thought his fever might have gone down too. His eyes were back to being hazel as well, though he wouldn't quite look at her.

Helena retrieved a handkerchief to tie around her arm. "How are you feeling?"

He took a deep breath. "Better," he admitted. "I...cannot truly repay you for your kindness..."

"You did your duty, Victor. You got Lillian to safety and suffered greatly for it. I can't help but feel responsible for that."

He surprised her by reaching out and tying the cloth around her arm. His hands were still slightly shaky, but he managed it, tying a neat bow that looked very similar to the one she had made the last time she had tied a handkerchief around his wound on that mission that seemed so long ago now.

"I am always happy to serve you and your cause, my lady," he said.

"I'm only sorry those hunters will likely not be punished for what they did to you," Helena said, unable to help the darkness that shrouded her voice.

Victor shook his head as he lay back against the pillows. "I am used to it, my lady. Justice is not something my kind are familiar with. Which is why people like you are very... important to us."

An odd look passed over his face, but his eyelids were drooping. He seemed to already be slipping off and his words were rather soft, leaving a warm feeling in Helena's chest.

Victor seemed to sleep a little easier, more heavily. His fever was still there, but his temperature had gone down a bit at least. She continued to bathe his brow, seeing that it soothed him, and checked his bandages regularly to make sure there was no blood soaking through and that his wounds were not showing signs of infection.

His fever spiked again in the middle of the night and as she was renewing the cloth, he turned toward her in his sleep, pressing his face into the coolness. His lips moved, barely imperceptibly, but she could have sworn she heard him whisper her name.

Helena's cheeks heated slightly at the sound. While she always insisted Victor called her by her name during missions, he rarely did even then and now, hearing it when they were in such an intimate setting...

She swallowed hard, and settled the cloth on his brow, sitting back for the moment. Had she grown...too attached to her footman? She shook her head at the thought. She had only broken professionalism to tend to her injured employee. She would have done the same for anyone else who worked for her.

She picked up a book to pass the time, trying to push aside the thoughts dancing in the back of her head. But she soon found herself to be so exhausted, that she finally laid her head on the side of the bed and closed her eyes.

***

Victor wound in and out of sleep, not really aware of the passing time. He barely recalled waking to Lady Helena by his bedside, allowing him to drink her blood—had that been a dream after all? He wondered as he slipped further into unconsciousness. He did feel a little less weakened, as if he had been given fresh blood. But surely that was some fever dream—it had to be anyone else.

When he finally opened his eyes, sunlight spilled past the edges of the curtains, indicating that it was already late morning. Normally, he should be up and about his duties, but he couldn't find the strength.

His sharp ears caught on the sound of breathing at his shoulder and he tilted his head in curiosity.

His eyes widened in shock as he saw the ash blond hair and the familiar purple silk of one of Lady Helena's favorite dresses. Her folded arms rested on the side of the bed, her head laying on them as she slept.

A modestly embroidered handkerchief was wrapped around one of her arms and his fingers recalled the sensation of tying it in place.

A sense of brief mortification welled up inside Victor. Had he actually drunk from his mistress? Surely, he would not have—

The door opened quietly and he felt like a deer caught in a hunter's sights as Rose poked her head inside.

"Oh, Mr. Victor," she said quietly, relief in her voice, before she stopped, noticing Helena sleeping in the chair. Her own eyes widened, but she simply lowered her voice. "I'm so glad to see you awake, can I get you anything?"

He swallowed, throat dry, then said. "No thank you, Miss Rose. I'm...quite all right."

Rose glanced back toward their lady and shook her head. "I don't think I have the heart to wake her."

Victor shook his head in agreement, already feeling the exhaustion pulling at him again. "I hate to think of her exhausting herself with my care."

"That's what Lady Helena does," Rose said fondly. "I'll be back later if you need anything."

Victor nodded and Rose slipped out of the room, leaving him behind.

He was too exhausted to think any longer about just how inappropriate the current situation was, and simply fell back to sleep.

***

Helena woke around mid-morning and stretched her back out. She checked Victor, seeing him sleeping soundly, then went to have breakfast and check that everything was all right.

She saw a telegram waiting on her desk from the Hunters saying that one of the unlicensed hunters had been caught and it would be helpful to hear Victor's testimony to convict the man. She wrote up a quick reply and handed it off to Daniel to send.

Rose brought her breakfast to her at her writing desk.

"Mr. Victor seems to be feeling better this morning," she said.

Helena nodded. "His fever broke before dawn. We'll need to change his dressings, but for now I'd rather let him sleep."

She finished up her breakfast and her correspondence, then went back to check on Victor.

To her surprise, he was sitting up, talking to Daniel who had brought his breakfast. The boy looked relieved to see the footman in better condition and grinned at Helena as she came in.

"My lady! Mr. Victor is feeling a lot better today," he said.

Helena returned his smile. "I see that. I'll need to speak with him now, though. Cartwright asked for your help in the stables."

Daniel nodded and hopped up. "Let me know if I can bring you anything, Mr. Victor."

"Thank you," the dhampir replied. He watched the boy leave the room before his gaze landed on Helena and darted away.

Helena stepped forward, taking the seat by the bed. "If you're feeling up to it, I'd like to discuss a few things now that you're awake."

"Of course, my lady," Victor said, though his voice still sounded a bit weary.

"I got news that one of the thugs who attacked you was apprehended. The Hunters have asked that you give your testimony when you are feeling well enough."

"And what should I tell them if they ask what I was doing that night?"

Helena thought for a moment. "Tell them that you were delivering a message to someone at the hotel for me."

Victor nodded. "Very well, my lady."

Helena pressed her lips together, moving on to the question she had been wanting to ask this whole time.

"You had your papers of employment on you, why didn't you show them when those men attacked you?"

He exhaled softly as if he had been expecting this question. "They were the kind of men it would make little difference to."

"They should have known to follow the law," Helena said sternly.

"Those papers had your name on them," he said in a pointed voice. "I did not want to expose you."

"Foolish," Helena snapped before she could school herself.

To her surprise, Victor looked up to meet her eyes. "What you do is important, my lady. I would not be the one to ruin that."

Her heart was pounding in her chest still, a pain she could not entirely place. "You could have been killed," she insisted, then took a deep breath to steady herself. "I would have had to find another footman as useful as you."

"So, I am useful to you," Victor said, voice flat. "That is good to know, my lady. Tell me, do you spend hours sitting beside all your tools when they are being repaired? Do you let them drink blood from your veins?"

She felt as if a dagger had found her heart. "Victor, you know very well I do not feel that way."

He looked down, nodding slightly. "Very well then. I spoke out of turn, my lady, I apologize. This fever has exhausted me."

She exhaled slowly, carefully releasing her hands from where they had gripped in her skirts without her realizing. "Then rest. You need to heal."

"I'm sure I will be back to work in no time."

Those words stung for reasons Helena couldn't place. She took a deep breath and began carefully. "What I meant, Victor, is that I would not want to have to seek out another footman as *trusted* as you Someone who would risk his life for a girl in desperate need, who would go where I told him, no questions asked, and help me in my endeavors." She swallowed hard. "It means everything to me to carry on where my father left off. His dying wish was that I follow in his footsteps. I do not think of any of my employees as tools, Victor. I care very deeply for all of you. You are all I have."

Victor seemed surprised to hear her sincerity and Helena berated herself for being so vulnerable, yet at the same time, it felt good to speak her piece.

"Lady Helena, may I ask..." Victor began, hesitating before he pushed on. "Why your father chose this cause?"

Helena was quiet for a long moment before she began to speak. "His stepmother was a dhampir, and no one knew, not even his father. She died in childbirth with my father's sister and it wasn't until the girl grew older and her inherent traits began to show that they realized what she was.

"My grandfather felt utterly betrayed. The instant he found out he cast her aside, had his own daughter sold at an auction. My father was devastated. He loved his little sister so much and she adored him in return. I believe he spent the rest of his life looking for her as he made it his mission to save other dhampirs from sharing her fate."

Victor was silent, taking in her words. "Your father sounds like a fine man, my lady."

"He was," Helena replied quietly. She cleared her throat and sat up straighter. "Since I told you about my father, I would like, in return, to know about the scars on your back."

Victor froze a bit, but finally nodded, gathering himself before he spoke.

"Ironically, my past was not much different than that of your father's sister except I was not sold—I think my mother thought it her cruel duty to see that I was not let loose on the world," he said wryly. "I do not remember my father—I don't know if he was a good man who was killed, or a bad one who ran off, but my latent dhampirism manifested when I was quite young and my mother became incredibly cruel toward me. She would beat me consistently, refusing me blood until I was close to feral, and then it was always cold pigs' blood. It was only later when I was around twelve that I managed to run away to work for a butcher. He never asked if I wasn't human and it was easy enough to sneak blood.

"I lived without suspicion for a while until I was recommended to work at an estate. There, I was discovered to be a dhampir when I fell ill from lack of blood and my employer took it upon himself to make my life misery. I was always beaten for the smallest thing, locked in the cold cellar to sleep. When the old man died, his estate went to his children and it turned out to be a mercy for me that they left all of his staff to fend for themselves. That was when I came to London. I am not proud to say that I faked my letters of recommendation to get a job as a footman, but I had no other option at the time."

"This was your previous employer?" Helena asked.

He nodded. "Yes. They were good people, they treated me well, until I was caught drinking blood. You know the rest." He took a deep breath. "Despite all of it, I dare say I had a rather blessed life compared to many."

Helena listened, her heart aching for a young Victor who had been made to feel like an animal not just by a previous employer, but by his own mother. "That does not mean it was easy," she commented.

"No, my lady, but it led me here to your employ, and meeting you showed me that there are still people in this world who are decent and kind."

Helena didn't know what to reply to that. She stood, adjusting her skirts, and finally met Victor's eyes.

"I am truly glad you found your way here, Victor," she said quietly.

***

The days passed and Victor's recovery was aided by the attentive care everyone showered on him. Helena even gave him another dose of fresh blood, though this time she bled into a cup. It seemed...different now to let Victor drink from her veins when he was not in the throes of fever.

Once he was back to work, however, she couldn't help but feel that there was an intangible tension between her and the footman now. She wasn't sure how to place it or where it originated. He had always shown the utmost professionalism in his duties, but now he seemed to be almost too formal. She wondered if his convalescence had made him feel too vulnerable—she could certainly understand the feeling.

Still, she was surprised when Victor knocked on her study door one morning.

"My lady...may I have a word?"

Helena pushed her chair back from her desk and turned to look at him. "Of course."

Victor stepped forward and held several neatly folded papers out to her. Helena took them instinctively, but felt her stomach drop as she saw they were his papers of employment.

"What is this, Victor?" she asked.

He took a deep breath, standing very straight, hands clasped behind his back. "My lady...I'm afraid that I can no longer serve you. I only ask that if you have been pleased with my service that you would consider writing a recommendation for me for a house that would not mind one of my kind in their service."

Helena stared at him, dumbfounded. "You want to leave my service."

"Yes, my lady."

Helena stood quickly, trying to push down the irrational feeling of panic that was rising in her chest. "Are you unhappy here, Victor?"

"No, my lady," he said softly, an earnest look in his eyes. "I simply think it's best that I leave."

"I will not allow it," Helena snapped. "Not without an explanation, at least."

Victor took a deep breath. "I'm not sure I can give one."

"I understand if this job contains more danger than you assumed when I brought you here," Helena probed. "You were injured badly, it is only understandable that you would not want that to happen again."

"I am no coward, my lady," he said firmly. "At least...not in that way."

Helena looked at him with a deeper furrow in her brows. "Explain."

Victor closed his eyes with a sigh, his shoulders slumping at a very unprofessional angle. "The fact is, my lady...I have...feelings that I can no longer quell, and serving you in any capacity of professionalism is no longer within my capabilities."

Helena froze, her heart stuttering in her chest. She stared at her footman, his downcast eyes, his reddened ears.

"Is this true, Victor?" she asked, her voice barely above a whisper.

He nodded. "I'm afraid so, my lady."

"Then I suppose I'll have to let you go."

He let out a shaky breath, and nodded. "Thank you for your understanding, my lady—"

Helena stepped forward and stopped him, a hand on his arm. "On the condition that you'll stay on...as more than just my footman."

Victor's head shot up, eyes wide in shock. "My lady, I don't understand."

Helena's cheeks tinted pink as well, but she smiled up at him. "Victor, I fear that I also have feelings beyond that of your employer. I have been...considering them over the last few days without truly realizing it until now." She handed him back the papers, pressing them into his hand. "I cannot marry as one of my station normally would, not with my mission, not someone I couldn't trust. But you,

Victor, if I may be so bold, I think we are a good match." She looked up at him a little shyly. "You do not have to say yes if the idea does not please you."

"Helena," he whispered and she felt a shiver of delight run through her at the sound of her name on his lips. "I must confess that the idea pleases me greatly."

Helena took his hand in hers and Victor threaded their fingers together, finally allowing himself to smile.

"You would still act as my footman for public appearances," Helena said. "But I would very much like the honor of calling you my husband while in the privacy of this house."

"And I..." Victor said as he sank to his knees and kissed her hand tenderly. "Would like nothing more."

About the Author

LadyWallace is a long-time artist and writer--and nocturnal creature. When she's not drinking coffee, or crafting, she's usually dreaming up whump scenarios for her favorite characters or OCs. She is currently working on a series featuring vampires set in the same universe as The Footman.

Red

Nanda Writes

CW: Character death, mentions of childhood abuse

Whumpee: Man, Whumper: Man, Caretaker: N/A

Ulrich Richter didn't have a brother anymore. Sometimes, he wasn't really sure if he had ever had one at all.

The memories from his childhood were vague, sparse and dissonant, his young mind struggling to comprehend the two sides of his parents he somehow saw.

How could the father that was so loving and played with him with such care sometimes sound so angry and strike at that other boy with such violence? How could the mother that was so kind and was loathe to deny her baby boy anything he wanted sometimes turn so vengeful and lock the boy in his room for days, screeching like a harpy she hoped he would finally die this time?

He saw that other boy so rarely he sometimes wondered if he even existed at all.

But then, again, who else could be that person that attacked those older kids that were picking on him? That fell from a tree with a smile because he had managed to grab the ball Ulrich had kicked there?

Perhaps an imaginary friend. A figment of his imagination.

Not much longer after Ulrich had been able to form such memories for himself, the older boy disappeared for good.

To the army? He thought he heard a neighbour comment something of the sort one day, but his parents didn't seem to know what she was talking about. He had probably just gotten too old for imaginary friends.

Until some years later, the monster appeared.

He had sharp claws and fangs and eyes as red as the blood dripping down his hands and his chin, dried in his clothes and hair. Even if Ulrich had been able to forget the scenes from that night, he could never forget the sharp, nauseating smell of fresh and old blood.

He had played with his parents like they were prey, torturing and killing them slowly, relishing in their screams.

He had seen it all through a crack of the door separating the living and dining rooms. The noise had disturbed his sleep and he had gone to take a look, only to fall frozen, kneeling behind the door, forgetting even to breathe.

After the monster had finally thrown to the floor the rag dolls that had once been his parents, his eyes turned to him.

The house was dark, but Ulrich was sure it wasn't his imagination. The monster had looked right at him, features so similar but so different from his own staring into him for a long time. Then the monster had turned away and left.

Ulrich remembered his breath returning to him all at once then, and he screamed for ages until finally one of the neighbours showed up.

He knew what the monster was now. Vampire. One of those creatures from the neighbouring country.

But vampires that killed humans were hunted and killed either by a human king or their own. And one that had been on such a rampage like *he* had?

He should have been long gone.

But if that was so, then who was that person Ulrich was staring at on the other side of the ballroom?

Words passed by him in whispers, completely meaningless. "General", "Lord", "Envoy to the King".

The only thing he heard was when the stranger bowed to their host and said:

"Heinrich Richter, at your service."

A lie, was the only thing he could think, that creature was in no one's service but his own.

A stream of dancers obscured his view for a moment, and then the creature was gone, nowhere to be found.

He felt like he couldn't breathe.

Darkness descended, compressing his heart, squeezing the life out of him with icy claws.

Those blue eyes, those features so similar but so unlike his own, untouched by the passage of time since that night. Like looking in a mirror of twenty years ago.

He saw red, down his mother's nightgown, pooling around his father's feet, splattered on the walls, sliding down the monster's throat as he licked his lips.

Red eyes piercing into his very soul, ripping it to shreds with the force of its hate.

Blue eyes piercing into his very soul, tearing the fragile stitches he had patched himself with over the past decades.

How? Why? Why now?

Someone called his name, breaking the spell. The ball came back to him in full swing. Too colourful, too loud. Someone called him again, asked if he was alright. He shook his head as if warding off a curse. Breathed deeply. Forcedly shut the door.

No, he must have been mistaken. It was but a memory, a ghost, a figment of his imagination.

Ulrich Richter didn't have a brother anymore. He wasn't really sure if he had ever had one at all.

About the Author

Nanda is a writer, translator and English teacher from Brazil. Passionate about building narratives (and getting lost in them, too).

Consumption

Willow Nichols-Capra

CW: Death of a parent, body horror, suicide
Whumpee: Woman, Whumper: Woman, Caretaker: Woman

It has been years since this tale has been told. Generations have come and went, born then given back to the earth to continue the ever-flowing cycle of life. Now, this city is filled with skyscrapers and bustling crowds with technology-brimmed pockets. When I was young, I resided in a small town on the cusp of Boston with my family. Everything was much different then. Cobblestone streets with quaint wooden structures lining them, and the hardworking villagers that resided inside. My father was a merchant; he owned a small shop on the outskirts of our village. He was a stoic man but caring in his own strange way. He loved my mother deeply and provided everything my sister and I needed and wanted. I never knew much about him or his life before us, but I knew that he adored his family. He built the home we lived in as a way to prove to my mother and her father his commitment to her. Shortly after they wed, I was born; my sister brought into this world five years my junior.

I was fifteen when my mother became ill. She first suffered a bout of melancholy—as the doctors referred to it then. She spent most of her time in bed, howling sobs often seeping their way through our thin walls. My sister, Victoria, used to sit in the dark with her. For hours she would hold her gaunt hands, brush her golden hair, and tell her exaggerated stories of her days and nights away from Mother. I never visited with Mother often. Her room carried an eerily heavy feeling, as if I'd been pressed under rubble. Darkness shrouded her figure lain limply on her bed, covered with a thin sheet of cotton. Her hair spilled behind her in a knotted mess of mats and curls. She didn't speak much once she became ill, only murmuring an incomprehensible monologue repeatedly when one of us sat in her presence.

After the melancholy came the consumption. Father had sent for a doctor after my mother started experiencing violent episodes of coughing. Sometimes blood speckled her handkerchiefs

that littered the side of her bed. Dr. Pickman, a celebrated doctor of the time, assessed her one dreary afternoon. We sat in the front room, wringing our hands and hearing our mother's distant coughs. When he returned to the parlor the news was grim.

"Your wife," he paused for a moment, facing my father. "Consumption, it has her, sir." He glared at the floor, not daring to meet the eyes of our patriarch.

"Well, what can be done?" my father asked, completely void of emotion.

"The best I can suggest is to let her rest. Sleep is all that can help her now, for she is incredibly weakened by this illness," Dr. Pickman said.

"There must be something else!" I cried. "I've heard people in the village speak of remedies, rituals to keep her *safe.*" The last word of my sentence emitted as a weakened whisper. Before then, I had not discussed my findings with my family. I was ever growing curious about consumption; it had taken more than ten in our village alone, mostly infesting families like fruit flies. Many mothers buried their children, and many men buried their spouses across New England. Families were torn apart, each week the tabloids reporting even more deaths in surrounding towns. There had been gossip amongst the affected, rumors that the dead were waking again, and infecting their families under the cloak of the night. Many discussed ways to keep their families safe and cure them of the ailment. One particularly ominous remedy being the exhumation and burning of an infected corpse's organs, which were then to be consumed by the sickly.

"You surely don't mean *that* nonsense," the doctor said wearily, while my father looked increasingly confused. "I apologize sir, but what your daughter suggests is simply a step further than my qualifications. Good day and God bless," he said as he tipped his wide brimmed hat and retired from our home.

"Emily," my father turned to me. "What is it that you suggest?" As I told my father of the recent happenings of the affected, he sat patiently and absorbed the information.

"Absolutely not, and not another word of it," he said once I finished. I opened my mouth with a rebuttal prepared, but he walked swiftly away ending the conversation indefinitely.

My mother's health declined rapidly after the doctor's visit. She spent her nights covered in perspiration, lolling and crying for help. Victoria was hurt most by this. She was still so young; she needed our mother. Days turned into weeks and Father was around less every day. Eventually, Victoria and I only saw him for breakfast and dinner. Soon after, his plates would sit uneaten at the head of the table, Father staring at the wall behind me with no sign of conscious thought. He became a man drained of everything, never speaking and losing weight rapidly. These events thrust me into the position of being the household's sole provider, matriarch and patriarch to my sister as best as I could achieve.

Our mother died on a frigid afternoon in February 1822, the exact day I do not recall for it has been ages since the last visit to my mother's resting place. The gravediggers worked tirelessly with shovels and pickaxes to break ground where she was to be laid to rest, ultimately deciding to store her body until the first signs of spring when the ground had thawed more. This sent my father further into his spiral. He did not attend her wake, his weak coughs heard upstairs by the attendees. People left Victoria and I food and shared their condolences, and I thanked them all graciously, careful not to present the pain that plagued me through my expressions.

April of the same year, not a week after they buried our mother, Victoria began to show signs of consumption. I sat by her bedside each night desperately trying to lower her temperature with cool cloths. Her cheeks burned crimson, and she was feverish, crying out for Mother and rambling nonsense of seeing her shortly.

One morning before dawn, while Victoria and Father slept, I left our home and thought of Anthony Graham. Graham had lost his entire family, save his younger brother, to consumption. A young man of just seventeen, we lived symbiotic, tragic lives. Recently, I spoke to him at church, he explained to me that he fed his sibling the ashes of his mother's heart and how it indeed saved his life.

"You must exhume her, mash the ashes into a paste with water and blood. And pray. This will save her from harm," he told me, as he gripped my shoulders tight. I wanted to honor my father, who thought the practice was barbaric, but I was desperate. Victoria was just eleven, times were changing, and she had her whole life ahead of her, she was my priority. I loved her dearly, she was fiery; a true force to be reckoned with. I needed nothing more than for her to live on. She was meant to have a fulfilled life, full of laughter and love, in which she would retire from peacefully surrounded by those who loved her most, not like this.

I walked by the church, navy blue darkness still blanketing the yard, a faint shadow of the steeple cast by the dull moonlight. I slipped into the cemetery where my mother rested eternally. I savored the walk up the hill, glancing at the first headstones planted in the ground. They were violently slanted and cracked, lichen consumed the text on each stone to varying degrees. As I approached my mother's freshly dug grave, I saw mounds of dirt piled to the side of her plot. Her headstone was partially buried in the earth, tipped fully on its side. My stomach lurched, heart beating faster with each step I took. Approaching the hole where my mother should have been, I balled my hands into fists, nerves taking over my body. Each step I took was unstable as my fingernails dug into my palms, drawing drops of blood from my shaking hands. What I saw was not my mother, but a man splayed out unnaturally in her open coffin. His limbs were twisted behind him in an insectile fashion. His skull was exposed and blood flowed from his cranium and neck. He was covered in handprints, branded into his skin in various tones of purple and red. I gagged to my side and fell, feeling the dirt and gravel dig into my knees as I collapsed to the ground. The inside of Mother's coffin was engraved with blood-streaked scratches, an attempt to claw her way out. A single fingernail splintered the destroyed and bloodied wood. She clearly had succeeded in such a matter based on the gravedigger's body in place of her own.

I cried, feeling confused, not fully understanding. Was my mother one of the beings that they whispered about? Had she come back to the land of the living to consume the rest of her family? *Victoria.* The thought hit me as though I had been shot. I fell back, digging my hands into the soil, desperate to catch my bearings and stand. My legs were terribly weak, barely able to hold the weight of my body as I pulled myself from the ground. Gravestones sped by as I sprinted in the direction of our home. My only job, my purpose as a sister was to protect Victoria, and in that moment, I feared I failed her. I pictured our mother bent over Victoria's frail body, gargling and swallowing in sickly gulps as she drank the blood from my sister. Tears filled my eyes and ran down my face in hot streaks, a burning reminder of my failure. *I'm so sorry,* I thought, praying that my message would reach her somehow.

As our home came into view, I heard Victoria's frantic screams. The sun began to rise over the horizon, casting rich hues of pink and orange across the sky as I pushed harder with my last bout of energy. The door slammed against the inside wall, making a booming *crack* as the doorknob connected with the bricks. I rounded the corner sharply and came face to face with the thing that was once my mother. She stood, hunched over, each vertebra outlined by her paper-thin skin. Lesions peppered her body; some bore so deep that her bone was visible through the rotted holes. Her hair was stringy and knotted, caked in earth and pieces of moss. She wore an inhuman smile plastered on her face, one of her cheeks was fully decomposed. Victoria let out a strangled sob behind her and I sprung into action.

Using all of my weight I threw myself towards the mother-thing, she shrieked as she received the blow of my body against hers. I gripped her arms tightly; her skin was moist and sticky with decay. Smell permeated around us while I tried to wrestle her body to the ground. A cacophonous snapping sounded in my ear as my mother writhed and gnashed her teeth together in a desperate attempt to bite me. I cried and slammed her rotted body against the floor. She jerked, digging her mud-covered hands into my back and pulling me closer to her chomping mouth. I couldn't help but look at her mouth, the metallic stink of blood wafted from her throat and her teeth were sharp, broken into pointed daggers.

The sun began to rise more, the first signs of daylight entered the window. A warm glow cast over the mother-thing and I. She screeched as a ray of sunlight touched her cheek, and her skin began to bubble and char. I took advantage of her moment of weakness and, gripping her as tightly as possible, I flipped her writhing body on top of me. Her back, exposed to the sunlight, sizzled as she screeched. As if time had slowed, I watched her head shake frantically, her eyes were filled with fear. She looked down at me, into my eyes and paused for a moment, as if to say *I'm sorry,* before plummeting her teeth into my neck. She drank, growling against me as the sun slowly took her forever. I closed my eyes and let her drink, knowing that any distraction from my dear Victoria would be worth everything. Slowly, the mother-thing turned to ash as my heart slowed and I became one of the consumed.

I believed that my story had ended there, until I jerked awake in darkness. I frantically felt around me, feeling splintered wood against my fingertips. I had to break my way free, no different than my mother, starving for the blood that was stolen from me.

Two hundred years have come and gone, and I have consumed many lives, some human, some animal. I stayed away from Victoria, only sometimes watching from the woods behind her homestead. I watched her marry, bare children of her own, and die peacefully surrounded by them in her old age. She lived the full life she deserved, and for that, all the years of consuming were worth everything. Now, here I lay on the grave of Victoria, her passing having been over a century ago. I watched humans grow, I watched humans destroy, and now I am tired and must enter my eternal rest amongst my kin. Sunlight speckles the sky above me and I smile, ready for whatever is to come.

About the Author

Willow Nichols-Capra is a New England based writer and bookseller. Many of her stories are formulated by her experience as a BIPOC queer woman. Find her on Bluesky @novella.menagerie.bsky.social

The Velvet Curtains

Okay Savage?

CW: Sexual content, noncon/sexual assault, character death, suicide
Whumpee: Woman, Whumper: Woman, Caretaker: Woman

I can feel the weight of her next to me when I wake up. She lies still as the night. I'm mesmerised by the way her chest fails to rise and fall. Her skin is cool and pale, like frost on a winter morning. I want to kiss her. I don't, though. It isn't right. None of this is right. As I know the sky must be starting to grow pale outside the window, I try to decide whether I should get up to open the thick, black velvet curtains or just leave them be. I wonder how she'd feel if she knew I was thinking these thoughts. She doesn't move an inch. I can't help but hate her.

It all started with her, after all. Evelyn. It's all been about her. And us.

What abominations we became together.

***

We met in a bar. It wasn't entirely unusual for me to hit it off with a girl in a bar, especially that bar. It was a favourite haunt of mine, after all. Grimy and loud, it's a place I could go with my friends to drown out and swallow down the stress and monotony of everyday life. We'd meet, the three of us, and spend most of the evening outside in the beer garden, which was more of a carpark with picnic tables installed. The bar had a speaker outside as well as in, blasting out metal and classic rock. The owners clearly acknowledged the fact that at least half of their clientele were chronic chain smokers, and the other half would probably pop out for at least a social smoke or a vape at some point in the night. Or maybe the bar staff had requested it, considering they were all clientele too on their nights off and always seemed to be outside. I never thought to ask. It was nice, though - familiar music and familiar faces.

We'd been joking around, just having a bit of a laugh really. Harry and Debs had been at each other's throats all week. They'd each messaged me relentlessly behind the other's back about some nitpicky mess of drama they'd concocted between them. It was nice to see them out, having fun together. I may have encouraged it along a little by providing the first few rounds.

Speaking of which.

"Right, what'd everyone want?" I asked. My glass had been empty for around five minutes, and that was five minutes too long as far as I was concerned. Debs looked into her own half full pint of cider.

"I'm still working on this," she said. I looked to Harry.

"Oh no, Angie, you can't get this one as well, you got the last two!" he protested. It didn't sound very genuine, and I didn't bother to correct him on the number.

"What do you want?" I asked. He straightened himself up a bit.

"No really, it's ok. I feel bad at this point - you must have spent a fortune."

I shrugged.

"I just got paid," I replied.

This was true.

"It's no big deal."

This was probably not true.

I hadn't been very sensible with my money recently and I knew it. I really wanted to save up a deposit to move. The flat where I was living was, putting it nicely, a shithole. Falling to bits, tiny, cramped; whatever words someone could come up with to give a realtor nightmares, my flat fit the bill. I could afford the rent on somewhere nicer - I worked enough hours at my stinking greasepit of a job - but it was saving the deposit that I kept getting stuck on. Nights like this one didn't help. Where I'd go out, finally having a bit of spare money to save, then get over-excited and leave myself wrung dry by the next day. It turns out I'm not a friendly drunk, or an angry drunk, or even a particularly flirty drunk (most of the time). I'm the worst sort of drunk for one's wallet - a generous drunk.

Neither Debs nor Harry knew my finances so intimately, of course, so Harry just took me at my word, and sent me off with a request for a fruity cider and some crisps, preferably chicken, but plain would do. I swung the door open to a throng of people, standing, chatting, and drinking. People didn't dance very often here - it was a bit cramped for that - but it was more than lively in there, all the same. The music was louder in here, and I had to push my way through to get to the bar when my "'scuse me"s went unheard. Nobody seemed to mind.

At the bar, there were more people. There were only ever two bartenders on at once, and people here liked to chat, so it could take a while to get served on a busy Saturday night like this one. I shuffled as close as I could and waited. I was more than tipsy at that point, and it felt so good to be surrounded like that. All that sweat and noise. I felt alive! I let the music rip its way through me, smiling and swaying.

I wasn't familiar with the song. I loved the singer's voice, though. Gritty and sharp, hitting stupidly high notes, and holding them until they squirmed. It reminded me of the style I'd tried to master, back when I thought I could be a rock star. That was one of those dreams that sounded totally unattainable, but not quite totally enough to stop me from wasting all of my free time between the ages of 17 and 19 writing songs and playing gigs. Well, I suppose wasted is a little harsh. I had met Harry and Debs through different bands we'd all been in at points. And it had been good at times, despite the crushing disappointment of never getting the big break I was always desperate for. The one I was always convinced was right around the next corner. God, it had been good.

The music had taken me so fully that it took me a moment to notice someone was talking to me.

"Eh?"

"What are you having?" the woman next to me repeated herself. I was taken aback for a moment. She looked at me with such wide, piercing, blue eyes, I almost thought she was angry with me before I processed the question.

"Oh no, that's really sweet thank you, I'm fetching though," I explained.

"Okay," she said, turning back round to the bar. I felt disappointed that it was that easy. I'd thought she might insist; that we might get talking. I shook the thought off and made my order when the bartender asked the same question of me.

I tucked the crisps under my arm and picked up a pint in each hand. I nearly dropped them when I turned round and found the woman was right behind me.

"Hello again," I said with a startled laugh.

"That's a lot to carry, let me help," she said. She had her own drink in hand already, something clear in a short glass, so I'm not sure why she believed herself more able than me to carry two at once. Those shocking blue eyes were the crown jewels in an even more shockingly beautiful face though, so I didn't think twice before thanking her and handing her my drink. She smiled, slow, wide and toothy, and I almost melted.

Outside, I set Harry's drink down on the table and climbed onto the bench. The woman placed my drink in front of me and sat herself down beside me. I couldn't help but notice how lithe and athletic she looked swinging her legs over the bench. She reminded me of a big cat, elegant and long, with the suggestion of powerful muscles underneath her sleek surface. Harry and Deb looked at each other, then at her, then at me.

"Sorry, you don't mind if I sit with you, do you? We were just chatting at the bar," she said. Her tone was sweet, charming, and just a little bit apologetic. I'm not sure if I'd agree that we were chatting, had I been sober, but in my drunken state, I didn't blink at the inaccuracy. In fact, I just felt stupidly giddy that she wanted to sit with us. *With me.*

"The more the merrier!" Harry beamed. He was a little louder than necessary. I looked at Debs and was quite proud of her when she managed to restrain her eye roll to a small twitch.

"I'm Debs, this is Harry, and you seem to have met Angie," Debs said. As fed up with Harry as she could get, she really was lovely, and she'd never say no to someone joining the table.

The woman smiled.

"I'm Evelyn," she said.

"Like Evelyn Sharp?" Debs asked brightly. She was very keen on history, especially political history.

"Who?" Evelyn replied.

"Oh she was this amazing suffragette! She did loads! She was born in 1869, you see, when-" Debs started. I zoned out and stared at Evelyn as she was swept up into one of Debs' impromptu lectures. She really was beautiful. She had long, straight hair, cut into low bangs over her brow. Her cheeks were high and rounded, giving her face a loveheart shape that seemed pleasantly at odds with her wide, salacious smile, which was painted black, matching her hair and nails. She was very pale, but a smattering of freckles decorated the bridge of her nose, with the odd outlier planted here and there upon her cheeks.

Evelyn seemed to be a lot more interested in what Debs had to say than I was. She listened patiently, nodding, then interjected with her own points. Sometimes Debs would say something that made Evelyn frown, but it was a good-natured, curious sort of frown. Like she was considering each point and chewing it over. I noticed that just before she would ask a question, every time, she would do this little frown, purse her lips, and take a big breath in through her nose, as though she really wanted to make sure she was asking her question with just the right words. I could have watched her chatting with Debs all night and been quite content.

As such, I was a little bit annoyed when Harry decided to interject.

"Hey Debs, don't we need to get an early night tonight so we can be up for that thing in the morning?" he cut across them.

"What th-" Debs started to say. Harry gave her a look and darted his eyes over to me.

"Oh the thing!" she said. "Yeah, no, we'd better get going soon actually."

In hindsight, I imagine that Harry had probably noticed me staring at Evelyn like a lovesick puppy for the past twenty minutes and was trying to be nice, but through my beer goggles, I didn't quite get the memo.

"What?" I cried. "You can't leave me this early! We were having a good night!"

Debs did not restrain her eye roll when it was aimed at me. Harry was more diplomatic.

"You can still stay out," he said. "After all, you've got Evelyn to keep you company." He gave me a wink that both made me realise what he was doing, and made me want to throttle him for being so obvious. I took the offer though, looking imploringly at Evelyn to make sure this was OK. She giggled and shifted her weight to angle herself toward me.

"You're cute," she said. I faked a grouchy look over the top of my drink at this appraisal but internally I was glowing. *She thinks I'm cute!* My pink cheeks probably did little to keep this feeling internal, actually.

"Right, come on," Debs said, pulling Harry up.

"Nice to meet you Evelyn," she said warmly.

"You too. Get home safe!" Evelyn smiled at both of them.

Debs led Harry past our side of the bench to give me a kiss on the crown of my head. Harry bent down and gave me a hug with one arm.

"You're down bad," he whispered into my ear. I smacked his arm and glared.

"Shoo," I said. He laughed boisterously and gave me an extra squeeze. Dickhead.

"They seem really nice," Evelyn said to me, after we watched the couple disappear through the door into the bar. I smiled.

"Yeah I love them," I said.

"They're lucky," she replied. I felt my cheeks heat up even more and I was stuck for words. Meanwhile, she looked cool as a cucumber, staring into my face with just the hint of a smile.

"I, uh..." I started. I'm not sure where I was going with that but my words stopped dead when she laid her hand over mine. Her fingers were cool and smooth and just a little bit longer than my own. Usually when I meet a girl with a nice manicure, I get a little bit self-conscious about my own nails, which are nearly always a ragged mess where I've picked at them. The thought didn't even cross my mind this time though, as I watched her glossy black nails stroke the back of my hand, mesmerised. I'm not even sure if I was breathing. Movement pulled me out of the daze, and I looked up to see she'd shuffled closer to me.

"Hello," I said dumbly.

"Hello again." Her voice was a whispered breeze over satin, with just the barest hint of mockery, and her smile was wicked. Was she looking at my lips? I took my chances and leaned in slightly, barely breathing. My heart was dancing a samba at the bottom of my throat, and my head was spinning. The moment it took her to close the distance between us lasted an eternity.

I'd never quite understood what people mean when they talk about seeing fireworks and sparks flying when they kiss. And I still didn't. There wasn't any light in this. It was dark and hungry. It felt like falling into an abyss. No light, no air, no end in sight. Just the feel of her perfect lips moving confidently against my own. She was firm and unforgiving as she devoured me, and I matched her force greedily. I never wanted to come back up. I don't remember moving, but when she finally pulled away we were clinging to each other, each straddling the bench with our arms around one another and my fingers buried in her leather jacket, as though we really had been falling together.

Someone at the picnic table across from ours wolf-whistled, so I cleared my throat and untangled myself from her, embarrassed by my own enthusiasm. She looked dazed and delighted. She was staring at me as though we were the only people there. The only people anywhere. I felt I should break the silence before it became awkward.

"That was lovely," I said in a low voice. She grinned lazily. My heart skipped a beat when I saw how her black lipstick had smudged at the corners of her mouth. *I did that.*

"Wasn't it?" She put her hands on my knees and I could have fainted. She leaned in, and I parted my lips automatically, ready for another round, despite the rude reminder that we weren't alone. That wasn't her intention, though. She leaned past my waiting mouth to whisper into my ear.

"Let's go somewhere more private."

I shivered. For a split second, the sensation of her breath at the corner of my jaw and the clean, sweet smell of her perfect hair in my face overshadowed her words. But when they hit, it was like fire in my belly. She pulled back and I nodded furiously.

"Please," was all I could say. She giggled and got up. Before I could stand on my own, she'd taken my hands to help me up. My head and chest were a swirling shipwreck of attraction and arousal as she led me by the hand to the door and out through the bar. *She* didn't seem to have any trouble getting through the crowd, and I stayed close behind her, watching the confident way she moved with awe. We must have ordered a taxi at some point, because one eventually arrived, but all I remembered of the wait was a slew of desperate kisses as we tried to climb into each other's souls, mouth-first, on the cold metal bench out front.

***

When I woke up, my head was pounding. The room was dark, so it didn't occur to me that anything was unusual at first. Then I caught a smell on the pillow that surprised me. Who...? The previous night came rushing back to me and I grinned from ear to ear.

The room came into focus a little bit more as my bleary eyes grew accustomed to the dark. We'd gone back to her place. I was laid on a big double bed under black and white paisley sheets. The room was spacious, with old-fashioned wooden furniture and a large window hidden behind absurdly thick, black velvet curtains. I laid still for a minute or two, replaying the night giddily in my mind. Some of the details were a little fuzzy, but others came back clear as day, stoking my excitement. I thought Evelyn must still be asleep, so I rolled over as carefully and gently as

I could. I didn't want to wake her, but I couldn't wait to see her beautiful face again.

Finding myself alone in the bed was a disappointment. I frowned and sat up. I could just about make out a lamp on the bedside table, so I fumbled around for the switch and turned it on. I realised then that I was completely naked and got up hurriedly, trying to figure out where my clothes had ended up. I found my oversized Iron Maiden t-shirt thrown over a high-backed chair on the other side of the room. After a little more searching, I found my underpants, which had somehow got knocked under the edge of the bed. My trousers, socks, and bra were still a mystery, but I felt a little more at ease having the essentials covered, at least. I didn't mind not having any socks on either, as the carpet was thick and plush. I sat on the edge of the bed, digging my toes into the soft fibres, as I tried to clear my head and figure out what to do. After an indeterminate amount of time spent pawing at the carpet and zoning out, I decided to get up and see if I could find Evelyn. I spotted a glass of water on the bedside table and downed half of it, then heaved myself up from the bed again.

There was a light on in the corridor outside the room, but no natural light. The window at the end had the same sort of thick curtains as the bedroom. I wondered what time it was. It could have still been night, but I felt like I'd slept through, despite (or possibly because of) the hangover headache.

There were two doors on the wall at the other side of the corridor, one further towards the end with the window, and one the other side. Beyond that, at the other end of the corridor, there were two sets of stairs. One led up, and one down. The carpet out here was high quality too, and the walls were covered in flocked, embossed wallpaper with more paisley patterns. These ones were in dark, muted burgundy, with silver accents. If the bedroom hadn't smelled so strongly of Evelyn, I might have worried I was in a hotel. Everything here dripped with luxury.

I walked down the corridor cautiously. The house was dead silent, and the way the deep carpet and flocked walls swallowed up the sound of my footsteps made me nervous. I decided that going down the stairs was my best bet.

Both the bannister and the stairs were made from dark, polished wood and felt sleek to the touch. I padded my way down and found the stairway opened up to something that resembled a foyer. It was tiled in black and white, with wood panel walls, and an impossibly high ceiling. There were large double doors across from the stairs, and two regular doorways, one to the left and one to the right. The door to the right was ajar, and I could hear a whisper of song creeping out around it. I wondered if I was dreaming, as I followed a compulsive pull towards the sound.

Through the door, there was a kitchen. The lights were brighter and cooler in here, though still synthetic, so it took me a moment to orient myself. It was a huge kitchen. Marble counter tops lined three sides of the room, and a great big dining table stood in the middle. Everything was white marble, polished chrome, and black steel. The singing was coming from the enchantress, who stood by the stovetop with her back to me. She was dressed in a long, white satin robe, her dark hair spilling down over it in sharp contrast. The song she sang was some kind of folk tune about lost love. She swayed gently as she sang. She had a voice like wilting roses; mournful and sweet and so beautiful it made my chest ache. I stayed in the doorway listening until she finished her song.

She still didn't turn around. I couldn't see what she had on the stove, but she seemed to be waiting for something. I thought about saying hello, announcing my presence, but decided that I shouldn't miss my chance to romance her. I walked up behind her softly, doing my best to emulate her own cat-like grace. I could see now that she had an old-fashioned kettle over one of the gas hobs, and was waiting for it to boil. I wrapped my arms around her wordlessly and laid my cheek against her shoulder. I felt her startle and tense, but only for a fraction of a moment before she relaxed her body against mine.

"Hello again," Evelyn said contentedly. I kissed her shoulder before I replied.

"Hello."

"Mmm."

She put her hands over mine and we stayed like that, holding each other in relaxed silence until the kettle started to whistle.

"I'd better get that," she said with the ghost of a laugh. I let her go, reluctantly, and stepped back as she busied herself filling up a cafetière. She got two mugs out from a cupboard overhead, and the sight of her stretching up to reach, with the sleeve of her robe slipping down her arm, was mesmerizing. When she turned round, I was still staring, slack-jawed, at her. She laughed prettily.

We sat at the dining table together to drink the coffee. There were six chairs, three on each side, and I expected her to sit across from me. She scooted in right next to me instead, pushing her chair up to the side of mine. I wasn't about to complain. I blew on my coffee and took a sip. It burned my tongue, but it was delicious, with a rich, complicated smell. I couldn't resist taking another few careful sips before I set it down to cool.

"Your house is beautiful," I said. In truth, the house puzzled me. Rents weren't cheap in my city, and I wondered just how many roommates she must have to live in a place like this.

"Thanks, it's been in my family a long time, but I did some renovations a couple of years ago," she replied. She said this casually, as though it was the most natural thing in the world for someone to just drop into conversation that they came from old money. I balked.

"It's yours?" I asked incredulously. At 32, only a couple of my friends had managed to buy starter homes so far, though a fair few of them had been thinking enough about purchasing to complain constantly about how unaffordable it was. She laughed again. She seemed to find me endlessly amusing.

"Yeah, I know, it's embarrassing," she said. She had the good nature to look slightly abashed, but not as much as her words would suggest.

"No it's cool," I replied. "I'd give an arm and a leg to have my own place. Not having to deal with a landlord sounds great."

She looked down at her coffee and waited a moment, running a long black nail around the rim of her cup, before she spoke again.

"So, where do you live at the moment?" she asked. "I mean, is it just you or...?"

I cottoned on to her meaning surprisingly quickly. It normally takes me a bit to parse questions that aren't direct, but it was like Evelyn had a line wired straight into my head.

"Are you asking if I'm single?" I teased. "You know, that's normally the sort of thing people try to find out before taking someone home to their fancy gothic mansion."

She shot me a look of genuine embarrassment this time, mixed with trepidation, and I nearly fell over myself trying to walk my comment back.

"I am, though! Single, I mean. Right now, anyway. Not that I have to be. I mean, I'm available, you know. Not that - I mean... Umm, yeah. Sorry," I stammered. The relief on her face was instantaneous, though my own cheeks were burning.

"Me too," she said softly.

"Eh?"

"I'm available."

Somehow, her eyes were even more intense, freed as they were from the thick black eyeliner she'd worn the previous night. There was no lead-up to the kiss.

***

My legs were tangled up in sweaty sheets, and one of my arms was pinned under Evelyn's slender neck. I'd just about regained my breath.

"You know, I have no idea what time it is," I mused.

"I can check," Evelyn offered.

"No, I don't care," I said. She hummed happily and shuffled closer to lay her head on my bare breast. I ran my fingers through her silken hair, petting her idly. My own hair felt like a rat's nest, with my dip-dyed blonde ends shooting off in all directions. I had black hair too, naturally, but I'd done the dye job thinking that if it was only the ends I dyed, the bleach couldn't do too much damage. As it turns out, the ends are where hair splits, funnily enough, so it had turned my shiny shoulder-length waves into a frizzy mess that often left me feeling self-conscious.

I couldn't care less right then, though. It occurred to me how odd this was. We were basically strangers, but I felt so comfortable there, with Evelyn. I could have stayed there forever. It was only when my stomach grumbled loudly that I had to acknowledge the impossibility of this.

"Oh no," Evelyn joked. "I think your tummy cares what time it is."

I laughed instinctively at her use of the word "tummy". It was a funny word to hear from a grown woman anyway, but especially from someone as cool and elegant as her. The laughter turned into a groan of commiseration when Evelyn moved to get up.

"No, don't leave," I grumbled.

"I'm just checking the time." She leaned over me to grab her phone off the bedside table, and I wondered where I'd left mine. Trouser pocket, I thought. *Wherever my trousers were.*

"It's just coming up to half twelve," she said. I started, and sat up.

"Half twelve as in lunch?" I asked. I hadn't even been sure that it was morning yet when I woke up, so knowing that half of my Sunday had already passed was a bit of a shock. Not that I was complaining about how it had been spent, of course.

"Yes, lunch time, hungry girl," she teased, poking my soft belly. I laughed.

"I was just surprised it had gotten so late."

I explained how I'd been unsure of the time since I woke up, what with the lack of natural light in the house.

"Should I open the curtains?" I asked.

"No, I'm not really a sunshine kind of person," she answered. I looked at where her pale white hand was laid across my own dark olive thigh, the contrast making her pallor all the more shocking.

"Yeah, that tracks," I said. She stuck her tongue out playfully.

"So, do you have somewhere to be, or should I feed you, hungry girl?" she asked. I wasn't sure about this new nickname, but I liked the playful tone she took. I looked at her, sat on the bed with me... Dishevelled and naked.

"I could eat," I said.

***

It was nearing four by the time I finally left. We'd forgotten about food, so I found myself ravenously hungry on the way home. Her grand house was on the other side of town from my pokey flat, so the taxi ride took a good half an hour. I chose not to think about the further hit on my bank balance. I held my phone in my lap the entire ride, checking it anxiously every so often. Harry and Debs messaged to check in with me, and I assured them that I was fine, but spared the details. It wasn't them who I wanted to talk to.

I'd given Evelyn my number before I left, and it was only when I got into the taxi that I realised I wouldn't have hers until she decided to message me. I didn't know when that would be. Would she play it cool and wait until later? Or even the next day? What if she didn't message at all? This thought was more worrying than my battered bank balance, so I tried to shove it away. Despite my efforts, it kept resurfacing in the exhausted, hungover swamp of my mind like a bloated corpse. Maybe Harry had been right. I was down bad.

At home, I let myself in and went straight to the fridge. My flat was open plan, with a little galley kitchen separated from the pokey living room by a counter and nothing else. I made myself the most disgustingly stacked sandwich I could manage and slumped onto the couch to shove it into my face. God, I was tired. The food seemed to make me even more sleepy instead of re-energising me, so I put my plate on the floor, kicked my jeans off, and let myself drift off on the sofa.

I woke to a knock at my door. I pulled my jeans back on clumsily and stumbled over to the door. Through the peephole, I could see a little old lady dressed in an aggressively pink cardigan.

"Hello Maggie." I opened the door tiredly. My neighbour looked me up and down.

"Oh I didn't mean to intrude," she said.

"No, no intrusion, I was just having a nap," I said. She gave me the once-over a second time.

"Of course you were, my dear." Her tone was suggestive, and it made me feel grubby.

"What's up?" I asked.

"I picked up some of your mail by accident, I just thought I'd drop it off. I haven't opened it, don't worry!"

The mail room was downstairs in the entrance to the block of flats, and we all had our own numbered post boxes. However, the current postie didn't seem to have noticed these letter boxes, as he had an annoying habit of just leaving everyone's mail in a stack on top of the side table.

"Oh, they never get it right, do they?" I said.

"Don't get me started, love!" she jibed back. I took the letter from her and thanked her. It looked like a bill.

"I won't keep you. I'm sure you've got better things to be doing," she said. There was that tone again. Had she noticed that I never came back last night? I felt awfully self-conscious.

Indoors, I went to the bathroom to check how I looked. There hadn't been a mirror in Evelyn's, so I'd not really gotten a good look at myself all day.

"Oh god," I groaned out loud. To say I looked a mess would be the understatement of the century.

I'd taken a shower before I left Evelyn's house. We both had, in fact. But without a mirror, I'd clearly not been able to remove my makeup as thoroughly as I thought I had. Evelyn must have liked the panda eyes and specks of black lipstick though, because she hadn't said anything. That was nothing though, compared to the state of my neck. It'd been such a long time since I last actually went home with someone, that I'd not stopped to think, when she was going to town there, of the marks involved. Up and down my throat on both sides, my neck was red and purple. I pulled the collar of my t-shirt down on one side, and there, sure enough, were even more hickeys scattered across my collarbone. I didn't even bother to check the other side of my collar.

"Fuck me," I swore at my own reflection.

No wonder Maggie was waggling her eyebrows at me. I realised the icing on the cake when I tried to leave the bathroom and something caught on the door handle. I'd not been careful enough putting my jeans back on and my bra, that I'd shoved deep into my pocket before leaving Evelyn's place, had shuffled up and been flapping about at my side, it seemed. Great.

Evelyn still hadn't messaged by the time my alarm woke me the next day. I got ready for work, worrying that maybe I'd offended her somehow as I was leaving. Had I said anything weird? Was I too clingy? It didn't sit right with me, and I ended up zoning out in the shower for about twenty minutes and nearly setting off late. I didn't get a chance to grab any breakfast, but that was fine. I felt too exhausted to have much of an appetite anyway.

I managed to grab a bite to eat at the restaurant where I work just before they opened for lunch, which was good. I'm a pot washer (and general dogsbody), but I'm pretty friendly with both chefs, so I made a point of casually dropping into conversation that I hadn't had time for breakfast to Jerry, the old line cook. Thankfully, and somewhat predictably, he snuck me a tub full of various bits that I wolfed down on my break.

I don't like days when I have to go in early to help with prep at the best of times. They always seem to drag. Plus when I'm not as busy, I feel a little more aware of my surroundings, and the surroundings there were pretty grim. The kitchen was clean enough most of the time, but it had an air of dinginess that wasn't the sort of thing you could wash off. Scorch marks, peeling paint, old burnt stoves, and the smell. God, the smell was intense. All the different bits of prep going on created a chaotic underlayer to the pervasive, and ever present, scent of onion that overwhelmed everything in that kitchen. It got worse as opening time approached, and they'd start heating up the deep fat fryers. The fryers really needed changing daily, but were done twice a week instead to save oil, on the boss man's specific instructions. It would be nice to say that it became unnoticeable again when the place got busier, but in fact it was a strange infohazard of a smell, in that once it had asserted itself fully, it became impossible to ignore.

The one good point of the early shift was that I got to swap out with Dave, the other lackey, at five. This meant I could still have my evening to myself, instead of working all night. Sometimes this back and forth played havoc with my sleep schedule, depending on what pattern of shifts the boss man put me on, but I wasn't going to complain. What I was going to do was find a better job and quit that shithole. I just hadn't quite got round to it yet.

I got the bus straight home at five. I wanted to shower the grease out of my hair and I didn't have any plans for the evening. I was still thinking about Evelyn all the way home, oscillating between giddy recollection of our time together and anxious spiralling over why she hadn't been in touch yet. By the time I'd finished in the shower, it was nearly seven, starting to get dark out, and she still hadn't messaged. I caught sight of myself in the bathroom mirror and frowned. *Maybe it's for the best if that was a one-night stand,* I thought, touching my bruised neck. I'd caught Jerry and Enid looking at the damage, earlier on. I pretended not to hear them snickering about it with each other on the other side of the kitchen.

Maybe it's for the best.

As if she'd read my mind somehow, it was at that moment that my phone buzzed, nearly vibrating its way off the side of the sink. I wiped my hands down on my towel and grabbed it.

"Hey, it's Evelyn. Would you like to meet up tonight?" the message read.

Tonight?! Seriously? We'd gone from no contact all day to - what? Booty call? I felt I should be offended in some way, but it was hard to concentrate on that when I was already busy ripping through my wardrobe, looking for something to wear, less than a minute after reading the message. I was fully dressed in one of my favourite pairs of jeans and a rather fetching button down within five. I messaged her to ask when and where, and tried to do my eyeliner hurriedly, as though I thought she was about to message back instantaneously saying, "Here, now". In my hurry I smudged it several times, swearing to myself and taking longer in total than if I'd just done it calmly.

I needn't have worried. Half an hour passed by before she got back to me.

"Why don't you come over to mine whenever you're ready and we see what we feel like?" I swallowed thickly and replied, with shaking hands, that I was on my way.

Her doorway was a grand affair. Double doors up a set of four steps, with curly iron handrails on either side. The steps were tiled with old flagstones, and I wondered whether they were original or just a quirky touch to the renovations. It was an odd thing to be thinking about, looking back, but I was probably just trying to think about anything that wasn't my own sweating palms or the butterflies in my stomach.

She was radiant when she opened the door. Seeing her face, I wanted to kiss her then and there but I held myself back. I was certain that would be far too fast.

She held the door open and invited me in.

Inside, she led me to the kitchen. I was happy to follow, admiring how she looked from behind in the outfit she'd worn. Tight leather trousers and a dark purple, off the shoulder t-shirt. She looked fantastic.

The kitchen was very dark, a contrast to what I expected of it after last time. The only light came from a cluster of candles in the middle of the dining table. Evelyn beckoned me in.

"What's all this?" I asked, grinning. She looked a little nervous, not as confident as I remembered her being.

"I thought you might like to have dinner with me," she said. Her voice was a lot cooler than her face, betraying no hint of nerves. I don't know why, but I found myself making a mental note of the mismatch. I reached out and grabbed her hand.

"I'd love to," I said, stepping toward her. She smiled and squeezed my hand then lifted it up and, ever so gently, kissed the back of it. My heart flipped in delight and I returned the gesture. Her hand smelled of pomegranates, and it took a lot of restraint not to immediately move to kiss her lips. She obviously wanted a proper date though, so I played along and kept a little distance between us.

She sat me down at the table and grabbed a full plate off one of the counters. Well, full is maybe an overstatement. It had some sort of interesting vegetable dish on it in a portion size that went some way, in my mind, to explaining why Evelyn was so slim. She put the plate in front of me and then brought two glasses and two wine bottles before taking a seat across from me.

"This looks delicious, thank you," I said. I meant it too - it looked very nice indeed. She smiled.

"I hope it tastes as good as it looks." Her tone was playful but she looked nervous again. I imagined it might be hard to tell if Evelyn was nervous, but having seen the relaxed way she held her body around me before, the tension suddenly present in her shoulders and jaw felt palpable. I put it down to first date nerves. It made sense - god knows I was nervous enough, trying to avoid any major cock ups. And it wasn't like I was the one who'd gone to all the effort of providing a candlelit dinner that the other was about to eat. *There* was an interesting point though...

"Where's yours?" I asked. Evelyn had a glass in front of her that she was fiddling with, but no plate.

"I uh, I think maybe I should tell you something," she said. Well, this sounded concerning.

"What is it?" I asked.

"I don't really eat..." she said. There was a long pause.

"I'm uh, I'm sorry?" I said. I wasn't expecting this. Uncertain on how to proceed, I tried a gentle probe, hoping for a little more context.

"Do you mean, like, on purpose?"

She must have understood what I was worried about because she jumped in quickly.

"Oh not like that," she said. "I mean I don't really eat people food."

OK, that didn't clear anything up. Thankfully she wasn't done yet.

"Angie..." She spoke softly with a serious expression. "I'm a vampire."

I laughed.

"You're a vampire?" I asked, still laughing. She didn't join in, so I went quiet. It kind of made me feel like a bit of a dick, but surely this must have been a joke?

"I am a vampire. I'm not joking," She announced, with uncanny timing. I wondered what the fuck was meant to be happening.

"Is this a roleplay thing?" I tried to keep my voice gentle and curious, but I felt a bit like I was being messed with, and I didn't like it. She gave me an imploring look. I genuinely wasn't sure what she wanted me to say. She sighed heavily, staring into her glass.

"Yeah, if you say so," she said. She looked resigned and upset, and I felt like even more of a dick. A great, big one this time.

"Hey, we can do that. I'm sorry, I just didn't catch on. That's fine," I tried to reassure her. I reached across the table to touch her hand. She looked up at me and smiled but it didn't quite reach her whole face. I leaned in further.

"I'm kind of into it," I said conspiratorially. She laughed and I felt my shoulders drop an inch or more in relief. The thought of upsetting her and ruining the night when she'd put so much effort in, well, it was horrible.

It was weird eating dinner while she drank whatever was in that bottle. She poured wine for me out of the other one, but the stuff she poured for herself from that one was thick, red, and utterly convincing. We got into more of a rhythm though, when she asked how I'd been, and I told her about Maggie catching me with my bra hanging out of my pocket. We laughed together and everything started to feel more natural again.

When I asked about her day, she mentioned having gotten up at sunset and messaging me straight away, and how she would have done it the previous night but she'd been so exhausted from staying up in the daytime with me on Sunday, that she'd slept right through. It rubbed me up the wrong way, to be honest. I'd have appreciated a *real* explanation for why she left me hanging without her number when she had mine, but her game conveniently got in the way of that. Not that I thought I was owed such a thing, of course. But it stung a little, after waiting to hear from her all day, to have it rubbed in like that. I didn't want to upset her again by breaking character though, so I played along.

"Isn't it inconvenient having to sleep in the day?" I asked. "Do you always have to work nightshifts?"

"Oh I don't work," she answered. She said it so thoughtlessly and automatically that I figured this part was probably true. *Must be nice,* I thought. I took a mouthful of my vegetable delight.

"Tell me more about what you do," she said quickly. I finished my mouthful, and told her about my restaurant job. This lightened the tone again, as we laughed over sweet old Jerry, and snarky Enid, and my feckless boss.

After dinner, and another glass of wine or two, we ended up going to her bedroom, to my exhilarated delight. I thought I'd play into her game by waiting until she had me undressed underneath her, and then stretching my neck out for her.

"Bite me," I said in my most seductive voice. It didn't quite have the effect I'd intended.

Evelyn's face dropped and she rolled off of me to sit on the edge of the bed with her pale boney back facing me. I scrambled up after her.

"Hey, I'm sorry. I thought you'd be into that," I said softly, placing a hand on her shoulder. She turned to face me and the serious look on her face caught me off guard.

"It's dangerous, you know," she said.

What? Was this still part of the game? I did my best to sound as flirtatious as I could, but I was getting a little frazzled trying to keep up.

"Maybe I don't mind danger," I said.

Evelyn eyed me critically. She was deciding something, definitely, but I'm not sure what. She did that curious little frown.

"I can't tell if you're being serious," she said. *Here's my chance to prove myself,* I thought. I leaned forward to whisper in her ear.

"Serious as a heart attack."

I nibbled her earlobe for good measure, and she gasped. I felt an enormous swell of pride at the noise, and it made me grow bolder. I kissed and licked my way down her neck, sucking gently at the juncture where it met her shoulder. She squirmed, pressing her legs together and breathing heavily. I kissed my way out to the round of her shoulder. Then, throwing caution to the wind, I bit down firmly. She let out a high-pitched moan and spun round to throw herself at me.

Before I knew it, I was pinned underneath her again. I lost it when she started kissing me, moaning wantonly into her mouth and bucking my hips beneath her. Whatever she wanted from me, I was more than ready. When she pulled away, I stretched my neck out again and shot her a challenging look.

"Do you want me to beg for it?" I asked demurely. She growled, and before I could even register just how attractive this noise was, her head was in the crook of my neck. Her hot breath teased at the sensitive skin there.

"Please," I whispered. I'm not sure what I was even asking for at that point, but Evelyn took it as her cue to bring our little game to a head. She sank her teeth down into my neck.

For a moment it was nice.

Then it hurt.

Then it *REALLY* hurt.

It occurred to me that this was rougher than I'd expected, much rougher than the activities that had left my neck looking like an abstract painting previously. I instinctively pulled away. She kept one of my arms pinned down under her, though. I was trapped. Then, her hand was between us doing things that, while they didn't dull the pain, distracted me enough to allow it. By the end, I was encouraging it, groaning and whimpering and begging her not to stop. She heeded my request, and kept going until my whole body was quaking and spasming beneath her clever fingers and her horrible, wonderful mouth.

When it was over, she laid herself down next to me and tucked her arm around me. She pulled my head onto her breast. I kissed wherever I could reach, lazily, between laboured breaths. I felt like my soul had exited my body towards the end of that, and it left me lightheaded and breathless. The room was spinning slightly.

"How much wine did I have?" I asked jokingly. My words sounded far away and slurred, like someone else was saying them and not very well. Evelyn went very still.

"Shit," she said suddenly.

She jumped off the bed.

I looked up at her and saw there was something red dripping from her breast down her side. Red. Was that... I opened my mouth to scream but instead found the room slowly falling away from me into darkness.

When I came round again, the first thing I heard was Evelyn's voice.

"Please be ok, please be ok."

She was muttering these words to herself over and over like a mantra. I opened my eyes and found her over me. She was pressing something into my neck. I didn't get chance to try and see what it was before she was hugging me and weeping.

"Oh my god, I was so scared you weren't going to wake up," she cried. Her body shook. I wanted to put an arm around her and tell her everything would be OK, but my arms felt heavy, like they were full of lead.

"S OK," I managed to mutter.

"It's not OK," she sobbed. "I didn't think of the wine. Alcohol thins the blood."

It took me a minute or two to parse together what she was saying.

"Wait, so you did break the skin?" I asked, voice still slurring somewhat. "I did... I did wonder. At the time. You know." For some reason, in my delirious state, this seemed rather funny, so I laughed. It came out more as a series of huffs.

"Oh, Angie. How do you think I'd feed without breaking the skin?" she asked.

"Beats me." I laughed again. Then I took a moment to consider what she was saying.

"So you're really a, umm... Really vampire?" I asked. I was still too out of it to really understand anything. Everything just seemed surreal, and oddly funny.

"What?" She withdrew, keeping pressure on whatever she was pressing against my neck, but sitting up to look at me properly.

"I told you it was dangerous! You said you were being serious!"

"Serious as a heart attack." I giggled.

She recoiled further like I'd struck her. Pain wrote itself in every corner and fold of her face, and I felt the need to smooth it out immediately.

"Wha' sup?" was my rather eloquent attempt at this.

"I thought you knew," she whispered. She looked so heartbroken. I wanted more than anything to make it right.

"It's gon' be ok. You can just turn me into one and we'll be fine, right?" I murmured clumsily. The room was getting darker and darker around me. Evelyn said something, but she sounded so far away that I couldn't quite catch it.

The next time I woke up, I was in a hospital bed. I don't remember much of my time there. I do remember having to embarrass myself in front of a couple of doctors, several nurses, and even a police officer by admitting that my wounds were caused by an accident - a sexual situation gone wrong. No, it was nobody's fault, and no, nobody was pressuring me to keep quiet or making me feel unsafe at home. I certainly did not want to tell them who had bitten me. I said all of this to the professionals, but I merely told my friends I'd fallen and hurt my head. Yes, I was fine. No, I'd rather they didn't visit. Evelyn was nowhere to be seen or heard from, and after a day passed by in hospital, I deleted her number. There was no excuse that would make up for her leaving me there by myself in that state.

Thankfully, I hadn't lost enough blood to need a transfusion, but only just. They gave me a couple of stitches and some antibiotics - just in case - ran some tests, and kept me in for a day and a night to make sure I was steady and stable. They sent me home with some iron tablets, and the advice to stay off work for a few days and rest up. I didn't have any problem with that. Time off that I had a valid excuse for? Don't mind if I do. Then again, by the second day stuck in at home, I found myself longing for a distraction. I ended up falling asleep in front of my laptop watching reruns of Kitchen Nightmares. It made work seem a lot more tolerable than usual when I went back.

Just because I deleted Evelyn's number, it didn't mean that I stopped thinking about her. She floated into my head unbidden at all hours of the day and night.

I only deleted her number - never blocked it. The choice to leave me injured and alone, without ever checking in to see how I was recovering, was entirely her own.

Ghosted by a "vampire". How ironic.

Luckily, I never did get round to sharing any details of what happened that Saturday night and after to Debs and Harry, so the next time I saw them, I just made out that it didn't go very well, in the end. I shamelessly implied that Evelyn and I had gone home to our separate houses, and never seen each other again. The last thing I wanted was to have to talk about her, or what had happened. They were much more interested to hear how my head was doing, and the fictitious story of how I'd managed to trip up on the stairs, anyway. I took to wearing fashionable scarves while the worst of the *actual* damage healed, and nobody commented on it except to say it suited me.

***

Three months later, the scars from the bite had faded enough to be unnoticeable to anyone except myself. Better yet, I'd just about managed to convince myself that Evelyn had been nothing but an irresponsible creep with a fetish that had gone way too far. Just about. There was still a part of me that couldn't help but wonder - what if? After all, there was the old house, the lack of mirrors, the wine bottle, the way she'd actually drank... I couldn't even think of the last part without bile rising in my throat. I clung to the little scraps of evidence that painted her as a fraud, a freak, and a pretender. The way she drank coffee and spirits, before I ever saw her drink blood. I remembered her excusing herself to use the toilet too, which didn't seem particularly vampiric. There were other tells, heat and breath that became oh so noticeable when we were -

No.

If I let myself think about those sorts of things, it always left me feeling pan-icked and nauseated. I didn't want to acknowledge it or deal with it, but some part of me was still attracted to her. It repulsed me.

I started taking a lot more showers, despite the weather growing colder.

With all of that time and work trying to get past what had happened, I should have been more prepared. I thought I would be prepared; I knew we both lived in the same town and chances were I'd see her again some day. But even after three months, it was still too soon, and I was still too fragile. So fragile.

This is how I broke.

It was a Friday night. I'd been on an early at work, so I had the whole evening free. Unfortunately nobody else seemed to be free. Harry and Debs were having a date night, which I couldn't begrudge them for. Honestly, it was nice to see them nurturing their relationship on purpose like that. I sent a couple of messages out to other friends, nice people who I wasn't as close to as I was with Harry and Debs, but who nevertheless, wouldn't mind me tagging along if they were going out. Nobody was though. They were either skint or tired. *Isn't that always the case?*

I sat about and considered having a night in to pamper myself. Maybe I could get a takeaway, watch a movie, have a nice candlelit bath... For some reason when I pictured the candlelit bath, I started to panic. I think maybe it was imagining the candlelight. It brought me back on some level to the start of that night. The dinner. When things had begun to go wrong. Before I'd even consciously figured this out though, my heart was already fluttering in my throat and my stomach was twisting into knots. *Well, there's another thing I've accidentally ruined for myself,* I thought. I decided to just go out regardless of if anyone was free to go with me. I felt I could do with a drink. I washed the workday off myself in the shower, with all the lights on and the bathroom door open.

I went to my regular haunt. Even though it was where we met, it was one of the few places that still felt safe after dark. I suppose I'd just been going there so long it was like a second home. With the familiar faces and the familiar music and the loud, busy, predictable unpredictability that I'd come to expect.

I got a cocktail in a pint glass with something fruity in it and sat outside. I didn't smoke myself, but the outdoor speaker was a touch quieter than the indoor one, so it was a good place for eavesdropping on other people's conversations if you were bored. Plus, I just liked being out in the fresh air. I tended to avoid what had been my regular table these days, of course. Debs and Harry had noticed this the last time I was out with them, but I'd explained how my back wasn't what it used to be, and I liked sitting on the bench by the wall now so I could lean up against it. They'd teased me for getting old then said no more about it.

So there I was, nearly at the end of my cocktail and still alone. I was torn. I was cold and bored and thinking that maybe I should just go home. Then again, the group at the table over to the left of me were loud, messy, and boisterous; they seemed, overall, to be having a jolly good time. Maybe I could go over and introduce myself, make some new friends for the night. If I was going to do that, I'd need a little liquid courage.

That was it, I decided - I'd have one more drink and make my choice then.

I was nearly at the bar when I noticed her. I wasn't sure at first. From the back, she was just a tall thin lady with long black hair. Not exactly out of place in a setting like this. There was something about her though. I had a feeling. I hung back and waited for her to turn around. She did. It was her.

It was Evelyn.

She caught my eye and suddenly the previously comforting noise of the bar was too loud. The music thumped and pounded at my ears like it was trying to batter its way through my skull. My neck twinged under its tiny scars. I stood, frozen, for an amount of time that could have been a second or a minute or an hour for all I could discern. It felt as though every nerve in my body was switching on, fire running through my veins. The feeling filled me up, overwhelmed me, and spilled out of my limbs. I bolted.

I don't remember anything except my feet pounding against the sticky floor, then the pavement; the wind rushing past me, and my pulse roaring in my ears. When I finally stopped, I'd gone down the street, turned onto an alley, gone down that, and found myself behind an industrial bin. I slumped onto the ground with my back against the brick wall, and the skip blocking my view of the street. My breath started to come back to me in jagged, heaving sobs. I did my best to muffle them against my sleeve.

What was wrong with me?

The cocktail threatened to come back up, but I held it down, counting my breaths in and out like I used to do as a kid, when I was scared of the shadows in the corner of my room at night. My heart began to slow, eventually, to a rate that didn't make it feel as though it was about to burst open inside my chest. I let the tears flow until they dried up by themselves. Then I wiped my snotty, wet face clean on the sleeve of my coat. I was sweating from the exertion of the run. The coat felt like it was trapping me in my own muggy, claustrophobic microclimate, so I took it off and let the cold night breeze touch my arms. I shook like a leaf, but the cold helped to calm me at least.

I took my phone from my pocket and opened up the app to order a cab when something stopped me. What was that? I'd picked up on a sound, growing louder. Was that...? It was. Footsteps in the alleyway. I wiped my face again, ridding myself of any last stray fluids and smoothing it into a look of neutrality. I scrambled to my feet, and held my phone against my ear. I had no idea who was approaching, and I certainly didn't want the wrong sort of person to see me looking as vulnerable as I felt, in that dark alleyway, with nobody else around.

"Yeah, yeah, I know. No, I'm just off Saxon Street, just popped into that little alley on the left to have a smoke. Great, yeah, I'll see you in two minutes then. No, yeah, of course I can stay on the line," I said loudly into the phone. I stepped out from behind the bin as casually as I could. I was still shaking, but I hoped that could be excused by the cold, seeing as I was clutching my coat against myself instead of actually wearing it.

I don't know what sort of person I was expecting, but it wasn't the thin, pale woman who I saw before me. My stomach dropped. How had she found me? The energy that fueled my previous panic was depleted. Instead of fire and sparks, all that filled me this time was a heavy dread. I let my arm fall down by my side, knowing the pretend phone call wouldn't be any use. Not now. I just stood there, numb and exhausted, as Evelyn approached me.

I felt as though I wasn't quite in my body as the interaction unfolded. I was there, of course. But I was also an inch above myself, like body and mind were layers that overlaid on one another, and mine had got knocked out of place. None of the corners quite lined up anymore.

I watched as she walked towards me, stopping a couple of feet in front of me.

She was still beautiful. I noted this dispassionately. It was a fact, not a feeling.

"Hey, Angie," she said. She sounded like she wasn't sure if I'd want to talk to her. I did want to, though. There were so many things I wanted to say to her. So many questions she should have to answer. Things I wanted to tell her about what she'd put me through. They screeched out in my head, angry and buzzing.

I watched myself stand there and say nothing.

She took another step closer.

"I saw you run off. I've been out looking for you," she said. She sounded concerned. The angry voices swirling round my mind yelled and thrashed against this.

Who does she think she is?

What the fuck gives you the right to follow me when it's you I'm running from?

Why can't she just fuck off and die?

Why won't you leave me alone?

Leave me alone!

Fucking freak!

Fucking monster!

I felt myself shaking violently, but I still didn't speak.

"Angie, I'm scared," she said softly, taking another step that brought her nearly nose to nose with me. The voices screamed and roared like wild animals at this remark.

I closed my eyes so that I wouldn't have to look at her face. Her piercing blue eyes were too intense, too focused. They made me feel like it was really her and really me and we were really there, and I didn't want that at all. If I could just keep my eyes closed, I could keep this from being real. I could wait until she left, then go home and pretend I'd never met her at all. I put all my resolve into remaining like that - still, unfeeling and blind - a statue.

I could have done it. I know I could have. But then I felt her hand on my cheek. Cool and soft. Trying to comfort me. I scrunched my eyes tight, but the tears spilled out from the corners of them anyway.

"Oh, Angie," she muttered. She sounded so gentle. So sorry. I felt her thumb wipe some of the tears from my cheek, and then her soft lips pressed against my forehead. I broke.

My resolve shattered into a million cut-throat shards. The statue I had been was lying broken on the pavement.

First, it was just a gasp. I raked in the air like I'd never tasted it before. Then I was wailing like some dying creature, still scrunching my eyes shut tight. Suddenly her arms were around me. I buried my face in her shoulder, breathing in the sweet, clean scent of her hair, and clinging to her for dear life, or so it felt. She held me and rubbed my back as I sobbed into her hair. I must have dropped my phone and my coat on the ground, but it didn't matter. None of it mattered. All that mattered was right here, right now, her and me.

She rocked me gently, swaying back and forth as I cried out all the hurt and pain from the past three months. I could feel it leaving my body in waves, crashing up from the pit of my stomach, building into animalistic wails and howls that rolled their way up my throat and roared out of my gaping mouth.

"Shh. Shh. It's ok. You're alright now," she whispered. Her voice was thick and gravely, unlike her usual silken tone. It didn't occur to me then, but I think she might have been crying too.

My keening turned to childlike sobs, then eventually died down into wet hiccups and snuffles. She pried herself away from me and held me by the shoulders. Her eyes sparkled in the dim light.

"Do you want me to take you home, sweetheart?" she asked.

I nodded, still blubbering.

She sat me down against the bin, then collected my things up in her arms. She ordered the cab on my phone, talking me through everything she was doing. I didn't say a word. I just nodded and did whatever she asked. In the taxi, I felt numb and empty. And so, so incredibly tired. It wasn't until we were back at her house that I spoke.

She took me into the foyer and showed me to the door on the opposite side from the kitchen. I hadn't been in there yet, and it turned out it was a cosy lounge.

There were two big sofas, a squishy armchair, soft brown carpet, and a plethora of blankets, books, and cushions scattered about over the furniture. There was no TV, which was a bit odd for a living room in my experience, but I didn't really question it. The room was lit by a floor lamp that gave off a pleasant yellow glow.

Evelyn laid me down on one of the sofas and put a velvet cushion under my head. She took my shoes off, unlacing the converse and pulling them off one by one. Then, she pulled a blanket from the arm of the sofa and tucked me up like I was a child. She smiled at me and I managed a weak twitch of my lips in response. She explained how she'd be up in the bedroom and I could come and get her if I needed anything. She assured me that I was welcome to go anywhere in the house and that if I wanted to leave, she'd understand. *Like I was in any state to coordinate getting myself anywhere.* I'd remained silent up until that point, but when she turned and made to leave, I grabbed her hand. My voice was hoarse from crying and my words came out in a gruff croak.

"Was it true?"

She looked down at me with a strange expression. It was something close to pity but not quite. It certainly wasn't unkind, but it made me feel uncertain and off-balance. She leaned down and kissed my head. I closed my eyes and let myself relax into the smell of her that wafted over me, and the sensation of her dark curtain of hair tickling my face and neck.

Then it was over.

I kept my eyes shut, waiting for an answer, but all I heard was the lounge door closing. When I opened my eyes, she was gone. I was so exhausted. It didn't take long to cry myself to sleep.

When I woke up, it was the same as last time. The dark house remained totally unchanged by the passage of time. It could have been midnight or midday and I'd have no way to know. My eyes felt hot and dry and my throat was sore. I hoisted myself up and made my way out, across the foyer, and to the kitchen. The hard floor was cold, even through my socks.

She wasn't there this time. There was no song, no coffee. Just me in a room that felt far too big and far too posh to accommodate me. I poured myself a glass of water and drank it in two big gulps. I refilled it to take it with me, back to the lounge. I hesitated outside the door to the cosy room, though. My eyes were drawn to the stairs. I wasn't sure how I was supposed to feel. I wasn't sure how I'd let myself end up back here again. Hell, I wasn't even sure what was real anymore. But one thing I was sure of, was that if I wanted answers, I was going to have to talk to Evelyn.

Up the stairs, I had to summon all of my courage to knock on the door.

"Come in," her voice answered. As though in the habit, I followed her command.

"Hello," I said quietly. I stood in the doorway awkwardly. Evelyn sat up against the headrest of the bed with her legs crossed in front of her. She was fully dressed but in different clothes to what I remembered her wearing the previous night. Those had included a fancy red and black dress with chains and tassels. In her bedroom, she wore a loose cotton shirt and linen trousers, all in black. Her feet were bare, showing off how her toes were painted glossy black just like her fingers. Her face was bare too and her hair was tied back. It made her look both older and younger at once, somehow. She held a book in her lap, which she closed and placed on the bedside table, next to the lamp.

"Hello," she replied tentatively. I wasn't sure what to say. All of the questions and accusations felt so inappropriate now I was here in her bedroom. She looked so vulnerable. It made me uncomfortable.

The silence went on too long and I felt the need to fill it up, fearing it might stretch on and on until it became so thin it snapped and something fragile got broken.

"What - Ermm," my voice was still hoarse and I had to pause to clear my throat. "What are you reading?" I asked lamely. She looked at the book on the nightstand with surprise, like she'd already forgotten all about it.

"Oh that? Just a dusty old history book. Nothing very fun. It's got Napoleon in it," she said. She offered me a smile and I made an effort to return it.

"No wonder you got on so well with Debs," I joked. Her smile widened and she made a noise that was somewhere between a hum and a laugh. I felt the ice between us start to melt a little, and it made me braver. I came in and let the door fall shut behind me.

"Do you want to sit down?" she said. She patted the bed with a long-fingered, black-clawed hand.

"Sure."

I sat on the edge of the bed at the foot of it. I angled myself round, leaning on my arm so that I didn't have my back to her entirely. She solved the problem for me by scooting over and swinging her legs down to sit beside me on the end of the bed.

"We've got some things to talk about, haven't we?" Evelyn said. I nodded. She waited patiently. She didn't try to touch me or hold me. I stared down at my own hands in my lap and took a deep breath.

"Why did you leave me? Why -"

My breath hitched as I struggled to articulate my fears and pain into civil conversation.

"Why didn't you call? I thought... I felt like you didn't care if I lived or.."

There was an uncomfortable pause. She didn't say anything. I had more to say, and we both knew it. When I did, it came out in a voice that sounded much smaller than my own.

"I thought... I thought maybe that's what you wanted. You wanted me to die."

When she still didn't answer, I looked up from my hands to see why.

She was staring down, just like I had been. Her blue eyes, normally so strong and intense, were wide and shining with tears that spilled out and rolled down her sharp nose. They dripped off and landed in her lap.

"I'm sorry," she whispered. "I'm so sorry."

My immediate feelings of sympathy and heartbreak told me to hold her, to comfort her, and try to make it all ok. But the pain from the last three months must have hardened something inside of me, because I stayed strong. I looked away from her to make it easier on myself.

"That's not an answer," I said simply.

Out of the corner of my eye, I could see the movement as she nodded.

"I know, I'm sorry. I know." Her voice didn't exactly suggest she'd collected herself, but she was clearly at least trying to. She sniffed wetly and took a deep breath in.

"I can try to explain. I owe you that much. A lot more probably."

She paused as though she expected me to say something, but I just waited for her to finish.

"You might not believe me, though. And you might still hate me."

I took a moment to think about this.

"I know," I said finally.

I reached out and put my hand in hers. She squeezed it and started her story.

***

As she told it, she'd been enamoured with me from the moment she laid eyes on me. She saw in me a free spirit with a joy for life, and an "impossible beauty". It stirred things inside her. It had been decades since she'd last felt like this. It was overwhelming for her. She said she'd noticed the way I listened so intently as she spoke with my friends, I was hanging off her every word, by her reckoning. It made her feel seen.

She said she regretted moving so fast. That she wished she'd asked me out on a date, instead of whisking me away to her bedroom. This stung, and I had to remind myself to keep calm. Not to extrapolate her regret in moving fast into something more generic that she hadn't actually said.

Was that my own feelings surfacing and projecting onto her? All the times I'd laid in bed wishing we'd never met at all?

I put the thought away and did my best to hear her out.

Apparently, that first night had been both heaven and hell for her. She didn't remember ever feeling so good just touching someone and being touched. Being so close it felt as though we were one. I was uncomfortable listening to this. It felt too close to my own recollection of the night; a memory that I'd spent the last three months locking away inside myself, for my own sense of sanity.

Hell came in the form of temptation. So many times, she said, she'd wanted to throw caution to the wind, to rip my throat wide open, and drink me dry until we really were as one. She described how she'd longed to leave me with only enough blood left to force my own weaker teeth into her. How she couldn't stop imagining what it would be like to feel her dark essence pouring out and filling me up.

All she'd wanted, then and there, was to turn me into one of her own, so we could stay wrapped around each other, inside of one another, for eternity.

She knew it was wrong though. Her life was hard and lonely. She couldn't inflict this curse onto somebody else, especially unknowingly. So she'd been good. She'd restrained herself - only barely - but she had. She settled for ravaging me in other ways and trusting that if she could just make it good enough, please me enough, I might come back for more. She'd even waited to message me until the day after I gave her my number, worried she might come on too strong and scare me away if she wasn't careful. Evelyn said she was used to scaring people away.

On the Monday night, she couldn't resist the urge to see me again. She said she felt like she was being called to me - drawn by a force with a deeper gravity than the Earth itself.

She was used to living in seclusion, isolation, and secrecy. There was something about me though, she said, that told her I would understand her situation. That free spirit and joyful energy she'd been drawn to - surely someone like *that* wouldn't be cynical enough to reject her outright, without hearing her out?

She spoke of her disappointment when I'd failed to take her seriously. I felt an anger rise inside me. It seemed so unreasonable, from my perspective, for her to expect me to just accept something that went against all logic and reason. I tamped it down and reminded myself that I was here to listen. I could judge when she was done.

She said that, as the night went on, she came to believe that maybe I'd come round to accepting her truth. She'd doubted it again when I asked her to bite me, though. She said it felt like I was making a joke out of her - mocking her for the very thing she hated most about herself. But then, when I'd reassured her and asked her again, she realised that I actually meant it.

She said it was like all of her dreams had come true at once. Here was this wonderful, magnetic person - she said - who not only believed her and accepted her, but wanted her. Truly, deeply, wanted her. Not a human facade of her, she said, but the real her. And so she'd given herself, and taken what she was offered in return.

She said it was the most wonderful experience of her life. She'd never fed like that before. She didn't even want to think about some of the other times she'd fed, before she'd managed to find a clean supply of blood, siphoned from sources that didn't make her want to rip her skin from her bones after choking it down.

That was what it had been like before me, she said. Bad, or neutral, but never good. Never right.

And then there I was, offering her what she hated to crave but needed to live. Not only with my consent, but with affection, maybe even love.

It was the most perfect thing in the world.

She said.

She explained how she'd been careful to bite where she could feed, but not where it would cause me to bleed out. She'd taken every care to avoid that. She described how if she'd so much as nicked the carotid artery, my insides would have squirted out, gushing like a hosepipe, until I was dead and cold within minutes. I rocked back and forth slightly as I listened to this part, fighting the urge to get up and run.

Hear her out. Hear her out.

She said it should have been fine. She hadn't taken enough to harm me. Less than they'd take at a blood donation centre, she said. But she had made one nearly fatal mistake. She'd forgotten about the alcohol thinning my blood.

A bit of leakage afterwards would have been normal, she said. Harmless. But when I started to talk like I was drunk, she got worried. I mentioned the wine, she said, and her heart sank. She suddenly realised the growing pool between the two of us. She said she'd never felt fear like it, which was, apparently, saying something after some of the things she'd been through in her countless decades.

She thought at first that maybe she could stop the bleeding herself. She'd grabbed a towel and pressed it against my neck. She said she was praying and pleading with me to stay with her. Her heart jumped with relief when I woke up, but she could tell I wasn't right. I'd lost more blood than I should have.

She said that *I* said some things that were... Hurtful.

She braved it though, keeping the towel pressed down and trying to keep me conscious. When I dropped again, she'd gotten dressed at lightning speed and rushed me to the hospital.

She said we flew.

We flew through the night sky, under the stars and above the buildings, me cradled in her arms.

She said.

She left me there and disappeared into the night. It wasn't ideal, but she was terrified that the small-minded human doctors would think she was some sort of deranged murderer, and call the police to come and take her away.

I didn't mention how I'd had to skirt the issue of her identity when the police questioned me, having been afraid of exactly the same thing.

She said that when she got home, she tore through the house, howling and ripping things apart. She was so scared, and ashamed. She was convinced, more than ever, that she was nothing but a monster. A demon with a curse from hell that should have thrown itself on the mercy of the sun and burnt away into dust years ago.

Something that never should have existed.

She said she became convinced that she was a danger to me. To everyone. Not only that, but obviously, she thought, I would hate her. Why would I want anything to do with her after she'd treated me so carelessly? After she'd shown me what sort of a monster she really was? She said she kept coming back to the words I'd said in my nearly-unconscious state, feeling that I'd already rejected her, even then. She said she realised, now, how wrong she was to never reach out. How I must have felt abandoned by her. But in her eyes, she'd been giving me the only gift she could, by way of remaining absent.

Apparently, she'd locked herself in after that. Refused to leave the house, and spent her days doing nothing but reading, sleeping, and feeding from her delivered supply whenever she couldn't take the hunger any more.

I couldn't help but notice, when she said that, that she did look even thinner than she had before. I tried my best to keep this fact separate from the story she was telling me.

She said she'd wanted to reach out to me so many times. She mourned my absence like a death.

She knew I wasn't actually dead, of course, because she'd allowed herself one brief outing to return to the hospital and check on my wellbeing, floating outside my window in the night while I slept.

I had slept next to the window. I didn't say this though. I kept listening.

Evelyn finished her story by telling me how her outing to my favourite bar had been a lapse of restraint in the face of temptation. She craved me more than she'd ever craved anything else, even blood, and it had been ridiculous to think she could stay away forever. She'd gone there looking for me, sensing that it was where I'd be that night.

She wanted the chance to see me, even if I never wanted to see her again after this.

Now she had, she was prepared to let me go forever.

She didn't want to, of course. It may even destroy her. But she would.

If that was what I wanted.

There was a long, heavy silence after she finished, while I let her words sink in. My mind was racing. Working fast, trying to stay logical in the face of more emotions than I could deal with, I figured out that there were three options.

Option one was that she was mad.

She was a deranged lunatic, who genuinely believed she was some sort of mythical creature, and had concocted this fantastical story - with unnatural lifespans, and blood drinking, and the power of flight - to explain her horrific actions to herself. I looked at her critically.

She looked exhausted, defeated, shamed, and unhappy.

She didn't look mad though. God knows I wasn't qualified to judge and I didn't know nearly enough - or anything really - about such matters to make an accurate appraisal, but she'd never struck me as insane.

The second option was that she was lying.

In a way, this would make her more dangerously insane than option number one - to be able to be so calculated and manipulative as to put on a show of this calibre. I didn't like this option at all but there were a number of facts that supported it.

Obviously, all I knew of vampirism was what I'd gleaned from pop culture, but I'd never heard of vampires drinking spirits or coffee. It was a fact that she did these things.

It was a fact that her teeth looked quite normal, which isn't what I'd expect from a vampire. Oddly perfect - gleaming white and straight as a row of gravestones - but nothing a good cosmetic dentist couldn't do with enough time and money.

It was also a fact that I'd felt her pulse, heard her breathe, and seen her cheeks flush red.

None of these were what I expected from a vampire.

But then again, why would I assume that I should have any idea what to expect? The words, *"closed-minded humans"* and *"so cynical"* floated through my mind in her voice. And the cruelty and precision required to weave such a tale, told with such emotion, well, it wasn't the sort of thing I'd ever run into before. It was the kind of thing one would expect from a supervillain in a movie, not a real person who was sitting next to them. I looked at her again. A fresh wave of tears rolled down her cheeks but she stayed still and silent, looking into her lap and waiting for me to decide what to do with her. I really didn't want to believe that another human being was capable of being manipulative enough to fake that.

More importantly, *what sort of person would it make me if I accused her of such inhuman cruelty?*

Which brought me to option three.

Maybe she was telling the truth.

Vampires were real.

She was a vampire.

This option was horrible. It shattered my view of the world. It went against all reason and logic and experience. *Vampires are real? Pull the other one, it's got a tooth fairy on it.* But I couldn't deny that there was a certain appeal to it, as well. The romance of it. The whimsy. If vampires were real, what else was real? What other boundaries of common sense could be shattered to reveal the magic hidden just beyond them?

This made me wary of option three. In a way, it was too horrid and too good to be true.

I weighed the options against each other.

Option one just didn't ring true to me. Maybe it was inexperience or naivety, but I just couldn't see her as deluded.

Maybe, deep down, it was because I was afraid of the implications if this was true. That maybe *I* had been the one taking advantage of *her* all along. Indulging her. Encouraging her. Hurting her.

No, that couldn't be right.

Of course she wasn't mad.

I would know.

Which left two and three.

Three was preposterous; a ridiculous flight of fancy that only a fool would believe.

But if it wasn't three, it would have to be two.

This beautiful woman who was trying to keep her tears silent, merely to allow me more emotional space to judge her, was actually the worst kind of human monster. *That person* was devious and devoid of empathy. The woman who had made me feel so good, who had trusted me to make her feel good too, was lying to my face through crocodile tears.

The thought of allowing this to be true shattered a much more fragile part of my worldview than option three could hope to touch.

In the end, I didn't know. I couldn't know. I just had to choose what I would rather believe. There was only one option I could live with. Only one that wouldn't break me in a way I couldn't rebuild upon. Only one that would redeem us both.

And, it occurred to me, it was the only option that came with a way to test it. *A way to finally, actually, know.*

"I want you to bite me," I said. Evelyn looked at me with shock. I don't think it's what she was expecting from me.

"W-what?" she asked. Her voice trembled.

"I want you to bite me. I want you to drink long and deep," I said.

"And when you've had your fill, I want you to show me how to bite you. I want you to pour yourself into me and let me stay with you forever."

I don't know how I managed to say this so calmly. My words shocked me, never mind her.

They were out now though, and I couldn't take them back.

I tried to keep my fear in check, reminding myself that, one way or another, I needed an answer. To know. This was the only way I could think of.

Evelyn moved closer and looked up at me through dark, wet lashes.

"Does this mean - " She hesitated. "Does this mean you believe me?"

She sounded so hopeful. I smiled sadly.

"I don't know what I believe," I said. Her face dropped again.

"But I know what I want to believe,"

I cupped my hand and lifted her chin to look into her eyes.

Those beautiful eyes.

"Help me believe, Evelyn," I whispered.

Before she could answer, I captured her mouth in a kiss. We melted into one another, and I knew there was no turning back.

***

I can feel the weight of her next to me when I wake up in her bed. She lays, still as night. I'm mesmerised by the way her chest fails to rise and fall. Her skin is cool and pale, like frost on a winter morning - splashed and stained with stale blood. Just like the sheets underneath her.

Just like me.

I wish I could kiss her. I don't, though. It isn't right. None of this is right.

I check the time and see it's nearing seven. As I know the sky must be starting to grow pale outside the window, I think about opening up the thick curtains that cover it.

The black velvet fails to show it, but I know they must be drenched in blood too. There's barely a corner of the room that isn't.

It would be so easy to open them.

I wonder how she'd feel if she knew I was thinking these thoughts.

She doesn't move an inch.

Maybe this is normal. Maybe this is part of the process. Maybe we would both burn up and *die* the moment the sun touched us.

I still don't know. Why can't I ever know?!

I hate her so much.

I hate the uncertainty. The fear.

Damned if I do, and damned if I don't.

I hate what she's made of me, and I of her.

What would be worse? Opening the curtains and burning up?

Or waiting patiently for her to wake, and seeing her start to rot, instead?

I lay my hand on the bloodied parting in the curtains.

I've been through too much not to get my answer now.

One way or another, I'm going to find out what's real.

About the Author

Okay, Savage? is a neurodivergent, queer artist and writer from Leeds. They have a small daughter and an even smaller dog. They used to take long nature walks, but they developed CFS/ME, so now they watch David Attenborough and the like instead. It's far less muddy and tiring. Okay's art and writings are an exploration of the surreal, the sublime, and the macabre.

Sanctuary

Nox Spacey

CW: Eye gore, starvation, impalement, abandonment

Whumpee: Man, Whumper: Multiple and Environmental, Caretaker: Man

"I want to thank you all for being here in my banquet hall." The young lord held up his goblet, his sharp nails clinking on the chalice. The liquid inside was deep red. "A toast!" he said with a be-fanged smile.

Those around the feast table all retrieved their glasses—some filled with the same metallic scents, others with the heady smell of rich wine.

"My castle will now be a sanctuary for..." The young lord's ears twitched, hearing the jingling of metal on belts and the rustle of wooden stakes at the front door. "Wait. Something is wrong."

***

If it had been anybody else, he would have been staked through the heart first thing.

But no. Lucillian Varitan Ironsong had been the son of the richest family in Aucraven before he'd died and been resurrected as a vampire, so the monster hunters knew better than to kill that particular beast. His family was extremely vocal about how they wanted to keep him alive—undead—in the hopes that a cure could be found, something to bring him back to warm flesh and blood and purify him without losing him.

The whole family was fucking rich and spoiled. Nobody ever told them no. Their rich fuck of a spoiled son had had everything handed to him his whole life. Then he dies and he has undeath handed to him, *then* when the monster hunters got a whiff of him killing innocent people, he had a stay of execution handed to him because his family can never cope with not getting exactly what they want.

So instead of staking the vampire to kill it, they sealed it inside its mansion. They caved to Mommy and Daddy's demands just like everyone else in the country and spent way too much time, money, and effort that could have been spent saving *living* human lives storming the castle. It'd been far in excess of what one vampire would merit, to make sure he was taken alive—they'd weakened him, then covered the young lord's manor house with arcane runes that would bind the vampire inside. He'd been rendered unable to leave and untouchable until a cure for vampirism was found and the oh-so-important family could have their foolish, selfish son back.

So now the vampire hunters had this ill-tempered bird in a gilded cage that nobody really wanted. But not for long. Because Nathaniel was going to end it.

He was tired of his children living in fear. The residents being menaced by that castle on the hill, the trapping runes glowing dark red ominously throughout the night, hadn't been asked if they were okay with having a pissed off vampire living next to their farms.

Nobody had ever liked the Ironsong family when all the members of it were *alive.*

Nathaniel was going to kill the vampire and piss off the monster hunters and the powerful, asshole family, and he didn't give a damn what anyone had to say about it. He was tired of people in power making decisions for the poor without any regard for their quality of life.

Not to mention, no matter how much the powers-that-be insisted everyone had been evacuated from the mansion before they'd sealed it shut, Nathaniel wouldn't put it past them to sacrifice a few peons and doom them to being trapped in there with a vampire. Servants, maids, groundskeepers, anyone a lord would think expendable. This thing probably still had victims, and he had to take matters into his own hands.

Nathaniel reached the gates of the castle, wrought-iron things overgrown with vines. The property hadn't been abandoned for long enough for it to fall into disrepair. Lucillian Ironsong had just let it get like that before he died.

Nathaniel coaxed his horse into stepping onto the grounds despite how spooked she was. It was daytime, but the thick overgrowth of trees this deep in the forest made the light perpetually dim anyway. Again, it had been like this even before Lucillian had become a vampire. He had been a ridiculous man.

The trapping runes glowed deep red around the entryway, laced around the doors and windows and in a line circling the entire building. Nathaniel pulled his horse up to clop parallel to it, looking for the easiest way in.

And stopped, because maybe he didn't need to find a way in.

There was a hunched-over figure crouching in one of the entryways, on the stone path just at the edge of the runes. Its face was hidden by its long, stringy hair, but Nathaniel could see drool dripping down onto the stones. Its hands ended in blackened claws, which scratched at the ground. It was dressed in clothes that had been fine, once upon a time, now ruined, stained, and torn.

Nathaniel pulled his horse to a stop and dismounted, retrieving his shotgun. It wouldn't kill the beast, but it would slow it down enough for Nathaniel to safely get at it with his wooden stake, which would finish the job.

The monster's ears twitched at his footsteps, and its head tilted in his direction. The hair cascaded like a waterfall away from its face, revealing that where its eyes should have been, there were two silver spikes jammed into its eye sockets.

They must have blinded the thing to keep it from reading the runes to figure out how to undo them. It was trying to get out anyway, though. It'd managed to get past the barred doors, so maybe it would eventually figure this out, too. He'd come just in time.

Nathaniel retrieved some shells out of the fold of his cloak and fed them into the shotgun. The vampire uncrunched itself from the ground and started clicking its tongue to echolocate.

"Yeah, you see me, huh, you bastard?" Nathaniel said, snapping the shotgun shut. "I'm gonna kill you now, so just stand still and make this easy for both of us."

The vampire lord let out a savage hiss and threw itself in his direction. Chains of arcane red electricity spiked out of the runes and dragged the vampire down to the ground. It shrieked in pain, and its hands dug trenches in the ground as it fought to try and continue forward despite it all.

Nathaniel pointed his gun directly at the vampire's chest and pulled the trigger.

The blast sent the creature tumbling back into the wall of the castle, thunking meat onto the stone. Despite the injury, the creature had no blood in its body to bleed. Still snarling savagely, the vampire slunk away as Nathaniel broke his gun back open to feed more shells into it. Still clicking its tongue, it retreated back through a window into the shadowy depths of the house.

***

Lucillian's boots clicked on the floor as he ran with rapid speed away from the entrance, where the monster hunters were battering the door down. "Run!" he shouted. "You all have to get away!"

His preternatural hearing allowed him to hear the rustle as the vampires scattered, their same hearing allowing them to hear the command before the human guests. The human guests, who'd have no way to flee in time. They would be helpless.

He had to protect them.

He slid to a stop inside the feast hall, where all the remaining guests stood at attention, alarmed.

"Master Ironsong, what's happening?" said one of them. A woman who'd been fleeing arrest for handing out medicinal herbs to wives fearful of their husbands and the chains that motherhood would bring.

"Where should we go?" said another. A man nearly stoned to death for stealing one too many kisses from another man where they could be seen.

"Are we in danger?" said another. A woman from a family of nomads despised and persecuted for practicing witchcraft.

"We'll help defend you," said another. A man who'd fled execution for levying some well-deserved criticisms upon the king.

Lucillian looked at them all. His flock of black sheep. His family despised them, no matter how much he tried to keep his help to them discreet. He had to protect them.

But he was a fledgling vampire, turned on his deathbed by a loving friend as repayment for helping the outcasts, to save him from death at the hands of disease. He was young and inexperienced and did not know how to be a proper vampire lord yet. How to use his powers. How to rain terror down on mortals who dared defy him.

So a few minutes later, he was still fighting the authorities and losing badly as his guests were chased out of the feast hall, amid panicked sounds and fleeting footsteps. From under the table, Tabitha hissed fearfully.

Lucillian was in the process of wrestling a spear out of the hands of the lead monster hunter when a bola from behind swept his legs, slamming his skull on the tile. The spear came down next, going clean through his guts. A second, third, and fourth spear came next, pinning him to the ground.

Lucillian struggled wildly against the metal eviscerating him, clawing at the spear to try and free himself. A man approached–grizzled with bite scars all over, clearly a monster hunter experienced in fighting vampires. Lucillian hissed and spit up blood, the very limited supply of the stuff he had running through his veins emptying out onto the floor beneath him, his body turning cold, cold, colder than anyone had the right to be.

The monster hunter took out two enormous silver spikes.

Lucillian gripped a spear and bent it with his hands, kicking his legs and trying desperately to get up and mobile, because those silver spikes were coming right at his head-

White-hot pain exploded across his vision, blotting out every sight and sound and smell. Someone cried out before Lucillian realized it was his own voice. The agonized wailing was undignified for a lord of the night like him–it happened all the same.

The last of the precious lifeblood emptied out of him. Metal tinkled nearby as someone took his rapier. The pain in his face continued as the silver burned away the last of his eyes and melted to the inside of his sockets.

"Stop!" he screamed out, thrashing against the polearms still skewering him. "Stop this at once!"

One of the polearms was pulled out, taking a chunk of his intestines with it. He wailed and writhed and pulled on the one sprouting from his left clavicle, but another hand had already started prying it out.

"Release me!" he shrieked.

The remaining polearms were pulled out, leaving him a bloodied, punctured body on the ground. His ragged chest heaved in and out, the vampire unsure of what to do now that his demand had actually been fulfilled. The burning silver in his eye sockets remained.

Human voices murmured elsewhere in the room. With considerable difficulty, Lucillian rolled himself over and got up on his hands and knees, the remnants of his blood–his friends' blood, really–dripping down onto the tile beneath him. "Remove this-"

A kick to the ribs interrupted his command halfway through, shoving him back down to the ground. He lay there where he'd fallen, like a defeated dog.

It was quieter now. Just the sound of the monster hunters. They must have won, chased everyone else out or killed them. Lucillian was next.

The footsteps of the head monster hunter approached. Lucillian clutched his side through his tattered waistcoat and pushed himself back, fumbling sightlessly.

The expected stake through the heart did not materialize. Instead, there was just the gravelly voice saying: "Be good and stay in your cage now, hear?"

"Wh-what?"

The footsteps were already retreating. The other noises had died down, leaving him in agony on the ground as silence fell.

"Wait—I demand you come back here and…"

They were gone. His voice echoed in what was clearly an empty feast hall.

"Hello?"

He managed to pull himself up by a nearby chair and wobble to his feet. "Hello?" Blood and tears dripped down his face and off his chin to patter onto the ground. "Hello?"

Distantly, the front doors boomed shut. His ears twitched at the hammering sound that followed, the sound of someone clearly boarding them up.

Huffing in agony, Lucillian's hands ghosted over the burning hot metal in his eyes. He spent a few minutes clawing at it, burning his hands over and over to try and get them out. Hissing in pain and frustration, he gave up and stumbled out. Past the kitchens, into the drawing room, through the hallway, down the grand staircase, into the foyer. All empty.

Something burned him when he tried to open the front door. Something burned him when he tried to open the windows. Something burned when he tried to wiggle out through a hole in the wall, or through the servant's passage. Something cutting down to the unholy part of him that wouldn't hurt anyone if it'd just been left alone.

Lucillian hung upside down from the rafters of his abandoned castle, once a sanctuary, now a prison.

***

Nathaniel stepped over the trapping runes cautiously, keeping his gun pointed towards the floor. The house was dark and dusty inside. There were bloody footprints everywhere, evidence of the vampire's activity in its isolation. Broken and overturned furniture littered the foyer, the entryway, the hallway. Nathaniel followed the faint sound of the vampire clicking its mouth to echolocate.

Into the feast hall, the tallest room in the house. A beautiful golden room with elegant chandeliers, broken and unlit, and soaring buttresses. The vampire had hooked its feet from the rafters and hung with its hair dangling downwards like a ribbon. Its chest heaved in and out in a labored way, arms crossed. The clicking sound continued for a few moments, before its gravelly voice said:

"Get out."

"No," Nathaniel said.

The vampire's lips peeled back in a snarl. "I will kill you."

"You'll try."

The vampire unfolded itself and landed heavily on the table below, among the rotting scraps of the last meal, exposed bones and half-eaten fruit and dirty goblets. "You took *everything* from me," it wailed, exposing his blackened, snaggly teeth.

"Me?"

"The monster hunters. And now you're going to finally finish me off."

"I ain't no monster hunter," Nathaniel said, raising his gun. "But it can't be that hard. Just sit still and it'll be fast."

Nathaniel unloaded a shot, but it only grazed the vampire's arm as it darted away, shredding its already mangled clothes.

"You ruined everything!" the vampire's voice echoed. "Now I'm feared and hated!"

Nathaniel broke the gun open and fed more shells into it, scanning the dark room to try and find the thing's hiding spot.

"Just get out! Leave me alone! Haven't you done enough?"

Nathaniel snapped the gun shut and walked forward cautiously. "Haven't *you?*"

"Get out!"

A meow sounded in the hall, and a cat flashed past, running by Nathaniel's legs. He cursed and kicked, his boot missing the connection.

"No!" The vampire's voice was different now, and he materialized seemingly out of nowhere to pounce on the cat. At first Nathaniel thought he was going to eat it, before the vampire merely held the squirming creature close and backed up defensively. "Don't hurt Tabitha! What's wrong with you? You'll abuse a helpless animal?"

"It was a reflex! I'm in battle mode here!" Why was he so defensive? Why did he feel the need to justify himself to a vampire? "I wouldn't hurt a cat on purpose!"

"Oh... Well–well, good."

The two stood there awkwardly as the cat continued to struggle.

"You...said you aren't a monster hunter?" the vampire said.

Nathaniel didn't lower his gun. "Yeah."

"Then why are you–"

"Because I'm tired of being menaced by damn monsters if the monster hunters won't finish their job."

"I've hardly *menaced* anyone... Oh, who am I kidding? Anyone who could be convinced I'm not a monster is long gone." He lay down on the floor and crossed his arms over his chest. The cat darted away. "Just–just make sure Tabitha goes to a good home? I can't bear the thought of her having to catch mice in the castle all alone now."

Nathaniel lowered his gun slowly, squinting suspiciously. He was looking at the vampire as a different, much more relatable type of creature now: a man trying to care for and protect someone precious to him. "You'd let yourself die and worry about your *cat?*"

"She's always been there for me."

"Hhhgn." Nathaniel brought the gun back up. "Speaking of. You're really alone in the castle? No servants stuck in here with you for you to drink their blood?"

"Do I look well fed? It's nobody here but me, Tabitha, and whatever mammals we can happen to catch. Recently we managed to catch a raccoon. So that was a delight."

He *didn't* look well fed. He looked positively starved. That was another relatable type of man: someone struggling and going hungry. Nathaniel lowered the gun a little.

"And for the record," the vampire continued, "I never fed on my servants. Only my friends."

"Is that supposed to make it less goddamn ghoulish?"

"Well a servant would be afraid to say no. I know my friends did it willingly."

Nathaniel lowered the gun even further. "You are... really not what I expected."

The vampire smiled sadly. "You're not the first to say that to me, although you are the first since I've been turned undead."

Nathaniel sighed and set his weary bones down on the floor to sit next to the vampire. "How am I supposed to kill a monster that's not fighting back? Hardly seems sporting."

"None of this was ever about sport."

"What's it about then?"

"My family's image."

"Yeah, they wanna keep their precious son alive until they can figure out how to reverse vampirism. Can't have a member of the great Ironsong family being a vampire."

"Is that why they did this? I thought it was to punish me."

"...for what?"

"For tainting my family's image by associating with undesirables. They flushed all my houseguests out before imprisoning me here and-" His voice got choked up. "They had nowhere else to go. All I wanted to do was protect them."

Nathaniel sighed. "Well. Hell. I know what that feels like."

The cat walked back in, tail held aloft in a question mark.

"So you really ain't going to prey on the innocents?"

"I have no intention of it."

"Cuz that's what they told us you were gonna do."

"I suppose they would."

"Cuz I never knew you were a kind soul taking in strays."

The cat approached and rubbed its cheek against Lucillian's boot. "I tried to keep my business discreet. My castle was well-known in underground circles. My family still didn't like the blight on their image." Lucillian groaned and levered himself into a sitting position. "I was on death's door due to illness, and one of my compatriots revealed themselves to me as a vampire and offered me the gift of undeath for the kindness I'd done for them. I had plenty of people willing to offer me their bodies-"

"The hell is that supposed to mean?"

Lucillian's face spasmed as his body tried to send blood it didn't have to his face to make him blush. "I had a cadre of intimate acquaintances with rather eclectic tastes-"

"You're telling me you already had a convenient castle full of freaks who liked being bitten?"

"If you're a good enough lover, you can make almost any experience into something people beg for. I never wanted for human blood."

"Uh-huh."

"Everybody was happy with the arrangement! Everything was fine! Until my family decided they knew what must be best for us. Ooooh." He shielded his ravaged face and turned away. "I'm so parched I couldn't cry even if my tear ducts were still intact. But I'm weeping on the inside, I assure you. We had something beautiful. A sanctuary for those who had no sense of belonging elsewhere."

Nathaniel sat there uncomfortably, liking the situation now even less than he did coming into the castle.

Lucillian folded his legs up to his chest and rested his head on his knees. "So... may I ask... will the monster hunting be continuing anytime soon?"

"...Come here, Mr. Fancy Pants. You ain't dying today."

A few minutes later, Lucillian was laid out on the feast table screaming as Nathaniel pulled on the stakes in his eyes. "Great God above in Heaven whose name burns my unholy tongue! The agony!"

"You got a better idea?"

The first stake came out, stringing gore and bits of skin after it from Lucillian's eye socket. Lucillian immediately rolled over and curled up. "Hail Mary, full of grace, the Lord is with thee; blessed art thou among women-" His tongue started to smoke even as he said the prayer.

"Stop being overdramatic. We're already halfway there." Nathaniel threw the silver spike on the ground. "Now let me see the other one."

"I've decided a man can go through life and undeath perfectly fine with only one eye. Eyepatches are in fashion-"

Nathaniel grabbed him by the lapels and rolled him over. "Come on, you big baby." He braced one hand on Lucillian's temple and used the other to start pulling.

The seared flesh melted to the metal started to tear. "-and blessed is the fruit of thy womb, J-J-J-You know-Holy Mary, pray for us sinners-"

The second spike tore free, leaving two crusty, sightless sockets gaping in his skull. Lucillian rolled over the opposite way, kicking feebly and hiding his face in his hands. "-*NowandatthehourofourdeathAmen.*" His tongue caught fire as soon as he finished. He yelped and clapped his hands over his mouth, smoke wafting out.

"There," Nathaniel said. He took out a rag and started wiping the gore off the silver spikes. They might be worth something. "So how's this work? You're torn up pretty bad." In part because of Nathaniel's own buckshot, but that was neither here nor there.

"I'll heal if I have blood," Lucillian said. "There are enough vermin in the castle that I can surely get a goblet's worth in...a few months or so."

"That long?"

"Well I would heal faster with human blood, but..."

"You're a glutton even as a vampire, ain't you? Vermin ain't fit for a lordly sir such as yourself."

Lucillian's face did the thing where he was trying to blush again.

"It won't turn me if you drink some of mine? Unless you bite me?"

"No! Not unless I drain you completely."

Nathaniel sighed wearily yet again. "Fine. I don't see why it's always gotta be me stuck with doing these things, but someone's gotta."

He picked up an overturned goblet from the feast table and withdrew his knife, pricking a cut open near his elbow and squeezing the blood out into the chalice. Lucillian's face took on a manic look as drool pooled in the corner of his mouth and dripped down. He politely wiped it with his hand and took a step back.

"Here," Nathaniel said. He set the chalice down on the table. "I'll come back and check on you in a few days."

He turned and left without looking back.

***

True to his word, he was on his horse riding back to the ominous castle later that week. Despite his wife being right that this was a foolish risk to take. He should have just killed the damn vampire. It's what a wise man would have done, and would do now.

Nathaniel wasn't wise. He just saw what was in front of him.

What was in front of him now was the elegant entryway where he'd seen Lucillian the first time. He tied his horse to the gate and kept his shotgun down to the ground, ready to pull it up. "Lucillian? I'm back."

He crept further into the entryway, peering into the darkness. A pair of red eyes opened and peered back.

"Lucy?"

"I don't go by Lucy." Lucillian stepped out of the darkness. He was clean now, with a fresh outfit unstained by blood, a face whole and unmarred and with a *smile* on. He was handsome. Nathaniel could see why he'd entice so many people with *eclectic tastes.* "I do go by *friend,* though."

"That's the dumbest thing I ever heard."

Lucillian laughed and brushed his hair back. He approached to the edge of the runes, his boots a millimeter short. "I would invite you in for a proper thank you, but nobody's been by to bring in the proper wines and fancy cheese I set out to entertain in ages. I'm afraid all I can offer you is my finest selection of rodents. If you'll wait around a bit, though, I'm sure Tabitha and I could catch another raccoon. The height of the hospitality I'm currently capable of."

Nathaniel laughed, relaxing his grip on his gun and stowing it. "You're something else, aren't you?"

"I like to think so."

"Glad I was able to help. You clean up nice."

Lucillian twirled and put a hand to the frilly cravat around his neck. "Well, I was finally able to pick out clothes that matched in color! I'll need to see a tailor since, ah, most of my clothes are too loose on my frame now. Once I can... be about town again, I suppose."

Nathaniel squatted down by the runes, examining them. "Yeah. I got no idea how to break these things. Sorry." He ran a hand over them, but they were carved into the earth and bound by magic light. He couldn't just kick the dirt over them.

"It's hardly your fault." Lucillian sat down on the other side cross-legged. "It's good to see you again. I've been so terribly lonely for a kind face."

"Yeah... about that. I was thinking. You know how you said your place was a sanctuary?"

"Yes?"

"Well... it can still be that. We'd have to see if these... spells affect it at all. But hey, you don't have to be able to leave to get all those people back in here, right?"

"...If I can gather them up again, I suppose. They must have scattered to all corners of the globe by now."

"You could get in some new people. There's never any shortage of creatures that need help."

"Creatures?"

"Yeah, well... I was just thinking the monster hunters don't always have the best judgement, you know? Because the powerful families buy them off to do or not do certain things."

"What are you saying?"

"Well... I got wind of a werewolf down in Langfield who tangled with monster hunters despite not wanting to fight. If I can get it up here to your castle, think you could take care of it?"

"Well... I'd have to make sure they wouldn't chase Tabitha around, if they're a wolf."

"That a yes then? It could be a monster sanctuary as well as for whatever washed-up folks you take a liking to."

Lucillian gave a be-fanged smile. "I think I would like that."

About the Author

Nox is a lover of all creatures and people in sci-fi and fantasy and loves stories about persevering through horrors to come out better on the other side.

Never Fight a Woman in Spurs

Robin Rose Graves

A bullet rips past him, whistling as it ricochets off the nearby wall. Jackal's luck pointed in his favor yet again. He bares his teeth in a grin. Unsteadied by whiskey, he holds the same wall as he turns to face the woman who failed to shoot him.

There she stands in the dusty road, revolver in hand. Her with dark hair pulled into a ponytail beneath her ten-gallon hat. Her with her trousers - such a peculiar woman. He already likes her.

"Need to work on your aim," he taunts her.

She moves nine yards in a blink of an eye. The shock further unsteadies him and he leans heavier onto the wall. It was just his mind playing tricks, thoroughly saturated in the drinks, and maybe some other substances as well.

She grabs him by the collar of his shirt, shorter than him, but having the strength to throw him against the wall.

"That was a warning shot!" The air is crushed from his lungs. Jackal knows what little else to do but laugh, thinking lady luck was still going to smile on him.

"You lost. Accept it," he tells her. He had a knack for cards, for gambling, and he seldom lost.

"You cheated." Her dark eyes narrow with the accusation. She throws him to the ground, before digging the spur of her boot into his ribcage. He grunts at the pain, no longer laughing, but he could take a beat down. "I want my fucking money back!"

Jackal rolls onto his back. Her face is entirely blacked out, backlit by the moonlight. "Or what?" he taunts her. He knew a bluff when he saw one. 'Warning shot' his ass. She wasn't going to kill him. He wasn't afraid of her.

She spits on his face. Jackal laughs. He sees the sole of her boot rise above his face. She brings it down hard on him, smashing her heel against his face as if he were a venomous viper. He closes his eyes, turns his face away, but the battery continues until her heel collides with his nose. He hears a snap. Blood fills his sinuses. He can taste it in his mouth.

"Not laughing now, are you mister?"

Jackal is quiet. He will wait this out. Not the first person he pissed off, and she isn't going to be the last.

His vision is blurry by the time she stops. He blinks a few times to clear the blood from it. She is gone. It was one of the worse beatings, he would give her that.

Jackal is slow to sit up. His head feels like hell, blood pounding in his ears. He hears horse hooves on gravel. It halts before him. Jackal looks up. His stomach drops as he sees that it is her again.

He should have ran when he had the chance.

She dismounts as Jackal rolls onto his stomach, attempting to crawl away, though he knows it will be futile. She grabs his ankle, holds tight on to it.

"I'll give you the damn money! Just-! Leave me alone!" he shouts. She declines to answer. He hears a 'Ya!' in time with a flick of reins - peculiar, given that there is still pressure around his ankle.

He makes the connection a moment too late, as suddenly his entire body is yanked along by his ankle. His leg pops from the socket at his hip as Jackal is dragged through the dust by the horse. He claws into the ground, attempting to gain purchase. Dirt wedges beneath his nails. It cuts his fingertips.

He quickly learns that his best defense is to go limp. Any movement causes him to roll, banging his elbows on hard earth passing too fast underneath him, or worse, his head.

The pain steadily increases in his leg where bone had split from joint. The weight of his body resting on it, he could feel himself slowly ripping apart, sinew by sinew. And just when he thought he was going to lose his leg entirely, the horse came to a stop.

He smells a burning fire smoldering to coals. There are two other horses tethered at this makeshift camp. Two other dark figures rising from where they sat by the fire to take stock of their newest addition.

"He's bleeding," one states. Though he cannot see faces, the voice sounds feminine. He also notices that despite her words, she does not sound concerned.

The woman from the bar unties his ankle. Jackal quickly collects himself. His leg hurts with every movement, bone still disconnected. His chest aches, his skin feels raw, yet still he wills himself to move.

"Drink up, girls." She grabs him by his hair, drags him a little bit closer to the campfire before letting him fall prone again. "Though I must warn you, this one has been drinking."

"Aren't you going to drink, Nisha?" the other asks. Nisha mounts her horse, shakes her head.

"I have business to take care of," Nisha answers, her horse begins to trot in place. "Mabel...Clem...Don't drink too much. I need him alive." The horse gallops, ferrying her away.

Jackal reaches for his revolver. He is still soggy from the alcohol, disoriented from the dragging, but this is his last hope for freedom. He draws, fires two shots just as the women turn back towards him. He watches as the shots rip into their torsos, blood bursting from the entry spot. He can't believe his luck.

Jackal stands, shaky, like a newborn calf. Any weight put on his leg hurts horrifically. He makes no progress towards the two other horses before he notices the women still close in on him. They are bleeding, yes, but otherwise unaffected by the gunshots.

"W-what?" His eyes squint, as if he were just not seeing things right. Maybe he is higher than he originally thought.

They speed towards him, nearly jumping from one spot to the other, like he had seen Nisha do. The one named Mabel grabs him by the hair. The other, Clem, digs her fingers into his dislocated leg. Jackal cries out in pain. He feels his revolver leave his hand as one of them takes it from his pain-weakened grasp.

"It's alright. We'll take care of you," Clem says. Jackal's vision is marred by the flaring pain. She leans into his neck. He thinks she might kiss it, but instead he feels a sharp pain cutting into his skin.

"Ah!"

"Shh..." Mabel hushes him.

His eyes move wildly about him, unable to comprehend, unable to see a way out of the trap. He feels added pressure to the wound and realizes that she is sucking, pulling out more blood. Jackal groans in discomfort. He wants it to end. His hand twitches as he remains held by both women, now weaponless and severely weakened. He would not underestimate them again.

Clem's lips are red and bloody. She laps the extra from them, like a cat after drinking milk. "Nisha was right. A bit boozy, but it does in a pinch."

Mabel is already eager and reaching for him for her turn. "I've gone hungry long enough, I don't care what it tastes like!" She latches on to the same wound Clem bit into him, with a new pressure that earns a noise from Jackal.

"What's...wrong with you!?" Jackal gasps out, eyes meeting with Clem's, as she watches her partner drain him.

"Are you just figuring it out now?" Clem answers. The smile she gives him is wicked. Mabel drinks with much more enthusiasm. He can almost feel the blood being pulled from his veins. Excess blood drips from around her mouth, dripping hot down his neck and onto his shirt. He groans again. He is starting to feel a little lightheaded. "She's new. Don't mind her," he hears Clem say, though that made just about as much sense as everything else did. He feels a heaviness in his head. Clem says something else but he can't make out her words. The night grows darker. The fire seems nonexistent now. Gravity is calling him back to the ground, and as Mabel releases her hold on him, he obeys.

***

The blood on his face is crusted and dry by the time he comes to. His head feels delicate, swollen and bruised. Like the worst hangover combined with a pair of invisible hands clapping over his ears. He longs for numbness, for sleep, but the sun shines relentlessly on his face, pressing through closed eyelids.

Jackal was used to sleeping outdoors and in the desert. He preferred it to enclosed shelters. Even the most innocent of rooms could remind him of a cage. The one they had put him in when he was very little. Freedom looked like waves of sand interrupted by sparse vegetation and extending on towards infinity.

He blinks in the oppressive sun. His tongue, a rough and dry thing inside his mouth. He attempts to roll over but is stopped by the rough braiding of rope around his wrists, securing them together. His head seems to be the only thing he can move. All he is able to do is pan between the oppressive sun and the wooden chair he is strapped to.

How did a chair get in the middle of fuck-knows nowhere?

His company offers a clue. Two figures, covered from head to toe in dark garments. Their faces are shadowed beneath the wide brims of their hats, but Jackal has a guess. It must be those two women: Clem and Mabel - the ones who drank his blood. Or was that just a bad trip?

"What do you want with me?" he croaks the words out. Their expressions remain hidden.

"Nisha told us to watch you."

"And then what?"

They turn to look at each other. Jackal imagines a smile forming in each dark abyss where a face should be. They refuse to answer.

Even the slightest movement makes his leg hurt. His skin itches with sand and blood, small abrasions from being dragged. His nose simultaneously numb and yet still throbbing in pain.

"Can I at least have some water?" he asks.

"No you can not." He recognizes the voice to be Clem's. He can hear the smile in her tone.

"You're not the only one who's thirsty!" Mabel hisses at him. She circles him, like a vulture.

"You just fed last night," Clem reminds her. "And Nisha said-"

"To hell with Nisha!" Mabel growls. She grabs Jackal's head from behind, pulling it back towards her. Jackal grunts, his neck bent to its limits. The sun continues to beat down into his eyes. "Food is food! I don't care what he did to Nisha! She already got all his money!" She adds pressure onto his strained neck. He anticipates the quick snap. Maybe then it'd all be over. Better a quick death than being kept alive for further abuse.

"That's enough, Mabel!" Nisha scolds, seemingly materializing from thin air.

Mabel releases her hold. Jackal lets his head fall forward. It still hurts from the strain.

"I don't mess with your targets and you don't mess with mine," Nisha reminds Mabel.

"Sorry Ma'am," Mabel shies away. He can hear the poison in her words, as if submitting to Nisha was eating her alive. "New Blood, hunger s'all."

"You two are dismissed," Nisha says. She stands in front of Jackal, wearing the same dark, flowy garments the other two women were wearing. "How are you holdin' up?"

"Could use some water."

She laughs. "I bet you could." She begins to walk away from him.

"You got your money!" he calls to her. "And my gun. Let's call that even."

She clicks her tongue at him. Suddenly she's standing before him again, holding his face in her hand. His breath catches. She has red eyes, just like the other two. He's realized by now some sort of devil's play is at work here. "Cheatin' is a crime..." Her head cocks. "I don't believe I got your name."

"Jackal."

"Very well, Dog. I'll be back when you've learned your lesson."

"Wait!" Jackal calls out again, but he's staring at an empty patch of sand. The wind carries dust as it blows. The breeze gives him no respite from the heat. Sweat mingles with his hair, drips down his face, sticks his shirt to his back.

His throat is dry. Swallowing hurts. His lips are cracked. Delicate tissue within his nostril splits, blood that he can't spare drips down his face.

Jackal screams. It's all that he can do. No one is around to hear him, but he hollers and wails until his lungs feel as if they are folding in on themselves. Mabel should have just killed him. This death is unmercifully slow.

There is no more noise left in him. He can not seem to make tears, though he wants to cry. Instead, he hangs his head in defeat, catching his breath.

He flails against his bindings. The rope digs into his wrists, but it's much friendlier than what else he has been through as of late. The sand gives under the chair, tipping. He collides with sand, impact resonating through his aching body. His mouth is so dry it doesn't even feel like a mouth anymore.

He's tired and panting. Jackal closes his eyes. The sunlight still persists through. He wishes he could fall into eternal sleep.

The sand before him crunches. Shadows relieve him of the sun for a moment. Jackal peels an eye open. How long had Nisha been away for? She holds a canteen.

"W-water?" Jackal asks. She kicks him in the ribcage. "Please! Please, I'll...die." She leans down, grabs him by the collar and is able to right him and the chair with a single arm.

She unscrews the canteen. "Drink. Without wasting a drop," she commands. He opens his dry and blistered lips, waiting for the touch of metal against them as she brings the canteen close. She has to hold it for him, still tied up. She tips it and he accepts the liquid with gratitude, hungrily gulping it down. It washes over his tongue and is already down his throat before the taste hits him. The consistency was thicker than he expected, but water was water, except this wasn't. There was a distinct bitter taste of iron. Jackal gags. The canteen still empties out into his mouth. He's choking against the stream, unwillingly imbibing more despite his protests. She doesn't stop until it's empty Half of it had spilled onto his shirt and pants, soaking in and feeling sticky against his skin. Jackal gags again once she pulls the canteen away. He spits out what is left in his mouth. It is dark and red against the sand.

He feels like he can't breathe, and not just because she almost made him drown in it, but because he knows what it is, yet he can't comprehend it. She tricked him. Tricked him into drinking blood.

Black spots bloom in his vision. Everything goes dark.

He wakes in the night, still bound to the chair. There is a campfire with two figures seated around it. Clem and Mabel keeping watch. Watch for what?

His mouth is an empty canyon and he wants to ask for water but is afraid to catch their attention.

Where is Nisha and what has she planned for him next?

The night air is far colder than it has been the previous nights. Teeth chatter in his skull. Hands shake against their restraints. He is covered in a sweat and groans in a new sort of discomfort.

The women snap to attention, grinning their coyote smiles as they press in on him.

"Awake now, Doggy?"

He can't distinguish the two from each other. The world spins on its axis and it's a dizzying ride like a spooked horse.

"What have you done to me?" he moans. He wants to spill his guts along with his words. His body has become his worst enemy. Everything feels so terribly wrong.

His weighted eyelids fall shut and when they open again, the sun is rising. The sickness is passing. No longer does he feel the ache in his hip nor the swelling of his broken nose. He is miraculously a new man and Jackal begins to suspect the past few nights were all a drunken nightmare.

The first touch of the sun is hot, but he is caught up in his sudden gratitude for life he barely notices. But it steadily becomes a more demanding presence as the sun gradually climbs. The skin on his knuckles itches with the first signs of sunburn. He isn't surprised. He has been left out to dry in the sun for the past few days with only nightfall to relieve him. He scratches his thumbnail against the itch and skin peels off in a white husk. He feels his cheeks tighten and peel. His shoulders. His arms. Every inch of exposed skin transforming under the sun's rays.

The discomfort eases into pain as toughened skin chips away to reveal pink sensitive skin underneath. It burns as if a hot brand were pressed to his shoulders and back. He grits his teeth, clenching his fists.

By high noon, his blood feels like it is boiling inside of his veins. His skin is bright red like the skin of an apple, though warped in blisters that form and then pop.

Despite the pain, he finds the rage and strength to fight against his restraints. The rope cuts through his skin like a hot knife through butter. He drowns out all senses, threatening to break his bones as he pulls against the wood of the chair. He manages to throw his weight back on the chair hard enough the wood snaps and collapses. He lays supine under the sun, splinters of wood poking into his skin.

The woman dressed in black appears in front of him, offering him shade under her large, brimmed hat.

"I wondered how long it'd take you to figure it out," Nisha says. Beyond her face, he sees the two other women. "Get him, girls."

They close in on him. His body has become strange to himself, and so his movement is uncoordinated as he scrambles to flee. Mabel and Clem catch him, gripping the tortured skin of his arms. He yields under the pain and with little contest, he is thrown into the back of a carriage and sealed inside.

The shade is so delicious he pays no mind to the cage he is put in. The cab rocks as the horses begin to pull it along. Jackal analyzes his skin as it transforms in reverse. Wounded skin pulls together until it closes. Redness returns to sun-kissed brown. Blisters flatten into valleys.

What have they done to him? What will they do to him next?

The panic begins to crawl up his throat. The six walls of his container press in on him. Of course he tries the door over and over again. It jiggles, but something has it barred. The carriage continues to rock. He hears no voices but knows the wicked women steer him to his unknown destination and towards new horrors.

Jackal can't breathe. There are no windows. He loses trust in gravity and begins to question if down is really down or is it perhaps up? All logic in the world has been subverted in the past few days, there is no belief he still holds to be true.

All physical pain from his body is gone, magically healed away. He has nothing to focus on besides, perhaps, the newfound hunger tearing at his throat. Odd that he is no longer thirsting for water when he has had none in far too long.

The carriage halt is sudden. He is left alone for some time. He thrusts his shoulder against the wall and the whole vehicle sways under the effort. He tries again and again until he hears a crack and a sharp pain shoots through his shoulder. Jackal curls in on himself, focusing on the pain rather than the smallness of his cage.

When the door opens, he is subdued like a child after a tantrum. He looks towards the sunlight pouring in and almost can't believe his window of opportunity for freedom. His shoulder still aches as he crawls towards the open door. No black shrouded women in sight. The sun would burn him, but it would be brief before he'd find shade again. He is free. He is free!

Jackal leaps from his cage, grinning as luck spun in his favor once more. He finds himself in the same town where he cheated Nisha at cards. He is so happy he wants to grab the nearest person and kiss them. There, a man in proper garb stands. Jackal rushes to him, holding his arms between his hands. A person! A real person and not a wicked blood sucker! The man's eyes widen. Jackal is still grinning as his mind processes in slow motion the knife tracing along the man's cheek, the crimson line it draws as blood beads. Nisha stands behind the man, smiling as she disappears behind the swing doors of the saloon.

Something animalistic takes over in Jackal. Feast. Feast. Feast, the wilderness inside him says, and then he is biting the bleeding man, ripping chunks of his flesh from his face. His nails dig into the soft flesh of the man's torso. He has him pinned to the ground and is devouring him piece by piece as a crowd forms around him.

Once his starvation is sated, Jackal meets their collective gaze and knows he has been set up.

***

For one beautiful day, he is safe from the sun and Nisha alike, tucked away behind bars. For once, the cage feels like sanctuary. Jackal finally comes to terms with what happened to him. The damned woman took his soul and now he was a blood craving creature of the night, the kind which cowboys traded stories about over whiskey. Cattle would go missing in the night, turning up drained of every last drop of liquid life and not even flies would touch the corpses.

Just to confirm his theory, he climbed to the high barred window and stuck his hand out. Within moments, the itching began.

So it wasn't just dehydration the other day. The sun was now his enemy.

"Get down from there!" the sheriff clangs at his bars with the butt of his revolver. "No use trying to escape."

"Wouldn't dream of it." Jackal settles back onto the hard mattress, crossing his ankles. The sheriff eyes his dinner left untouched since yesterday. The bread turned into a stale, hard shell.

"You're entitled to a last meal," the sheriff says.

"Don't need one," Jackal says, his stomach full of slaughter. The rich man was his final meal. He has no need for the grub of the mortal. "Help yourself."

The sheriff initially hesitates, but within an hour, he's munching on the clearly undesired food.

"You seem decent. Why'd you do it?" the sheriff asks.

Jackal debates telling the truth. He was set up. Or close to the truth. Long days lost in the desert drove him to madness. He has the inkling he might be able to sway the sheriff. In the short time before, he would use his silver tongue to get out of most trouble. Now, he thinks himself lucky to finally be out of Nisha's reach.

At sunset, the preacher arrives and blesses his damned soul. His wrists are bound in rope and his cell is unlocked. An audience of all ages is already gathered at the gallows. Many had witnessed his murderous rampage and now are hungry for justice. They watch him ascend the stairs, his skin prickling in the last rays of sunlight on his final day. Jackal holds his head high as he takes position over the trap door. Only death can save him now. His eyes meet the silver dollar moon in the sky as the rope is laid around his neck by the sheriff. He tightens the rope until it's snug, like a lover's embrace.

"Any last words?"

The desert wind whispers in his ear. Suddenly he notices the black garbed figure at the back of the crowd. Jackal grins and then reaches for the lever himself. The floor drops from underneath him with a loud mechanical clang and he is falling and yet it feels like flying.

His head yanks back and his neck snaps. He loses feeling in his fingertips and toes. His body swings with inertia. He has no control over his body, but yet remains fully conscious as he dangles before the cheering crowd. His eyes stare blankly at brittle bush.

The sound of the crowd dwindles as darkness falls, and he knows it's only because they've lost interest and wandered off to the saloon for drinks. Jackal is only beginning to fear being buried alive when someone walks into his line of vision. She pulls the black bandana down from her face and allows him to get a good look at her.

Nisha. She knew this would happen. That he can't die. Yet she allowed him to experience death. She smiles and she has teeth like a viper's.

"Cut him down, girls," Nisha orders.

Something saws at his rope and he falls, this time into Nisha's open arms. She loosens and removes the rope from his neck and then holds him close. "You're mine now, don't you ever forget," Nisha hisses into his ear. His stomach drops. He thinks she might kiss him with the way she holds his head between her hands, but she snaps his neck back into place. It aches for a moment, then feeling begins returning to his limbs and he knows he will fully heal in time, only for Nisha to break him again.

About the Author
Robin Rose Graves' work has previously appeared in 100 Foot Crow, Dark Matter Magazine and Simultaneous Times Podcast among other publications. Her first book comes out from Graveside Press in 2025.

Shadows in the Light

Todd Sullivan

CW: Character death, terminally ill parent

Whumpee: Man, Woman, Whumper: Man, Caretaker: Man, Woman

Ossie stood in the shadows of his sister's porch, his hand raised to ring the bell. Seconds passed into minutes, and only when the minutes had matured into an hour did Ossie finally stir. He tapped the faintly glowing button, and a melodious chord filled the house.

"Who could be here this time of night?"

His younger sister, Ruby, muttered the question on the second floor. Ossie still heard it outside, just as he heard his mother's labored breathing in her bedroom. The effort of each desperate breath made Ossie's heart constrict with grief. She had been healthy, vibrant in her early 60s when he left home to move into the city. He had stayed away too long, but he'd been given no choice by the Tribe that had adopted him one dark night in an even darker club in midtown Atlanta.

Through the glass panes of the front door, he saw lights flare to life upstairs and flow down to the living room. Ossie picked up the sound of hinges creaking and Ruby in socks stepping across the floorboards of the loft. She paused by the upstairs windows, and Ossie looked up to see her peeking down at him. Their eyes met, and he heard her sharp gasp.

"Ossie?" she whispered. With his new ears, it was as if she yelled his name.

The downstairs lights blinked on, then the porch lights. Ossie squinted against the sudden glare and resisted the urge to put on his sunglasses. He meditated instead as his sister came downstairs. Using his training, he adjusted his mind to dampen the extreme sensations his new body experienced. He must appear human to his sister. She couldn't discover that he had changed—that he was an animated corpse only pretending to be human—or his clan would kill his little sister to keep their existence secret.

Ruby's shadow preceded her down the stairs. She touched the bannister as she turned and hesitated a moment before continuing to the front door. Her gaze never faltered from his face. She looked older than he remembered, though she was only nineteen. The edges of her eyes showed tiny wrinkles when before they had been smooth with youth, and her twists were frazzled at the ends and loose at the top. Ruby had always attracted his friends, which drove him crazy. He would threaten anyone who flirted or paid her too much attention. She would tease him about it, but Ossie knew guys and the desires that drove them, and he didn't want his little sister to have anything to do with it.

"Ossie?" She said his name quietly to herself as she approached the door, yet still he heard it. He refrained from reading her thoughts, but he couldn't block the waves of resentment washing off of her and submerging him in her anger.

She was not happy to see him.

He wanted to put her at ease, so he smiled. He must have done it wrong, as she abruptly paused, distaste sweeping her features. Ossie tried to rearrange the upward tilt of his lips, the feeling unnatural even to him. He hadn't made the gesture in years, not since joining the Tribe. In that time, he'd committed such inhuman, monstrous acts for the ecstatic high he absorbed from those he terrified. The damned no longer smiled easily after causing so much suffering to the living.

Maybe his attempt to reassure her worked; maybe his presence there so late at night simply left her curious. She continued forward until she stood at the locked door, but she made no move to unlock it.

"Ruby. You going to let me in?"

She took longer to consider the question than he liked, and he feared she would turn him away. Upstairs, their mother moaned, long and low like a wounded animal slipping away from her mortal coils. He had to see her. He would not be refused. Yet would he force his way past his sister who already hated him?

"Ruby," he tried again, "it's kind of cold out here. You planning on letting your brother freeze to death on your porch?"

"So now I got an older brother again?" She said this loud enough that even a normal human would hear the reproach directed at him through the glass panes. After a few more moments, she reached out and turned the lock. She stepped back and opened the door just wide enough so that he could slink in. They stood face to face, he taller than her by two feet. When they were younger, she used to summon him to get things she wanted out of cabinets and down from shelves. Sometimes he would complain, but often he enjoyed helping his little sister, who would look up at him with those soft brown eyes, her tiny hands outstretched.

Those same eyes were narrowed now, their roles reversed this night. He needed to ask her for something, and he wasn't sure if she was going to give it to him.

"Don't make a lot of noise," she warned as she closed the door behind them. Ossie almost laughed at that. He moved without sound when he travelled with his clan hunting their human prey.

Ossie went into the living room. It looked the same but smelled differently. The acidic aroma of disinfectant perfumed the counters and tabletops. Mingled in that was the smell of medicine and sickness. His mother had vomited recently, and soiled clothes ran through the washer in the laundry closet next to the kitchen.

"Why you here, Ossie?" Ruby asked. She went to the electric fireplace and flipped the switch to bring the dark hearth to crackling life. She sat down in the chair beside it and stared at him as the room warmed.

"I'm here to see momma."

Ruby gave him a brittle laugh. "Come to see her before the funeral, huh? I thought you'd wait a little longer than that, maybe when we were already at the cemetery lowering her coffin into the ground."

Ossie stared at the flickering flames, wishing he had a shield for his sister's venom. His body could take extreme damage, physical blows that would kill any human. Getting here tonight had been proof of that. Each clan in the Tribe had a leader whose role was to ensure that lesser members like Ossie didn't falter from the righteous path of darkness. The Tribe didn't want him weakening and doing something stupid like trying to see family again. For clan members, brothers and sisters, mothers and fathers, cousins, aunts, and uncles, no longer existed. Ossie's new reality revolved only around one of the clans that made up the Tribe.

And of course, the hunt and the blood, the need to create terror that filled him with ecstasy.

"Is momma awake?" he glanced upstairs. He already knew the answer, could tell from her irregular breathing that she wasn't asleep.

Ruby leaned back into the chair cushion, incredulous. "You're serious, aren't you? You really came to see momma right before she passed away."

"I wanted to come sooner, Ruby," he said.

His little sister laughed. "You're just in the city, Ossie. I called you a year ago when momma found out about her cancer, and you sent back a single message: Busy." Her fingers curled around the arms of the chair. "Fucking busy!"

To be fair, the message had been a few words longer than that. Ossie remembered the night well. The Tribe had taken his old phone the night he joined, but his sister had called him over a messenger app that he'd downloaded on another phone he'd stolen from one of their victims. He'd wanted to call Ruby without his clan discovering, but the opportunity never arose. Then one day, Ruby left a recording telling him that their mom had been diagnosed with Stage 3 cancer. Ossie had wanted to rush right home, but he couldn't escape the constant presence of their leader. When he was sure no one would see, he had sent her back the message: Talk to you later, busy now.

He had hated doing it, but he'd wanted to protect her from the truth. He knew the text would upset her. Until tonight, standing under the withering assault of the rage that whirled off her with a palpable force, he hadn't understood how much.

The fire warmed the room, and Ruby said, "You can take off your jacket, you know."

Instinctively, Ossie zipped the leather jacket up further. It hadn't belonged to him until an hour earlier when he'd taken it from the human whose car he had stolen. He hadn't wanted to kill the man, but he'd had no choice. He'd made a desperate escape from his clan as they hunted a young college couple downtown. It had only taken a second for the members to realize what he was doing, and they'd left their prey to dash after him. Their leader carried a machete, the only one of them allowed to be armed, and he'd slashed out at Ossie with the sharp blade. The blow would have severed his torso had it landed. Ossie had twisted as the blade cleaved through the air, evading the worse of the attack. The machete sliced through his underarm, nicking his torso but leaving him mobile.

Blood gushed down his side when he fell from the roof of a convenience store. He landed on his knees in front of a startled human climbing into his car. Ossie grabbed the man and tore into his neck even as he shoved him inside. He started the car and drove off into oncoming traffic, leaving his clan behind.

Ossie's dead body had been busy healing the wound, but his shirt was stained red. The man had had a black leather jacket in the backseat of his car, and Ossie had taken it up when he dumped the vehicle on the side of the highway. It hid the blood as long as it remained zipped. He couldn't let his sister see or she would ask questions. He couldn't remain here long. His clan was still hunting for him, and he couldn't let them find him here.

"I have to go soon," Ossie said, putting his hands in his jacket pockets. "I can only stay for a moment."

His sister hissed, "Get out!" She leapt from the chair. "Why did you come all this way to act like this? You're not needed, Ossie, and you're not wanted here!"

"Ruby," he began, but she cut him off, grabbing his wrist.

"Leave!" She tried to yank him to the door. Ossie didn't allow his body to move, and Ruby almost toppled over as she jerked back into him.

"Ruby." He attempted to make his voice sound gentle, but it came out in a low growl. As a member of the Tribe, he had tortured so many humans to the brink of death. Clans seldom killed. Prey left alive caused less interest from investigating police, and no one believed wild tales of monsters hunting the night. At the convenience store this evening, it had been different. Ossie had been desperate. Nothing made Tribe members more dangerous to humans than when they were left without options.

"I'm not going anywhere," he firmly told Rudy, who still tugged at his arm. "You can't make me leave until I see momma."

She slapped him, hard, across the face. The blow made her wince in pain as her palm made contact with his cold flesh. She stepped away and clutched her hand to her chest, her eyes wet. "Why don't you just go?"

The first tear to slide down her cheek opened the flower of time. Ossie felt as if he tilted forward and fell past this moment with his sister to the time when he had first moved into his own apartment in the city. He'd been twenty then, Ruby only sixteen. He'd packed his old Honda with everything from his room, and she'd watched him silently as he sat with their mother talking about the classes he would be taking and the barista job he had gotten. Before he left, Ruby asked him if he'd visit often, and he'd said of course, he was only an hour away.

Ossie continued to descend through the petals of time to when their parents had divorced. He'd been in high school. Their parents had fought constantly over money back then, or the lack thereof. Ossie used to let Ruby have the lion's share of what little food their mom prepared for them. It wasn't until their mother got a job at the chemical plant that that their financial situation reversed, and they moved into the two-story house they lived in now.

Further down into the bud Ossie tumbled, to summer days when he and Ruby played in the park where neighborhood boys smoked pot, their stares following eleven-year-old Ruby. They made Ossie overprotective of his little sister, and he used to have her change into his bigger clothes with a cap on her twists to hide her figure from the male gaze.

Still further he slid down the stem of time to when he and his little sister sat strapped in car seats as their parents drove them to visit distant relatives, or to the beach or the zoo. Ruby always asked Ossie to tell her stories, about anything, about nothing. The sound of his voice seemed to comfort her as the adult world passed outside the car windows.

Ossie hit the stems at the bottom of time and bounced back out again into this present moment to see his sister's tears glowing orange in the firelight. He had to say something to make her understand, and all that was left to him was the truth.

"Ruby," he said, "I'm a vampire."

He studied Rudy's face, a grimace twisting her lips.

"Momma always used to make sure we stayed away from the druggies," she said. "Those losers who tried to sell us shit in our old neighborhood. You remember those guys hanging out on the corners. You're the one that used to make sure none of them came around me."

Her voice wavered, her tears pattering the wooden floorboards. "But when you disappeared for so long in the city, I figured that's what happened to you. Out there in midtown with all those nightclubs and party people. I once tried to tell momma, but she wouldn't believe it. What are you on right now, Ossie? Acid? Coke? God! Are you some kind of crackhead now?"

"Ruby," Ossie said again, "I'm a vampire." He reached up, took the zipper between his thumb and forefinger, and slowly unzipped it. His sister followed the movement, and when her eyes widened, he knew she saw the bloodstained shirt.

She frowned with disgust. "Ossie, you really lost your mind, haven't you? You think I'm going to let you see momma when you come here this time of night bleeding and high?" Worry crinkled her brow. "You joined some kind of gang, didn't you? What trouble are you bringing this way?" She backed away to the phone on the counter. "I don't want to call the cops, Ossie, and you don't want me to call the cops. You know they're liable to shoot you before they arrest you. Don't break momma's heart, just go away. Now!"

Before Ossie could respond, the front door shattered. A dozen shadows exploded into the room, and Ruby screamed. One of the shades darted at her, but Ossie moved faster. With a roar, he launched forward, his fist connecting with the attacker's jaw and flinging him through the wall with a crash and back out into the cold night. He pushed Ruby behind him and prepared for the onslaught from his clan.

The members had taken positions along the walls. A couple crouched upside down on the kitchen ceiling. Altogether there were twelve, and Ossie made thirteen, a sacred number in the Tribe. The leader stood before him, his thick locks tumbling down his shoulders, his eyes glowing bright red, his incisors extended.

"Ossie," he said, his voice a deep baritone filled with menace, "why did you turn your back on the clan?"

"I came here to see my mom," Ossie said, keeping track of each vampire, watching for the slightest move. He couldn't let them separate Ruby from him, couldn't bare to watch what they'd do to her. Screaming victims intoxicated the Tribe. He had to do all in his power to protect his little sister, but how could he get past all twelve of them?

"You lost your momma when you joined the clan, Ossie," the leader said. "You knew the price when you took the vow and drank from the bloodline of Father Adam flowing in our veins."

Behind him, Ruby whimpered. The shadows surrounding the vampires swirled with life of its own.

"I must be dreaming," she whispered. "This is some kind of nightmare."

"We are some kind of nightmare, human," the leader replied, his bright red eyes streaking the darkness shifting around him. "And your foolish brother has dragged you into the heart of darkness."

"Let her live," Ossie said, eyes darting from one member to the next as he sensed them gathering their power to strike. "Do whatever you want to me, but let her live."

Even as Ossie said it, he knew what the response would be. His clan members laughed, and the leader's lips twisted with a wicked turn of his lips.

"You've sinned against the Tribe, Ossie, revealing our existence to a mortal and breaking our highest law. The punishment for her is a slow death to invigorate the clan. The penalty for you is penance for your transgression." The leader stepped forward. "Hand over your sister so that we may spill her organs and share her blood amongst clan. Then you will come with us back to the temple and pray to Caine and Abel for forgiveness."

Ossie bared his fangs, a desperate growl rumbling in his chest.

"Is this real?" Ruby's terror rose from her to perfume the air. "This can't be real."

The leader focused on Ruby with his crimson gaze. "Our reality is divine, human, and beyond your mortal comprehension." To Ossie, he said, "She's pretty. She'll make grand entertainment for the Tribe. Her pleas for mercy will be music, her screams of pain a symphony."

They had run out of time. Ossie had to do something, anything, no matter how futile. He tensed, preparing to throw himself forward and fight, when a light touch on his shoulder made him freeze.

"I get it now, Ossie." Ruby's voice was broken through sobs. "Why you couldn't come home. I get it now, and I'm sorry."

Forgiveness. After all Ossie had done to humans since he joined the clan, to have one forgive him now despite his many sins ignited a spark that burst into a flame. He gazed at his clan members and saw that they were but shadows in the light.

Ossie spun around, wrapped his arm around Ruby's waist and charged forward. He slammed his shoulder into the leader, knocking him across the room, and flew upstairs. Flinging open his mother's bedroom door, he sat Ruby on the bed, bent down, kissed his mom on the cheek, then spun as the clan burst into the room and surrounded him and his family.

"Thank you, Ruby," he said, a fire igniting in the darkness that had existed inside of his soul for too long now. "Your brother is back, and he'll protect you again."

Until the end.

About the Author

Todd Sullivan taught English as a Second Language in South Korea and Taiwan for sixteen years. His fiction, poetry, and non-fiction have been published internationally. He was listed on the preliminary ballot for the Bram Stoker's Awards in 2018, and was nominated for a Pushcart Prize for poetry and fiction in 2023.

Tunnels of Sin

C. W. Stevenson

CW: Character death, drugs, addiction, reference to death of a child
Whumpee: Man, Whumper: Man, Caretaker: Man

"God, grant me the serenity to accept the things I cannot change, the courage to change the things I can, and the wisdom to know the difference."

John was relieved when the two addicts on either side of him mumbled the closing of the Serenity Prayer. He'd made a mistake coming here, thinking it'd help. It never did.

Carol, the woman to his left, gave him a sad smile as the others turned to get more coffee or left.

"You okay, hon? You're pale as a ghost!"

"Just tired," John lied.

"Well, you go rest. We hope to see you back. Maybe next time you'll share something with the group? It's good to talk. We've all been where you are now."

Turning to leave, John said over his shoulder, "Yeah, yeah maybe. So long."

Outside, the glow from the Las Vegas strip shone bright as dusk turned to darkness. John ambled down the sidewalk contemplating his choices. Coming to the meeting had been an act of desperation. He'd emerged from the tunnels he called home that evening to buy some new socks—his only other pair without holes had been washed away in last night's flood, along with most everything else. After returning from the shelter, he and the others had been staying at throughout the storm, he'd found that at least his chair had survived.

God he was hungry. It'd been days since his last decent meal, and the free coffee the local N.A. provided wouldn't cut it.

He bought some new socks, AA batteries, and a box of peanut butter crackers with the rest of his cash. Munching on one of the packs of crackers on his way back to the tunnels, he suddenly doubled over.

"Almost back," he muttered in pain to himself and stood upright. "Almost home."

A limo came to a halt and someone rolled the windows down. John was just beginning to cross the street when the group of drunken females inside yelled after him.

"Got some coke?" one asked.

"C'mon!" another said.

Sending them a sideways sneer, John kept walking, ignoring the slew of insults coming from the limo. He was used to it, as were his neighbors. There were good folk down there. In fact, he'd met some of the most creative minds down in the underground community. Of course, one had to be inventive to live in the darkness, having no source of clean water or electricity.

He was getting close now.

Cutting through a gap in the fence, he scrambled down the rusty ladder into the canal and its dank standing water. Still clutching his stomach, he forced his way toward the entrance.

If someone had to categorize it, these were one of the many "meth tunnels". John had never touched the stuff.

Down here, few stayed for long because floods cleaned house a few times each summer. Addicts also tended to drift from tunnel to tunnel. Only a durable few stayed in this span of tunnels for more than a year or two. So, it suited him. It was quiet, save for the squeaking of rats and the occasional tweaker making a ruckus.

Most people kept to themselves, but those who'd been here for a while took care of one another.

Hob, an obese one-legged veteran of Operation Desert Storm, had been staying down in the tunnels for twelve years. He'd kicked his addiction but found he couldn't tolerate living amongst the "normies" of society. Next to Hob, John was the second longest permanent resident.

Seven years in this section. He'd been underground for far longer. It had gone by in the blink of an eye. Time was like that.

He was starting to sweat now. The pain in his stomach was screaming at him to satisfy his cravings. Trying to keep his composure, John sidestepped to avoid the two newcomers. One grabbed his arm.

"Hey, it flooded last night," the young man said through his remaining teeth. The rotting stench of meth mouth hit John square in the face.

"No matter, it'll have dried by now, I live here. Now let go of my arm," John growled.

The other man flicked a cigarette to the ground and got in John's face.

"Say," he began, "what you got in the bag?"

"If I tell you, I'll have to kill you," John said, and jerked his head down at the hand still gripping his arm. "I'm not going to repeat myself."

Without breaking his gaze, he lifted his hand as if to surrender. "Calm down buddy, we was just askin' a question."

"Mm-hmm," John mumbled and continued on his way, listening for any footsteps close behind.

None followed him into the darkness.

***

"Hold up John, I wanted to say thanks!" Hob wheeled himself through a deep puddle to shake his hand.

"Anytime," John replied. "Didn't want you to run out of light in your torch. Damn though, batteries are costing an arm and a leg nowadays."

"Well, they can't have my other'n."

Both men laughed.

Hob's smile soon disappeared. "You alright, man?"

"No," John said, shaking his head slowly. He clutched at his stomach.

"Ah, that. Well, there's one thing that can fix that."

"No," John repeated.

Throwing up his hands, Hob said, "Had to try," then changed the subject. "Say, you talk to them boys? They still out front?"

"Yep, I did. I was going to tell you to be careful with them wandering about. Thought they were about to try and knife me over some batteries and crackers."

"Mary-Anne said they took a pass at her, but she fought'em off."

"I'll have a word with them tonight."

"Shit, coz this gawdamned flood... I won't have my alarm system up until tomorrow."

Hob had constructed one of his "alarm systems" for him too, not that John needed it, it was just something for Hob to do, to feel useful—all it required was some sort of thick thread and some cans or bottles. It was an early warning system for minimalists, but damned if it didn't work.

"Don't worry, I'll take care of it," John said.

Leaving the old-timer, he wandered down the tunnel further.

With hundreds of miles crisscrossing under the city, the tunnels weren't just a part of the sewer system—but abandoned mineshafts, and unused service routes. John knew them all. Seven years was only the time he'd spent in *this* section.

Tossing Mary-Anne a pack of peanut butter crackers, she grunted her thanks and closed her eyes. She was still stoned.

John kept walking, the squeaking of the rodents his only company now. He climbed a short ladder to the large space he called home. Using a dry shirt from an old toolbox he used as a storage container, he sopped up the remaining droplets of water.

Taking a crate with him, John climbed back down the ladder and began collecting rats.

***

They'd squirm at first, but John made short work of them. Quick and painless, that was his way. Humans didn't give rodents enough credit for how intelligent they could be. Hell, he'd kept some as pets that might be smarter than a few people he knew. And they had their own personalities. So, he snapped their necks, one after the other.

Call it population control, but the others didn't complain. John was providing them with a service.

Taking the crate back up with him to his room, John sat in the La-Z-Boy recliner he'd set up for himself and leaned back. Starting with the fresher rats on top, he sucked them all dry.

***

John dreamed of long ago, when he'd gone by a different name, had lived in a different land. The memory was more than any physical pain he could endure. He and his son had discovered their village in the Congo razed to the ground, and his youngest son dead on the pile with the others near modern-day Kolwezi. Today, his once remote home was being run rampant with cobalt mines and the greedy corporations who needed the precious ores of heterogenite to be refined so they may keep producing lithium-ion batteries.

Long dead was his family. Everyone he knew. The man he once was, gone forever. He'd lived a different life since. A darker one. But then everything was dark in the tunnels.

John woke to the sound of raised voices echoing down the length of the tunnel.

He hadn't meant to fall asleep on the chair, but sometimes after a meal it just happened. In a panic, John shot up from the chair, spilling several dead rats he'd neglected to place back in the crate in his half-starved state of being.

Hob.

With blinding speed, he made it to Hob's campsite—as many of them referred to their spaces. Hob's tent had been torn and the cardboard boxes filled with useless trinkets the old man had kept lay strewn about on the damp floor.

On the ground, Hob struggled to flip his wheelchair upright. He had a bloody nose.

After helping Hob into the chair, John growled, "Where are they?"

His anger must've frightened the old man because Hob's voice shook as he spoke. "Took C-Route to Dominic's camp."

John didn't bother with a reply, he just needed to get away. Hob's blood was too enticing, and the rats had done little to sate his hunger. It was why he frequented meetings for addicts of all kinds. The occasional human was fine, considering they were one of the undesirables in the tunnels no one would be missing. But too many too often would bring about questions, threatening his very way of life. John couldn't have that. He was a slave to his addiction, like so many others.

Speeding through the tunnel down the path he and the others had dubbed C-Route for its eventual connection near Caesars Palace, John picked up their scent. There was no escaping him, not in this ravenous state, driven by anger and out for blood. He'd stalked this city and its underground for decades. And before that, its canyons of desert, and hills, thinking one day he'd have the courage to step out into the sun and end it all once and for all. When the tunnels came, he'd found purpose. No one left or entered the darkness without his say-so. If there was a hierarchy in the tunnels beneath the city, he was its unnamed king, whether the others knew it or not.

John slowed as he approached Dominic's camp, keeping to the darkest part of the shadows, careful not to step into a puddle or run into a piece of trash.

His vampire eyes searched the darkness where the scent told him they'd be. Dominic wasn't home.

Stepping from the shadows, John revealed himself.

"Greetings," he said quietly.

"Wellll," it was the same youth who'd grabbed at his arm. "I was hoping we'd run into you ag—"

John bared his fangs and hissed, the terrible sound reverberating off the walls. He leapt into both of the men at once and they began to scream. Using both arms, he kept the men from wriggling free as he gorged himself, feeding like a pig at the trough.

This would not be quick. This would not be painless. These were not rats, but worse. These were intruders, unwanted vermin who'd slighted the King. The screams of agony and desperation sent a feeling of euphoria pulsing through his body, reveling in the pain he'd inflicted, a feeling not so dissimilar to sexual gratification.

They screamed for help, for loved ones, for their god. John could've silenced them, crushing their windpipes with a swipe of his hand. But he did no such thing. His mind lost in the blood, in the darkness, John let instinct take over as any semblance of a man disappeared.

He ripped flesh with his teeth, with his hands, drinking their polluted bodies free of blood, the taste of their addictions coming through each gulp—one of the downsides of hunting in the tunnels, or Las Vegas for that matter.

Dragging the shriveled corpses along, John traveled deep, deep into the tunnels until he made his way into the tight confines of a connected abandoned mineshaft, where eventually, after the bugs and rodents had eaten their fill, only their bones would remain.

Heading back to camp, John licked his fingers clean, washing himself in the shallow waters the floods had left behind.

Finally sated, he would sleep well.

About the Author

C. W. Stevenson resides in Texas with his wife and two sons. His work can be found in Summer of Sci-Fi & Fantasy Vol. 4, Creepy Pod, and Monster Fight at the O.K. Corral Vol. 1. His debut short story collection "Lost Lambs: Tales of Darkness" will release in 2026.

Death Becomes Him

Booker G.A. Feniks

CW: Character death, self-harm
Whumpee: Man, Whumper: N/A, Caretaker: Man

He opened the door to the smell of blood and decay.

Wind had picked up speed in the few hours since Yorrick had turned in for the night. His pigs had all warned him of trouble to come, squealing and crying when he herded them back inside, into their sties. The little cottage at the edge of the thick, pine forest did not see the worst of the storms that this side of the Continent harboured. But neither did it see the best of the winter weather, snuggled as it was beneath the canopies above his roof.

The wind had picked up speed, and the rain hammered at his wooden walls like waves against the hull of a ship. The fire burning in the hearth did little to warm his addled mind.

Soon after, there came a knocking at his door. It had been incessant, and he had tried to scare the intruder off with threats of swords and axes, to no avail. Now, he stood face to face with a man for whom swords were little better than toothpicks.

The giant before him stood swaying, hunched over as if the faintest of breezes could topple him over. And yet, even when he tried to make himself seem small, Yorrick had never seen a bigger man in his life. Moonlight gleamed from the delicate jewellery he wore, making his jet black hair shimmer. A considerably long beard hid his mouth from view, but Yorrick could easily tell that the stranger pained and suffered. His red, shining eyes told of that easily.

"Помогите мне," the man said in a voice that reverberated through Yorrick's body. He had lived on the Continent, away from his kinsmen, for many a year now, and he had not once heard a voice as deep and rich as the stranger's. Even with whimpers of pain, it proved to boom out like a clap of thunder. And yet, the words were nonsense to his ears, for the giant spoke a language Yorrick had hardly encountered before. But it was the urgency held within that voice that brought fear and unease to his heart, and forced him to act.

"Get in." He ushered the stranger inside.

Vaguely, he heard the man speak, "Спасибо." But he knew not what the word meant. Only once he was alone, watching the trees fighting against the wind upon the dark sky, did he notice the blood trailing behind the man, as if he had bathed in it. Beneath cloth and furs, the giant was clutching onto his side, hissing any time his wound was jostled by his own movements.

Yorrick slammed the door shut behind them, for fear of beasts smelling out the blood. He grabbed the table to push it against the door, doing the same with both of his chairs. He almost brought his cot to the door too, before remembering that he had a guest who required it far more.

He turned back to the giant, to find him collapsed upon the floor where the table had stood. In the haste to reach him, Yorrick tripped, falling besides the giant. "Milord? Are you alright? Milord!" The man still breathed, his massive chest rising and falling, albeit faintly. Yorrick managed to grab a hold of the wounded man's arm, as thick and heavy as a young pig, even by itself. The stench of decay clung like a bad omen to the rich, soft furs Yorrick pressed himself against.

With a heave, he managed to get the man onto the cot. It creaked and groaned in protest, but held steady. The giant's bloodied boots grazed the floor, hanging limp over the head of the cot. Yorrick grabbed his own winter cloak, shoving it beneath the black tresses of the man's heavy head, hoping to make his rest more peaceful.

The man did not stir for the rest of the night.

***

Bloodsuckers did not ask for help of the humans they feasted on. After all, neither did a human ask for help of the cattle he kept, or the hounds he fed.

The man, who slept on for three days without stirring, bore the fangs of a wolf and the eyes of a cat, and his breath stank of blood.

Yorrick heard, once, of the royal families of the Continent. That each generation birthed an heir to the throne, and a cursed whelp for the slaughter. A whelp to give to the bloodsuckers that hid within the shadows. The crown would remain safe, protected by forces more powerful than any king, and in turn the beasts would have something to feast on.

Marta, however, claimed they didn't eat the child.

She was a bright, redheaded thing with as many freckles as there were stars in the night sky. To Yorrick she was like a little sister, although the village folk enjoyed their gossip. He knew that she was a homely sort of beauty, a simple village girl for a simple pig farmer, with rounded hips and a small bosom. He, however, had no interest in her affections, only in her words.

"They call him Vasiliy," she whispered against his ear. "He was a beautiful boy, they say. With hair so dark, not even the moon could illuminate it, and eyes so bright they look golden or crimson under the right light. The northern tribes surrendered him to the bloodsuckers as they did with every newborn. I hear that, in their culture, women make better rules, so he was sacrificed at his sister's birth, even though he was older. But the bloodsuckers did not feast on him, oh no. They say..." They were alone, yet her voice dropped lower, so quiet that the hares in the fields around them would struggle to hear. She came closer, her lips brushing against the shell of his ear.

"They say the bloodsuckers made Vasily their king. That under the power of their cursed blood, that small, handsome infant grew into a giant. A man so feared, no ruler dares speak his name. No one dared summon him, for fear of having to greet him in their court."

Yorrick did not know, then, how much he believed her. The week before she had told him of an old man with hair woven out of vines, and legs made out of tree bark, that roamed the forests near town. And the month prior she had regaled him with tales of a land so vast, and yet so empty, that it held nothing but sand, despite having no ocean near it. There, people worshipped gods with the heads of animals, and built structures so high that they touched the heavens.

Now, Yorrick sat before the wounded stranger, dabbing his face with a cold, wet cloth. Vasily had sweat through his clothing, and Yorrick had nothing of his own to spare. He had left the man in just his shirt, to hide the still bleeding, festering wound in his side. The stench of decay had permeated his home in those three days, and Yorrick knew he would never get it out again.

***

Vasiliy's eyes followed Yorrick like a beast. He had come in from the cold, stamping his feet by the entrance to dislodge the freshly fallen snow from them. And then he looked up, and found himself being scrutinised by golden eyes.

"Milord?" Yorrick approached Vasiliy, whose visage was pale, and whose white lips had parted to allow him to pant like a tired dog. Vasiliy watched him approach slowly, making his way around the perimeter of the room. He felt like the mouser his parents owned when he was still an Islander child, sneaking up on a rodent.

"Голодный." A hand shot out from beneath his blanket, wrapping lightly around Yorrick's wrist. There was barely any strength behind it, a lose sort of bracelet of frigid fingers. But the anguish within the man's voice brought a tightness to Yorrick's heart.

"I do not understand, milord," he whispered, kneeling down beside the cot. "I do not know what you want."

"Помогите мне." Despite the fatigue within his tone, Vasiliy had a booming voice that shook Yorrick to the core. Something within him told him to run, some part of his brain that was neither rational nor human.

"What do you wish for, milord? I do not understand."

"Больно." He spoke in a lilting, swift tongue, so different to the Continental languages Yorrick had come to learn and exist around. Who could he even ask for help, when his mind could not make its way through the syllables, or parse apart each individual word? He could hardly bring another human to his home, anyway, dare to risk Vasiliy's life.

Yorrick lifted his arm, watching Vasiliy's fingers slip from his wrist. Those golden eyes closed, and his face twisted in pain. Yorrick brushed a strand of hair from his face, wiping sweat from his brow, and rested a hand on his cheek. Pain contorted Vasiliy's visage, and he turned his face away from Yorrick's searching eyes. He pressed his lips to the strong beat of Yorrick's pulse point, his nose flaring at the scent of hot blood rushing through his veins. But there was no movement from him to indicate danger, no flash of sharp teeth. The bloodsucker did not sink his fangs into Yorrick's wrist.

"You are weak, milord," Yorrick murmured, pulling a knife from his belt. "Too weak. Will this help?" The blade had dulled over the years, streaked with salt and lime. Yet it glinted faintly when the sun fell through Yorrick's window at just the right angle.

Then, he dug the very tip of it between two delicate wrist bones, just above where Vasiliy's mouth rested. The blood wept down his skin, painting the blood-sucker's lips crimson, and only then did Vasiliy move. A pink tongue gently lapped up the blood, as sluggish as the flow of the red nectar. Yorrick sat there with his arm slowly going numb, watching him.

And when Vasiliy had, had his fill, he said only one word, "Спасибо."

***

A storm slammed against his windows, billowing wind wailing through the trees. It was never a good day when the skies wept, especially in the winter, especially after snow fall. Yorrick sat before a fire, staring idly at an empty cooking pot as his fingers worked away on the knots in the rope. Up, around, twice over, he went through every knot he had ever learned, from the ones that held up his hammock to the ones that kept the sails flying high.

Vasiliy sat behind him, pressed up against the thin, wooden walls. "Yorrick." He kept repeating it, getting his tongue accustomed to the sound, the shape of his name.

"Yorrick." He said it wrong, however, put too much emphasis on the I, elongated it into a high EE.

"Yorrick." He rolled his Rs like the thunder rolling outside.

"Yorrick." It was the same way Marta said his name, the same way Olaf the Trader and Mateo the Fisher said it.

"Yorrick." It was so Continental, that Yorrick feared he would never get used to it.

"Yorrick..." He turned, hearing the difference in Vasiliy's tone. Not quite a question, but not just repetition.

"Yes, milord?" he asked, dropping his ropes. A crack of thunder drowned out Vasiliy's next words, but no lightning followed to brighten his form. He was a dark silhouette, untouched by the flames Yorrick's own body hid from him. The cot bent beneath his massive form, but he remained still, like the stone gods on the outskirts of town. Yorrick could hardly even see the glow of his eyes like this.

"Меня зовут Vasiliy, а не milord." His voice was a guttural growl, choked up from pain. It hardly compared to the voice Yorrick heard on the first night.

He looked up into the shadows of the cottage, seeking out Vasiliy's eyes, for he had a feeling that was what the bloodsucker was telling him. A living legend sat within his room, holding one massive hand to the bleeding, leaking wound in his side that Yorrick had already cleaned three times that day. Now that he looked closer, he wasn't sure if Vasiliy even held his eyes open.

"I understand, Vasiliy," Yorrick said in a low, quiet voice. "I shared my name with you, it is only right you did the same."

"Я не понимаю," Vasiliy said quietly. "Но мне нравится твой golos." Yorrick stilled, holding his breath. He searched and searched, but could not find Vasiliy's eyes.

"My voice." He recognised the word. "Something about my voice. It is the word a bard from the North used once."

"Ya частлив, когда ты говоришь." Vasiliy's voice echoed. Were it not for his state, Yorrick would not be able to tell where he was, for his voice came from everywhere and nowhere at the same time.

"You," Yorrick echoed. "You react to my voice. In a good way, I hope." He was met with silence, and the cottage grew still once more. Yorrick hardly even noticed when Vasiliy slipped down his cot, giant body laying limp halfway across the floor. When approached, he didn't steer, but for the first time in four days he seemed relaxed.

Yorrick grabbed his legs, and pulled him back up onto the cot. He did not return to the fireplace, for the thunder had grown silent, and the wind had died down. The fire caressed Vasiliy's face, playing with the gauntness of his cheeks and the hollowness of his eye sockets. But there was something proud to the curve of his nose, and there was beauty in the lines in the corners of his lips.

Yorrick sat down beside Vasiliy, letting the fire bathe him in its light. He, on the other hand, hid himself within the darkness, working away on his knots long into the morning. He only fell asleep once the rain no longer hammered against his door, and the ghosts of long ago no longer wailed to be let in.

***

"Нет." Vasiliy did not quite growl, although Yorrick did not care for the difference. There was hardly a difference between being a cornered beast, and simply feeling like one, his heart hammered within his chest for both.

Vasiliy's grip did not grow slack, despite the weak hold he had on Yorrick's wrist. The wrist where a wound still festered, skin pulling apart regularly as he worked. Vasiliy's eyes were wide, completely black, and he flared his nose at Yorrick.

"Alright," Yorrick whispered, pulling his hand back from Vasiliy's face.

"Спасибо," he muttered, releasing Yorrick's wrist. "Spasibo."

"Alright. I cannot touch you. Cannot touch your beard." He brought his hand to his chin, stroking it as if he weren't clean shaven.

"Нет." Vasiliy repeated himself, smoothing a shivering hand down his beard.

"Can I touch your arm?" Again, Yorrick stroked his shoulder, tilting his head at Vasiliy in question.

"Net."

"And your side. Can I touch your side?"

"Net."

Yorrick dropped his head in a half nod. "Net. No." He lowered himself onto his knees upon the cot. He offered his hand out, silently.

Vasiliy swayed, his big, black eyes staring upon Yorrick's calloused palm. He approached sluggishly, arm hanging in the air yet moving as if through honey. Yorrick missed honey from the Islands, he missed it so.

Finally, Vasiliy dropped his hand into Yorrick's, heavy paw resting limply within his human grasp. "Da. Держи это."

***

Yorrick slept in fitful bursts often. Nightmares woke him on many a night, and dreams could not keep him. Solid beds could never quite compare to the places he slept on, on the ship. No stillness could put him to sleep as well as the calming sway of the waves.

He found himself waking once more to the stench of decay pressed right against his face. The bandages around Vasiliy's midriff were soaked through, although the position itself was what worried him more. He thought he had fallen asleep, as he usually did, on the floor at the foot of his cot. Except, this wasn't true, for he had been wearied so by his pigs, that he had dropped parallel to the cot like a plank of wood.

Yet here he was, now, upon the cot. The bloodsucker had brought him onto it, letting him rest his heavy head across his chest. The gentle sway that accompanied his low, pained breathing was... soothing, Yorrick found.

"Вы заслуживаете комфорта." He could not begin to fathom what Vasiliy said, spitting it out through clenched teeth. Pressed so tightly against him, Yorrick heard a rattle within the man's chest, cradled between pained panting and the sluggish beat of his still human heart.

Yorrick pressed his face into that heartbeat, counting the seconds between each thump. "Thank you, Vasiliy."

"Пожалуйста."

***

"Ya..." A frown marred Vasiliy's pale face, his hands shivering around the book in his lap.

Yorrick bowed his head, holding his own hands out. "I'm sorry, m... I'm sorry, Vasiliy. I thought a book might entertain you while I tend to the pigs." The leather journal felt heavy when it was deposited in his hands. The worn, rough cover still smelled faintly of sea water, with its pages hard and brittle from sea brine. Yorrick hardly even remembered what colour the book was originally.

Vasiliy lay upon the bed like a damsel, black locks haloing out around his head, one arm resting daintily across his abdomen. He stared at the space above Yorrick's head, golden eyes unfocused and hazy. A smile played at the corners of his pink lips, hidden by the long, uncombed hairs of his beard.

Yorrick knelt beside him, his heart clenching uncomfortably within his ribcage. The faint rise and fall of Vasiliy's chest reassured him, although only faintly. "Vasiliy, are you alright?"

"Ya…" A shuddering sigh fell past his lips. "Мне скучно. Почитай mne. Твой golos. Ya люблю это."

"Voice." Yorrick held the journal up. "You want me to read it?"

"Da," he said with a faint smile, eyes falling shut. Yorrick sat down upon the cot, in the crook of Vasiliy's hip, with the bloodsucker's arm wrapping loosely around his waist.

So Yorrick read to him notes and observations, and told him of the many journeys he took across the world's seas. He knew not what Vasiliy understood, or how much of it he was awake for. Journeys of distant lands were recounted in the form of diary entries, to which Vasiliy hummed and hawed.

And, eventually, he fell asleep to the sound of Yorrick's low, monotonous voice. And for what felt like the first time in days, the scent of decay did not seem quite as stifling and choking.

***

The wound ate away at his body. Skin had turned grey, flesh had turned black. Veins bulged out from between melted, rotting muscles, and they pulsed with fervour and fear.

"Ya умираю." Vasiliy brought his hand down to the wound, no longer wincing when he grazed his fingers against it. Yorrick's hands were stained black. Vasiliy no longer flinched away from him.

"You are dying," he said, struggling to breathe through the tightness within his throat. So soon…

"Почему ты обо mne заботишься?" The low rumble of Vasiliy's voice came closer, crimson eyes staring right into Yorrick's soul. Although his hand was so much bigger than Yorrick's, it was gentle when it grasped his fingers, threading them together like stalks for a wicker basket. Yorrick found that Vasiliy had such soft hands, so unlike his own, unmarred by callouses and scars.

"I do not know if the legends are true, Vasiliy," he began, feeling the need to hold Vasiliy's hand to his chest, to let him feel his own pulse hammering beneath his ribcage. "I can only guess if this was silver, a wooden stake, or The One God's blessing that brought your demise. If only you could tell me who hurt you." For he had axes and swords on hand, and he did know how to make good use of them. And, when needed, rope always did the trick well enough.

Vasiliy's eyes turned golden in the dark, remaining crimson when the light hit them just right. And they were red now, as he bent low to press his cheek against Yorrick's, and his lips against the shell of Yorrick's ear.

He felt those lips, cool and cracked, twist and rise into a smile. "Твой доброта вызывает благоговение. Spasibo, что остаётесь со мной."

Yorrick felt his heart slow and his mind grow quiet. "You're welcome, Vasiliy. I do not understand, but you are welcome."

***

"Yorrick." A familiar, yet unwanted roll of the R. Yorrick opened his door, as he had done so many days ago now, to someone knocking at it incessantly. Marta stood with a basket in hand, holding some of the wildflowers up to her nose.

"Marta, why are you here?" Vasiliy was asleep behind him, having supped on but a few droplets of his blood. He could hardly stomach a larger meal.

Marta smiled, radiant like the sun that climbed the horizon behind her. "I heard some of your piglets died during the recent storms. I came to see how you are, and how the sows are doing."

"They made good eating," he said simply. "And the sows have many more piglets to care for. I make sure my brood is always large, you know that."

Her smile faltered. "Yorrick, I miss you. You haven't been coming around recently. What is wrong, friend?" Her hand was pale, dainty as it wrapped around his wrist. But there was strength in her grip.

Yorrick peeled her fingers off him, gentle as could be. He did not offer her a smile, or a nod, but his tone was soft as he spoke. "I am not feeling very well, Marta. I wouldn't wish to infect you with whatever ails me. I'm sure you can smell the stench that has overtaken my farm, a fox or a hound must have died in the vicinity and now the miasma made me sick. You should leave before it takes you too, I can manage until it clears out." For just a moment, he feared she would not leave.

Then, finally, she held out her basket of wildflowers, and wrapped his fingers around it. "Take it, then. And get well as quickly as you can, alright?"

After a nod, Yorrick closed the door. He set the basket beside his cot, but the pungent smell of decay could not be masked. Vasiliy could hardly keep his eyes open, pale skin hardly able to flush with the force of his fever. And he was feverish, painfully warm to the touch. He was losing strength, for every time Yorrick lay beside him, head upon his chest, Vasiliy felt thinner, and thinner.

He barely registered the basket, but reached out for a particular shape within it. Tulips symbolised gratitude, according to Marta, and the pink petals of the small bud looked nothing if not vibrant, clutched between Vasiliy's ashen fingers. Yorrick took the flower when it was offered to him, and sat back down to his vigil.

"Для tebya."

Yorrick took it, holding it up to insert into his cap. "Thank you."

***

"Yorrick." There was no strength behind that word. It was but a whisper of a voice, and yet Yorrick woke to it being murmured into his ear.

"It's time," he said simply, turning to look Vasiliy in the eyes.

"Da." Vasiliy's face had grown thin and taut, skin stretching across his bones like a sheet spread too thin across the floor. His eyes had lost their lustre, no longer glimmering golden in the right light.

Yorrick sighed, brushing a stray lock of limp, black hair from Vasiliy's forehead. "I'm sorry you have to die. I'm sorry I could not save you."

"Мне жаль," Vasiliy muttered, pressing his sweaty, feverish forehead against Yorrick's cool skin. "Хотелось бы, чтобы у нас было больше времени."

"Let me tell you a story," Yorrick mumbled. "And you just sleep, alright?"

"Da, Yorrick."

His own breathing came to him slowly, with a shudder. "Once upon a time, there was a young boy. He came from a world without beasts or monsters. Once sheltered by a fearful mother, and a careless father, he ran away from home."

Vasiliy gripped the back of his shirt tightly, giant fingers digging into the cloth, ripping through its thin seams.

"Once upon a time," Yorrick continued, "there was a man. He became a sailor. With no home, no money, nor a family, he travelled the world. The Island that had been his home for seventeen seasons had turned out to be but a fraction of the known world. He travelled to worlds where people drank water made from herbs, and rode on greyish beasts so massive, no bison could compare. He saw cats as orange as the sunset, and people with skin so dark they must have been born of the night sky. And he loved everyone and everything he met, for it was new, and he was young and inexperienced."

Vasiliy's chest kept rising and falling, pressed against Yorrick's abdomen. He had buried his head in Yorrick's shirt, staining it with his sweat, and his tears.

"Once upon a time there was a sailor," Yorrick said, rubbing one hand down Vasiliy's wide back, and one hand against his own throat, threatening to close up on him. "He had travelled to so many places, owned so many ships. He had met many people, and survived many storms. But this one had been different. Everyone told him this would be his last voyage, and his last storm. He did not believe them, young and foolish as he was."

Vasiliy shuddered.

Yorrick kept talking. "Once upon a time there was a ship, and she was named after the sailor's mother. And one day she... simply sank. A lightning bolt had hit her hull, and the sailor, her captain, remained on board. They sank together, never to be seen again."

Vasiliy dug his fingers deeper into Yorrick's back.

Yorrick kept talking, choking back tears. "Once upon a time there was a siren, and he was as beautiful as the glittering waters around him. He had saved the foolish sailor from a death upon the ocean, nursing him back to health. His eyes were as golden as a sun setting across the horizon, and his hair was as black as the deepest depths of the seas. He and the sailor were in love, despite one being a human, and one a beast."

Vasiliy stilled, and for a moment Yorrick felt his heart stop too.

He continued talking, and Vasiliy took another breath. "Once upon a time, a man lived by the ocean, with a siren whom he loved. People said he was mad for loving a beast, but the siren had never hurt him. He wished that, one day, he could repay his lover's kind gift to him. He never received that chance, for hunters came to their house by the sea, and slit the siren's throat."

Vasiliy's wound wept, and his blood soaked into the cot.

Yorrick continued, even when he felt the pool growing and growing, staining his hips and his legs. "Once upon a time there was a pig farmer. He had lived a long life, not all of it very happy. The village gossiped about him, but none of their tales were true. Because once upon a time that pig farmer had been a young boy, then a man, then a sailor. And once upon a time, that man had promised to repay the kindness a creature of the depths had shown him, so he took in an ailing creature of the night. And even then, the man could not repay the gift his lover had given him, for he had failed, and he would continue to fail, for the rest of his days."

One last gasp of air, and one last sob. "Thank you, Yorrick."

Humans oft died loudly, in displays larger than anything they had done in life. Yorrick had not expected Vasiliy to go in this way, but neither had he expected the silence. For Vasiliy's chest had sagged and fell, rattling with the impossible act of keeping him alive. He left slowly and quietly. His eyes simply closed, and never reopened.

The smell of decay permeated the room, eating through the wood and settling into the walls with intent to remain. Outside, snow fell in flurries against his windows, covering the pig sties and paddocks in a thick blanket of white.

Tears fell thickly, hotly down his cheeks, wetting Vasiliy's hair. Like this, pressed against Yorrick's chest, they looked identical, and the bloodied sheets felt almost the same as the bloodied sand.

Vasiliy's body quickly grew cold, held within Yorrick's grasp. Words barely managed to fall past his lips. "I am so sorry, Albert. I'm so sorry, Vasiliy."

And then, just like that, Yorrick fell back onto the bed, closed his eyes, and didn't reopen them.

About the Author

Booker-Garet August Feniks is a queer, disabled writer of fantasy, comedy, and poetry. He writes stories that pull directly from their experience as a queer immigrant. Originally from Poland, Kielce, Booker writes primarily in English, and has a passion for storytelling and linguistics as a whole.

The Carpetbagger

Susan Shwartz

CW: Character death, noncon/sexual assault, suicide
Whumpee: Woman, Whumper: Man, Caretaker: Man

Legs askew, the dead woman lay in a doorway off Bourbon Street. Her head rested on a battered kilim bag, and her eyes stared up like a camera set for time-lapse photography. Gradually the images trapped in the glazed lenses faded — the krewes passing, gaudy and raucous, Rex on his horse, Isis with her crown, men flaunting evening gowns and women wearing almost nothing at all below bobbing breasts; the flight of flash of "throws," the plastic necklaces tossed out to onlookers; and the avid pale face of her last cavalier.

Constrained by her New England upbringing, she had found it hard to scream, but after the sun plunged like a counterfeit doubloon into the brown river water, her eyes had met the eyes of a man in weathered gray. He wore a hat with rifles crossed upon it, a saber, and a fringed gold sash, a Mardi Gras clone of Ashley Wilkes.

Not at all like Ashley then, but like the sailor in the *Life* photo at the end of World War II, the man in officer's gray grabbed her, spun her around, and bent her back until she felt splayed upon her spin; and that too was nothing all that abnormal for Mardi Gras.

"How's this for a taste of your own medicine, you bloodsuckin' Yankee?" Cold lips against her throat reeked gunpowder and bad blood.

Oh Jesus, just my luck if he's got AIDS, she thought. People danced on by, still screaming Mister throw me something, letting the bon temps rouler as she tried to roll him off her.

His face changed. She saw the gunshot-ruined mouth, bone and fangs protruding. His teeth sucked scream and blood and breath out of her throat.

She had time before her sight faded to wonder what she had done to deserve…

***

Silence, despite the jazz drifting from the bars.

Stars and streetlights shone down into drying eyes. The revelers picked their ways past her, cruising the Quarter like the pros. The Mississippi rolled on. Silent times for one more victim.

Hoofbeats down Bourbon Street: helmeted police with hard guts, Tabasco tempers, and faith in law, order, and LSU football clattered in a dead march two by two.

Mardi Gras is over. To your scattered bodies go.

A water truck whirred behind them, crunching discarded go cups, springling the dead along with the rest of the trash lying in the way: water over the damned.

Easter isn't for weeks yet. What we have here is premature resurrection.

Tears of wretchedness cleaned the dead woman's face. She turned her other cheek where it rested on her bag and vomited a puddle of reddish brown.

Jesus, the crazy hadn't even bothered to steal her bag. The contempt of that plucked at her nerves. She would have screamed if she had had the strength and no sense left. She fumbled in her bag: wallet intact, cash intact, plastic intact.

Was she?

Fucked over in New Orleans. God. This sort of thing would have been bad enough at home with swabs and doctors, bright lights, the stink of stale coffee and her own unshowered flesh, questions from female cops and rape kits as invasive as a second rape, if rape it was. Among the bubbas—didn't the cops beat up on people down here—it would probably be worse. You could scare hell out of yourself down here, if they didn't get to you first.

"Did you know the man, miss?" She could just hear the litany now.

She shut her eyes. That face before it changed and shattered ... the night before, she'd gone with friends to The Dungeon, just a few doors down.

"You don't want to go to Pat O'Brien's: it's for the tourists. And the line for Preservation Hall is just too long. This is neat, authentic, you'll really like it."

They ventured in at the narrow door, paid up, then headed down a sloping passageway lined with f'rgodsake cobblestone, and over a bridge as the picture of the horned and hooved patron on the wall. She was honestly tempted to throw the bounder a cake to let them pass.

Smoke and rock and roll assaulted them. So did The Dungeon's vibes. Very simply, they were the worst she'd ever felt.

"The hell with the cover charge. Let's go!" she nudged her friends.

But her companions were already shrieking at the choice of house drinks: Witch's Brew or Dragon's Blood or grosser. The man behind the dark, cramped bar wouldn't say what was in them. Complimentary roofies, anyone? They should have gone back to O'Brien's or Preservation Hall. Wasn't as if tourists weren't here, too. You could tell them in their dark shirts and pants, almost like New Yorkers. The few women among them were local with their big hair, dyed, fried, and pushed to the side. She wanted to leave now.

One man wearing gray and an Aussie hat swung down from where he sat near the dance floor, held out a hand.

"Go on!" one friend gave her a sly push. She saw herself in the mirror, out of place, dancing alone, her eyes enormous.

"You from up North, little lady?" His voice was honey over acid.

"Near Boston."

He danced tense and fast. Under the hat, he was pale, trim beard over a weak mouth held angry-taut. Well, she could always retreat to the Ladies' Room. Board of Health rules meant they'd have one. Wouldn't they?

"After 2:00 a.m., women drink free. You'll like that, won't you?"

What she didn't like was his hostility, only half disguised by the questions.

"I can buy my own drinks."

"Little Miss Independence. I just bet you can. All you Yankees, come down here with your own money, actin' like a queen. What you going to do here, sweetheart? Kick up your heels in those Sunday School teacher clothes, then go back and be a virgin again?"

Jesus, why'd she have to be the lucky one again? It wasn't an Aussie hat the man was wearing after all. She spotted some kind of Southern thing on the crown. A Confederate die-hard, wouldn't you just know? That war'd been over for a hundred years, but you wouldn't know it down here. They were still fighting it, them and their Sacred Cause, aided and abetted by book publishers. No wonder the Big Easy was such a mess. They were still fighting a guerrilla war against Reconstruction.

She turned and left the dance floor. "I'm out of here," she told her friends, now gyrating with partners of their own, and good luck to that!

This long after midnight, she knew to find a cab back to the Quality Inn. The driver, hunched over the wheel, had a slow islander's accent. "Lady like you shouldn't be walkin' around here alone. Shouldn't be alone. They's all kind of lowlife."

He drove off, made some turns, and she was lost. Down the road, past a darkness in which she saw blurs in which long structures with pointed roofs emerged.

"Now, doan' you go in there— " It was St. Louis Cemetery, Number 3, where Creoles, carpetbaggers, Cajuns, and voodoo queens lay above ground, their bodies protected from the seep of Lake Pontchartrain and the Mississippi for the short years until they decomposed or a hurricane snatched them. Whitewash, plastered over brick, coffins stacked within, tomb upon tomb, the dead yielded place to more recent dead and to the predators who hid among the green, shadowed lanes.

Her driver's eyes glazed sideways, and his hand went to touch something around his neck. "They hide behind the tombs. You starin' at some angel and they jump out at you!"

She tightened her grip on her bag, an expensive new one made out of a Turkish rug, and promised not to go anywhere alone. At the motel, she tipped him, and he waited until she reached the lobby before he drove away.

Yes, she had seen a pale face, twisted with anger beneath the shadow of a hat. And knew it before it changed. She wondered if any cop would buy that. Even if she said sir at the end of every sentence.

What did you suppose a Louisiana mental hospital would be like? Probably a snakepit. Like the bayou.

Sit up, why don't you? She struggled up, then rubbed her hands over her face to smear away the tears. Her fingers looked dark, as if she had worn mascara, and she knew she hadn't. Dark tears? She must be a worse mess than she thought.

She leaned out beneath the streetlight. The yowls of karaoke and rum-sodden drunks overpowered the blue notes of a jazz trombone, wailing like a train in the night. How pale her hand looked in the dark. She knew she'd caught some sun up on the levee by the Aquarium the other day, drinking Hurricanes and watching the dirty umber river flow by. Weird river, with its centuries of freight. Weird city, like the shards of mirror in a burnt-out funhouse. By the waters of Babylon. Buy the waters of Babylon— and anything else they'd try to sell her.

Again, she rubbed her eyes. Her tears were tainted almost red. Jesus.

She pulled a mirror from her bag to see the damages. And she saw precisely nothing at all. Oh, she saw the street, the pools of filth dissolving in the water from the truck. She saw the shopfronts. Saw a drunk embrace a post. But of herself, her reddened hands, her ruined clothes — not a trace of a reflection.

She could put a name to the type of creature that died, then rose and couldn't see its face in the mirror.

God.

That wasn't the name.

She rubbed her throat, at the rawness there from the bite. Her mouth tasted of salt and worse. Gagging, she made herself look down. She had retched, bringing up a tiny pool of blood. Dregs. Apparently, draining her the rest of the way hadn't been worth the trouble.

"Come to New Orleans!" Her friends had urged. "We can eat our way cross town. Let the good times roll—they make an industry out of it!"

That wasn't all New Orleans had turned into a cottage industry. She had taken the quaint old streetcar up St. Charles to the Garden District.

"Can we see Anne Rice's house?" some idiot had called, to suppressed snickers. The writer had lived here, behind a gate, amid lattices of painted iron and green trees and sunlight. And probably private security.

Sunlight. She would never see the sun again.

She forced herself to her feet, her eyes darting to the sky. When was dawn? Thank God, she had her watch. What if she went calling to the Garden District now to talk to a ghost? Excuse me, ma'am, but I've had this accident, you know, and I was wondering — do you have a spare coffin?

Right.

If she had to be turned into a monster, why'd it have to be a vampire?

There. She had said the word.

What time was it? Her eyes darted frantically from her watch to the night sky. Hours left till dawn. That wasn't a real long life-span, was it?

But she was dead already. Or undead. And she would die again when the sun struck her unless she could think of something.

For God's sake, think of something.

I don't want to be a vampire. Want to go home! She doubted that North American Van Line would haul coffins. After giggling that she'd probably run off with a man in romantic New Orleans, her girlfriends would have reported that she'd vanished. They'd track her down when she used her plastic to pay for something. Besides, what would she do, even if she could get home? Would an emergency ward test her for porphyria or give her standing appointments for transfusions. Would her insurance cover it if she were dead? Did shrinks have office hours at night? For certain, she would have to hit up the weirdo shrinks at Cambridge Hospital. Well, John Mack had switched from headshrinking Lawrence of Arabia to reporting on saucer people. He'd have gotten another book contract out of her — if he too weren't dead already.

When the hospitals and insurance gave up on her, would they at least sterilize the stake they brought into the OR?

You can't stay here all night, panicking under the streetlights.

Think it through.

She needed a place to rest, to hide. She needed a place to clean up, assuming running water didn't send her into screaming, steaming fits. The dregs of her own blood and the spoor of the one who changed her assaulted her nose. So that much was true: her senses were keener. Maybe she could track her killer, could ask him why.

I'll kill him. So help me God, I'll kill him.

Did she really think that was safe?

Safe? Was anything safe? She laughed. Several blocks away, dogs began to howl.

Well, did she have a better idea?

Food, perhaps. She was desperately hungry. There was nothing left in her to throw up. You can eat your way across town, they'd told her. Cajun cooking. Creole cooking. Dinner at Antoine's, yeah sure; and she'd just love to hear what that totaled woman Frances Parkinson Keyes' sweet wimps said about vampires, too: the tradgirls would probably faint on the spot. What about beignets with a veritable blizzard of powdered sugar at Café du Monde? Sometimes you get the beignet; sometimes, the beignet gets you. It had gotten her for sure this time.

It's much too rich! the well-fed types would cry at food down here, lifting soft hands in mock horror. Kale-eaters, all of them, examining each leaf as if a slug lay beneath it, maybe poking it with a fork just in case. Center-parted hair, sallow, muscles gone to ropey lines down arms and calves — but damn, they ate healthy. Bloodless.

Something, not her stomach, lurched hungrily.

If she could not eat, she would have to feed. And find some answers.

She started off down Bourbon Street, passing drunks and hookers like a wisp of dark cloud. Well, she had always had a talent for invisibility. It might help her now. A black man, rolling like a sailor too long from land, stopped. He shrank into himself, trying for invisibility too. The salt of his flesh and blood lured her. His pulse thudded in her ears: alive, afraid, terrifyingly magnetic. The woman with him drew herself up and placed her own powerful frame between them. Go away. She made the sign of the Cross.

***

Listen to that. The Dungeon's inmates would still be partying hearty. Perhaps she could put thumbscrews—no, she thought with a chuckle that appalled her too—perhaps she could put the bite on its denizens for information. Sounded like a plan. No one tried to collect the cover charge. The bouncer actually stepped back when she entered. His belly under his ripped tee shirt twitched visibly.

Her feet felt every roughness in the cobblestones as she crossed the bridge. Another myth: running water didn't hurt. If the Ladies' Room hadn't been empty when she entered, it cleared out fast as she washed. The sight of wall and towel dispenser and Purell bottles and the rest of the room where her reflection should have been turned her slightly queasy. Maybe that was the hunger speaking too.

When she was as clean as she could get (her clothes were stained beyond redemption), she walked into the bar. Her girlfriends were long gone. She half expected to see, beneath the slouch hat, the face of her attacker the vampire. The other vampire.

"He changed you. Why did he change *you*?"

The voice was breathless, magnolia over scraped slate, and it came from a woman crammed into a black leather — no, vinyl — dress. She was powdered pale, if sweaty, and she wore a ribbon around her neck. A black ribbon, not a yellow one.

Oh God, this vampire even had wannabes. She knew the type: the professional neurasthenic who read romance and popular history and quoted it like Gospel when she wasn't fluffing back her hair, or who combed genealogies to make herself look prestigious. Eager to party, but the most stalwart virgin in the sorority house.

Tonight, though, the spite — "he changed *you*?" — annoyed her. And it was even possible that "he" had left a message with this creature, who knew enough to recognize what she was.

"What do you know about him?"

"He says he'll make me like he is, when I am stronger. I am so sensitive, so delicate, he says." Woman had haunches on her like an ox. "And then we'll be together forever." Exaggerated rapture. Not so much a wannabe as a groupie.

The woman laid one tattooed hand on an ample breast, hiked up beneath the dress. Under the creaking heated vinyl, her heartbeat thudded.

The groupie stared at her with that look such women get when they eyed what they considered their physical inferiors, rendering them invisible with a flick of fake eyelashes.

"Why did he pick a wicked little nothing like you? And a Yankee to boot? You just don't think you'll do as he says. But you won't have a choice! You'll want to. And it will serve independent types like you right!"

She didn't have time for this. With a scream of rage that sent shards of mirror cascading down the walls, she pounced upon the woman. Her teeth closed on the ribboned neck, near the wound the vampire had left. She could smell him beneath the stale perfume.

Don't drain her.

If she drained this woman, she would never learn the message she'd sensed driven like a stake into her clouded mind. A shop on Royal Street? That was all?

In disappointment, she released the woman, who sagged against the bar, her eyes appealing for rescue from someone, anyone. Not even the bartender moved.

"You're not worth draining. You haven't got the guts to rise again. That's not protection you're bragging about. That's contempt."

Now, where had those words come from? She wasn't about to take them back.

The woman pushed away from the bar with surprisingly angry strength. She shoved her back easily. She was the stronger.

"Look at you! You despise your own life. I want mine." I want mine back.

Wanting her life was how she had survived her own transformation. Maybe the very force of her desire had pushed her back beyond the edge.

She glanced around the room. No one screamed. No one even moved. But their eyes glittered, not with fear or loathing, but with desire. She could feel the heightened pulses, the quickened heartbeats. They repelled her even as they drew her closer. Even the small amount of stolen blood she'd sipped had made her glow like a candle to these pathetic, sodden moths. One drink, one drunk. She didn't want to want them. But God, she was starving.

She made herself laugh and hit a scornful high note that would have turned Mozart's Queen of the Night bloodless with envy. Gathering her new strength about her, she stalked out as if a cape indeed trailed from her shoulders. The bouncer held his arms out in front of the crowd, trying to protect it. A cross actually gleamed around his neck.

Damn. The first time in her life she could make an exit, and it had to be Final Exit time.

She could not have drained that feeble rabbit. But the paltry sip of blood she'd taken would not sustain her for long. The encounter had left her disgusted. There might be some glamour to being the Bride of Confederate Dracula, but none at all in being a vampire groupie.

She headed toward Royal Street and prowled until she saw a shop that matched the image she had seized. An antique shop, selling not Creole memorabilia, but guns, bullets, pictures, papers, swords: costly relics of the Civil War for fans.

In the window lay a yellowed newspaper with crumbled corners, its print uneven and broken the way type was back in the 1860s and 1870s. Although the shadow of a tattered Stars and Bars half hid it, her changed eyes easily made out a restrained headline. Beneath it was a crude photo of a body lying across a floor, a blanket across it to conceal — what? A shattered head?

Beneath it ran the story, which could have happened today: a man broken by war, fighting in disguise in the West, but returning at last to his home and his old identity to take his life.

But he had failed even at suicide. Suicides sometimes rose. This man's anger had no doubt pushed him beyond the peace of death. No doubt, too, his people, those rational blond people who never let anyone forget how self-controlled they were, had despised what they would call mumbo-jumbo, weakness, worthy only of ex-slaves and immigrants. They had not taken proper precautions, and so he had risen.

Gave new meaning to "the South shall rise again," didn't it just?

Why had he chosen her? She was a Yankee, therefore, as he saw it, his enemy. Maybe he thought to play the old hatred out beyond the grave. She was strong enough to make the change so there might be, even in undeath, some satisfaction in bending an enemy to his will. It probably even helped that she was female.

You still want to die, Mister? You tell me how I can find you to drive a stake through your heart. Assuming you've got one.

Could you just imagine? If every suicide rose — think of Faulkner's Quentin Compson as a vampire. I don't hate the South, he said. I don't. I don't. She wondered how they'd have worked it out in Cambridge when Quentin threw himself off the Andersen Bridge into the Charles amid the odor of the honeysuckle, rather than the beer, sweat, rum, and tainted magnolias of this city, precarious beneath the level of the water. The Compson blood had thinned out. At least this way, a vampire Quentin would recover it after a fashion.

She'd always wondered if he and Shreve had ever been lovers. Buried in one coffin, roommates again, to rise and let straight-arrow Canadian Shreve live for the first time. Right.

Wasn't as if you didn't find that theme in the South, either. Just look at Blanche's husband in *Streetcar*, set here in New Orleans. Another suicide.

God, she was losing it ... Soon it would be dawn, and she had no leads at all, no place to wait out the sunlight. What was she going to do? Linger on Royal Street until dawn and then fry? It wasn't as if she outlived centuries so she could just fall away to ash. Maybe she was a wicked little nothing, and maybe she hadn't had much of a life, but she'd wanted it, never more than now. And she was damned if she was going to lose what she had left because someone had been too cowardly to stay alive and live past an old grudge.

What would become of her?

The panic she had suppressed flooded in on her the way Hurricane Katrina had burst the city's levees and inundated this gumbo Atlantis.

"Oh help me, God!"

A vampire praying. Imagine that. Dogs howled descant to her howl of anguish. The glass front of the store next to the gun shop shattered. A burglar alarm whooped. The white of old lace and muslin billowed from the darkness, to be restrained by iron grating.

Clean, fragrant cloth — yes! She tried the grates. The lock yielded to her new strength. She seized the gown that had caught her eye. Police would surely come soon. She peeled out of her soiled clothes (Sunday School teacher clothes, he had called them) and pulled the dress over her head. She eased its genteel folds down over waist, then squandered a moment smoothing her hair. The tag showed that the vintage dress would have cost more than a month's salary.

She wished she could see herself — lunar skin, dark hair, Giselle rising from the grave, not to save life, but to seek it. Her friends would giggle. Just think, she'd met someone and stayed out all night! Tomorrow, maybe, they'd achieve concern for her. But they wouldn't miss her long. She was a spare single. Next of kin would get her insurance. No, no home for her.

Where to? She still needed a place to stay, some place safely dark. What about that rusty, torpedo-shaped thing in Jackson Square by the Cabildo? A submarine, it looked like. It would be dark inside. Yes, and she'd bet the money she didn't have that it was sealed so people could not climb inside and screw, just to say they had.

As she wandered down Royal, she thought she almost fit in here now, here, in this dancing dress that might have belonged to some Creole *jeune fille bien élevée* who would not have been left out this late at night. It made sense. New Orleans spent more than half its time living in the past. Living and dead slept close together, and time here was twisty. It flowed sideways like a cat, to rub against the living or to jump them, out of the shadows, and sink in claws and fangs.

She could go to the cemetery the driver'd warned her to avoid. Surely, no mugger could harm her now or even meet her eyes. Perhaps there might be some familiar name there, some scalawag or Yankee trooper whom a fever had borne off, and she could find houseroom. She would rather not lie among strangers.

She shut her eyes, seeking the thread of awareness that she'd heard (when she'd bothered to think of it) must draw a vampire to her creator. She found nothing. It hardly seemed fair just to leave her on her own, but it didn't seem as if chivalry worked for vampire, even those who had been Southern gentlemen. This was his turf. He knew how to hunt and track and stalk. He might even enjoy her panic. Besides, she was...oh God, she was so hungry.

She would have to feed, regardless.

"Excuse me, *Mademoiselle*. Miss, are you all right?" At a respectful distance, addressing her with respect: heartbeats, blood, sweat, life, a starched shirt. Inclining forward in a half-bow, careful not to spook a woman all in white who should not be out alone before the earliest of Ash Wednesday's masses.

Go away.

He was coming at her: dark, reserved, more European then Southern. One of the Creoles, then, who mostly kept themselves to themselves, unlike the more boisterous Cajuns. Why did this one have to be out, strolling back, no doubt, to some discreetly inherited flat in the Pontalba Buildings or to an even more discreet house whose iron grilles barred it from city riffraff? Confident, or why would he investigate an alarm all by himself.

Hunger made her dizzier than she thought she could be, yet still keep her feet. She sensed the cleanness in this man's blood along with some subtle cologne. He wore a wedding ring. Even worse, she wanted to feed on a family man. She shrank away. Think of your children and run!

"Were you hurt? Did the thieves touch you?" he asked.

What a reward for his kindness to drain him till he died.

She shrank back. It was the wrong thing to do. She saw that in a flash. Now, he'd think she'd been raped, and he'd want to help her.

Carefully, he stepped toward her. Slowly. He could not know how that tantalized her. He held out his hand. "Let me help you."

She shook her head, mute.

Dear little one, rest easy.

She never could. Her back touched the wall. His outstretched hand touched hers.

She could not help herself. She pounced.

Grabbing him with that strength she had not gotten used to, she bent back his head for the unnatural kiss. She would take, she resolved, no more than would fill a go-cup. A *small* go-cup.

His blood had all the savor of the food here: bell pepper and red wine and rice and pork. Oh God, make that a big go-cup. The blood tide flowed over her, bright moments frothing in its wake like bubbles in sparkling wine. A dark-eyed son, a shy daughter. Generations passing serenely despite upheavals beyond his family's iron grilles, years and years in which the dead and the living danced together, Spanish and French — *Vive l'Empereur.* Casting a cold, punctilious eye on the blond invaders, withdrawing further into the land itself, a land of camellias, of sun upon the river that flowed past white homes, tumbling down in these latter years; a land of shadows in the bayou, of feu follet and lou garou.

Breast against her breast, his heartbeat making her even more drunk, he knew her, knew what she was, knew how she had come there. Anger at the lanky enemies fired the blood she kept drinking. They fought at our side, but they are still strangers.

J'ai peur, maman. Mother, I'm scared.

His eyes rolled up, and he knew she could not restrain herself. Hail Mary Mother of God and Into Thy Hands rang in his fainting mind. His pulse beat like angel wings.

In that instant, understanding blossomed in his mind, and a terrible compassion. Poor little one. Just tonight? *Fais dodo, chère.* It was Cajun, it was rowdy, and it stopped her dead.

She wrenched her head away, holding him lest he fall.

"Dear God," victim and vampire said at once, in different languages.

She released him. He took a step or two, testing his ability to walk, then returned. Of course: she might leave him if she chose, but he must wait to be dismissed, if she could.

"Hey! Excuse me, you two. Did any of you see anything?"

She whirled, but the man with her pressed her back and turned more slowly to face a large policeman, brother to the cavalry on Bourbon Street. His partner waited silent by his side. Could she take them both?

"Good evening," said her victim. He drew himself up, the perfect gentleman. "I very much regret, sir, but no. I was walking this lady home when we heard a noise. I am distressed I brought her down this street. What if the thieves had seen us?"

She followed his cue and took his arm, edging shyly behind him. Don't overact.

The police straightened, touching hat brims.

"But of course, I should be glad to give you my card if you have further questions. Perhaps tomorrow, since today is a Holy Day?"

He moved his hand. Aristocrat or not, the policeman raised a hand. Stop right there.

"Your name and address will do."

He gave it. Prosperous, well-connected, judging by the policeman's response.

"We may send a man around tomorrow, sir. But if you say you saw nothing..."

"Neither I nor this lady. Now, if you will excuse us..."

He turned and escorted her away.

"Thank you," she whispered.

He touched his throat. "Of course I shall assist you," he said, his voice husky.

"I am sorry," she whispered. Blood-tinged tears threatened.

"This is very terrible," her victim said. "You were a guest in my City."

"I am sorry," she said again. She had spent her life apologizing for inconsequential things. Here, beyond the end of it, she saw how foolish those earlier regrets had been when she still possessed her life.

"I am sorry too." Her victim reached out to her. He shimmered in the sudden flood of tears in her eyes. Then victim, knowing her need, comforted vampire, and she forbore to weep blood tears upon his crisp shirt.

At length, she pushed free and stood aside. She shivered at the touch of the grey air. He nodded.

"Those upstarts. *Canaille* with this money and their guns, their boots and their loud voices. And we had to listen to their bitterness when the war ended — a double bitterness, a double theft when the other thieves came down from the North. And you, a guest, are treated thus..."

Another feud, then, passed down the generations, not against the Yankees or modern tourists, but against the strangers who had barged in and actually bought this entire area without their consent. Who had trampled all over it with the barbarian they hailed as Old Hickory, and turned a sultry, almost French city into something more vulgar if just as sinister.

"I thought..."

"Because he was born here, and you were not? What is the likes of him but a Scalawag to us?"

They were allied now by blood. She had an image of centuries of dark-haired men and women, profoundly loyal to family, silent in the face of outsiders, but quick to seize advantage. "Remember how long we have lived here. Do you think you are the first? You are not."

It happens in the very best of families. It would have been impolite to laugh.

His was an older tradition by far, for which the Code Napoleon was still the law whenever the code duello was not. And this was what she, sensing his cleanliness and his strength, had made her servant.

For how long? Until his fear of her outweighed his fear of death? Longer? He had said that he was bound by honor as well as blood. He had said she was not the first.

Perhaps his kin had a way of handling this, handing down the knowledge, and the bond in the blood, from son to son (the spare, not the precious heir) out of love for the man who had first brought home the pledge. Perhaps they had a family tradition: the special friend. Children, as they grew up, would be allowed to stay awake past bedtime to be presented to their night-time *Tante*. The bond would traverse the generations as family tended the vampire's coffin alongside the quiet graves.

It might just work. All those vampire stories had to come from somewhere.

The Creole gentleman eyed her shrewdly. "You are wondering if your life, even as you are, is worth the price. I should remind you: our Church teaches us that life is to be preserved. Even as..." A gesture worth one hand, so graceful that she almost saw lace swirl from his cuff. Life even for such as she. Apostle to the Undead. He smiled. She had not made a witless servant.

What did she want? Revenge? A stake through her maker's heart? He had left her one clue: the newspaper. And in it, the vampire's name, his history, his death.

"If he controls me..." A wind brushed the folds of her gown, her hair where it flowed past her shoulders. Almost dawn. Swiftly, she told him about her maker, his suicide, his rise from the grave.

"He had his life in the sun, and he despised it. And he hates this other existence too. So he chose you-- someone he could treat as an enemy, someone on whom he could take out his anger, yet someone strong enough to make him lose again. Because he wants to lose."

Like her maker, she would sleep during the day. But this man, so ready to serve her, so she that her enemy was his enemy, and had been his family's enemy for generations. He could check court records. He could search the graveyards in daylight. And he could enter a tomb by day, open the coffin, bring out stake and hammer...

He eyed her shrewdly. "Do you want to give him what he seeks?"

She flinched.

"I do not wish to kill," she said. "It strikes me as a paltry sort of vengeance."

He nodded respect and waited.

"He wants to die?" she said. "Let us not oblige him. When we find his grave..." She knew her eyes glowed like coals because the living man stepped back. "Do not stab him or burn him. But wrap his coffin in chains." A memory of old stories came to her. "With silver locks. Trap him until doomsday."

The gentleman smiled and kissed her hand. In the shadows and damp of New Orleans before dawn, the gesture did not seem absurd.

She heard stirrings as the Big Easy woke from a drunken sleep and returned to life. Ships' horns boomed over the Mississippi. Why should she not survive, dancing down the generations with this ally and his family? This seemed to be a convenient city for casual violence and ancestral feuds. Why not, for vampires — even for the likes of a Yankee vampire?

There would be an investigation when people missed her. Highly placed as this man's family seemed to be, she could evade it. They would protect her, would help her contrive financial resources. She could survive. She would.

"I must hide before dawn," she said. If worst came to worst, some of the tombs had been forced open. Or she could break in. Bodies didn't last long in the city's heat and humidity. She could have her choice.

Her ally touched his breast pocket. "My family has such a place, locked and tended. I will drive you there." So there was room in the inn after all.

"I've heard the graveyards aren't safe," she objected. "No one will attack me, or if they try, I think they will run the instant they see me. But once I am...Safe...You..."

His laughter startled her.

"After surviving tonight, how should I succumb to what you call a mugger? Come with me. Hurry."

Her victim held out his arm. The vampire took it. Lady and gentlemen out late at night.

His discreet black car purred over the road. The necropolis rose out of the dying night to reveal a whitewashed slum, tombs, some crumbling into their original brick: a morbid warren four coffins high, the merely dead and the living. She smelled only mud and rotting vegetation. The dead were stored above the level of the water.

Some day, she knew, another hurricane, worse than Katrina, would drive Lake Pontchartrain down upon this place. Coffins would stir on the face of the waters, the living clinging to their dead. Then, they would find her too.

Perhaps. First, survive.

They hurried, a guide and his anemic Juliet searching for her tomb, through the shadowed lanes of the cemetery, past a tumbled angel, a whitened Gothic arch, a low-branched tree. The setting moon glinted on a plastic necklace, a glinting fake doubloon, tawdry images of the sun from Mardi Gras.

She must preserve her memories of how the sun looked as best she could. She would not, she thought, forgive that in a hurry. Anger made her shiver.

"Not far now," whispered her guide.

If thieves or killers lurked beneath the bulk of the chapel to the left (she heard them breathe), they sensed her dangerousness and forbore to strike.

Drawing a tiny key from his breast pocket, he opened the door and bowed her inside a tiny chapel. He crossed himself. A Creole Notre Dame, she thought.

The approach of dawn was making her dizzy.

Visibly, he wavered. She suppressed a laugh. What should a gentleman do? Hold open *grandmere*'s coffin lid for his stranger guest?

"I must learn to do this for myself," she said. A lady solved such problems. She held out her hand again for his salute. He shut the door behind him and locked it. She would ask for an inside lock.

Yes. She would learn to speak the husky, softened French of her protector. And she would make herself at home here in the heart of this city of the dead. Perhaps her enemy would find her, or perhaps priests of police. Though she had not wanted life on these terms, she would not let them take it from her. At least, not yet. By God, she would lead them a chase and have herself a dance or two or five. Perhaps, she would dance one night outside that writer's house. Maybe its present inhabitants would invite her inside for tea or I-never-drink-wine. Or just to talk. She would have many years just to talk.

So it all was settled, at least for now.

She chose a coffin at random and opened it. Empty, or all but. The bones did not disturb her, but perhaps she should have one all her own. She whispered thanks to her host and made herself lie down.

So much could still go wrong. The tomb, the coffin, her servant, her enemy, her vengeance — was she really going to be able to shut the lid upon herself?

She must.

Darkness reached out to drawn her down. *J'ai peur!* She cried out to it, a frightened child. A memory from the night floated back into her mind. *Fais dodo, chère.*

There, my dearest. There.

Now rest.

Whimpering at first, the vampire sang herself a lullaby. As the deadly sun came up, she learned to sleep.

My thanks to the late George Alec Effinger for advice, research, and local...colors other than red.

About the Author

Susan Shwartz returned from a long sabbatical on Wall Street to her first love, writing fantasy, science fiction, and horror. She is a five-time nominee for the Nebula, a two-time nominee for the Hugo, with nominations for the World Fantasy Award, the Philip K. Dick, and the Edgar. In 1993, San Francisco chronicle cited her work for Best Novelette, and in 1996, best Novella with the late Mike Resnick for "Bibi," a 1995 winner of the HOMer award.

The Castaway

Kailey Alessi

CW: Shipwreck, burns, corpse, environmental whump, fantasy racism, language barriers, restraints, knives
Whumpee: Man, Woman, Caretaker: Woman, Whumper: Man

The first thing Cy knew was warmth. The second thing he knew was burning. Cy gasped awake, sputtering in the lapping waves. He was alive. But more importantly, he was currently burning in the sun. Cy forced his shaky limbs to crawl himself up the beach, towards the shade of the tree line. The sand under his fingers was hot, a scorching reminder that he had to get out of the sun. He had no idea how long he had already been exposed. He collapsed against the tree and let out a pitiful whimper. Cy raised a hand to the back of his neck and winced. Yep, he was burned all right. Ironically, it was a good thing that it hurt. That meant the burn hadn't edged into lethal territory. He looked out at the brilliant blue sea. The waves gently rolled against the sandy beach, giving no indication that just last night they had towered twenty feet high. Cy wrapped his arms around himself. Pieces of wood littered the beach, but he didn't spot any other survivors.

His entire body felt like a giant bruise, tender, sore, battered. It didn't help that he hadn't fed in almost a week. The crossing was only supposed to take about ten nights, so of course they hadn't bothered bringing humans along. Anything to cut costs for the shareholders. What was he going to do now? Cy leaned his head back against the tree and closed his eyes. Sand crusted his body and his lips were cracked from the saltwater. He desperately needed to bathe, as well as to drink some water. And blood.

Cy awoke to find his bare feet burning. He yelped, the sound scratching his throat, as he scrambled back further into the woods. It must have been late afternoon. Cy used a tree to help himself to his feet. He wobbled when he stood, the trunk being the only thing preventing him from collapsing back to his knees. Cy looked around him. The trees were primarily oaks, stretching taller than any he had ever seen. The only sounds were the lapping of the waves in the distance, the tweeting of birds, and the rustling of leaves in the wind.

"Hello?" he called, his voice a painful croak. He tried again. "Hello? Is anybody there?"

No answer. His heart sank, even though he wasn't surprised. There had been ten other sailors on the vessel. He had gone to sleep early, the others staying up to indulge in the sizable liquor stores and play cards.

He needed to find the others. They could be further down the beach. Cy pushed his battered body away from the tree and started back towards the water. He hovered within the shadows of the trees, not daring another brush with the sun. He walked parallel to the shore, scanning the wreckage for the others. Cy called out. There was no response. He had walked maybe half an hour when his eyes lighted on a lump of fabric on the beach, huddled next to a broken timber.

"Hey!"

The bundle didn't move. Cy grit his teeth and considered the shadows. The shade stretched further towards the water now. He would have to move fast, but he could reach the sailor before the sun got him. Probably. Cy took a steadying breath before dashing out of the shadows. The warmth of the sun enfolded him as he neared the other vampire, the heat caressing his skin like a threat. He dropped to his knees next to the sailor and reached out a hand.

"Hey, it's not safe here-"

Cy jerked back when he saw the missing arm, seemingly ripped from the socket. He fought down the bile in his throat as he moved his gaze up to the face. A burned caricature stared back at him. Flesh wept from the bones. Where the eyes should have been were half-empty sockets, half-deflated, reddened eyeballs staring back at him. Cy screamed and scrambled backward. The vampire was dead. Probably had been for awhile. He retched, tears stinging his eyes as bile burned his throat. The corpse was so mangled he couldn't even tell who it had been. The only mercy was that they had probably drowned, not been slowly roasted to death by the sun. Cy clutched his fingers in the sand and looked back at the vampire. The lips had burned away, so that one fang jutted out. Cy rose to his feet and retreated back to the safety of the trees.

He walked for hours. He found more debris but no vampires, dead or otherwise. Cy assumed he was on an island, and a large one at that. He licked his cracked lips and cursed himself for not paying more attention to the nautical charts. He knew there were some inhabited islands this far north, but had no idea if this was one of them.

Cy stopped walking, staring out at the empty beach. No wreckage littered the shore. He wouldn't be finding any help. Anxiety twisted his stomach and caused his hands to shake. He was alone. He was alone on a probably deserted island and no one was coming for him. All he had was the clothes on his back. He was burned, weak, and hungry. He was going to die. Cy sank to the ground and put his head in his hands. His shoulders shook, even as his cheeks were dry. His body didn't have the moisture to spare on tears.

Once he had cried himself out he laid curled up on his side, arms folded close to his chest. The way he saw it, he had two options. Wait here on the beach and hope that another ship would pass by. Or leave the beach, venturing into the woods to try to find a settlement. Both were fool's errands. He didn't know a ton about navigation, but he knew that they had taken the northernmost route, which was technically faster but was also more dangerous and thus less traveled. The odds of another ship happening across this exact island before he succumbed to starvation were astronomically low. As for the settlement ... that was also unlikely. He remembered from his history lessons that most of the islands had been abandoned over the past five hundred years as people migrated to the continent. It turned out that people generally preferred having cities to visit to living on an isolated island.

He stared out at the water. He was well and truly screwed. The sun was down now, the darkness enfolding him in a comfortable embrace. Then he smelled the smoke. Cy bolted upright. He sniffed the air. Yes, that was definitely smoke. And smoke meant ...

"Help!" he screamed. "Help! Please!"

The smell was coming from further inland. Cy stumbled through the woods. Branches stung his face and roots caught his feet, but he kept going. The smell was strengthening, he was definitely going in the right direction. An elated laugh bubbled out of his throat. He was going to be okay.

Then the ground opened up beneath him. For one sickening moment he fell. Then he hit the ground with enough force to drive the air out of his lungs and fold his ankle to the side. He couldn't breathe and his vision went white with pain. Cy gasped like a fish out of water, tears streaming down his face. He stared up at the sky, a good six feet farther away than it had been just a moment before. His breath returned with agonizing slowness. Once his breathing was back, he was able to take stock of the damage to the rest of his body. He had hit his head in the fall and sticky wetness coated the side of his face. He tested his limbs experimentally and immediately gasped at the pain in his ankle. It wasn't broken, but it was sprained.

Cy froze when he heard the voices speaking an unfamiliar language. He eased himself to sitting cautiously. There were people approaching the pit he had fallen in. He glanced around his surroundings. This wasn't a natural hole. It was a trap.

Suddenly all the old stories came back to him. Stories of isolated islands inhabited only by humans. Stories of how those humans hated vampires. Stories of how said humans enjoyed eating vampire flesh. Cy scrambled back to the side of the pit, jerkily getting to his feet, even as the pain in his ankle almost caused him to cry out. The people approaching might be harmless, but he wasn't gonna just wait here, where he would be unable to fight back if necessary.

He stretched up on the tip toes of his good leg to try to reach the lip of the pit. His fingers were only an inch away. He jumped and tried to get a grip on the side. The soil crumbled under his hands and he fell back into the pit with a jarring thump, a scream tearing from his throat as his ankle gave out and pain flashed up his leg. Then the orangey glow of firelight fell across his face.

He flinched backward and raised a hand to block the light from his eyes.

The people spoke in a harsh, guttural language that he had never heard before. As his eyes adjusted, he was able to make out that the people were carrying gnarly looking spears and knives. One of them was currently gesturing with a spear, clearly trying to speak to him, but he had no idea what they were saying.

"I'm sorry, I don't understand you," Cy said. The person stopped talking. Everybody had gone deafeningly silent.

Cy backed up. This was it. He had survived a shipwreck only to be killed by hostile islanders. Then hands were reaching down into the pit. Apparently the people wanted him to willingly go to his demise. He sank to the ground and pulled his knees toward his chest. Nope. He would stay right here, thank you very much.

The people were clearly irritated. They were insistently reaching out toward him. Cy tried to block out the angry yelling, even though his heartrate was increasing with every word. He should just turn himself in. At least then he wouldn't be stuck in the pit when the sun came up.

Someone jumped into the pit. Cy shrieked.

The person held up their hands and spoke in a soft voice. Like they were trying to soothe a spooked horse. Cy bristled at the treatment.

The person took one step toward him, then another. Cy was against the wall of the pit and didn't have anywhere else to go.

"Please don't hurt me," he whispered. Then he passed out.

***

Cy came back to consciousness slowly. He was cold, colder than he had ever been before. He shivered. It was quiet. He was laying on his back on something soft. He opened his eyes. He was inside. He was *inside*. Cy bolted upright, or at least tried to. His head swam and he groaned before sinking back down into the pillows. The humans had caught him. The room he was in was made out of stone. There was one window across from the bed, currently firmly shuttered. A wooden chair sat in a corner. The only other thing in the room was the bed.

Cy tested his limbs, wincing at the stiffness in his ankle. The humans hadn't restrained him. Another chill wracked his body. His skin hurt, probably from the burns. An all-consuming ache permeated his body, seeming to originate in his stomach and radiate outwards. He needed blood.

He pushed himself upright, more slowly this time. The humans had taken his clothes while he was unconscious and dressed him in a thin, sleeveless shift. Cy swung his legs over the side of the bed, took a deep breath, and stood up. His ankle couldn't take his weight and he fell to the ground with a cry.

At that moment, the door opened. A human gave a shout and rushed towards him, a child hot on her heels.

The human was speaking rapidly in that strange language. It sounded like she was scolding him. She gently picked him up under the armpits and dragged him back into bed.

She made a *stay there* motion and stepped out of the room. The child stayed, staring at him with wide eyes. Cy inwardly cursed.

The woman returned with a tray. She set it on the bed then took a seat next to him. She picked up a bowl.

His stomach turned. What were these humans playing at? She attempted to hand it to him. Cy just stared. The bowl was filled with a thick, brownish liquid. Little blobs of solid material floated in it. He couldn't eat that. He shook his head.

The woman made a tsking sound and held it out more forcefully. Nausea swam up his throat. He couldn't eat human food.

The woman sighed and turned back to the tray. She set the bowl down and picked up a cup. She held it out to him. The liquid was clear and scentless. Water.

Suddenly his throat was dry. He could have water. Cy reached his hand out and took the cup. It was more difficult than it should have been for him to raise the cup to his mouth and drink.

The woman was speaking to him, in a low soothing voice that reminded him of his mother. As he drank, he looked between the woman, the child, and the open door. He was too weak to escape without feeding. There was no way he would feed on a child, he did have *morals,* but the woman would be easy pickings. She was short and plump and he could almost see the blood pulsing through her neck. But if he bit her, the child would run for help. Cy grit his teeth. He would have to bide his time.

The woman took the cup and tried to hand him the bowl again. He shook his head and scooted backward. She sighed, put the bowl back on the tray, and left.

The next time the door opened, the woman was accompanied by two large men. She held a bowl in her hand and a steely expression in her eyes. She stopped at the foot of the bed and spoke. From what Cy gathered, she was telling him to either eat the fucking soup by himself or she would have the two intimating looking men help her to force it down his throat.

Tears of frustration stung his eyes. Why did these humans insist on torturing him? They surely knew that vampires could only eat blood.

Unless they didn't. Horror mounted as the realization dawned on him. These humans didn't know he was a vampire. They probably had never even *seen* a vampire.

Cy bared his fangs and hissed. One of the men jumped back. The other looked like he was trying to hide his discomfort. The woman looked at Cy with a disapproving expression.

She marched up to him and the men grabbed hold of Cy's limbs. They were just humans, Cy should have been able to fight them off. But he was so weak that his struggles didn't do anything besides exhaust himself. The woman grabbed Cy's chin and brought the bowl to his lips. Cy's eyes burned with frustration. He opened his mouth, but instead of taking the offered bowl he sank his teeth into the woman's hand. She cried out and then slumped as the venom took hold.

Cy gulped in one mouthful of blood, then another. The hot, thick liquid rolled across his tongue and down his throat and he almost wept in relief.

Then a punch hit him in the side of the head and his fangs jostled in the woman's hand. Another hit him in the stomach. Someone pulled the woman off of him as the other human continued punching him. Cy cried out, trying to curl in on himself as the blows rained down.

Then he was alone, the door slamming as the humans fled. Every breath was excruciating. Cy moaned. He had fucked that up.

When the humans came back, they were armed. There were five men, all brandishing weapons. Knives, axes, pitchforks, they all crowded into the small room. The leader's voice was menacing. Cy didn't know what he wanted. But the humans clearly were angry.

They grabbed Cy. Cy fought back but they easily tied his hands behind his back. Cy snapped his teeth only for a punch to snap his neck to the side. While dazed, they stuffed a wad of cloth in his mouth and tied a strip of fabric around his head to keep it there.

Cy's ears rang and his limbs shook. Two humans grabbed his arms and dragged him out of the room. Angry shouts filled the air and Cy couldn't take in his surroundings, as the world appeared to be spinning. Cy groaned.

The humans marched him outside, where the sun was shining brightly. They threw Cy to the ground and the dirt scratched his face. He instinctively curled into a ball, trying to keep as much of his skin out of the sun as possible.

All of this, just because he was hungry. The back of Cy's neck was starting to tingle. The humans stood in a loose circle around him. There was nowhere for him to go. Cy let out a keening sob, the sound muffled by the gag. These fucking humans were going to kill him. They were going to kill him, and there wasn't a godsdamned thing he could do to stop them.

Cy was so lost in his own terror that he didn't realize at first that the humans had gone deathly quiet. A pair of shoes stepped into view and Cy flinched back, bracing himself for a kick. It didn't come. Instead, the human knelt down beside him and put a hand under his chin. Cy met the woman's gaze. Her face was a bit pale, but she didn't look angry. *Please*, Cy pleaded with his eyes, hoping she would understand. *I didn't mean to hurt you. I was just hungry. Please don't hurt me.*

Something in the woman's expression softened. She spoke to him in quiet, soothing words. Then she reached up and untied the gag. Cy held still for her so she could remove the wad of cloth from his mouth. Her fingers brushed the side of his mouth and everything in Cy ached to bite, to feed, but he resisted. When his mouth was free he bowed his head.

"Thank you," he said.

A cloud had moved in front of the sun, blocking at least some of the burning rays. Cy breathed a little sigh of relief. Then he saw the woman held a knife. Cy scrambled backward until he hit the legs of the nearest humans. Hands came down to rest on his shoulders, making it very clear that he shouldn't move. The woman approached with the knife. Her voice didn't sound threatening, but the knife in her hand was sharp and it could easily slit Cy's throat.

Cy closed his eyes, trembling. This was it. He waited for the prick of metal against his skin. But it didn't come. Instead the metallic aroma of blood filled the air. Cy's eyes flew open. The woman knelt in front of him, a small cut running across her palm. She held out her hand to Cy. Cy hesitated a second. The blood welled from the cut, filling her hand like it was a bowl. One drop spilled over the side. Cy awkwardly got to his knees and pressed his mouth against the cut. The woman made a noise of encouragement and Cy began to drink in earnest. He was so hungry. The blood was hot and rich and it stained his tongue and filled his belly and he had never been more grateful in his entire life. He drank and drank until the bleeding slowed, then licked her hand, both to help the wound close and to get every last drop of blood.

"Thank you, ma'am," Cy said, meeting her eyes. She had a warm expression. She moved behind him and sliced through the ropes binding his wrists. He winced as his hands tingled and he brought them in front of him, rubbing his wrists. The humans were all staring at him, and his face heated. Then the sun broke out from the clouds and a stab of fear went through him. He slowly got to his feet, wincing, and the closest humans backed up a couple steps. Cy scanned the area. He was in the middle of a village, small stone cottages with thatched roofs arranged in a circle. Nobody made a move to grab him, so Cy ducked his head and headed back to the cottage they'd dragged him from, each step sending another jolt of pain through his ankle. Once he reached the threshold, he ducked inside. He headed back to the room was the bloody sheets. He stripped them off the rough straw mattress, piling them in a corner. He then grabbed the pitcher of water, tore a rag from the ruined sheets, and set about cleaning the blood off the floor.

Cy didn't know how long the woman had been watching him work. When he raised his head she was standing in the doorway, arms crossed, a slight smile on her face. Cy gestured sheepishly at the soiled sheets. "Sorry about the mess," he said.

She just shrugged. She said something in her language and strolled into the room, gesturing for Cy to get up. Cy got to his feet and she grabbed his shoulders, gently leading him out of the room. She swung his arm over her shoulder, letting him use her as a crutch. She led him through the next door, where a large bed sat against the wall, the sunlight streaming through the window. Cy missed a step. The woman noticed his hesitancy and released his shoulders, rushing to the window to pull the shutters. Then she gestured to the bed, repeating the word. It must mean rest. Cy sat down on the bed, unsure. The woman beamed at him. Then she grabbed his legs and pulled them into the bed. Cy gave a startled laugh. Then the woman spread a blanket over him. She repeated a word as she stroked his hair back from his forehead. It must mean "rest."

Cy repeated the word, the vowels and consonants strange on his tongue. The woman gave a soft chuckle. And Cy did what she had asked. He rested.

About the Author

Kailey Alessi is the founder and editor-in-chief of the Whumpy Printing Press, a publishing company whose mission is to publish the work of the whump community. She is also the author of the Of Vampires and Men dark fantasy series, and her short fiction has appeared in numerous anthologies. She is an archaeologist by day, and by night she writes all sorts of dark fiction. You can find her on tumblr @whumpy-writings

Your Love Like Iron Bars Around My Heart

Lux Thorn

CW: Noncon/sexual assault, NSFW, addiction, emotional abuse, kidnapping, captivity
Whumpee: Man, Whumper: Man, Woman, Caretaker: N/A

Gabriel leaned against the rusted-out back door of his car, sighing as it drank in gallon after gallon of gas. "You're an insatiable old beast, aren't you?" he muttered, patting the car affectionately—after all, they'd been through a lot together, him and it. "I don't know how to tell you this, but I think you may have a drinking problem. And it's not easy on the wallet, I'll have you know."

The car seemed to sag into the pavement. He sure hoped that was his imagination, and not one of his tires leaking air. "Oh, I don't mean it," he said, with another pat for good measure. "You know I love you."

He shivered. His thin jacket wasn't enough to keep out the winter air, and of course he'd left his winter coat behind when he'd left the apartment in a hurry three weeks ago. And he sure wasn't going back for it now, not with the way he and his former roommate had parted. Beyond the searing glow of the gas station's floodlights, the darkness seemed to creep in closer, bringing the tooth-chattering cold with it. This was the kind of night that used to have people huddled around campfires, fearing the monsters beyond the reach of the light.

Cars whizzed by on the road. So many people with someplace to go. Probably blasting their heat without any worry about the cost. On their way to a nice warm house where they'd cook themselves up a bowl of hearty soup and then snuggle up on the couch under a warm blanket in front of the TV. Living the dream.

Gabriel tore his eyes away from the road and back to the meter, where the number was still going up, and up, and up. The beast truly was insatiable.

If his car were a person, Gabriel would have cut it off several drinks ago. But when your car was the only home you had left—especially on a night like this—keeping it fed wasn't optional. So the greedy thing would get all the gas it wanted tonight.

At last, the pump clicked. He winced at the number and hooked the pump back into its spot. "I hope you're satisfied," he told his car as he climbed back into the driver's seat. He sniffed his hands and nearly gagged. Someday he'd learn the trick of pumping gas without getting the foul-smelling stuff all over his fingers, but today was apparently not that day.

He turned the key in the ignition. Nothing happened.

His heart plummeted down to his stomach. "Oh, come on, you know I didn't mean all that earlier," he said, stroking the steering wheel placatingly. "You know I'll always give you all the gas you want."

He tried again. The car made a faint grumbling sound. He wished it didn't make him think of a death rattle. Then nothing.

"Come on, come on. Please." He tried again. Nothing.

"I'll tell you what. Start for me, and next time I'll spring for the premium stuff. Maybe even a nice car wash. What do you think? Would you like that?"

Still nothing.

The car behind him honked, clearly waiting for him to get out of the way. "As if I want to be sitting here," he muttered.

What exactly was he supposed to do now? It wasn't like he could afford a tow to the nearest garage. Let alone what said garage would charge him for repairs. He glanced toward his phone lying on the passenger seat, but he didn't have anyone to call. The only person he had been remotely close with around here was the roommate who had kicked him out, and that bridge was well and truly burned.

And to his dad's frustration, he had never managed to learn his way around an engine, so fixing the problem himself was right out.

The person behind him honked again. He ignored them, ducking his head and tucking his hands into his sleeves in preparation for the cold. He opened the door and tried not to flinch as the wind slapped him in the face. When had it gotten so windy, anyway?

He popped open the hood. Without much hope, he stared down at its contents. A tangle of tubes and metal whatsits. That there was the... um... thingy, and over there was the... He shook his head. He didn't have the first clue what he was looking at.

"Come on," he urged the car. "You don't want to spend the night here any more than I do. So help me out here, will you? Show me what's wrong."

Yeah, right. What did he expect the old rust bucket to do—open its nonexistent mouth and tell him where it hurt?

He thought about the phone lying on the passenger seat. His dad would know how to fix this. Might even be able to talk him through it.

And offer a heaping helping of self-loathing along with his advice, no doubt. There was a reason Gabriel had moved halfway across the country.

But it wasn't like he had any other options.

With a growl that landed somewhere between frustration and despair, he crossed to the passenger side and flung open the door. He grabbed the phone. His dad was still saved in his contacts—now that was a lucky break. He had thought about purging his family from his phone, but had been too much of a coward to actually go through with it.

His finger hovered over his dad's name in his contacts list.

A sudden whining hum from above made him freeze. The floodlights sparked—and went out.

The convenience store lights were out too. A power outage? If so, it was extremely local—the grocery store down the street still had all its lights blazing. And what would have knocked the power out, anyway? It was supposed to snow later tonight—as much as six inches, according to that one asshole forecaster whose dire predictions always seemed to come true—but he hadn't seen a single flake yet.

As if in answer to his question, the wind picked up speed, whining as it sped through the trees that lined the road. That was probably it—that freak wind had probably knocked out a power line. At least it hadn't affected his cell reception—not that he'd be able to see what he was doing even if his dad could talk him through the fix. Looked like he would be working by flashlight.

"Pardon me," came a voice from *way too fucking close.*

He yelped. The phone flew from his hands to land facedown on the pavement.

Even as close as he was, the man in front of him was barely visible through the thick darkness. He was painfully thin, and a full head taller than Gabriel himself. His long black hair was tied back in a ponytail. His face was as pale as if he had been out in the cold long enough for it to leach all the color from him. And yet he was wearing short sleeves, and didn't look the least bit uncomfortable.

"Sorry about that," he said, feeling a blush beginning to form. "You startled me." He bent and grabbed his phone. The screen was cracked down the center—just what he needed—but at least it still seemed to work.

"You have nothing to apologize for," the man said, his words oddly slow and measured. "Do you need assistance?"

From some freak who wore short sleeves in the middle of winter, who had somehow snuck up on him without him noticing? Not his first choice. But he was the proverbial beggar without choices. "I don't suppose you know your way around an engine?" He offered the man a hesitant smile even as he took a step back. Just in case.

"Ah, but that isn't the help you really need, is it?" The man aimed his penetrating stare not at the car, but at Gabriel himself. "You have no place to live, isn't that right?"

Gabriel took another step back. "What makes you say that?"

"I've been watching you," the man said, as if this wasn't a totally unhinged thing to say to a stranger in the middle of a dark parking lot of a gas station during a power outage. "You slept in your car last night. And the night before."

Gabriel glanced over his shoulder for the car that had been honking impatiently at him a moment ago, but apparently that driver had decided to try his luck elsewhere. There was no one behind him anymore.

He was on his own.

Another few steps back, and he'd reach the driver's-side door. And... then what? It wasn't like he could drive away. "I'll be fine, thanks." He slammed the hood shut. "I don't need any help after all."

"Gabriel," the man said. "Gabriel, look at me."

Startled, Gabriel lifted his eyes to meet the man's gaze.

A wave of calm washed through him. What had he been so worried about? This man was here to *help* him. He had said so. Help was exactly what he had been hoping for, wasn't it?

"You're right," he said, because answering the man's question honestly seemed only polite. "I've been living out of my car for the past few weeks. But it's temporary. Just until I find another job, a new place to live. I'll manage."

"But at the moment, you have no home and no employment," the man said. "This is fortunate. It means you will not be missed."

Gabriel blinked, trying to shake away the haze of calm. He wouldn't be missed? That... that was bad, wasn't it?

He felt like he was thinking through pudding as he stared down at his phone. He had the overwhelming urge to put it away. Instead, he stretched a slow-moving finger toward the emergency-call button.

"Sleep." The man's voice wrapped around Gabriel like a warm blanket.

Gabriel's phone tumbled from his fingers again. He never felt himself hit the ground.

***

Gabriel woke enveloped in softness. When he opened his eyes, a four-poster bed cradled him. The mattress was light as a cloud under him, a cocoon of blankets wrapping him in warmth. The fabric was smooth against his fingers, silky as running water as it glided along his skin. It smelled like laundry fresh out of the dryer. He drew in a deep breath.

Only then did he wake up enough to remember he should be afraid.

He sat up, and the blankets fell away. He mourned the loss of the warmth even as his eyes darted around the room in alarm. The wallpaper was an old-fashioned pattern in a rich red and gold. A carved wooden dresser held a vase filled with orchids. A portrait stared down at him from one wall—a pale-faced, dark-haired man who stared at him as if he knew he was an intruder in his house.

Gabriel hastily looked away. "Look, it's not like I chose to be here." How *had* he gotten here? He peered under the blankets. He was still wearing the same clothes—good. Although he was sure the man in the portrait wouldn't be happy about his grubby jeans all over his expensive sheets.

He snuck another look up at the portrait. Something about that sharp-angled face, and that pale, pale skin... He wasn't the same man Gabriel had met at the gas station, but he shared a resemblance.

The man from the gas station.

His heartbeat thundered in his ears as the memories of last night crashed down on him. That man. He had made Gabriel want to trust him, and for a moment, Gabriel had. It didn't make sense. He hadn't gone home with the guy, had he? He was sure he had better judgment than *that*.

No. That wasn't what had happened. The man had told him to sleep, and he... had? His memory cut off there. But how could the man have...

Get out first. Figure it out later. Gabriel threw the covers off the rest of the way. He was about to swing his legs over the side of the bed when the door to the bedroom opened. Gabriel froze guiltily.

The visitor looked nothing like the man from last night. His skin was bronze, his hair a dull brown cut close to his scalp. His head was bowed, and he carried a covered tray in his arms, like hotel room service.

Gabriel sniffed the air. His stomach growled. Even kidnapped and in fear for his life, he had to admit, whatever was in there smelled like heaven.

"Is that for me?" Gabriel asked. "Thanks. Um, not that I can eat it, so I guess you might as well send it back." Although after getting a whiff of whatever was in there, a part of him was tempted, danger be damned. "I was actually hoping to get going. If you could just tell me where I am?…"

Giving no indication that he had heard, the man held the tray out to Gabriel.

Gabriel didn't take it. "Actually, I'm not hungry," he said, even as his stomach growled loudly enough to prove him a liar. "All I really need to know is where I am, and what's the best way out of here. Is there a bus stop nearby?"

After he left, he'd have to go back to the gas station and pray his car was still there. Not that there was any chance it hadn't been towed overnight. He might as well skip straight to calling the local tow yards. He patted his pocket.

His phone. Where was his phone?

Again, the man didn't react to his words. He set the tray down on the bedside table, next to a lamp with a tasseled shade. He turned away.

"Um… can you hear me?" Gabriel asked.

The man walked back to the door, which Gabriel took to be a no. He left the room and closed the door behind him, leaving Gabriel alone again.

His phone wasn't in either of his pockets. A glance around the room told him none of the rest of his stuff had made it here. He must have dropped his phone when he had fallen, and even if by some miracle his car was still there, there was no way his phone still was. A new phone: another thing he couldn't afford. And how the hell was he supposed to find a new job or a place to live without a *phone?*

Get out of here first, he reminded himself. Everything else could come later.

But that divine smell wafting off the tray. Without the snacks he had stashed in his car, and without—oh, shit—his *wallet,* he didn't know when he'd have his next opportunity to eat. There was no harm in taking a few bites, was there? It would fuel him up for whatever came next.

He uncovered the tray. Hot steam rose up, bathing his nose in delicious scents. The tray held two perfectly poached eggs sprinkled with fragrant herbs, thin strips of beef in a thick and creamy gravy, and a roll dripping with butter. His stomach gnawed at his spine, promising vengeance if he didn't at least try a bite of everything.

The food disappeared more quickly than he would have thought possible. His stomach purred in satisfaction, properly full for the first time in weeks. A wave of purely physical contentment came over him, even as he stared uneasily at the door.

He stood, and felt perfectly steady on his feet—no dizziness, no nausea. The food hadn't been poisoned, then. Or if it had, it was something slow-acting. Great. Something else to worry about. But the feeling of a full belly made it hard for him to regret his choice.

He took a step toward the door—and as if somebody had been waiting for him to do just that, the door opened.

It was the man from the gas station this time. He looked no less eerie in the light. Maybe more. He looked like a porcelain statue, not a living human. Gabriel took an involuntary step back.

"I apologize for bringing you here so abruptly," the man said gravely, closing the door behind him, "and with no explanation."

"I'd say you've got more than that to apologize for," said Gabriel. "It's not like kidnapping would have been any better if you had taken the time to explain it to me first. Although I have to admit, the food is excellent. So, you know, thanks. For that part, at least. Not that it excuses the rest."

He was babbling. His father had always told him his mouth was going to get him killed someday. Maybe today was the day.

"I would have preferred to be forthright with you," the man said. "But secrecy is of the essence. Hence the need for swift action, and for the cover of darkness."

"The power outage," said Gabriel. "That was you?"

Who was he, that he could have taken the power out like that?

His breakfast was no longer sitting well in his stomach.

"Let us begin the way I wish I could have begun last night," said the man. He strode to the bed with the grace of a dancer and extended his hand to Gabriel. "My name is Mattias de Vaignon. I am what you would call a vampire."

Gabriel blinked at him, nonplussed. He didn't shake his hand. "Please tell me you're just really into Halloween." And not, you know, crazy. Or worse, *not* crazy.

"A vampire is a creature who feeds on human blood to survive," said Mattias. "Some call us monsters, but we prefer to think of ourselves as close kin to humans. My own mother began as a human, and many who live here were humans in their first life before they were brought into the family through the rite of sacred death. Our weaknesses are many, but our lives are long. We—"

"Oh, I know what a vampire is," Gabriel assured him. "That's not the issue here."

"This is my family's home, and now yours," Mattias informed him, as if this were a perfectly normal thing to say when he had just announced himself as a vampire. "You will be treated well, have no fear of that. All your physical needs will be met, and you will be provided with regular mental stimulation. We have rules, you see. We not only take those who will not be missed, but those whose lives are bleak, on the edge of death."

"Hey," said Gabriel. "I wasn't doing *that* badly for myself." As if that were the issue here.

Mattias looked at him with pity in his eyes. "You were suffering," he said. "But for the next six months, you will want for nothing."

"Um... why six months?" Gabriel had a bad feeling he wasn't going to like the answer.

Mattias sighed. "Even with careful treatment, a food source lasts six months at most. No human can endure our needs forever. But until that time comes—"

He stopped. Probably because Gabriel had barreled past him and toward the closed door.

Gabriel didn't see Mattias move, but suddenly he was between Gabriel and the door. "I'm afraid you cannot leave," he said. "But take this as consolation: there is nothing out there for you but hunger and cold. Here, you will be warm and fed. You will—"

"I'll die," Gabriel interrupted. "You'll drink my *blood,* and then you'll kill me." The man was crazy. He was crazy, and he was going to kill him. Either that, or...

Or monsters were real, and he meant what he said, and Gabriel was going to die anyway.

"Look at me," Mattias urged. "Look at me, and still yourself."

Against his will, Gabriel's eyes found the man. Instantly, his limbs felt heavy, his thoughts sluggish. Why was he in such a hurry to leave? It was cold out there, and he had nowhere to go. The bed was probably still warm. Maybe he would just lie down for a little while...

Mattias took his hand. His skin was cold as ice. Gabriel recoiled. Mattias's fingers tightened around him.

He led Gabriel to the bed. Gabriel tried to resist, but trying to think felt like wading through mud.

With exquisite tenderness, Mattias helped him into the bed and tucked the blankets around his body. Warmth suffused him. He was so tired.

No. He had to get out of here. He had to... to get up... to go...

"I will treat you gently," Mattias promised softly, running a cold finger down his cheek, "and you will know no pain. Let me show you."

He opened his mouth. Gabriel caught a glimpse of white fangs that ended in needle points.

He tried to shake himself free of the blanket cocoon. Mattias held him down easily with a hand on his chest. With his other hand, he swept Gabriel's hair aside to bare the side of his neck.

No. No, he had to get out of here...

Mattias bent over him. Gabriel felt a sharp and sudden pressure in his neck—but as the man had promised, no pain. A quick burst of panic shot through him—

Then peace. An ocean of peace, calm and unending. Cradling him. Drowning him.

He was one with the ocean. His blood was salt water, and as it flowed out of him and into Mattias's waiting mouth, he sank into the welcoming mattress. His eyes fluttered shut as he exhaled all the tension he had ever known in his life.

His parents. His roommate. Last night—the dark and the cold and the fear. All gone.

He was drowning, and he had never felt more at peace.

***

The food was always as delicious as that first morning. The bed was always soft enough to swallow Gabriel, the blankets always warm enough to wrap him in a sedating haze of warmth. He floated in that haze now as Mattias murmured to him, stroking his hair, occasionally bending down to sip from his neck.

Mattias was sitting on the edge of the bed where he had lovingly tucked Gabriel under the covers. His hands were so cold. Gabriel was so warm. He floated in the endless sea of peace and let the waves carry him where they would.

Mattias kept stroking his hair, but didn't bend down to drink again. The waves grew choppy. The haze began to lift. Gabriel blinked his eyes open. This room—so ornate, so luxurious, so wrong. He shouldn't be here. He didn't belong here.

He had to get out of here.

"Hush," said Mattias, as if he had sensed his tension. "It doesn't taste as good when you're so tense, you know. Relax—nothing will hurt you here."

He relaxed into Mattias's arms, as if the words had been a command. In the next second, he flinched away. What was he doing? This was sick. It was wrong. It was so, so wrong.

Mattias held him in place easily with one hand. He bent over Gabriel's neck, and Gabriel relaxed bonelessly into Mattias's arms as the sea swept him away.

"You were a good choice," Mattias murmured, his breath cool on Gabriel's neck. "So delicious. So comfortable. I could sit here with you all day. You're like... like a big, fluffy dog. I always wanted a dog. But we make dogs nervous—vampires, I mean. We smell dead to them. You're the next best thing, though. I'm so glad I chose you," he murmured happily as he pulled Gabriel closer against him.

Gabriel tried halfheartedly to squirm away, fighting in vain through the waves of peace dragging him under. "It... wasn't..." It was so hard to talk, when all he wanted to do was lie still. "It wasn't exactly... my choice."

Mattias continued as if Gabriel hadn't spoken. "My family thought I would choose badly. My mother thought I would pick someone too strong or too skittish—someone I wouldn't be able to control. My father thought I wouldn't be careful enough about who I chose, and would pick someone who would be missed. They had no faith in me." He let out a mournful sigh. His fingers tightened in Gabriel's hair. "Just because it's my first time."

Gabriel blinked at that. The vampire had seemed to him like an ageless creature. Even before finding out what he was, it had never occurred to him to think of the man as old or young. Now he wondered—just how young was his captor, by vampire standards?

"First... time?" he asked. His tongue was thick, his brain fuzzy.

"It's a rite of passage in our family," said Mattias. "Choosing our own food for the first time, instead of feeding off the humans the family keeps for all the children to feed from. It's a different experience, having a human of your own. Choosing them, then bringing them home to belong to you and only you. I didn't expect to feel so connected to you."

He bent and took another drink. Gabriel tried to fight the wave of wellbeing that washed over him. His whimper of protest turned into a sigh of contentment.

"I'm not surprised my family had no faith in me," Mattias said when he drew back up. "That's how they've always been with me. I'm the youngest of five children, and three of my older siblings already have children of their own. I've always been the baby. It's not easy, being looked down on by everyone around you."

As he rhythmically stroked Gabriel's hair, Gabriel seethed under his touch, anger breaking through the haze of peace. His captor thought *he* had problems? At least he hadn't been kidnapped and told he had six months to live. Did he really think Gabriel cared about his problems?

Mattias didn't take another drink, too wrapped up in what he was saying. With every word, the sedating calm receded—not enough to let Gabriel fight his way free, just enough to let him think clearly. Just enough to let him be angry.

"They don't actually see who I am," Mattias said sadly, curling a lock of Gabriel's hair around his fingers. "They never have. All they see is the person they want to see. The person they wanted me to be. They wanted someone sweet and pliable, I think. Someone who would be the baby forever, and be happy about it. They wanted someone to take care of for the rest of their lives, because they knew I would be their last child. My siblings, too—I was their practice for having children of their own. They all wanted me to remain a child forever."

Against his will, Gabriel's mind traveled back to a small white house at the end of a cul-de-sac. Cold hallways, stark white walls. No siblings, not for him—just him and his mother and his father. His father had wanted a miniature copy of himself. His mother had wanted him to be the man she had thought she was marrying, the man his father had failed to be. Someone who would be her knight in shining armor, who would dote on her the way she felt she deserved. Neither of them had wanted him.

Neither of them had seen him.

He shook his head sharply. He wasn't actually sympathizing with this creature, was he?

Mattias held Gabriel's head down, stilling him. The movement seemed absent-minded, like scratching his back or swatting a fly. "It would be easier if I had other people to turn to, the way you humans do," he said. "I've always envied you that. But we're forced to keep to ourselves. There's too much about us that could reveal our secrets. Our intolerance to sunlight, for one. Our inability to eat human food.

It would be so easy for someone to find us out. So we stick to our homes and our families. The ones who understand us. If only they really *did* understand."

Not all humans had other people they could turn to. Gabriel had moved far away from everyone he had known, which had seemed like a good deal at the time because it had gotten him away from his family. But new friends had never materialized. The only person he had known well enough to really talk to was his roommate, who had seemed like a decent guy at first. Until the job Gabriel had moved here for had fallen through, and he was stuck in the apartment most of the time. Enough of the time to see how much control Jason had started exerting over his life, little by little.

And as soon as he had tried standing up for himself, he was homeless. Homeless and with no social connections within a hundred miles.

"I'm so glad I have you to talk to," Mattias said, running a finger over the punctures in his neck. Gabriel shivered. The spot was sensitive, like a scrape or a burn, but without the pain. It was more of a tickly feeling. Not pleasurable, exactly, but not unpleasant either.

"Of course I'm a good listener." The words came more easily now that it had been a few minutes since Mattias's last drink. "I'm your captive audience."

Mattias's hand stilled in his hair.

Gabriel forced his head up from Mattias's lap. "And every day I'm here is another day you're slowly killing me," he continued, "so I'd say your problems are pretty minor, comparatively."

Too late, his heart pounded out a warning. Here he was again, saying the thing that would only get him hurt. Hadn't he learned his lesson with Jason?

A flash of pain crossed Mattias's face. "I don't like it when you say things like that," he said. "I like you better when you're relaxed. Relax for me."

He tangled his fingers in Gabriel's hair and drew Gabriel's neck down to his fangs.

Gabriel tried to fight. But before the message could reach his limbs, it was over. A sharp pressure, and then the calm. He sank into Mattias's arms and let the vampire's cold skin ease the heat of his anger.

"That's right," Mattias murmured when he finally came up for air. "That's so much better." He pulled Gabriel close and made a contented noise. "Oh, I chose so well with you."

***

Gabriel was growing used to Mattias's cold arms around his, to the vampire throwing one leg over him like he was a full-body pillow. The vampire's smell was familiar to him now, incense and old books underlaid by the faint tang of blood. He was well-acquainted with the sensation of fangs penetrating the flesh of his neck or the inside of his wrist.

There was never pain, only pressure, and after that came the calm. When Mattias wasn't around, when Gabriel was alone with nothing to distract him from counting down how many more days he had to live, sometimes he would press at the wounds. He would imagine he was feeling Mattias's fangs sinking into his skin. But it didn't work when he did it. The peace never came.

There was no peace now, either, even though he was curled in Mattias's arms. Mattias hadn't so much as taken a nibble yet. Without the contentment that came with the vampire's feeding, Gabriel was uncomfortably aware that he was trapped in the iron grip of a monster, with the ornate wallpaper surrounding him like the bars of a gilded cage. He longed for the pressure of Mattias's fangs, because that would mean the waves of peace were coming to carry him away. To make him forget, even if only for a few moments.

Mattias was quiet today, too. He hadn't said anything in several minutes. He was just... lying here. Holding Gabriel like someone was threatening to snatch him away.

"Is something wrong?" Gabriel asked. He hated the question, hated showing concern for his captor's welfare. But he couldn't breathe lying here in this silence, listening to his own breath squeeze in and out.

Why wouldn't Mattias just take a bite out of him already? Why wouldn't he just make him forget?

Mattias raised his eyebrows. Gabriel felt it rather than saw it, the movement of Mattias's forehead against his cheek. "Thank you for asking," he said, faint surprise in his voice. "It feels good to have someone who cares enough to ask." Mattias ran a soft fingertip down the back of Gabriel's neck.

Gabriel held himself rigid in Mattias's arms to keep himself from shuddering.

"It's nothing," said Mattias. "Nothing serious, at any rate."

He lapsed into silence again. Gabriel's breath droned in and out, in and out, like the rhythmic buzzing of a cloud of angry bees. His heart pounded a dull, resigned rhythm against the bars of his ribcage.

A frown from Mattias—again, Gabriel didn't see it but felt it. "You don't want to hear about it, I suppose."

Had he been waiting for Gabriel to ask him a follow-up question? Gabriel didn't know why he didn't just say whatever he wanted to say—it wasn't as if Gabriel could stop him. He thought about asking the question Mattias wanted to hear, but didn't.

"These times we have together," said Mattias, and ran his finger along the half-healed wounds at the side of Gabriel's neck. Gabriel's breath hitched in anticipation. He needed that peace, that forgetfulness. He craved it.

But Mattias didn't shift into position to bite him. "I've told you so much," he said instead. "About my family. My feelings. My innermost thoughts. You know more about me than anyone else in this world. Even my family—the people who have known me since I was born."

Gabriel didn't know what Mattias wanted from him, so he stayed silent.

"And you," said Mattias, drawing his hand away, "you've told me nothing. I barely know anything about you."

Well, what exactly did he want Gabriel to say? That he had a family too, one he couldn't exactly say he missed or even loved, but that he had hoped to maybe see again someday—even if only to show them he had turned out better than they ever believed he could? That he sometimes dreamed about shivering in his car, and woke up with tears on his face to find himself in this luxurious captivity instead?

That no matter how bleak his life had been out there, he would have traded away all this in a second just to have it back?

That he didn't want to die?

Was that what Mattias wanted to hear?

It wasn't as if Mattias had ever given him the space to say any of that. He was always talking about his own life, at least when he didn't have his fangs buried in Gabriel's flesh. His own petty complaints. His family treated him like a child. He was bored, trapped here in the house. He was lonely.

As if he was the only one who was lonely. As if he was the only one who was trapped.

Mattias pulled back to look at Gabriel. Gabriel realized the vampire had been waiting for him to respond.

"I've given you my blood," said Gabriel. "I give it to you every time you're here." If it could be called a gift, when he never had the opportunity to refuse. "Isn't that more intimate than talking? Isn't that what I'm here for?"

Mattias looked hurt. "That's not the same," he said. "That's food. It's not personal. Not like the things I tell you."

"You kidnapped me," said Gabriel, too restless in Mattias's iron grip to be discreet with his words. "I'm your captive. We don't have a relationship. I'm your living, breathing milkshake, and in a few months I'll be dead."

Mattias put on an expression that Gabriel had come to recognize as a pout. He released Gabriel and swung his legs over the side of the bed.

Gabriel should have felt relieved. But the absence of Mattias's arms, paradoxically, made him feel like a fresh weight had landed on his chest. He felt colder than he had when Mattias's chilly flesh had been pressed against his own.

Mattias was leaving. He was leaving without feeding from him, without giving him another taste of the ocean of serenity that was the only thing holding madness at bay. And how long would it be before he came back? Hours? Another day? Gabriel might start throwing himself against the walls by then.

"No," Gabriel found himself saying. "Stay."

Did he crave the vampire's chemical peace that much?

He wasn't sure he wanted an answer to that question.

Mattias stood. Gabriel wasn't sure he had heard him.

"I'm sorry," Gabriel said. "You're right. I should have been more open with you."

What was he doing?

He was finding the only bit of peace he could find in this place, that was what he was doing. He was keeping himself sane any way he could.

Mattias sat back down. He perched on the edge of the bed, not touching Gabriel. The wounds on Gabriel's neck ached. The phantom sensation of pressure was maddening—the fangs going in, the waves preparing to sweep him away. But there were no fangs. There was no ocean of peace. There was no respite from these four beautiful walls.

"Will you be more open with me?" Mattias asked. "Will you share with me the way I've been sharing with you?"

Gabriel hesitated. Even the craving couldn't wipe away his resistance at the thought of baring his soul to his captor. "I'm not like you. I'm a private person."

Mattias raised an eyebrow. "The way you cuddle me when I feed says otherwise."

Gabriel looked away. It wasn't him, he wanted to say. It was whatever the feeding did to him. It wasn't him who held the vampire like he never wanted to let go. It wasn't him who relaxed into the arms of his captor, into his invisible chains.

It wasn't him now, all but begging for Mattias to drain away a little more of his life force and leave him that much closer to death.

"Here," said Mattias, "I'll show you." He bent over Gabriel's neck.

Gabriel held his breath. Here, now, finally, it was coming. The brush of Mattias's lips against his skin, the feather-light kiss of an icy wind. Then, at last, the delicious pressure of fangs sinking into flesh. And then—

The restlessness faded. He sank into the mattress, sank into Mattias's waiting arms. He gazed into his captor's dark eyes and felt only contentment. He missed nothing of his old life—not the loneliness, not the cold, not the fear for his survival. This was the only place he ever wanted to be.

Even his own death held no fear for him. Surely dying in Mattias's arms would feel like being swept away by the ocean, by the kindness of its numbing waves.

When Mattias pulled away, Gabriel clung to him, his head in the vampire's lap. Mattias stroked his hair slowly. "You see? You're not so private after all."

Gabriel wanted to protest, but why would he? Mattias was right. He had wanted Mattias closer, as close as a vampire could get to a human, and he had gotten it. Intimacy was a small price to pay for a little peace. At least when he had nothing else remaining to him.

"Tell me your troubles." Mattias's words were soft, but to Gabriel, they sounded like an order. "I'll listen. I'll be here for you, the way you have been for me."

Gabriel shook his head, something still holding him back, although he couldn't say what. "There's nothing to tell."

"You told me once," said Mattias, "that I only talked about my own problems and ignored yours. I'm trying to fix that. To be more considerate. Will you not let me?"

His fingers brushed Gabriel's neck. Maybe a thoughtless gesture, but Gabriel chose to take it as a promise. He craved another touch of peace. He craved oblivion.

"My biggest problem," Gabriel said, "is being here. You took my freedom from me. You took away the future I thought I would have." When Mattias frowned, Gabriel added, "you asked me to open up to you. Doesn't that mean honesty?"

"I did ask for that," said Mattias. The frown disappeared from his face. "And this is a problem that is easily solved."

He bent over Gabriel's neck again. "Tell me," he said, "when being here with me no longer feels like a problem."

When that moment came, Gabriel could no longer remember how to speak.

Much later, when Gabriel lay trembling from blood loss in Mattias's arms, Mattias asked him the question again. "What troubles you?"

This time, Gabriel couldn't remember why he had ever refused to answer. He knew this should bother him. It didn't. He was at peace. For this, he was grateful. For this, he would give Mattias anything he wanted.

"Why were you living in your vehicle?" Mattias prompted.

"My roommate," Gabriel said easily. "I didn't know him when I moved in. I just needed a cheap place to live. But soon he was the closest friend I had—not because we were *close,* exactly, but because I didn't know anyone else around here."

He could have stopped there. Mattias didn't prompt him for more. But the words spilled from his mouth as easily as the blood had spilled from his veins at Mattias's prompting.

"He started making rules for me," said Gabriel. "First what kinds of foods were allowed in the apartment. He had allergies, he said, but the restrictions changed from week to week. Then he started deciding when I could and couldn't go out—it woke him up when I got home too late, he said, but soon I would be locked out until the next morning if I got home from work even a minute late."

Mattias said nothing. He offered no judgment, no advice. Gabriel began to understand why Mattias found confiding in him so appealing.

"Then it was about what I could do in my room," Gabriel continued. "My typing was too loud for him. He didn't approve of the books I read—they didn't have literary merit, so he didn't want me financially supporting the publishers. Same with the TV shows I watched, plus the TV was too loud. He didn't want me writing, because I could be writing bad things about him. Finally, I'd had enough."

Mattias stroked Gabriel's cheek. "And he forced you from your home?"

"*His* home," Gabriel said bitterly. "He wouldn't even let me pack any of my stuff. Which has got to be illegal, but what was I going to do about it?"

"Let me take your troubles from you," said Mattias, and drank from him again.

The peace swept Gabriel away. A reward for his confession. The pain drained from him, and if Gabriel remembered that his life was draining away along with it, he no longer cared.

***

Gabriel lay in Mattias's arms and felt his heartbeat slow. His breath came evenly for the first time since he had woken at dawn from a nightmare about his own death. He had known it was dawn because that was what the old-fashioned grandfather clock in the corner said. He hadn't seen a sunrise in weeks. He hadn't seen the *sun* in weeks. There were no windows in this room.

He didn't need to think about that now. Because now Mattias was here, nibbling on his neck, taking away the horror for a little while. These days, he felt it as soon as Mattias entered the room—the slowing of his heartbeat, the easing of his breaths. Like Pavlov's dogs, salivating at the sound of a bell. The sight of his captor was what made him salivate, craving his own destruction.

Every drop of blood Mattias took hastened his demise. He knew that. But the vampire's feedings were the only times when he could forget.

It was wrong. It was purely chemical. An escape, an addiction. But it was also all he had.

He nuzzled Mattias, burrowing into the vampire's neck, breathing in the crisp scent of him. He felt sick.

Mattias responded with a noise of contentment, pulling him closer, leaning his head down to take another quick drink. Gabriel's breath caught for a second at the sharp pressure, then released all at once as the tension left him. There was nothing to fear here. That was what he could tell himself, at least, until the end.

Mattias pulled away from Gabriel's neck to rest his head on his shoulder. His lips were still sticky with Gabriel's blood. "You're the only one I can really be myself with," he said, his voice sleepy—he got like that sometimes after he had drunk from him. "You're the only one who understands."

Gabriel made a wordless encouraging noise. Sometimes, if he made the right noises, Mattias drank more—until he was fully sated, until Gabriel forgot even the memory of fear.

This time he didn't, though. He stroked Gabriel's hair, pushing a lock away from his eyes with a cold finger. "And you?" he prompted.

Gabriel's mind was sluggish from the effects of the feeding. The ocean called him away. There was no need for thought there. "And me, what?"

"Aren't you glad you're here with me?" Mattias asked. "You have someone to talk to now. Someone who understands. Are you grateful?"

Mattias had pressed him for more confessions, after that first time. More pieces of himself, given over to Mattias along with his blood. Always, he hesitated, and always, he gave Mattias what he wanted after a long feeding. And always, Mattias rewarded him with a feeding even deeper and lengthier, until he wondered why he had hesitated at all.

And yet he was always just as reluctant to speak the next time.

He had waited too long to answer—Mattias frowned, tensing slightly against him. "I thought you felt the same connection I do between us."

"I do," said Gabriel. "I'm grateful."

He thought about Jason. About all the apologies Gabriel had offered him. The excuses for what, in retrospect, had been ordinary things—coming home ten minutes late, reading a trashy novel instead of a literary classic—but which had, at the time, seemed like unspeakable sins. He had lost himself in Jason's rules, lost the ability to tell what was reasonable and what was not. He could lose himself in Mattias, too, he sensed—lose the ability to tell what he really felt and what he was willing to say for another taste of peace.

"You don't say so very often," said Mattias. "Maybe you're just saying what you think I want to hear." He pulled away sharply and stood, leaving Gabriel abruptly alone in the bed.

"I'm not," said Gabriel, although it was a lie. When Mattias didn't look convinced, he added, "When you drink from me, I feel more at peace than I ever have in my life. I feel…" Like he would rather drown than go through the painful effort of taking another breath of cold, hostile air. "Like there's nothing to fear. Like nothing can ever hurt me."

"Good," Mattias murmured. "Good. I'll never hurt you. I hope you know that."

Mattias never hurt him—but every day, he was killing him. "I know."

"But do you mean it?" Mattias asked. "Do you really mean it?"

"I mean it," said Gabriel, because saying anything else risked Mattias walking out the door in a sulk and leaving Gabriel alone with the horror of his captivity.

Mattias slid back into bed and cradled Gabriel against him. And then, what Gabriel really wanted—he lifted Gabriel's wrist to his mouth and took a long, slow drink. Gabriel melted against him. Yes, this peace was worth lying for.

Mattias yanked his fangs away abruptly, leaving a small tear in the skin. Blood leaked out over the sheets. Gabriel pressed his thumb to the wound, feeling cold all of a sudden. "Did I do something wrong?"

Before he had moved out, he had always been asking Jason what he had done wrong.

"Hush," Mattias said sharply. The cold spread through Gabriel's body, hardening his skin into goose-bumps on his arms and legs. Then his ears picked up a faint sound, which Mattias must have heard before him.

Footsteps.

The door swung open.

A woman stood in the doorway. She had Mattias's pale skin, and Mattias's eyes. Cold seemed to radiate off her, like the wind that heralded a winter storm, like the chill of the grave. Her eyes landed first on Mattias, then on Gabriel next to him. Her lips pressed together into a colorless line.

Gabriel fought the urge to hide under the covers like a child.

"Great-grandmother," said Mattias. His voice, normally slow and soothing or filled with an immature petulance, trembled with fear.

"What," the woman asked, "are you doing?"

Her voice was as cold as the rest of her. Each word pierced Gabriel's eardrums and drilled down into his brain to lodge there like spikes of ice.

"I'm feeding," said Mattias, and there was the petulant tone Gabriel was used to. "And feeding is *private*. You taught me that."

The woman swept her gaze over the two of them. "There's no need to *cuddle* as you feed. And you've been up here too long. You could have slaked your thirst in half this time." She narrowed her eyes. "You often spend a strange amount of time up here, I've noticed. If you were spending all that time feeding, your human would be long dead."

"I like to take my time with my meals."

"Your sisters say they've heard you in here with your human," the woman said. "Talking."

"They're listening outside the door? Don't *they* know feeding is private?"

"You know better than to play with your food." The woman pinned Mattias to the bed with her gaze until he went still. Gabriel, too, felt the weight of it, even though it wasn't directed at him. "Would you lie down in a barn with a filthy pig? If not, then get out of the human's bed. You've taken what you need from him tonight."

Mattias hesitated. The woman made a sharp gesture with her hand. "Get up." This time, Mattias obeyed as if he couldn't help himself.

"I wasn't—" Mattias began.

When the woman closed her fingers together, Mattias's mouth snapped shut.

"No excuses." The woman chilled the entire room with her words until Gabriel thought he might never be warm again. "Just break this filthy habit. Unless someone needs to help you break it."

Mattias hung his head. When the woman beckoned him out the door, he followed without a backward glance.

The door shut. The cold remained. Gabriel wrapped himself in his blanket, trying to banish the chill in his bones. Wondering when Mattias would be back to banish his fear.

If he ever would.

***

Mattias came back hours later. Gabriel had been trying to nap, and had finally managed it. He came awake at the sound of the door, his half-asleep brain supplying images of the woman with her cold aura and colder voice. But it was Mattias he saw instead. He relaxed into the mattress, his body warming at the thought of being held, even though there was no warmth in Mattias's touch.

But touch wasn't what he was really craving.

Gabriel's neck and wrists ached eagerly. His heartbeat slowed in anticipation of the peace that was to come, even as his senses sharpened. Time slowed down, the seconds dragging by, each one too long to wait.

This was wrong. He knew that. And still, he pulled the covers back to allow Mattias in, and sighed happily when Mattias settled in next to him.

"I can't believe she did that," Mattias said as he pulled Gabriel against him like a teddy bear. "She interrupted me while I was feeding. You don't *do* that. Feeding is private. You never interrupt another vampire while they're feeding unless they're too young to be able to feed without harming the human. I know what I'm doing. I'm no child."

Gabriel, only half-listening, made his usual encouraging noises. He waited for the pressure, and the relief that would come after.

But the relief didn't come. "What's so wrong with what I'm doing, anyway?" Mattias's mouth was close enough to Gabriel's neck that his lips tickled the small hairs there, and yet he didn't bite. "I just want someone to talk to. Why can't she understand that?"

Gabriel tried not to betray his impatience. He stroked Mattias's arm and made noises of sympathy. He listened to the seconds tick down in agony.

"It's so lonely in this house," said Mattias. "And she's the one who made it that way, with her rules about not risking contact with humans. The humans we feed on are all we have, all but our family, and I can't talk to *them*. Why doesn't she understand how lonely it is here all the time?"

A memory broke through his craving, his mother sitting at the kitchen table with her head in her hands. Midnight. She hadn't known Gabriel was awake. Gabriel had gone still at the sight of her looking so weak, so vulnerable. He had backed away as slowly and silently as he could, forgetting about the drink of water he had come downstairs for. He had felt slimy and vaguely ashamed, like he had seen something he wasn't supposed to see.

"Maybe," he said, "your great-grandmother is lonely too. Maybe she's been lonely for so long she's forgotten what it's like to feel any other way."

Mattias went still. Gabriel thought he had said something wrong, and jeopardized his chance at a little peace tonight. But then Mattias said, "Maybe you're right."

"My mother was lonely, too," said Gabriel, when what he wanted to say was, *Take a drink. Please. What are you waiting for?*

"She's lonely," said Mattias. "They're all lonely. They're all so lonely, and they don't even see it."

An unfamiliar feeling tugged at Gabriel's heart—a strange affection for the vampire who had him locked in his unyielding grip. He had never heard Mattias consider anyone else's perspective even to that extent before. Maybe there was hope for the vampire yet. Maybe he was capable of growing up.

"I wish I could just leave," Mattias mused. "Live out there in the human world. Meet new people. See something besides this ugly wallpaper for once."

As he said it, Gabriel wanted it too, craved it so badly he could taste it. Craved it more than he craved the feeling of his blood flowing into Mattias's mouth. The walls seemed to draw closer. Mattias's grip compressed his ribcage, suffocating him. He was trapped. Trapped. He would never see the sun again.

He bared his neck to Mattias. "Drink," he urged. "It will help you feel better."

Mattias shook his head. "It's too soon since my last feeding. I'm not hungry."

"Then why are you here?"

A flash of hurt crossed Mattias's face. "I needed someone to talk to. Isn't that enough?" A nervous frown; a flash of worry. "Is that all right? You were sleeping. I woke you. You weren't expecting me at this time of night."

Now he was taking Gabriel's feelings into account. Maybe he really was growing up.

If only he would feed from him. Just a little.

If only he would let him go—

But that would never happen. Better not to think about it. Better to think about what he could have instead. The ocean. A gentle drowning.

"It's all right," he said, even as under his skin he writhed in agony.

Mattias pulled him closer, burying his nose in his hair. "I'm glad," he said. "You're all I have."

The horror crested—then receded. His heartbeat slowed at the pressure of Mattias's tightening arms, even though he knew no feeding was coming. His breathing relaxed at the sound of the vampire's voice. That Pavlovian reaction.

After so many feedings, Mattias's presence was enough to hold the horror at bay.

There was something very wrong with that.

"Talk as long as you like," said Gabriel. What he meant was, *Please don't leave me.*

***

Normally, Mattias seemed as calmed by Gabriel's presence as Gabriel was by his. He would walk into the room, and he would smile, his posture softening, his movements slowing. He would slide into bed and reach leisurely for Gabriel, first drawing him into his arms, then drawing the blood from his veins.

But one night, a few days after the confrontation with the cold vampire woman, the pattern broke. The door opened, and Mattias rushed in, all but running to the bed to grab for him. He burrowed under the covers as if they could warm his cold body, and clung to Gabriel like he might snap him in two.

Gabriel wasn't comforted, not this time. His breath came quick and ragged; the grip around his torso felt like prison bars. "What's wrong?" he asked, and then wasn't sure why he had asked it. He didn't care about his captor, only about getting his fix. Otherwise this situation would be even more fucked up than it already was. And it was already plenty fucked up.

"The same as ever," Mattias murmured against his neck. "My family. This house. I don't want to talk about it. Not today."

His fangs pierced Gabriel's skin, and Gabriel no longer cared what was troubling Mattias, so long as that peace never left him.

But Mattias pulled back too quickly, and clung to him again. He held him tighter this time, tight enough that Gabriel thought his bones might snap. He struggled to draw in a full breath. "You're stronger than me," he reminded the man in a wheeze. "You'll break me."

But he snuggled into the vampire anyway, still riding the wave of the feeding. If he died here, in Mattias's arms, it wouldn't be such a bad way to go. Just as long as Mattias didn't let the peace fully fade before the end.

"I'm sorry," Mattias murmured, and loosened his grip. "I'll be gentle." He ran a hand down Gabriel's torso. The touch was feather-light, but there was nothing relaxed about it. The movements of his fingers were quick and urgent, sending alarm bells ringing in Gabriel's hindbrain.

"I'll be gentle," Mattias repeated as his hand moved lower. His fingers, cold as ice, brushed past Gabriel's belly button, then quested lower.

Gabriel pulled away—or tried. Mattias's other arm still had him locked in a vise grip. But Mattias's hand stilled. "Is something the matter?"

Was he allowed to object? He didn't know. He had figured out the rules of this strange relationship, or he thought he had—what he was allowed to say, what he wasn't, how to do and say the things that would get him what he wanted. But those rules hadn't included how to respond to something like this. Even though all their feedings took place in bed, despite how closely they held each other during their long talking-and-feeding sessions, the possibility had somehow never occurred to him.

"If your family doesn't like the way you talk to me," said Gabriel, the first objection he could think of, "they'd like this even less."

"My family," said Mattias, screwing up his face in disgust. "Maybe I *want* to do something they wouldn't like." His fingers drifted lower again. Gabriel suppressed a startled yelp.

"Take my blood," Gabriel urged. "You're restless. Angry. You're probably hungry. You'll feel better if you feed." It felt uncomfortably like he was bargaining for his body, for which parts of himself he was allowed to keep. *Take my life, my blood—I've already surrendered that to you. But leave me this one thing.*

"Later," Mattias murmured. His hand burrowed under the waistband of Gabriel's pants. The cold of his fingers met the heat there. The ice of his touch was a startling burn—startling, but surprisingly, not unpleasant.

Gabriel fought the urge to press himself closer against Mattias, to press against the bracing cold of his fingers. To ride a different ocean, less peaceful, more exhilarating. The sudden and unexpected urge sent a shudder through him. What was wrong with him?

He pulled away, more insistently this time. There was no way Mattias could mistake his meaning. But Mattias held him in place. Cold fingers closed around him, stroking softly but insistently. His other hand shifted to the center of Gabriel's chest, pressing him down, holding him in place.

If Gabriel fought, he would lose. Mattias had a vampire's strength, and Gabriel wasn't exactly a paragon of fitness, even before the past few weeks of not being allowed to move outside this room. If he fought, maybe Mattias would leave in a sulk and not feed off him, and the last lingering remnants of his peace would fade, leaving him alone with the horror of his captivity. Or else Mattias would hold him down and take what he wanted from him, which would be its own kind of horror.

If he did nothing, Mattias would take what he wanted anyway. But that was nothing Gabriel hadn't experienced before. He knew the rules. Relax into the vampire's touch, let him take what he was going to take. It would feel good. It always did. It would let him forget.

He forced his muscles to relax. He let himself sag into the mattress, and let out his breath in a long sigh. It was a sigh of resignation, but Mattias must have taken it as pleasure, because his lips curled in a smile.

"That's it," he said. "You don't want to fight. We're connected. It's about more than feeding, with us. You can feel it. Can't you?"

"I feel it," Gabriel confirmed, because it made Mattias happy to hear that, and when Mattias was happy, he was more in the mood to eat.

But he didn't feed from him this time. He brought his lips to Gabriel's and kissed him, long and deep, as his fingers worked. The cold of the vampire's touch did nothing to quell the heat in him. If he closed his eyes, if he let himself forget where he was, he could almost pretend he wanted this. He let the heat build, and build, and build.

There was no luxurious prison surrounding him. No clock ticking down the minutes left of his life. Otherwise he would never be able to bear this. He would have to fight, and that would only end badly.

So he let him himself forget everything except the sensations. He made himself forget.

Mattias stroked him with terrifying expertise, wringing gasps of pleasure from him, swallowing them with his kiss. It wasn't enough to take Gabriel's blood. He would take this too. There would be nothing of Gabriel he didn't devour.

Gabriel went tense under him. Mattias pulled back with a frown. The hand inside Gabriel's pants paused, curling around him like a threat.

"I don't..." Gabriel hesitated, weighing the risks of saying no against the risks of saying nothing.

Mattias's face grew troubled. Gabriel thought about their conversation a few days ago, when Mattias had—however briefly—seemed to care what Gabriel felt. Maybe he would see that Gabriel didn't want this. Maybe he would care. Maybe he would stop, and bring his fangs to Gabriel's neck, and let him have the simple peace he craved.

"Would you like me to feed from you," Mattias asked, "to make it easier?"

A full-body wave of nausea crawled outward from Gabriel's gut through his limbs.

Mattias knew he didn't want this, or he wouldn't have made the offer.

He knew, and he wasn't going to stop.

And why would he? Gabriel was here for him to consume. What did it matter which parts of him he took? He had already resolved to take Gabriel's life, and seemingly thought nothing of it. Why, then, would he draw the line at this lesser violation?

At least Gabriel knew the answer now: he could not refuse.

"Yes," he said, and bared his neck for Mattias's fangs.

Mattias drank. His hand moved in the rhythm of the ocean waves. Gabriel moaned as the warring sensations carried him away—peace and desire, contentment and ecstasy. There was no room for fear. No room for awareness.

That was how he wanted it.

He was glad Mattias hadn't stopped. The more of him Mattias took, the more easily he could forget.

He clung to Mattias and prayed, in a wordless cry, for Mattias to consume him whole.

***

"Have you ever been in love?"

Mattias was curled against him as he asked the question, holding him carelessly, like a child who knew his stuffed toy wouldn't break no matter how it was treated. He had only taken little nibbles so far today, and had only touched Gabriel with simple affection. Gabriel didn't know whether he was relieved or frustrated. He wanted to keep a few scraps of himself. He craved the escape that came with being consumed utterly.

Gabriel shook his head. "No," he said, then revised the statement. "Maybe. I was a teenager. I thought it was love. Looking back now, I wouldn't call it that. But maybe all that matters is how it felt to me then."

He no longer hesitated before answering any question Mattias asked. Giving up these pieces of his soul made Mattias happy. That made Mattias more likely to stay longer. Feed longer. And just as Mattias's simple presence made him feel peaceful, so did giving up these small confessions. It was a different kind of intimacy, a different way to be consumed, but similar enough to make his breath calm and his heartbeat slow.

If he told Mattias enough about himself, maybe soon there would be nothing left. Nothing left of him to rage at his captivity when he was alone. Nothing left of him to fear death.

"I've always wondered what it would be like to fall in love," Mattias mused, his hand moving in lazy circles across Gabriel's chest. "But I never thought I would get the chance. Not trapped in this house."

"It has to happen sometimes," said Gabriel. "Your family has to grow somehow."

"Occasionally someone breaks the rules," said Mattias. "Falls in love with a human. Sometimes it ends badly. Sometimes the human agrees to be turned, and comes to live with us for eternity." His breath whistled past his fangs. "It's so romantic, don't you think?"

Gabriel thought it sounded like a nightmare. "Romantic," he echoed, and hoped Mattias would take it as agreement.

"But I could never break the rules like that," he said. "They watch me so closely. They all think I'm still a child."

The old familiar complaints. Gabriel tuned him out, focusing instead on the sensations of Mattias's hand against his skin. The cold, too, was starting to cause an automatic reaction in him, stronger every time he felt it. A rising heat, a craving.

"Drink," Gabriel urged. "Feed. You'll be calmer afterward."

Mattias's hand stilled. "I think I'm in love with you."

Gabriel went stiff against him. "What?"

Mattias frowned. Hurt flashed in his dark eyes. "Is it that shocking?" he asked. "You must have suspected it. Don't you feel it too? This connection between us—it's like something electric. Something alive. You must feel it too. You *must*."

Gabriel would have described his teenage puppy love that way, too. The object of his affections, a shy boy named Alec, had not in fact felt the same. It had seemed unimaginable to Gabriel, that a feeling that strong could exist only within his head—that it wasn't some new law of physics, a basic fact about the universe. He had withdrawn into himself for weeks. A short year later, he had laughed at himself.

When he didn't answer, the hurt in Mattias's eyes spread into a frown, a tightness at the corners of his lips. "Oh," he said flatly.

He was going to leave. He was going to leave, and take Gabriel's peace with him. Or worse. A person could be dangerous when their love wasn't returned. Especially a person who was already volatile. And Gabriel was already his captive.

"Don't go," said Gabriel. "You misunderstood."

"What did I misunderstand?" Mattias bit out the words. "I confessed my love to you, and you said *nothing*."

"Because I didn't know what to say," Gabriel said hurriedly. "I... I love you too. I love you."

Hope lit Mattias's eyes, as painfully bright as his hurt had been sharp and deadly. "Then why didn't you answer me?" His voice was guarded. "Don't you know how hard it was for me to say it?"

What was so hard about it? He could say anything he wanted to Gabriel. Do anything he wanted.

"I never expected you to feel the same way," said Gabriel. "I was afraid you would reject me. Laugh at me." He spun the words out of nothing, hoping Mattias would believe him. Because if he sold this, Mattias would stay. If he sold this, Mattias wouldn't turn on him and make his captivity a living hell.

What had Gabriel's life come to?

Skepticism lingered on Mattias's hopeful face. "Do you really mean it?"

"I mean it," Gabriel said.

Mattias kept watching him, like he was waiting for more.

"I love the way I feel when I'm in your arms," he said, and that was true, however much it made his skin crawl to acknowledge that truth. "I love how you can make me forget everything else in the world." Also true. "I love *you*." A lie.

Mattias hesitated for one single, endless second.

Then his face lit with a radiant smile, out of place on the sun-starved features meant for shadows and solemn old-fashioned portraits.

"I'm so glad we found each other," said Mattias. "It's fate, don't you think? That *you* were the human I found, my very first time?"

"Fate," Gabriel said, trying to make it sound like agreement.

As Mattias reached more insistently for him, a thought flashed into his mind. He was a captive, at Mattias's mercy... but Mattias was in love with him. That was dangerous for Gabriel, but it was also power. Maybe he could use it. Maybe—

Then Mattias's fangs sank into his neck, and icy fingers slipped into Gabriel's pants, and Gabriel turned away from thoughts of effort and let himself be devoured.

***

Cold hands on Gabriel's chest, between his legs, running up and down his inner thigh. Cold lips on his, drinking in his heat, moving lower to drink his blood. The ocean roiled. The waves swept Gabriel under; he opened his mouth and welcomed the drowning. Then the waves spit him back up to the surface for a gulp of air, a taste of Mattias's bloody mouth, before sending him under again with the painless pressure of Mattias's fangs.

Gabriel's eyes opened. Mattias's hair hung around him like a curtain. Those long black strands, the beautiful bars of his cage.

Gabriel hastily closed his eyes. He tried to lose himself in the sensations once more. Too late—Mattias stilled. "Is something wrong?"

Gabriel didn't want to speak. Words would remind him that he had a voice, a body, that he had thoughts. But Mattias wouldn't drink from him again, wouldn't touch him again, until he answered.

"Everything is fine," he said. No, that was wrong—Mattias liked more enthusiasm from him than that. He wanted his prisoner happy, breathless, in love. "Sometimes I get overwhelmed by how lucky I am. I love you. I love you so much."

He kept his eyes closed. He didn't want to see the walls. He didn't want to see Mattias's face.

Mattias didn't answer for a long moment, and Gabriel feared he had oversold it. He didn't open his eyes.

Then a ragged gasp from Mattias, and Gabriel knew he had gotten it just right. "It wasn't luck that brought us together," said Mattias against his neck, his lips brushing the place where he had bitten less than a minute ago. "It was fate." The skin was still tender. Not painful, never painful, but sensitive like a healing wound. The wound never fully healed. Gabriel's neck was a mess of bite marks these days. He tried not to look at himself in the mirror.

"Do you believe in fate?" Mattias asked as his hands resumed their roaming.

"I do now," said Gabriel, because he didn't want Mattias to stop.

But Mattias did, freezing with his fingers halfway up Gabriel's thigh. Gabriel tensed in response, his breath catching in fear. Had he given Mattias the wrong answer? What would his punishment be? The withdrawal of Mattias's touch, the cold horror of his captivity settling over him again with nothing to hold it at bay?

He opened his eyes.

Mattias rolled off him as the door opened. The cold vampire woman stood in the doorway. Her eyes swept over the scene, her gaze sharp and accusing.

"I can explain." Mattias was already scrambling out of bed, pulling the sheets with him to cover himself. Leaving Gabriel cold and exposed. Gabriel didn't try to cover his body—what would have been the point? He was here to be consumed. His body didn't belong to him anymore.

The woman curled her lip. Her sneer flashed a glimpse of glistening fangs. "I don't want to hear your explanations. It was plain enough to me what's going on here. It would have been plain enough to anyone with eyes." She sniffed the air theatrically. "Or a nose. It smells like human sweat in here. It smells foul, and now so do you." She directed this at Mattias, but it was Gabriel she was talking about. His sweat. His foulness.

As if he had chosen any of this.

Mattias hurried for the door, babbling apologies the whole way. "I don't know what came over me—it won't happen again—"

The woman didn't move from the doorway. As Mattias tried to squeeze past her, her hand shot out and slapped him across the face. The crack was like thunder. The blow snapped his head sideways and sent him sprawling across the floor.

Mattias lay in silence for a moment, stunned. While his lips worked, plainly trying unsuccessfully to speak, the vampire woman strode past him to catch Gabriel by the wrist. As her frigid flesh met his, her lips puckered like the touch of his warm flesh made her sick.

She yanked him toward her, and he saw why a single slap had sent Mattias to the floor. She wasn't strong the way Mattias was strong. She was strong the way a hurricane was strong, the way an avalanche was strong. He had no hope of resisting. Before he could register that she had moved him, he was lying naked on the carpet at her feet.

She didn't look him in the eye.

Her hand remained clasped around his wrist, keeping his arm raised at a painful angle, as she turned away from him to face Mattias. "Clearly you can't control yourself, so I'll have to do it for you. I'm taking this creature away to where he won't be a temptation anymore. One of your sisters will choose a new specimen for you. You clearly can't be trusted with the responsibility of selecting your own food source."

Mattias's desperate eyes darted from her to Gabriel. "No—please—I'll do better—"

"You had your chance." The woman strode toward the door as if the weight she was dragging behind her meant nothing. Gabriel gritted his teeth as his sensitive flesh scraped across the carpet. He struggled to right himself, but it was like fighting a gale-force wind. He flopped in her grip, and made a few noises of protest, and accomplished nothing else.

"Gabriel!" Mattias called after him as the woman dragged Gabriel out into the hallway. "Gabriel!"

Gabriel didn't answer. He didn't look back.

"I love you," Mattias called, apparently no longer caring whether the woman heard him. "I'll never stop loving you! Have faith in our love!" He was performing in his own private drama. Gabriel, rapidly receding down the hallway, had no part in it anymore.

At least now Gabriel wouldn't have to pretend to love him.

That would have been a relief if it didn't also mean he had lost his only means of escape—the fangs at his neck, the hands on his body. He cared nothing for Mattias's declarations of love. But as the woman dragged him deeper into darkness, the thought of never feeling fangs pierce his neck again drew a scream from him that echoed through the shadows.

The woman didn't react.

***

The woman dragged him down a flight of stairs, and another, and another. Down to a room where cold emanated from the walls. Down where the floor was rough concrete, where the air smelled of mold and the iron tang of blood. Down where moans of despair filled the air, never resolving into words.

The only light was the faint sliver of illumination at the top of the stairs where the woman had left the door open a crack. She dragged Gabriel across the concrete, heedless of his cries of pain. She hauled him to his feet and raised his arms above his head.

Cold metal locked around his wrists. Rust scraped across the tender skin where Mattias's fangs had opened his flesh again and again.

Her cold grip loosened, then withdrew. She left him without a word. She was only a shadow as she turned away and strode up the stairs. Then the faint sliver of light disappeared, and he saw nothing.

He tested his bonds. Above his head, chains rattled. He winced as the rusty shackles tore open one of his scabs. He cringed at the thought of rust inside his wound—as if infection was really his biggest problem right now.

He took a deep breath to calm himself, then regretted it. He wrinkled his nose. Underneath the smell of blood, the room smelled like stale human and bodily fluids of all kinds. The smell of blood was strong enough to turn the other sharp odors into an afterthought. He shrank away from the implications. How much blood had been spilled in this room?

"Who's out there?" His voice came out small and quavery. "Where are we?"

A thin cry of fear answered him. A moan of despair. A terrified shushing. No one answered in words.

"Please," he said. "I just want to know..." Know what? What was going to happen to him? He already knew—he was going to die. So what was he so desperate to find out? Maybe whether it would hurt. Or whether he would have a chance to taste that ocean of peace again before the end.

A few more wordless cries, faint, halfhearted. The voices of people who had given up. Then silence. All he could hear was his own breathing, and others' ragged breaths, and the occasional rattle of chains.

Then a click. Above him, a sliver of light. Someone had opened the door again.

Chains rattled. Voices screamed or sobbed. Gabriel tensed. It was already plain to him that an opening door meant something bad.

"Who will I choose today? Who, who, who? You all smell so tasty." A girl's voice, light and mirthful. A pigtailed silhouette at the top of the stairs. What had Mattias said about vampires too young to choose their own food sources?

The stairs creaked as the girl descended. "I smell someone new," she said. "Someone fresh."

Gabriel stilled. He didn't allow himself to breathe.

The footsteps came closer anyway. The silhouette drifted through the darkness toward him. Cold hands dug into his bare chest. A sharp nail tore his skin open. He screamed.

All around him, voices quieted. The chains no longer rattled. His fellow captives had relaxed, now that they knew they hadn't been chosen.

A tongue lapped at his chest. He shuddered. The girl laughed; the vibrations sank into his flesh. "You taste so new," she said. "I want you all to myself."

Hands in his hair, pulling his head down at an angle. A gasp of pain from him, covered by a giggle from her. Nails digging into his scalp; pressure at his neck; the sensation of tearing flesh, but no pain, never pain—

And the ocean swept him away.

No. Not here, not now. Not when he could feel her savaging his flesh like she was a puppy and he was her chew toy. Not when he could feel his neck ripping open to pour his blood into her mouth, too fast, fast enough to make him dizzy, to make him wobble on his feet and sag against his chains.

But there was nothing he had to worry about, nothing he had to fear. He was at peace. He was safe.

He was dying—

Safe, the ocean whispered. He was safe.

All he had to do was drown.

His shackles dug into his wrists. The girl made a noise of greedy pleasure deep in her throat as she savaged his flesh.

He couldn't fight. Even if he tried, he couldn't fight. She had a vampire's strength, even as a child, and he was chained, at the mercy of her killing fangs.

He couldn't fight. So why not let himself feel at peace?

He let out his breath, long and slow. He let himself drown.

As he drifted, a thought came to him, slow and lazy, bobbing on the waves. This was not, he realized, actually any worse than Mattias's feedings. She was drinking faster than he had, and the foul smell gagged him every time he tried to take a breath. But really, there was no difference. Mattias was a vampire, a monster. The girl was a monster. Mattias had been killing him, little by little. The girl was killing him; she would just show him the mercy of doing it faster.

He relaxed into the waves, and let his head slip under the surface.

He relaxed into his death.

The sensation of life drawing out of him vanished all at once. A cry; the sound of flesh on flesh; a girl's voice raised in protest. The scuttle of feet. A slammed door.

Cold hands at his neck, holding his blood in.

The ocean receded slowly. He blinked in confusion. "What—"

"It's all right," Mattias's voice murmured in his ear. "She's gone. You're safe now. You're safe."

He bit back a cry of despair. He had been so close.

"Let me—" And Mattias's tongue came down over his neck, licking away the blood. Like the girl had licked his chest. He didn't know whether to shudder or lean into him.

"That will slow the bleeding," said Mattias. "You're going to be all right. I got here in time." Arms encircling him, imprisoning him. "I'm so glad I got here in time."

Hands on his shackles. The rattle of chains. The scrape of a key in a lock, and then his hands fell free.

"Didn't I tell you to have faith in our love?" Mattias nuzzled his neck, but didn't drink. Gabriel wanted to scream in frustration.

"I'm here to save you," said Mattias, his voice full of self-satisfaction. "To save the love of my life."

***

Mattias ran his hands over Gabriel. His fingers lingered on the ruin of his neck, which had already stopped bleeding. "Are you all right?" he asked urgently. "Oh, my love. Did she do anything else to hurt you?"

"I'm fine," Gabriel interrupted, and tried not to sound too sour about the fact. Mattias had saved his life. He should have been grateful.

But the darkness at the bottom of the ocean had beckoned so temptingly.

"I'm here now, my love. I'm here." Mattias's fingers, wet with Gabriel's blood, came up to stroke his cheek. One finger drifted across Gabriel's lips.

"We don't have long," Gabriel reminded him, itchy and restless inside now that the peace was receding. It had never left him so fast before. But he had never been yanked up from such depths so quickly before. "She'll go crying to the rest of your family. They'll wonder what happened."

"They'll know what happened," said Mattias grimly. "Everyone knows now that I'm not to be trusted. As if it's any of their business what I do with the human

I chose!" He wrapped an arm around Gabriel's waist. "Come on. I'll help you get out of here. I'm here now, my love, and I'll never leave you again."

Gabriel wanted to protest that he could manage it himself, but he wasn't sure he could stand on his own for much longer. And anyway, Mattias wanted to help him. Letting him do it would make him happy. When Mattias was happy, Gabriel got what he wanted.

What he wanted was the oblivion his rescue had cheated him of.

Mattias led him toward the stairs, his arm a vise around his ribs. The sobs of the others followed. It sounded like they had figured out no rescuer was coming for them.

"Wait," said Gabriel.

Mattias paused, his grip tightening. "Are you hurt?"

"The others. We should bring them with us."

"The others?" Mattias sounded like he genuinely had no idea who Gabriel was talking about.

"The other captives," Gabriel said, gesturing with his now-free arm toward the walls where indistinct shadows writhed. "They don't deserve to die down here any more than I did." He tried not to linger with too much bitterness on the death he had almost tasted. Instead, he focused on the others. He could save them, and maybe they even wanted to be saved.

Or maybe not. Maybe they would prefer the ocean's embrace. Just like he—

No. They wanted to get out. They *all* wanted to get out. Him most of all. This was what he had barely dared to hope for, when he had thought briefly that he could use Mattias's love to his advantage. This was a better outcome than he could have dreamed of.

It *was* better.

Mattias frowned. Gabriel could barely see the shift in his face, but he felt the changes in his body, the subtle pattern of tension that meant he was confused. He had learned Mattias's body so well over the past few weeks. He had never known anyone so intimately before.

"The humans down here?" Mattias spoke the word *humans* like someone else might have said *cattle*. "They're just food."

"So am I," Gabriel reminded him. "Or I was when you brought me here."

"But I love *you*," said Mattias.

"Is it right to leave them here to die," Gabriel asked, "just because they aren't as lucky as me?"

Lucky. He was lucky that Mattias had rescued him. That his perfect peace had been snatched from him just in time. He was so, so lucky.

"You said it yourself," said Mattias. "There's no time. If we linger, we'll be caught. You'll die, Gabriel. I can't bear it. If you died, I think my own heart would stop."

Theatrics aside, the vampire did have a point. Gabriel couldn't tell how many people were down here, but his best guess was close to a couple dozen. If they stopped to save all of them, chances were good they would end up saving none.

He couldn't risk that. He wanted his freedom.

He did.

"You're right," said Gabriel reluctantly. "Let's go."

The tension left Mattias's body as he led Gabriel up the stairs. He guided Gabriel's every step, never releasing his grip.

They emerged from darkness into light. Or so it seemed at first, after the utter darkness of the basement. But the light was only a dim candle flickering in a holder on the wall. Another candle quivered far in the distance. Between the two, a patch of shadow. But of course, vampires could see in the dark.

They turned from one dark hallway into another. Then another, and a long and narrow staircase up. Another staircase down, and one more hallway, until Gabriel was half-convinced they were going in circles. Maybe this was a game Mattias was playing with him. Maybe this had all been some kind of game.

His breath quickened. His heart sped up. The walls seemed to press in on him from either side. He was trapped, trapped in a house of monsters. He was their captive, he was their *food*. He was dying. He needed, he *needed*—

He opened his mouth, but stopped himself before the words could escape. *Feed from me.* They caught in his throat. Why would he ask for that now, when they didn't have a moment to spare? But he knew why. Why would he ask when he was so close to freedom? But he knew the answer to that, too.

Another staircase up. Then down. Then up again. How much longer? Maybe there was no exit. Maybe the outside world was only a thing he had dreamed.

With every step, the possibility seemed more likely. He couldn't remember how it felt to stand in the open air, with no walls surrounding him. He could barely remember how it felt to stand under his own power, without Mattias's imprisoning caress. And how had he lived without Mattias's touches and Mattias's fangs, and the oblivion they brought?

How would he live without that oblivion once he was free?

A wave of dizziness came over him. He couldn't breathe.

Once he was free, would he never taste peace again? Would he always be conscious of the horrors around him, and never be allowed for a second to escape their grip?

Maybe, once he was free, there would be no horrors.

But he could not imagine a world without horrors. And when he tried, all he could remember was his father's fists. His mother's look of deep disappointment as she regarded the boy in front of her. The slam of the door as Jason tossed him out into the cold.

"Down this hallway," Mattias whispered. "We're almost there." They turned the corner—

And a wave of cold swept over Gabriel. His teeth chattered.

The vampire woman stood in front of them, her eyes glittering in the darkness.

Gabriel felt Mattias's shiver. But Mattias stood straight, maintaining his grip on Gabriel as he faced his great-grandmother. "I'm leaving." His voice barely shook at all. "We're both leaving."

The woman's lip curled. "You would leave your family," she said, "for a *human?*"

"For the man I love," said Mattias. "It isn't as if it's never happened before. My father—"

"Your father," the woman said, "did not think he was in love with his *food*."

"Which only makes it all the more romantic," Mattias insisted. "We'll tell the story to our great-grandchildren someday."

"You will not," said the woman. "Because if you leave now, you will never return. You will be cast out, alone, with no ancestors and no home. We will close our ears to your name and our eyes to the sight of you. We will burn your portrait and strike your name from our books."

Gabriel thought of the anger on Jason's face, the slam of the door rattling through his bones. He thought of cold nights shivering in his car, wrapping himself in the thin jacket that was the warmest thing he had managed to bring with him. "You don't have to do this," he told Mattias.

Maybe he had developed more sympathy for the vampire than he had thought. Maybe he was still picturing himself back in that basement, with the girl's fangs ripping him open, tasting how it would feel to be allowed to stop.

"Then so it must be," said Mattias to the woman, giving the words a formal weight. He pulled Gabriel past her.

Gabriel shivered as he passed within an inch of the woman. But she made no move toward him. She shuddered away from him as if he were diseased. She turned her back on them both, and said not another word as Mattias strode to a thick set of double doors.

He pulled the door open—

Gabriel pressed his lips shut before he could say the words on his lips—*no, not yet, feed from me first, it will calm us both*—

The cold wind enveloped them. The full moon shone through the trees, bathing them in white light.

He was free.

***

It wasn't until the door slammed shut behind him that Gabriel remembered he was naked.

The cold bit into his bare flesh. He remembered leaving his apartment that was no longer his. He had been too stunned to think about knocking and going back for his things, asking for his warm coat at the very least. Not that Jason would have opened the door for him anyway. At least then he'd had his thin jacket. And underwear, socks, pants. Tree branches stretched toward his vulnerable anatomy, seeming to reach for him. He cringed away from the jagged twigs thrusting out at him like tiny knives.

There was nothing but trees in any direction. Only the mansion behind him broke the monotonous view—tall and imposing architecture from a much earlier era, jagged towers stretching toward the sky. Gabriel hadn't even known there was any building around here that looked like that. Probably no one else did either, except the ones who had built it. It looked like it had been brought here straight out of some dark forest in Europe. He looked around at the trees, and suddenly wasn't sure he wasn't standing in that European forest. How far had the vampire taken him?

"Where are we?" he whispered. His voice blended with the thin whine of the wind as it passed through bare branches.

"You don't need to whisper," said Mattias. "Not anymore. We're free." He laughed exultantly into the wind, spreading his arms wide. "We're free!" He took Gabriel into his arms, lifted him as easily as if he were a piece of kindling, and swung him in a circle. "We made it, my love. We made it."

Gabriel let out a cry of pain as a twig caught his ankle. Instantly, Mattias set him down, peering into his eyes with theatrical concern. "My love? Are you all right?"

"Just a bit... you know. Naked." The brush under his feet dug into his bare soles. He shifted, trying to relieve the poking pressure.

"Oh! Of course. You poor thing, you were cast out with nothing." Despite having just lost his home, Mattias seemed to be enjoying this. It fit his star-crossed lover fantasy, no doubt. "Don't worry, my love. I'll take care of you." Before

Gabriel could protest, he lifted him into his arms again, this time cradling him against his chest in a bridal carry.

Gabriel squirmed against the vampire's iron grip. He didn't want to walk barefoot through the dark forest, but somehow he wanted this even less. Not least because being so close to Mattias's fangs made the craving start whispering to him again. They were out; he was free; he had no need to seek oblivion anymore. And yet he still *wanted*, wanted as fiercely as he had inside. The dark forest felt as full of horrors as the house they had left behind. Whether or not the danger was imaginary, he wanted nothing more than to escape.

"I can walk," said Gabriel.

Mattias paid him no mind, planting a whisper-soft kiss on his temple. His fangs didn't come anywhere near Gabriel's neck.

"Anyway," Gabriel said, unsure whether to lean into Mattias's touch or pull away, "don't we need to get out of here? That woman—your great-grandmother—she could come after us."

"She won't come after us," Mattias assured him. "I've been exiled. She will never speak to me again. I can never go home." Mattias spoke the words slowly and with relish, like he was savoring the taste of them. "You are my home now."

He nuzzled Gabriel's hair. His hair had grown long in captivity, he realized. Unruly. It covered his neck completely, draping over the very spot where he wanted Mattias's fangs to bite down.

No. He would never have to be a food source for a vampire again. He didn't have to endure his life being drained away little by little. He was free. He was going to live.

But he didn't feel free, held in Mattias's arms like a songbird in a cage.

Far in the distance, a wolf howled. Gabriel shivered, pressing instinctively against Mattias's chest. Then he realized what he had done, and tried too late to pull away. Mattias's arms tightened around him, comforting him, quelling his struggles.

"We should get out of here," said Gabriel. "Somewhere safe. Somewhere I can get some *clothes* on." Mattias still hadn't told him where they were. "Are we close to the gas station where you..." *Kidnapped me.* "Found me?"

"It's all right," Mattias assured him. "I know these woods. There's nothing here that can hurt me. The wolves have learned to fear *us.*"

That didn't make Gabriel feel any safer. The wolves could run from the vampires. He couldn't. "My car must be gone by now, but there was a Target nearby. I guess I could borrow your clothes and sneak in. I don't suppose you have any money?..." What he really wanted to know was if they were still anywhere close to that Target, anywhere close to the world he had known.

"We can worry about our physical needs later," said Mattias. "And take our time in meeting them." He planted a row of kisses along the curve of Gabriel's ear, letting Gabriel know he was thinking of needs other than clothing. Feeding apparently wasn't on his mind either, because his fangs didn't so much as brush Gabriel's neck. "For now, we should savor this moment. This is a victory for us. For our love. We never have to follow anyone else's rules again."

Mattias was still so young.

And cradled in his arms like this, Gabriel was still his prisoner.

"That doesn't help me much." Gabriel added a little chuckle to his words, trying to make light of his fear. "I'm just a fragile human. A wolf would think I was a tasty treat."

Mattias's arms tightened around him. Gabriel's body tried to tense and relax at the same time. Conflicting impulses warred under his skin, making him squirm under his skin even as Mattias pinned him in place until he couldn't move.

"I'll protect you," said Mattias. "You have nothing to fear."

Gabriel took a deep breath. The air still smelled like that house, underneath the crisp scent of the cold air. He thought it was the aura of that place stretching toward them, until he realized he was smelling Mattias.

He had been trying to breathe in courage, but the smell made it fizzle in his chest. Even so, he spoke the words. "I'd like to go home now." A softening of his voice, weak, placating—he knew what Mattias liked. "Will you take me home?"

"Home?" Mattias echoed. "You had no home when I found you, remember? You were shivering in the night. You were starving. Freezing. Dying."

And then Mattias had taken him and drained his life away little by little.

He had made Gabriel crave it.

He had brought Gabriel to the edge of oblivion, and then snatched it away.

How Gabriel wanted a taste of that oblivion now.

He longed to run into the dark woods and never see Mattias again. Or else feel Mattias's fangs pierce his neck and swim to the depths of the ocean until there was nowhere left to go.

"I am your home now," said Mattias. "And you are mine."

Fear prickled over Gabriel's skin, more potent than the cold.

Why had he ever imagined Mattias would let him go?

He had feared the absence of the vampire's fangs, of his touch. He hadn't thought to fear that his cage would follow him out into the open night.

The walls of the mansion had never been the true bars of his cage.

"We'll find a place to spend the night," said Mattias into Gabriel's hair. "Just you and me. I know you're cold—humans are fragile—but I'll find a way to keep you warm." His hand explored the contours of Gabriel's bare backside.

It would be so easy to say yes. All he needed was the pressure at his neck, the touch of oblivion. In the morning, the woods wouldn't look as scary. Neither would Mattias, maybe. In the morning, he could figure out what to do. Tonight, he could take solace in Mattias's arms.

No. If he didn't object now, he would be trapped forever. He would never escape his cage. Although it nearly made him sob in despair to do it, he shook his head. "I'll always be grateful for what you did for me." Tell him what he wants to hear, he reminded himself. "I'll always remember how your love saved me. But it's time for me to go back to my own people now."

Mattias tensed against him. When Gabriel looked up at him, his eyes were dark in the moonlight, his forehead creased with hurt. "You want to *leave* me?"

"No," Gabriel said, even though he wanted to scream *yes*. "Your love will always live in my heart." That was what Mattias liked, wasn't it? Flowery, romantic, meaningless. He had spoken Mattias's language so many times to get his fix of oblivion; he could do it now to earn his freedom. "Our love isn't meant to be. We belong in different worlds. I'll always remember you and wish it could have been different. And I know you'll do the same."

Mattias's arms tightened around him until he couldn't breathe. Those dark eyes were unreadable as they bored into his. Mattias said nothing.

Gabriel fought the urge to look away. He stared into Mattias's eyes, and felt the craving come over him, stealing his breath. He hoped Mattias took that craving to be the yearning of doomed love.

"Do you love me enough to sacrifice for me?" Gabriel asked. "Will you sacrifice the thing that means the most to you—the chance to be with me?"

If anything would convince him, that would.

"Oh, my love," Mattias said softly. "You see such a bleak future ahead for both of us. But it doesn't have to be that way. We won't always belong in different worlds. You can join my world whenever you like. In fact, why wait? We can do it tonight." He nuzzled Gabriel's neck, but didn't bite. For the first time in longer than he could remember, Gabriel suddenly didn't crave the pressure of his fangs.

"No," said Gabriel, too cold with horror to think about making his words sufficiently poetic. "No, that's not—I don't—I'm human."

"So was my mother," said Mattias, "until she fell in love with my father, and sacrificed everything. Do you love me enough to sacrifice for me?" He echoed Gabriel's own words back to him, his lips caressing Gabriel's neck.

"I love you," said Gabriel, and hoped the words would save him, "but I—"

Mattias pulled him close and swallowed his words with a kiss. "Hush," he said when he pulled away. "Love needs no excuses."

"Please," said Gabriel, forgetting the pretense of poetic love. "Please let me go."

"There is nothing to fear, my love," Mattias promised, his soft words like a smothering pillow over Gabriel's face. This time, the touch of his body did nothing to calm Gabriel's racing heart, his ragged breath.

Mattias bent toward his neck. This time, Gabriel knew, there would be no oblivion waiting for him. The promise of death, the escape he had tasted in the basement, would forever elude him. What Mattias promised—what he threatened—was eternal life.

The moon shone down coldly on his goose-bumped flesh. He still hadn't seen the sun. He would never feel the sunlight on his face again.

"Please," he tried one more time.

"I love you," Mattias murmured against his skin, not hearing him.

A sharp pressure at his neck. Then, for the last time, the ocean swept him away.

About the Author

A hermit at heart with a twisted mind, Lux Thorn is a lifelong whump enthusiast with a weakness for death scenes. They live in northern New England with their partner and child. They love swimming in the ocean, staying up late reading, and big floofy dogs.

Acknowledgements

First and foremost, I'd like to thank the slush readers who helped me tackle the giant pile of submissions for this anthology: Asidian, Ari, Havilah, Nox, withstrangeaeons, alchemistsarego, Tina, and Zipper. Y'all are literally the best!

Thank you to Nicole Alessi for the gorgeous cover art!

Thank you so much to all of the backers on BackerKit who helped to bring this book to life: AK Momster, Asidian Morris, Astoria, BubblyishYoshi, Cat Castillo, Chris Muir, Coy C, Coffee, Cats, and King, E.K., Joey B., Khadija Hussain, Lex Chimervera, Meera S., Megan, NQ, Nox Spacey, Reeby, Robin Lynn, Ronan Noctis, Ruth., Scott W., Stephen Ballentine, TastyPieceOfPastry, Vik B, carryingstarlightinherwake, seelieAce

Also by The Whumpy Printing Press

Anthologies

Hurt and Comfort

Once Upon a Blade

The Whumpboratory

Zines

ABCs of Whump

Novels and Novellas

Bloodbag

Cry of Fangs

Magnanimous Moonrise and Savage Sunset